Buddy O'Hara was tall and broad and big-boned. His size had always given the impression of strength, of raw power; but now, pacing nervously back and forth, he seemed diminished, as if he'd received some terrible blow.

"Buddy, what is it?" Patrick asked his stepson.

Buddy ran a hand through his blond hair. He took a handkerchief from his pocket and wiped his face. He looked at Patrick and then looked away.

"For God's sakes, Buddy, *tell* me."

"All right. My father. He's not dead. He's sitting in your library right now. I don't know what this will do to Ma. She'll go crazy."

Patrick stood very still. He felt the uneasiness roll over him as he thought about Ann, wondering how he would tell her. "How did he find you?"

Buddy shook his head. "He knew all about us. About you and Ma. And he's not alone. He brought his daughter. He wants to leave the kid here, for *Ma* to take care of, while he finds a job."

Patrick looked at Buddy in astonishment. "After all he put your mother through? Has he forgotten?"

"No, I think there's more to it. He's going to cause trouble. I don't know why or how or when, but I know him." Buddy mopped his wet forehead again. "You have to do something. It'll kill Ma to see him again."

"Nobody is going to hurt your mother again. Nobody!" he shouted—but there was very little conviction in his words . . .

Rhinelander Center

By Barbara Harrison

ZEBRA BOOKS

KENSINGTON PUBLISHING CORP.

ZEBRA BOOKS

are published by

KENSINGTON PUBLISHING CORP.
21 East 40th Street
New York, N.Y. 10016

Printed in the United States of America

For my father, Alex Harrison
With love

1

Patrick Dain was in the library of his duplex apartment high above Sutton Place. He stood at the window, watching as thick, fierce snow bore down on the city. A raw January wind whistled across the East River, sending swirling clouds of whiteness in every direction. The sky, in the gathering twilight, was dark polished silver.

Patrick smiled, remembering a similar snowstorm three years before, on the day he'd married Ann O'Hara. He remembered that day, as he remembered almost all their days together, with clear, uncomplicated joy. One happy memory tumbled on another until he laughed out loud. He was a lucky man, he thought now, a man head over heels in love with his wife.

He was still smiling when he turned from the window and went to his desk. He sat down, gazing contentedly around the library. It was a large room, with high, beamed ceilings, but he and Ann had arranged it to their tastes, making it a snug retreat.

Many hundreds of cherished books nestled against rich dark mahogany paneling. There were overstuffed wing chairs and ottomans in warm browns and tans and reds, their colors picking up the colors of the rugs scattered on the gleaming wood floors. Dozens of family photographs, each in silver frames, spilled over the tops of graceful mahogany tables. A fireplace ran half the length of one wall, antique bronze pokers standing proudly at its side. Near the fireplace was a deep, pillowed couch and a low table holding a silver tray, three crystal decanters, glasses, and a crystal ice bucket. There were baskets of dark green leaves, pots of tiny African violets, and several pampered, bushy asparagus-ferns.

Between the tall windows was an heirloom Hepplewhite desk, its red leather surface lovingly polished to a soft glow. Patrick reached across the desk, drawing too beribboned packages closer to him. They were anniversary presents for Ann and so he inspected the wrappings with care, a frown of concentration wrinkling his brow.

Patrick Dain was a handsome man, with dark hair and dark blue eyes fringed with thick black lashes. His features were strong and sure, with a firm jaw and a beautifully shaped mouth. He was in his early forties, though there was a zest about him which made him seem much younger. A tall man, over six feet, he had broad shoulders and a lean, rangy body, in the manner of all the Dain men.

The American branch of the Dain family had been founded more than a hundred and fifty years before by Edwin Dain, a robust, brashly charming man who'd believed in the young country and in the power of his own hard work and had built a vast fortune while still in his thirties. This he'd passed on to succeeding generations, along with a strong, sometimes stubborn, character.

It was said that of all Edwin Dain's descendants Patrick most nearly resembled him in temperament. Indeed, like Edwin Dain, he listened to his own voices and went his own way. Expected to follow his family into the law, or industry, or government, Patrick instead chose medicine. He made the decision early and passionately and never regretted it. Now, all these years later, the passion was still there, still a tall, bright flame. His devotion to medicine was absolute, matched only by his devotion to Ann.

The library door opened and Ann Dain quietly entered the room. She was a lovely, radiant woman of forty-two. Her skin was very fair, her eyes light, luminous blue. Her hair was silky and honey blond, parted at the side, falling in gentle waves to an inch above her slim shoulders.

She wore a long, black velvet dinner gown. The bodice was gathered into a V, the skirt, slit from ankle to mid-calf, swayed gracefully as she crossed the room.

"Darling." Patrick stood up. "I didn't hear you come in."

"This is the dress you wanted me to wear." She smiled. "How do I look? Okay?"

"Okay? You look wonderful. You always look wonderful."

"Because you're prejudiced."

"Who has a better right?" Patrick kissed her lightly. "If I weren't such a good friend of your

9

husband's," he said mischieviously, "I'd advise you to lock your door tonight."

"If I weren't such a good friend of your wife's," Ann smiled up at him, "I'd take the advice. Here, let's see how you look in your new dinner jacket."

Patrick turned around slowly. "Do I pass inspection?"

"With flying colors. How did I get such a handsome husband?"

"Some women—"

"Have all the luck." She finished the sentence, laughing. "I know. Ready for a drink?"

Patrick nodded. He perched at the edge of his desk, his arms crossed over his chest, watching Ann mix their drinks. They'd known each other almost four years. That was not a long time, Patrick thought to himself, yet in those four years they'd become markedly different people, their lives guided by laughter, by love, by happy camaraderie.

He remembered the day they'd met, two quiet, wary people leading quiet, wary lives, troubled by memories of the past. They'd both been refugees from disastrous marriages. Patrick's wife had been dead for many months, but the cruelty and bitterness of his marriage had remained with him, haunting him, persuing him even into his dreams.

Ann's husband had left her several years before, leaving her with no explanation, with no money, and with two children to support. To look into her eyes in those years was to see pain, and fear just barely held in check.

They'd met at Rhinelander Pavillion. An apt place, Patrick thought, for they were the walking wounded. They'd met because of Ann's son, Buddy O'Hara, then a medical student in danger of expulsion. Patrick and Ann, in trying to save Buddy's future, had found each other and saved their own.

Patrick had put his harrowing memories behind him. He was not so sure about Ann. Sometimes he would look at her and see a small, distant sadness. As much as she loved him, he knew he didn't have all of her. One small part of her was still in another time, unhealed, unresolved, hurting.

"Here we are," Ann said, giving Patrick his drink.

"To us," Patrick said, raising his glass to hers. "Happy anniversary, darling. Each year is better than the last."

"My sweet Patrick." Ann smiled. "You always know the right thing to say."

"My heart does the talking . . . or is that too corny?"

Ann laughed. "I can be corny too, as you'll see." She went to the closet and removed two packages, one large, one small, from a back shelf.

"Presents for me?" Patrick grinned. "Were they there all the time?"

"It's the safest place. You never look in the closet, you just throw your junk in there and run."

"I'm not that bad."

"You're that bad," Ann kissed him, "but I forgive you. Happy anniversary."

"And these are for you," Patrick said, holding out two boxes elaborately wrapped in gold foil.

They carried their presents to the couch. Patrick

11

tore the paper from the larger package. He smiled broadly, staring in delight at a framed watercolor painting. It was a painting of the two of them, sitting by the pond on the lush grounds of their Connecticut house. They were holding hands, watching a family of ducks play in the water.

"Ann, I hardly know what to say. It's beautiful. How ever did you have it done?"

"From the pictures we took last summer. On your birthday. Remember?"

Patrick remembered very well. They and half a dozen friends had picnicked at the pond. They'd stretched out in the sun, eating and drinking, telling tall tales and laughing until it was dark. He remembered the fireflies, and the sweet smell of the trees later that evening when he and Ann took a walk in the woods. They'd made love on a soft carpet of leaves, the red summer moon dipping in and out of the treetops.

"Patrick." Ann shook his arm. "Come back, you're a million miles away."

"You couldn't have given me a nicer present," he said softly.

"There's one more. Open it."

Patrick opened the other box. Inside was a solid gold keyring with a heavy gold disc. His initials were engraved on one side; on the other side were the letters ALPA. He looked curiously at Ann.

"It means," she said, "Ann loves Patrick always."

"Promise?"

"You have it in writing." She laughed, waving the keyring at him.

"And don't you forget it."

Ann turned to her gifts. She opened a long, flat box, gasping as she stared at a magnificent necklace of antique gold and rubies.

"My God, Patrick," she said, too surprised to say any more. Her eyes were enormous as she gazed at the necklace, transfixed by the fiery scarlet of the many stones.

"I was told," Patrick said, "the necklace once belonged to a Czarina. Now it belongs to you," he smiled, slipping the rubies around her neck. He fastened the filigreed clasp carefully, pleased at the way the necklace fit the neckline of her gown.

"Tonight you are a Czarina."

"I'll do my best," Ann said, her fingers brushing the smooth stones.

"Now this." Patrick gave her the last package.

"No, not another one. My heart won't stand it."

"This is not so . . . royal. Go ahead, open it."

Ann cautiously undid the wrappings. She peeked inside. "I love it," she squealed, lifting out an oval wood box, its top carved in a pattern of tiny flowers.

"It's a music box," Patrick said, raising the lid. "I think you'll recognize the tune."

Patrick and Ann smiled at each other as they listened to the first notes of *Always*. They'd heard the old song early in their courtship and ever since had thought of it as their song. It had been the first song played at their wedding reception, and the last, greeting their guests, later bidding them good night.

"What an anniversary," Ann said. "What a husband."

"You approve?"

"Completely."

"That's what I like to hear."

"Patrick," Ann said seriously, "I know these three years haven't always been easy."

"A piece of cake."

"No. It took me a long time to learn to fit into your world. I'm still learning, still making mistakes."

"Nonsense."

"And Buddy didn't help any."

"Buddy was a disturbed young man. And he disapproved of our marriage."

"He made it so hard for you. Too hard."

"That's all in the past, Ann. He's *Dr.* O'Hara now and the responsibility is maturing him. I know I have his respect, I think I have his friendship. It's even possible," Patrick grinned, "I have his affection. Ann," he took her hands in his, "we're no strangers to trouble. But our troubles are behind us."

"Don't say that."

"Why not?"

"You're tempting fate."

Patrick laughed. "I'll take my chances."

They turned their heads, distracted by a brisk knock at the door.

"Come in."

"Good evening, Hollis," Patrick said to the plump, silver-haired man who'd been his butler for fifteen years. He was a fatherly man of bounding good cheer, fond of Patrick, protective of Ann. "Come help us celebrate. Have a drink."

"I'd like to, Dr. Dain, but your guests are due any

moment. I thought Mrs. Dain might want to check the arrangements."

"Yes, of course." Ann rose. She looked toward the windows. The snow continued to bluster, blowing back and forth as if in some angry white dance. "I wonder if anybody will come," she said doubtfully. "Who'd go out on a night like this?"

"Ah," Patrick said, "we'll find out who our true friends are."

"You look very beautiful, Mrs. Dain, if I may say so. Your guests are in for a treat."

"Thank you," Ann said shyly. "It's the necklace."

"No, Mrs. Dain, it's you."

They left the library, going into the center hall. Ann and Hollis went ahead, disappearing into the living room. Patrick stopped at the doorway. He leaned against the doorframe, watching the two bustle about. He sighed in pleasure, touched by the splendor of the room on this night.

It was a beautiful room, the walls a warm beige, the wood floors buffed to a high gloss. A fire burned in the hearth, casting its golden lights on the polished rosewood and mahogany furnishings. The room was ablaze in candlelight, the flames leaping from gleaming silver holders. Gardenias floated serenely in sparkling glass bowls clustered throughout the room.

A long rosewood sideboard was arranged for a buffet. There were wheels of Brie stuffed with truffles, iced bowls of shrimp and crabmeat, and several kinds of pate. Shining silver flatware was stacked next to gold-banded china plates and rows

15

of snowy linen napkins.

Patrick watched Ann and Hollis move from place to place, chattering to each other, caught now and then in the flickering lights of the candles, in the deep glow of the fire. He smiled, for here was home and peace, comfort and safety. Here was all he had ever wanted.

Patrick turned at the sound of the doorbell. "I'll get it," he called, hurrying into the hall.

"Welcome, weary traveler." Patrick laughed as a bedraggled David Murdock strugged inside.

David Murdock was Patrick's closest friend. They'd been childhood companions, roommates at prep school and Yale, amiable competitors at medical school. Now they worked together at Rhinelander Pavillion, Patrick as Chief of Staff, David as Chief of Medical Services.

David was dark-haired and dark-eyed, a good looking man with neat, clean features. Always meticulously tailored and groomed, Patrick was amused by his present disarray.

"I'm so glad you're enjoying my misery," David said, shaking himself off like a terrior after a bath.

"You should have taken an umbrella," Patrick said, helping him out of his coat and boots.

"My umbrella was blown out of my hand on Fifty-seventh Street. It's halfway to Queens by now."

Hollis rushed forward, giving David a towel. "A bit wet out tonight, eh, Dr. Murdock?"

"British understatement at its finest." David smiled.

"Where's Lola?" Patrick asked.

"Still at the hospital." David dried his hands and face. He ran a comb through his wet, tousled hair. "She thought the weather might cause problems in the E.R. Lola's a doctor first, my wife second," he said, an unusual edge in his voice.

Patrick looked at David. "Is something wrong?"

"No."

"You know Lola's only doing her job," Patrick said as they walked to the living room.

"That's easy for you to say, Ann's always with you. Lola is *not* always with me."

"I'm surprised at you. You're actually angry."

"When I was single," David said evenly, "I never went anywhere alone. Now that I'm married I go everywhere alone. Forgive me if I find that odd."

"If they need Lola in the E.R.—"

"They don't. There is no emergency at the hospital. Even if there were, there's a staff of competent doctors and nurses to handle it. The hospital wouldn't exactly go to hell if Lola took a night off."

They walked into the living room. David relaxed, basking in the sudden radiant warmth. He felt better, glad he was there.

"Hello, David." Ann kissed his cheek. "How brave of you to come."

"I love a good snowstorm."

"I bet."

"I love a gorgeous woman too, and you are *gorgeous*," he said, stepping back to look at her.

"It's my magic necklace. Patrick gave it to me tonight."

"The crown jewels, I presume."

17

"As a matter of fact, yes." Patrick smiled. "Come get a drink."

Patrick and David went to the bar that had been set up in a corner of the room.

"Bourbon, please. Large," David said to the bartender. He glanced over his shoulder at Ann. "It's hard to believe that's the same woman I met four years ago. She was pale and thin and nervous then . . . Look at her now."

"I take full credit."

"I thought you might."

They took their drinks to the couch, sitting down with Ann. The doorbell rang again, ringing many times more in the next hour. The guests surged into the room, their voices raised in high spirits.

There were toasts and good-natured jokes and the easy conversations of old friends. By eight o'clock the storm had slowed outside and a second wave of guests arrived, quickening the rhythms of the party. Patrick and Ann smiled often at each other, and in those moments they might have been the only two people in the room.

It was nine o'clock when Hollis, looking worried, took Patrick aside. "May I have a word with you, sir?"

"Of course. What's wrong?"

Hollis drew Patrick to the edge of the room. "Dr. O'Hara is here."

"Good, Mrs. Dain was beginning to worry. Tell him to hurry."

"Sir, he wants to see you alone. Please, you'd best come with me. He's white as a ghost."

2

Patrick followed Hollis into the hall. He turned toward the library and then stopped, staring in surprise at Buddy. He frowned, puzzled, then alarmed by the young man's appearance.

Buddy O'Hara was tall and broad and big-boned. His size had always given the impression of strength, of raw power, but now, pacing nervously back and forth, he seemed diminished, as if he'd received some terrible blow. His moody blue eyes were dark with worry, his face drawn in anxious lines.

"You see what I mean, sir," Hollis said.

"Yes." Patrick nodded, for Buddy's normally ruddy complexion was dead white, his forehead shiny with perspiration. "I'll handle this, Hollis. Try to keep Mrs. Dain in the living room."

Patrick went to his stepson. "Buddy, what is it?"

Buddy jumped at Patrick's voice. "Where's Ma? he asked urgently.

"She's with our guests. What's wrong, are you ill?"

"I have to talk to you."

"All right," Patrick opened the library door, "but you'd better sit down before you fall down."

"*No.*" Buddy's hand shot out, quickly closing the door. "I have to tell you something before you go in there."

"Then tell me."

Buddy ran a hand through his blond hair. He took a handkerchief from his pocket and wiped his face. He looked at Patrick and then looked away.

"For God's sake, Buddy, *tell* me."

"I don't know how to start." Buddy's eyes darted desperately around the hall. He looked as if he wanted to escape, to run and keep on running.

"Calm down." Patrick put a steadying hand on Buddy's shoulder. "Start from the beginning. It can't be that bad."

"Well." Buddy took a deep breath. "About six months after Ma got her divorce . . ."

"Yes? Go *ahead*, Buddy."

"Six months after the divorce, we got word that Pop was dead."

"Yes? So?"

"He's not. He's not dead. He's sitting in your library right now."

Patrick stood very still. He felt the uneasiness roll over him, wave after wave, settling in the center of his chest. His heart began to pound.

"Your father is . . . here?"

"I don't know what this will do to Ma. She'll go crazy."

"Your father is here," Patrick repeated dumbly, thinking about Ann, wondering how he would tell her.

"He came to the hospital tonight. I was just going off duty. I couldn't believe it." Buddy spoke rapidly, his hands rising and falling with his words. "'I'm back, Buddy', he says, like that explains everything."

"How did he find you?" Patrick asked quietly.

Buddy shook his head. "He knew all about us. About you and Ma. About me being a doctor."

"Why has he come back?"

"He's not alone. He brought his daughter. He wants to leave the kid here, for *Ma* to take care of, while he finds a job."

Patrick looked at Buddy in astonishment. "After all he put your mother through? Has he forgotten?"

"He's nervy enough not to care. Besides, I think there's more to it. He's going to cause trouble. I don't know why or how or when, but I know him." Buddy mopped his wet forehead again. "You have to do something. It'll kill Ma to see him again."

"Nobody is going to hurt your mother again." Patrick went to the door. "Nobody!"

"You have to get him out of here. Ma will—"

"Ma will what?" Ann's voice came from the end of the hall.

Patrick and Buddy swung around. They saw Ann walking toward them. She was pale, her hands clasped tightly together.

"I knew something was going to happen," she said. "I felt it all day. Well, what is it? What's wrong?"

"Don't look so grim, darling," Patrick said. "It isn't that serious."

"What isn't?"

"Let's talk about this upstairs. It's quiet there, we won't be disturbed."

"Tell me here, now."

"It's Pop," Buddy blurted, anguish mixing with outrage in his voice. "He's here, the bastard's here."

The last of the color went out of Ann's face. "That's impossible. What are you saying, Buddy? You know that's impossible."

Patrick took her hand. "It's true, Ann. But you needn't see him if you don't want to."

"Why . . . is he here? What does he want?"

"We're not sure. Do you want me to send him away?"

Ann looked up at Patrick. He saw the confusion in her eyes, and the old despair. He put his arm around her shoulder. "Say the word and I'll send him away. He has no right upsetting you this way."

"No," Ann said slowly. "I'm okay." She looked at the closed library door. "Is he in there?"

"Are you sure you're up to it?"

"I'd . . . rather get it over with. I can't live under a sword. You understand that, don't you, Patrick?"

He smiled slightly. "Do you want to see him alone?"

She looked at the door again. "We're a family, we'll see him together."

"Ma, don't." Buddy stepped in front of her.

"I have to," she said, surprised by the harshness in her voice. "Buddy," she added quietly, "there are some things we have to do, whether we want to or not."

Ann led the way to the library. Patrick saw her

distress. He saw how hard she tried to keep her hands from shaking. He felt a chill, for he knew that three years of serenity had been shattered in this one moment. He wondered what damage had been done, what damage was yet to be done to them all.

"Hello, Bren," Ann said.

"Hello, Annie Laurie." He grinned. "I'm back."

Bren O'Hara was sandy-haired and brown-eyed, as tall and broad as his son. He was an attractive man, though time and a fondness for whiskey had blunted the stark handsomeness of his youth. His eyes had sparkled once; now they were quiet, wearied by too many failed dreams. His smile was unchanged, a crooked, lazy line. There was charm in his smile, and slyness, and something close to defiance.

"Ann," Patrick said, "do sit down. Let's all sit down."

"You'd be the husband." Bren smiled.

"Yes."

"I helped myself to a drink. I didn't think you'd mind, considering the circumstances."

"No."

Ann sat very straight, lacing and unlacing her fingers. "We got a letter saying you were dead. We believed it."

"I meant you to. I thought it was best that way." Bren spoke without apology. His voice was steady, soft with the accents of his Irish childhood. "We were divorced, after all. Best to forget the past and start fresh."

"Obviously you've changed your mind," Patrick said.

Bren shrugged. "Circumstances changed."

"Meaning you want something." Buddy threw up his hands.

Bren looked at his son. "I hardly know you this way, so hard and mean. What happened to you, Buddy? You used to jump in my lap and say 'Poppa, you're my best friend in the whole world'."

"Until *Poppa* took a walk and forgot to come back."

"Buddy, Bren, *stop* it," Ann cried. "This is hard enough."

"You're right, Annie, it's no way for grown men to behave." Bren took a swallow of his drink. He looked closely at Ann, studying her face, her gown, her jewels. A brief anger flashed in his eyes and then was gone. "You've come a long way in the world, Annie Laurie. In all my life I never saw such riches."

Ann looked away. Bren had always been able to make her feel guilty and now, she knew, he was doing it again. One glance had told her that Bren's life had not improved over the years. He wore a brown sports jacket and tan turtleneck sweater, both fraying and shabby. His slacks had long ago lost their crease and his boots were badly scuffed. She thought of the luxury of her own surroundings, of her life with Patrick, and she felt guilty.

Patrick watched her, guessing her thoughts. "Ann," he said gently, "I think you've had enough of this."

"No. Let him play it out."

"Play?" Bren frowned. "What do you mean by that?"

"You always played games," Buddy said angrily. "You played games with all our lives."

"Is that how you brought up the boy, Annie? To hate his own father?"

Buddy's eyes were very dark. "You walked out on us. You left us. What do you expect?"

"And what else could I do but leave? With your Ma nagging at me all the time? The kids need this, the kids need that. How much is a man supposed to take?"

A small cry escaped Ann's lips and Patrick jumped to his feet. "That's quite enough! I won't have my wife upset!"

"Don't get yourself in such an uproar," Bren said easily. "She was my wife before she was your wife."

"That was a long time ago."

"Everything's relative," Bren smiled slowly, "or so I've heard."

Patrick took a step toward him. "I think you'd better leave."

"I think that's up to Annie."

"Ann?" Patrick looked at her.

She sighed. "Bren, why did you come here? What do you want?"

"Well, it's like this, I need a favor."

"A . . . *favor?*"

"I've got my little girl with me. See, over there." Bren stood up. He went to a corner of the room. There, curled up in a wing chair, asleep, was a small blond child of about six. "This is Daisy," Bren whispered.

Ann and Patrick looked at the child and then at

25

each other.

"She's yours?" Ann asked finally.

"My own. Her Ma passed away two months ago."

Bren walked back to his chair and sat down. He took more of his drink and refilled his glass. "There was nothing left for me in Boston. I heard a friend of mine was starting up a small trucking business in New York. I decided to come to New York, but first I had to think what to do about Daisy. It's going to take a while to get started. I'll have no time for the child. Then it came to me."

"Well," Patrick said. He poured two drinks and gave one to Ann. "By all means, tell us what wonderful idea came to you."

"Dr. and Mrs. Patrick Grayson Dain, that's what." Bren grinned. "I knew about you because when you visited the Cape last summer there was a big article in the Boston paper. Pictures and all. Daisy's Ma was still alive then. I remember I showed it to her."

Ann sat back. She sipped her drink, staring into space, staring at nothing. She wondered if somewhere deep down she hadn't always expected Bren to turn up one day. Bren, irresponsible, careless, trailing trouble and pain, messing up people's lives. A deep exhaustion came over her. Her glass felt heavy, too heavy to hold.

"You want us to take care of your child," she said dully.

"She's not a stranger, Annie. She's Buddy's and Jill's half-sister, after all."

Buddy had been silent, looking out the window. Now he crossed the room and stood before his father. "It's not enough you dumped two kids, now you want to dump a third."

"Watch your tongue, laddie. You're not so big I can't take you, one on one."

"Buddy," Patrick said, "sit down. You're not helping the situation."

"Don't tell me what to do." Buddy spun around. "Who are you to tell me what to do?"

Buddy turned around, unable to meet Patrick's startled gaze. He was embarrassed by his outburst, for Patrick had been more than a stepfather to him, he'd been a friend.

"Sorry," he mumbled.

"It's all right."

But Patrick knew it wasn't all right. In less than an hour's time Bren O'Hara had managed to renew the old hurts, the old angers. The tension in the room was so real it was like a dark fog closing in on them, blotting out the light.

"I have a room in a boarding house on the West Side," Bren said. "It's clean and the supper's hearty, but still it's no place for a child."

"I see your problem," Patrick said.

"Daisy's no problem. She's a sweet little girl."

"Whom you are anxious to leave in our care," Patrick said impatiently. "Correct?"

"Correct."

"I think I have a better solution. One which will keep you and Daisy together."

"And what would that be?"

"We'll hire help for you. Someone to look after the child."

"A *governess?*" Bren laughed. "In a boarding

house? You want to put an English nanny in the last Irish boarding house in New York?"

"No," Patrick said, holding on to his temper. "We'll rent an apartment for you. With an apartment and live-in help, Daisy will be cared for, you can go about your business, and the two of you needn't be separated."

"I didn't come here for your fancy servant-girls. Nor for your fancy apartments. Daisy needs a home. She's just lost her Ma. The only friends she ever had are back in Southie. She needs a home, not a servant-girl."

"He's trying to help, Bren. Listen to him."

"He wants to turn my girl over to strangers, Annie."

"So do you," Patrick said cooly.

"Poppa?" a small voice came from the back of the room.

Bren looked around. "So you're up, Daisy. Well, come over here, little girl. These are the people I told you about."

The child hopped down from the chair and walked over to her father. She stood at a distance from him, glancing from face to face.

Daisy O'Hara had long, straight blond hair and choppy bangs that fell into her eyes. Her eyes were enormous, very gray and solemn. She had a delicate frame, dressed in jeans and a red t-shirt, none too clean.

Ann leaned forward, staring at her intently. She stared at the child a long time, hardly moving, hardly breathing. Patrick, too, looked at the girl. He'd seen many childhood pictures of Buddy and his sister Jill; the resemblance between Daisy and the young Jill was so great they might have been twins. He looked back at Ann. She was smiling, transfixed by the silent child.

Patrick walked away, trying to collect his thoughts. He knew without asking that Ann would agree to take Daisy. And so, he thought, Bren O'Hara would become a part of their lives. He would move insidiously through their days and nights, rekindling the hates and hurts, playing with their doubts and fears. Patrick knew Bren wanted something. Was it Ann, he wondered, or money, or revenge, or all three?

Patrick saw Bren looking at him. There was triumph in his look, and malice. "She's a dead ringer for our girl Jill," he grinned.

"Daisy," Ann held out her hand, "this is my husband Patrick. You've already met Buddy. I'm Ann."

Daisy ignored Ann's hand. She paid little attention to Ann or to Buddy, concentrating instead on Patrick. She looked at him closely, starting at the top of his head and working down.

"What about school?" Patrick asked.

"Daisy's just a baby, barely six years old. There's plenty of time for that later."

"Our house, our rules," Patrick said briskly. "That means school for Daisy."

"Patrick." Ann ran to him, her face alight with excitement. "Then it's all right? We can take her?"

Patrick stroked Ann's hair. "Speaking of school, what about your classes?"

"Classes?" Bren asked.

"I'm taking some college courses," Ann said, still smiling at Patrick.

"You're going to college, Annie? All this money and education too? Well, I shouldn't be surprised. You always wanted to be somebody."

Ann whirled around. "I wanted to *be* somebody so the children would *have* something."

Bren was about to reply when the library door opened. David Murdock walked into the room.

"I knocked. I guess nobody heard me." He hesitated, feeling the hostility in the air. "Hollis wanted you to know your guests are leaving."

"Oh, Patrick," Ann cried. "Our beautiful party. I forgot all about it."

"I'll make our apologies." Patrick went to the door. "I'll be right back."

"What in hell is going on?" David asked.

"*Hell* is the right word."

Daisy watched Patrick leave. She lifted her head and looked gravely at her father. "Am I going to live here?"

"For a little while," Bren said. "Until I get myself settled. You'll have a good time, too. It'll be like living in a palace. Won't it, Annie?"

"We'll do our best for her."

"I knew you would. I knew you'd want it this way. It wouldn't be right, leaving her alone all day."

"As if you cared," Buddy said

"Don't be talking about things you don't understand, laddie. There's two sides to everything. Your Ma has hers and I have mine, and that's the truth you wouldn't know anything about."

"Yeah, sure," Buddy said curtly, though a flicker

of doubt came into his blue eyes.

"All right," Patrick said, striding into the library. "Where were we? We'll make all decisions about Daisy while she lives here. Is that agreed?"

"Agreed." Bren nodded. "But I want to be able to have my say."

"We'll work something out. For now, it's time Daisy got to bed."

"Her things are at my boarding house. I'll bring them over."

"No," Patrick said. "Hollis will pick them up in the morning. We'll make do until then. Ann, Buddy, take Daisy outside. I want to speak to Bren."

"Come here, little girl, and give your Poppa a kiss."

Daisy did as she was told, though she did so without any emotion. They were surprised, for she seemed not to care that her father was leaving, that she would be alone with people she didn't know.

Buddy took Daisy's hand and led her out of the room. Ann took a few steps and then stopped, looking at Patrick and Bren.

"It's all right, darling," Patrick said, "go with Buddy."

Patrick waited until the door closed. He turned to Bren. "Is there anything you want to say?"

"Can't think of a thing."

"I can. First of all, don't think you can come barging in here any time you want. We'll make a schedule for you to see Daisy. You will stick to the schedule."

Bren's mouth twisted into a sneer. "Yes, *sir.*"

31

"And there is this: I am nobody's fool, least of all yours. If you are playing a game, you will lose."

"Would that be a threat?"

"Yes," Patrick said, his eyes as hard as stone. "It would."

Rhinelander Pavillion, in its one hundred and ten years, had grown from a single narrow building to a large graystone medical center occupying several city blocks. The clean, elegant lines of the hospital matched those of its east side neighborhood, an area of lovely, tree-shaded townhouses and handsome old apartment buildings.

Set back from the sidewalk behind a sloping driveway, its only identification was a small bronze plaque marked RHINELANDER PAVILLION; farther down the street was another entrance and another plaque marked CLINIC. The hospital's main entrance was tended, day and night, by neatly groomed doormen, their shiny taxi whistles resting on the cloth of their proper gray livery. At the end of the hospital structure was an unobtrusive underpass housing ambulance lanes on one side, staff parking on the other.

Patrick pulled his car into his parking space and slammed on the brakes. He hurried from the car, running along the ramp to the Emergency Room entrance. He darted inside, blinking rapidly in the sudden glare of the high-intensity lights overhead. It was seven o'clock in the morning, but there was none of morning's quiet in the E.R. Doctors and nurses scurried back and forth, quick flashes of white against the pale tan walls. Patients crowded the waiting room, some in obvious pain, others sitting quietly, their eyes full of fear. Medical machinery hummed and beeped, while all around them the hospital page droned on in staccato summons.

Patrick stopped at the nurses' station. "Professor Porter was brought in a while ago. Where is he?"

The nurse glanced at the admission sheets. She shook her head. "No, I don't see—"

"He's here. Look again," Patrick ordered. "Samuel Porter."

She ran her finger along the list of names. "Well, I don't see . . . oh, yes, here he is. Room 3." She smiled lamely. "I'm sorry, Dr. Dain, but we're really jammed up and—" She broke off, sighing, as Patrick disappeared down the corridor.

He was halfway down the corridor when he stopped, putting his arm around a slight, gray-haired woman. "Gracie, what happened?"

"Sam was shoveling snow, trying to dig out the car," she said, her eyes red and wet with tears. "I begged him not to do it, but you know Sam. All of a sudden he grabbed his chest and fell over. Patrick," she clutched his arm, "help him. *Please* help him."

"You know we'll do everything we can. He's a strong man, Gracie," Patrick said gently. "And he's a fighter."

"They won't let me inside, Patrick. Can't I go in? He shouldn't be alone . . . not now."

"It's best you wait here. I'll let you know when you can see Sam."

Patrick slipped into Room 3. Sam Porter lay on the examination table. His face was ashen, his eyes fluttering open as a doctor and nurse worked over him. There was a heart monitor at his side. An i.v. ran into his arm, an oxygen mask covered his mouth and nose.

Patrick's face contorted, for he and Sam went back a long way. Sam had been his favorite professor at medical school. He'd been teacher and friend and mentor, a shoulder to lean on during those first tough months. He'd been a vigorous man, in command always. Now he looked frail, helpless to stop what was happening to him.

"Dr. Rogers, what do we have?" Patrick asked, going to the table.

"M.I. He's had 5 milligrams MS i.v., and 100 milligrams lydocaine. I called CCU, they're ready for him."

Patrick pulled a stethoscope from his bag and bent over Sam. Sam's eyes fluttered open. He tried to speak.

"Don't talk, Sam," Patrick said quietly. "Save your strength."

He put the stethoscope to Sam's chest but then straightened up quickly, his eyes fixed on the heart monitor. The blips were jumping wildly across the screen, racing by out of control.

"He's in fibrillation!"

The nurse quickly covered Sam's chest with

cream. Dr. Rogers moved a defibrillator into place.

Patrick put the paddles on Sam's chest. "Give me two hundred."

Dr. Rogers adjusted a dial and then stood back. Sam's body convulsed as the electricity shot through him.

"No good," Patrick said, his lips compressed into a thin white line. "Dammit, give me four hundred and stand clear!"

Dr. Rogers sent the machine to four hundred and the force of the charge nearly hurled Sam off the table. Patrick glared grimly at the monitor. After a moment his expression relaxed.

"He's converting, but he needs CCU stat. Dr. Rogers, I want you to take him up yourself."

"I have patients waiting. I'll send a nurse along with the orderly."

"*You* will *personally* take Professor Porter to CCU and deliver him to Dr. Perkins. Is that clear?"

"Yes, Dr. Dain."

"Then call an orderly and prepare him for transfer."

Patrick grabbed his bag and walked into the corridor. Gracie Porter was at his side in an instant.

"Is Sam dead?"

"Sam's alive. They're going to take him to the Coronary Care Unit. You can go up with them."

"Is it very bad?"

"Sam's had a heart attack. But he's strong, and we're going to do everything we can. I have a call in to Dr. DeWitt. He's the best, he'll take good care of Sam."

"Is . . . Sam going to make it?"

"It's a little early to know too much, Gracie."

"What do you *think?*"

"Sam has a chance, a fair chance."

"Patrick, if you were a betting man . . ."

"I'm not."

"If you were. I want the truth."

Patrick looked at her. She, too, looked suddenly frail, yet her eyes were insistent, demanding to know.

"Sam has a 50-50 chance," he said softly, stepping back as two orderlies entered the room. "He'll be coming out in a minute, Gracie. He looks bad, but that's to be expected. Do you understand?"

"Should I call the children?"

"They should be here to keep you company. Call the kids, call the grandchildren. It's going to be a long wait, it's best not to wait alone." Patrick looked up as the page called his name. "I have to go. I'll keep on top of Sam's case . . . and Gracie, if you need anything, anything at all . . . if you have any questions, I'll be here."

"Thank you, Patrick."

"I'll see you later." He kissed the top of her head. "He's strong, Gracie. He'll fight."

"I know he will. He's fought all his life."

Patrick hurried away. His head was pounding, his hands were damp. He turned into the stairway and leaned against the wall for a moment, taking a deep breath. He'd been trained to accept death and he'd accepted it many times, but this, he knew, was different. This was Sam and the world had few enough Sams as it was.

Patrick wearily climbed the stairs. The year had begun so well, he thought, he'd taken it as an omen. But now Bren O'Hara was back, and an old friend was sick, and the year was turning ugly. He reached the second floor and turned into the corridor, his footsteps muted by the poundings of a dozen different typewriters in the dozen different offices around him. He opened the door to his outer office. It was a wide, deep room with offices to the right and left. He crossed it quickly, stopping at his secretary's desk.

"I heard about Sam," Jean Corry said. "I'm sorry. DeWitt called, he's on his way."

"Good," Patrick said, picking up his messages. "Were you paging me?"

"The staff meeting's already started. They're in your office."

"Jean, call Dr. Perkins. Tell him to make sure Gracie Porter is comfortable up there. Tell him I want to be kept informed of Sam's condition. If he *sneezes*, I want to know about it."

"Right." Jean smiled, tossing her short black curls.

Patrick went into his office. It was carpeted in dark gray and furnished with dark tweed couches and chairs. Paneling and cabinetwork ran around one wall, opposite a wall of medical texts and reference books. The desk was polished oakwood, the walls, hung with watercolors from Patrick's private collection, were a buff color.

Patrick dropped his bag on a chair and hung up his coat and jacket. "Morning," he said, loosening his tie. "Sorry I'm late."

"We started without you," David Murdock said. "How's Sam?"

"It doesn't look good. DeWitt's on his way." Patrick glanced at his messages and then put them on his desk. He sat down, looking at the typed agenda in front of him. "I don't have time for all this stuff today."

"We've covered some of it," Lola Shay said.

Patrick looked at her. Lola, Chief of Clinic and Emergency Services, was slim, dark and pretty, with lively green eyes. Now her eyes were subdued and he wondered if there might really be trouble in the Shay-Murdock marriage.

"With your usual efficiency." He smiled at her.

"Of course." She smiled back. "We were talking about the annual surprise inspection. It's due next month."

"What about it?"

"We haven't had a fire drill in a long time. I know everybody hates fire drills," she said, hearing the groans around her, "but I think we ought to have one."

"Fine, but this time let's not throw the hospital into a panic. David, you coordinate it with the services."

"You're too kind."

"Patrick, I have something." Paul Randolph spoke. He was the Chief of Students and Interns, a fortyish man of endless patience and good nature. "The intern committee is talking about right-to-strike clauses in all new contracts. It's still talk—"

"My attitude is unchanged," Patrick said firmly. "I don't believe *any* doctor has a right to strike. For

39

any reason. We'll have to have a policy meeting about this, but for now let them understand that any strike will bring extremely heavy penalties."

"Doctors have gone out on strike at other hospitals."

"I don't care! Lives are on the line! It's obscene!" Patrick shook his head. "These men and women will be making a fortune in a couple of years. If they have to suffer a little now, my attitude is: *tough*. I don't care, let them take me to the Supreme Court. I'm not budging on this one. Not with lives at stake."

Patrick looked at Eve Lawrence, the Administrator of Rhinelander Pavillion. She was a tall, sleek woman in her late thirties. She had calm, classic features, and short hair the color of gold.

"You've been very quiet." He smiled. "Don't you have anything for me?"

"The nurses' committee. They want more Spanish-speaking nurses on staff."

"That's fine. I don't want anyone fired, but as jobs open up, sure. I'd like to see some more black faces around here too, by the way." He looked down at the agenda. "The rest of this will have to wait. What I really want to discuss is the naming of a new Chief Resident. Any suggestions?"

"What about Majeski?" David asked.

"He's leaving to go into private practice."

"There's Joan Parker," Eve said. "It would be awfully good public relations if we could put a woman in there."

"She's not interested. In fact, I think we'll be losing her to Mass. General next year."

"We're talking about a *Chief Resident*," Lola said shortly to Eve. "How can you think about public relations?"

"It's my job to think about public relations."

"Not in this situation," Lola snapped.

Patrick stared at Lola, for it wasn't like her to be so abrupt. He saw the tightness about her mouth, the angry flush on her cheeks.

"Lola?" he asked. "Any suggestions?"

"I like Forbes."

"So do I. But he has all the tact of a Sherman tank."

"Candor never hurt anyone," she said, glancing quickly at David.

"The Chief Resident supervises the resident staff and coordinates the attending staff. That takes diplomacy. It takes," Patrick smiled, "a bit of a con man."

"Matt Lansing," Paul said.

Patrick sat back. "Frankly, he was my first choice. He's a brilliant young doctor, everybody respects him. And Lord knows he's a con man."

"Perfect." Paul laughed.

"I don't know. He's also headstrong. Cocky. Ambitious."

"That could describe any doctor in this room, at a similar age."

"Speak for yourself." David smiled.

"Well," Patrick said slowly, "I think I'll try Lansing in the job. I'll give it to him for three months. If it works out, I'll make it permanent. I have a few reservations, but we have to make a move. Unless there are any objections?"

"I've worked with him," David said. "He's good."

"That's settled then. I'll talk to Lansing and get a memo out. That's all for today." Patrick rose. "We'll meet later in the week on the rest of the agenda. David, will you stay a moment?"

The others gathered their notes together and stood up. Paul Randolph was the first to leave, followed by Eve Lawrence. Lola hesitated, then went over to David.

"Lunch?" she asked.

"I'll try."

"Call me. Patrick, join us if you can," she said, waving as she went out.

David looked at Patrick. "How's Daisy doing?"

"We've only had her three days, it's hard to say. She's a quiet child. I don't think she's said ten words." Patrick walked over to the window. He stared outside, watching a group of children build a snowman in Central Park. "Nothing seems to faze her, she's taking everything in stride. So far."

"And Ann?"

Patrick returned to his desk. He sat down. "It's a complicated situation. We're all a little off balance." He looked at the collection of photographs on his desk. He smiled at a picture of his son Tony, taken when he'd gone off to Yale. "Tony is twenty years old. It's been a long time since I had a child around the house."

"You'll adjust."

"That's part of the problem. We can't get too used to having Daisy around. She's not ours . . . But that's not what I wanted to talk about."

"Oh?"

"Lola seemed upset."

"I didn't notice anything."

"Then you're the only one who didn't."

"You mean that little thing with Eve?" David flicked a speck of lint from his immaculate blue blazer. "Lola's had her differences with Eve lately."

"So I've heard."

"If you've heard, why are you asking me about it?"

"I don't like tensions between members of the staff."

David was quiet, as if he were considering something. "It's nothing serious."

"Besides, I'm very fond of Lola."

"So am I." Again, David paused. "Patrick, people occasionally have . . . misunderstandings. Leave it at that."

"You're being evasive."

"Which is my right." David laughed.

"Agreed."

"Then I'll get back to work." David stood up. "About Matt Lansing . . . you know he and Buddy don't get along at all."

"They're too much alike to get along."

"There was a fight in the lounge a couple of weeks ago. I never found out who threw the first punch, but it took three guys to pull them apart."

"What? Why didn't you tell me?"

"It wasn't important then. I'm telling you now because Lansing's going to be Buddy's boss. And Buddy's not going to like it."

"I can't make hospital decisions based on

personal considerations. I never have. I won't now."

"It's not for nothing we call you Saint." David smiled. "Seriously, I thought you'd want to prepare Buddy for the news."

"Buddy will find out about the appointment when all the other residents do. What bothers me is that Buddy was brawling again. I thought he was learning to control his temper."

"He's been doing well. He still has a way to go. Lansing's no shrinking violet either."

"Would you want him to be? It's a hard job. To succeed, he'll have to be hard."

"I hear he has a hard left."

Patrick smiled. "That's not what I had in mind."

"You had a pretty good left yourself. Remember?"

"Ancient history. Although I do remember that you started all the arguments, then disappeared while I did all the fighting."

"Protecting my hands." David laughed. "In case I decided to become a surgeon."

"Or a concert pianist."

"That's good too."

The intercom rang and Patrick picked up the telephone. "Yes? . . . yes . . . I see . . . all right, thanks." He hung up. "Andrew DeWitt's with Sam. Sam's holding his own, but that's all he can say for now."

"Damn shame." David took his notes from the desk and turned toward his office. "I'll look in on him later."

"We'd better be prepared for the worst."

"The worst?" David paused. "I'm always prepared for the worst. In any situation."

David sounded distracted and Patrick looked at him. "Why do I suddenly have the feeling we're talking about two different things?"

"I'll see you later." David smiled slightly.

"One more question. Has Buddy been having trouble with anyone other than Matt Lansing?"

"No more than usual. He and Lansing just don't like each other. Lansing will be able to handle that. You'll be able to handle Buddy."

"I'll get out my whip and chair."

"Exactly," David said, going into his office.

Patrick stared down at his desk. He wasn't surprised by the animosity between the two young men. They were, he thought, opposite sides of the same coin. They'd both grown up in poverty and anger. They'd both grown up without fathers, feeling they had something to prove. Now, as adults, they shared a flinty determination, a driving *need* to succeed. That was their sameness.

Their differences ran as deep. Buddy had come out of his experiences a rainbow of raw emotions always threatening to boil over. Matt had come out of his experiences a smoothly private man whose emotions he, alone, knew. Buddy faced the world with a snarl. Matt faced the world with a smile. Indeed, the Lansing charm was well known around the hospital. He would need his charm, Patrick thought now, that and a lot more.

4

Matt Lansing was more compelling than hand-some. With thick, coal-black hair, flashing black eyes, and a tall, brawny body, everything about him seemed larger than life. His smile was so wide and white it was startling. The cleft in his chin was like a fissure in granite. His brows were slashes of black. There was a quickness in his movements, traces of a swagger in his walk. Both the quickness and the swagger were reminders of his past, of the street fighter he'd once been.

Matt Lansing was born and raised in New York. He was seven when his father died, eight when his mother started drinking her problems away. The loneliness had begun then. Mourning his father, his mother lost to him, he was shunted from relative to relative, welcome in their overcrowded apartments only for the few dollars he earned working after school. He couldn't remember a time he hadn't worked, after school, before school, weekends, summers.

It was a mean, poor childhood, but he'd survived because he'd sensed there was something better out there and he'd wanted it. Scholarships saw him through college, loans and a never ending succession of jobs through medical school. In all the years he'd made two promises to himself—that he'd never be poor again, that he'd never be lonely again.

Now, bent over a patient, Matt's eyes were two black points of concentration. His patient was sitting up in bed, clutching at the sheet, wheezing and gasping for breath. She was very pale, her lips almost colorless.

"I know it's hard, but try to relax," he said, adjusting an oxygen tube. "Nurse, 5 ml Epinephrine, 100 mg phenobarb."

Matt put his stethoscope to the woman's chest, listening carefully to her heart and lungs. "We're going to give you an injection. You'll feel better right away. Here it is," he said as the nurse hurried back with the medication.

Matt injected the woman and then smiled, for within seconds her exertions slowed.

"Better." She nodded weakly.

"Told you so." He listened to her chest again, then sat at the edge of her bed. "I'll be looking at your x-rays soon, and I have you scheduled for allergy testing. For now, we'll put you on a mild sedative."

"Allergy?"

Matt wiped her damp face with a tissue. "I think these attacks may have an allergic base."

"If it's an allergy . . . can you control it?"

"We can control these attacks in any case. The important thing is not to worry, not to panic. The more you panic, the worse it is."

She leaned back against the pillows. Her breathing was normal now, the color returning to her face. "God, I *hope* it's an allergy. You don't know what it's like when you can't breathe."

Matt patted her hand. "Let's wait and see what the tests say. Someone will be around to take a detailed history. The more information we have about you, the better." He took a paper cup from the table and gave it to her. "This is your sedative. I'd like you to take it now."

She looked at the pill suspiciously. "I'm afraid I'll choke."

"You won't choke. I promise."

She swallowed the pill quickly, chasing it down with large gulps of water.

"Easy," Matt laughed, "you'll get hiccups."

"That's all I need."

"You're going to be fine. Really. I wouldn't lie to you."

"I'll try to think positively."

"That's the spirit." He stood up. "I'll look in on you later. Try and get some rest, you're worn out."

Matt turned and left the room. He stopped at the door, surprised to see Patrick Dain standing there.

"Have you been here long?"

"Long enough. Very nice," Patrick said.

"Thanks. There's a pattern to her attacks. I think it's an allergy of some kind."

"Who's her doctor?" Patrick asked as they walked up the corridor.

"Clarke."

"He'll put you in charge."

"He already has. I don't understand that man. He

"dumps his patients and runs like a bandit."

"He doesn't like hospitals."

"Very funny."

"I'm not joking. He doesn't like hospitals. Never did. His residency was a torture for him."

"Now I've heard everything."

"Matt, I'd like to talk to you. Can you spare a few minutes?"

"Sure. Now?"

"Let's step in here," Patrick said as they reached the doctors' lounge.

The lounge was light green and sparsely furnished. There was a couch, a table and chairs, a coffee machine and an old television set. Medical journals were scattered on the table, along with the morning newspapers and a book of crossword puzzles.

Patrick sat down, crossing his long legs in front of him. Matt poured coffee.

"We're out of cream, and the sugar's a hundred years old."

"I take it black. Sit down, Matt, I'll get straight to the point. You know, of course, we have to name a new Chief Resident."

"We've been waiting for the announcement."

"Are you interested in the job?"

"Yes, I am."

Matt's voice was clear and calm and his expression had not changed. There was no eagerness, no surprise, no quickening excitement to betray his emotions. Patrick was amused, for he knew Matt Lansing would kill for the job of Chief Resident.

"Do you think you can handle it?"

"I know I can."

Patrick sat back. He sipped his coffee. "I'll be truthful. I have a few doubts about you. You're cocky, you think you can conquer the world all by yourself."

"I've been conquering the world all by myself since I was eight years old," Matt said with his dazzling smile. "Is that so bad?"

"It can be. That attitude can lead to mistakes."

"It hasn't so far."

"So far."

"Dr. Dain, I don't make mistakes."

"All doctors make mistakes. That's the difference between us and God."

"Are you unhappy with my work?"

"Certainly not. You're very gifted. But you're also cocky, headstrong, and, I suspect, stubborn as a mule. All the traits of youth." He smiled.

"You can't hold my age against me."

"I didn't say *age*. I said *youth*. They are not necessarily the same things."

"The traits you're talking about got me where I am now. And where I am now is a long way from where I started. I won't apologize for them."

"You'd disappoint me if you did. I'm speaking to you this way only because I want you to know where I stand."

"Fair enough."

"I'm offering you the job, but with this condition: The job is yours for three months. If it works out, I'll make it permanent."

"What makes you think I'd accept that condition?"

"You want a shot at the job. Chief Resident is a stepping stone to bigger and better things. I know you have your eye on the big medical centers. You're ambitious, Matt, a young man in a hurry."

Matt laughed. His laugh was deep, genuinely merry and warm. "I am ambitious, you're right about that. I want the good life and all the trimmings . . . but that's not all. I want my *work* to be important, to mean something. I'm determined that it will."

"I'm glad. You're good, you shouldn't waste it chasing dollar signs."

"I'll tell you something about that. I was a kid when I decided on medicine. I decided on it because it meant money, lots and lots of money. But when I got to medical school I realized I loved it. The practice of medicine was all I thought about, all I wanted to do. That's as true today as it was then."

"Money no longer interests you?" Patrick smiled.

"I still want the money, but it's my work that drives me. Are you testing me?"

"Not exactly. It's helpful to know how you think. I don't like surprises. Now, what about the job?"

"I don't know. Taking the job conditionally could be a step backward for me. I haven't taken many backward steps, I don't know if I want to take one now."

Patrick sipped his coffee. He looked thoughtfully at Matt. "I could call your bluff, you could call mine. Someone would lose. And that's foolish."

"Maybe."

"Don't let pride get in your way. Not if you're as confident of your abilities as you say."

"A little psychology, Dr. Dain?"

"We're in transition, you know that. This hospital was in bad shape a few years ago. Dr. Murdock and I turned it around, but we can't afford to be wrong. Not in something this important."

"Do I have time to think about it?"

"You don't need time to think about it. Either you want the job or you don't. Don't fence with me, Matt. Yes or no."

"Yes."

"Good. Now that it's settled, I can tell you you were my first choice."

"I thought as much."

"Oh?" Patrick smiled.

"Majeski was my only serious competition. He's leaving."

"You're honest, I'll give you that."

"I like people to know where I stand."

Patrick rose. "An announcement will go out to the staff this afternoon. No mention will be made of the three month trial period. I wouldn't want to give anyone a chance to sabotage you. Not," he laughed, "that I think anyone would. Everyone seems to like you. Half the women are in love with you."

"I think you should know that not everyone likes me. Dr. O'Hara and I had a fight recently. Why we fought doesn't matter. But it shouldn't have happened, and I take full responsibility."

52

"That's noble, but hardly necessary. Matt, having my stepson here at the hospital is sometimes awkward. So let's get it out in the open. I neither want nor expect special favors for Buddy. You will treat him the way you treat any other first-year resident."

"I'd planned to."

"But there will be no more fighting. It sets a bad example, and it's bad for discipline."

"It won't happen again."

"Friction between residents isn't unusual. Particularly if they're both talented. You know the old joke: How many residents does it take to change a lightbulb?"

"Two," Matt answered, smiling. "One to stand on a chair and put the bulb in, the other to knock him off the chair."

"There's a certain truth in that. From medical school on it's one long competition. Competition makes some people push too hard."

"There's no such thing."

"Of course there is. Everybody has limits. Nobody can control all the circumstances all the time. You'll learn that. We all do, sooner or later."

A rare frown creased Matt's brow. "I don't understand what you're trying to tell me."

"You will, sooner or later. Well," Patrick looked at his watch, "I have patients to see. Good luck, Matt. I'll be rooting for you. Don't be afraid to ask for help. I'm here, I'm available."

"Thanks. But I'm putting you on notice . . . three months from today you'll be apologizing for your doubts."

Matt's remark had been free of conceit, full of youthful earnestness, and Patrick smiled. "I will mark the date on my calendar. Meanwhile," he said, going to the door, "check with Jean about staff meetings."

Matt watched the door close. He stood up, then sat down again. He smiled broadly, savoring the moment. He'd been working toward this moment for many years and now those years came back to him. He remembered the first year in medical school—classes all day, cleaning labs at night to earn meal money, studying when he should have been sleeping. It had been a harrowing year, mentally and physically, but it had been the most exciting year of his life. It was then that he'd set out his goals, one after the other, like so many signposts on a long, twisting road. Matt smiled again, for with the Chief Residency he knew the rest of his road would be straight and smooth.

Matt left the lounge. He walked jauntily to the nurses' station. "Where's Holly?" he asked.

The nurse glanced up from her charts. "She's in 814. Hey, you look like the cat that swallowed the canary."

"I should. Dr. Dain just made me Chief Resident."

"Really, Matt? That's great. You were the betting favorite. I had a dollar on you myself."

"Only a dollar?" Matt laughed, walking down the corridor to room 814.

"Holly?" he called softly to a small, pretty blond nurse.

She looked away from her patient for a moment.

"Be right there."

Matt watched while she changed a dressing, wadding up the bloody gauze and tossing it away. She straightened her patient's blankets, said a few words, and then walked over to Matt, her white cap bobbing up and down.

"I thought you'd forgotten my name."

"C'mon, I told you I was sorry about the other night. I had something to do."

"I can imagine the something," Holly Masters said, her brown eyes twinkling. "Was she blond, brunette, or redhead?"

"And I told you it wasn't a woman."

"I know you, Lansing. It's *always* a woman. Your little black book weighs a ton."

"Holly, will you have dinner with me tonight?"

"Why? Did Bo Derek cancel out?"

"Will you be serious?"

"I will if you will."

"Holly."

"Okay," she laughed, "I guess you've had enough. But you had it coming."

"What about dinner?"

"You're on."

"I have something special to celebrate, and I want to celebrate with you."

"Don't tell me . . . Chief Resident?"

"Yep. Dr. Dain just left."

"I knew it! You deserve the job, Matt, nobody's worked harder. Congratulations."

"You can congratulate me properly when we're alone."

"You're incorrigible. What am I going to do with

you? You're too charming to shoot."

He smiled. "Pick you up at eight."

"Okay." She watched him walk away. "Today Rhinelander Pavillion," she murmured, "tomorrow the world."

It was past ten when Patrick got back to his office. He returned, as he often did, with a handful of notes and memos from various doctors and staff members. He flipped through the papers and then dropped them on Jean's desk.

"Do you have time to make some sense of these?"

"I'll type up a summary this afternoon."

"Jean, you are a treasure."

"I know it."

"Patrick." Buddy rushed into the office. "Can I talk to you?"

"I have a consultation in fifteen minutes." He checked his watch. "You'll have to talk fast."

Patrick went into his office. He sat at his desk, looking over his messages. "What can I do for you, Buddy?"

"Is it true?"

"Is what true?"

"Did you make Lansing the Chief Resident?"

"I only left him an hour ago. How did you find out?"

"It's all over the hospital."

"Western Union could learn something from our grapevine."

"Then it's true."

"Yes."

"How could you *do* that?"

Patrick looked up from his messages. "I'm not sure I follow you. *Do* what?"

"Why did you pick Lansing?"

Patrick regarded Buddy silently for a moment. "For many reasons. None of which are any of your business. Look here, Buddy, I'm aware of your problems with Matt, but they are just that, *your* problems."

"I can't work with that guy."

"You *will* work with that guy. Or you will be working at another hospital. Is that clear?"

Buddy threw himself into a chair. He stared down at the floor, kicking at the carpet.

"You're acting like a child," Patrick said. "Three years ago we decided you'd receive no special treatment. That means, among other things, that I won't disqualify a man because you dislike him."

"I've never asked for special treatment," Buddy said quickly. "I've never gotten special treatment."

"Nor will you. Buddy," Patrick smiled, "you're the best of the first-year group, Matt's the best of the senior group. That makes a kind of competition between you. Do I have to tell you my lightbulb joke?"

"Please, I feel bad enough."

Patrick laughed. "Matt's as much of a fighter as you are, he has the same steely will. But in his case the steel is tempered with grace. I am hoping that grace will rub off on you."

"Fat chance."

"*Give* it a chance. Buddy, you don't have to take him to the prom, you just have to work with him."

"I'm not going to make it easy for him."

"God forbid."

"He's not going to make it easy for me."

"He won't let you undercut his authority. So don't try."

"It's going to be a battlefield."

"It needn't be. Absit invidia . . . let there be no ill will."

"I hate this," Buddy said, going to the door. "I HATE this!"

The door slammed and Patrick sighed, sitting back. "Peace, it's wonderful."

5

The bedroom was silent, shrouded in predawn darkness. Patrick came awake slowly, and for a moment he couldn't remember what day it was. He rubbed at his eyes, trying to clear his head. Bits and pieces of his dream came back to him then. It had been a strange dream, full of ominous grays and blues. He'd been running, he remembered, running hard. There had been fog, and in the distance, the sound of a woman crying.

Patrick looked anxiously at Ann. She slept peacefully, the blankets drawn up around her chin. He longed to wake her up, to hold her, to talk to her, to dispell the uneasiness he felt. He kissed her lightly, smoothing back her hair. She didn't stir and he got out of bed, reaching for his robe and slippers.

The barest ray of daylight streaked the sky. The stars were long gone, the moon only a smudged shadow. Patrick peered at the clock and then left the bedroom. He started for the stairs, stopping when he saw the bright light under Daisy's door. He knocked softly and went inside.

"Daisy?"

Daisy sat at the foot of her bed, her legs crossed, her hands folded in her lap. She was watching television, straining to hear, for the volume was very low. Her bed was already made, and she was dressed for the day.

"Daisy," Patrick switched off the television set, "it's a quarter to six in the morning, what are you doing up?"

"I don't know."

He felt her forehead. "Couldn't you sleep?"

"I'm a good sleeper."

"Then why are you up so early?"

"I always get up early."

Patrick sat down next to her. "Why is that?"

"I always got up early with Mamma. We went to work."

"Work? What kind of work did your mother do?"

"She cooked things."

"At home?"

"At Eddie's Diner. She cooked the breakfast. She cooked the coffee break. She cooked the lunch. I helped."

"You did?" Patrick smiled. "What did you do?"

"I peeled vegetables sometimes. Sometimes I made toast. And I put the oranges in the juice machine. That was my best thing."

"I see. Did you go home after lunch?"

Daisy nodded. "We did cleaning and washing. Then we went back to Eddie's and cooked the supper."

"Where was your father?"

"Sometimes he was sick. Mostly he was sick. I

heard Mamma say it was because he drank too much of gin."

Patrick was beginning to get a picture of Daisy's early years. It was a bleak picture, he thought angrily, one without fun or diversion, without any of the high spirits of childhood.

He took her small hand in his. "When did you play? When you got home from Eddie's?"

"It was dark then. Me and Alfie and Eileen played on Sundays. Alfie had a skateboard. Mamma let me stay out 'til supper time. Alfie was my best friend."

"You start school in a few days, you'll make lots of new friends. And when you learn how to write, you can write to Alfie."

"I can write my name. Mamma taught me."

"That's a good beginning."

Patrick smiled at Daisy. She didn't smile back. He sighed, for she'd been with them a week and had yet to smile. He was troubled by her reserve, by the quietness in her gray eyes.

"Daisy is a very pretty name," he said. "But you're a droopy kind of Daisy. Don't you ever smile, or laugh?"

"I don't know." She shrugged.

"Well, until you do, I think I'll have to call you Droopy. Droopy Daisy O'Hara." He ruffled her hair. "Are you hungry?"

"A little."

"Then it must be time for breakfast."

Daisy jumped off the bed. She slipped into her shoes, bending over to fasten the straps.

"May I help?"

"I can do it."

"Sorry, my mistake." He held the bedroom door open. "After you."

Patrick took Daisy's hand when they reached the stairs. He noticed that she didn't run or skip down the steps, the way Tony had when he was little. She walked sedately, holding on to the bannister. That was typical of her, he thought, for in most things she seemed more like a small adult than a small child.

They walked through a hallway to the kitchen. Patrick turned on the lights and plugged in the coffee pot.

"Can I put the oranges in the juice machine?" Daisy asked.

"The juice is already made. Hollis always makes it the night before."

Daisy sat down at the table. "Is Hollis your servant?"

"He runs the household for us."

"Why doesn't Ann do that?"

"She has other things to do."

"What things?"

"Well," Patrick said, setting the table, "Ann was going to school. Now that you're here with us, she's put school aside to take care of you."

He poured a glass of juice for Daisy and one for himself. "Drink up while I start breakfast."

"You?"

"Why not?"

"Men can't cook."

"Of course they can. What will you have? Eggs, cereal?"

"Sugar Sparklers."

62

"I'm afraid to ask what that is."

"Cereal. Little cereal firecrackers with all shiny sugar outside."

"I'm sure we don't have any of that."

"I asked Hollis to buy it in the store. He says no no no. Will you buy it for me?"

"No no no." Patrick smiled.

"Why not?"

"Because your teeth will fall out."

"They'll fall out anyhow. Mamma told me."

"You're going to lose your baby teeth, but you'll be getting *new* teeth. The grownup kind. I'll make oatmeal for you."

"Oatmeal tastes funny."

"Trust me."

"It's sticky."

"Madam, my oatmeal is never sticky."

Patrick took a tin of Irish oatmeal from a shelf. He measured out a large helping, adding cinnamon and milk and handfuls of raisins and currants. He put the pot on the burner and turned up the flame, stirring the mixture slowly.

He glanced back at Daisy, pleased by her small quibbling. He felt hopeful, for she'd shown more animation in that brief exchange than she'd shown all week.

"Patrick, Daisy!" Ann rushed into the kitchen. "You scared me to death!"

"Good morning, darling," Patrick said. "How did we scare you?"

"I woke up and you were gone. I went into Daisy's room and she was gone. Oh," Ann said, her hand on her heart, "any new gray hairs are your fault. Daisy, what are you doing up so early?"

"We've already been through that." Patrick kissed her. "I'll explain later."

"Is everything all right?"

"The coffee is ready, the oatmeal is cooking. Would you care to take over? I think you'd better," he laughed, "Daisy doesn't think you're much of a housewife."

"What?" Ann shook her head. "I'm a few beats behind you this morning. What are you talking about? Is it important?" she asked, stirring the oatmeal.

"Not in the least."

"Good. I'm still asleep."

Ann unplugged the coffee pot and put it on the table. She set out butter and jam and a small tray of croissants.

"You're getting up earlier and earlier every morning, Patrick. What's going on?"

"Nothing special."

"You're making me feel very lazy."

"I was going to wake you up. Then I decided to let you sleep."

"That's why I love you." Ann smiled, going to the stove. "You always do the right thing."

"I thought you'd see it that way."

Ann served bowls of steaming oatmeal to Patrick and Daisy. Daisy sniffed at it, then took a tiny taste.

"Well?" Patrick asked.

"It's better than at Eddie's Diner," she conceded.

"I'll take that as a compliment. Aren't you having any, darling?"

"I can't eat this early. I don't know how you can."

"Years of experience. I'm sorry to get you up, but with Sam in the hospital I feel better being there. And I'm trying to keep an eye on Matt Lansing."

"How is Sam? I haven't had a chance to call Gracie."

Patrick put his spoon down. "You haven't called her?"

"I meant to, a dozen times. But I've been busy with Daisy. I'll do it today, I promise. How is he?"

"He's holding his own. That's more than I expected. Ann, about Matt, I think we should have a small dinner for him. It's customary."

"I don't know," she said slowly.

"We don't have to have him here. We can take him out, if you'd rather. If you're worried about Buddy—"

"It's not that." She ran a hand through her tousled honey hair. "I don't want to set a date just yet. Can it wait?"

"It can. But why?"

"I wouldn't want to make a date and have to break it."

"I don't understand."

"If something came up with Daisy."

"Hollis will stay with Daisy. He got his basic training looking after Tony. He knows what he's doing."

"Could we talk about this later?"

Patrick looked up. He saw Ann's hand moving nervously about the table. "No," he said, "I don't

65

think so."

"Patrick ... Bren and I haven't settled on a schedule yet."

"*What?*"

"Until we do, I don't want to make any dates."

Patrick stared at Ann in silence. He looked at Daisy then. She'd finished all of her juice and cereal. She sat quietly, her elbows propped on the table, her chin propped on her hand.

"Do you want anything else, Daisy?" Patrick asked.

"No."

"Then run along upstairs and brush your teeth."

Daisy slid off the chair and walked to the door. Patrick watched her, a little figure in a red jumper and white blouse.

"I'll be right up, honey," Ann called after her. "Patrick, I'm sorry about the schedule. But Bren keeps changing his mind. I haven't been able to pin him down."

"You told me it *was* settled."

"I thought so at the time. Then he changed his mind. What am I supposed to do?"

"You know the answer to that."

"Well, he's her father. I can't issue orders about when he can see his own daughter."

"Yes, you can. He will waltz you around forever if you don't. I don't want Bren coming and going as he pleases. I don't want him hanging around here."

"I've *tried* to get him to a schedule."

"You haven't tried hard enough."

"He's not ... an easy man."

"I'm glad you remember that."

Ann stared down at the table. She turned her coffee cup around and around. "I know this is a bad situation."

"Bad heading toward worse."

"What do you mean?"

"Our lives are being upset. Subtly, but surely."

"If you're mad because I didn't call Gracie—"

"I am, as a matter of fact. But it's more than that. Much more. We're not spending as much time together as we did. When we are together . . . you're preoccupied, and I'm afraid to ask too many questions."

"Afraid?"

"Ann, you've never resolved your feelings for Bren. Perhaps it was too painful at first. Perhaps, after a while, it didn't seem to matter. But he's back now. It matters."

"You're not suggesting I still care for Bren?"

"I don't know what I'm suggesting. I only know you're letting Bren take advantage of you."

"You're wrong."

"Am I?"

"Patrick, you don't understand. My life is so happy now. His isn't. I owe it to him to do what I can."

"You owe him nothing. He's manipulating you. He has you atoning for imaginary sins."

Ann twisted around in her chair. "I can't help what I feel."

"You don't *know* what you feel. That's the problem. You have to get your feelings sorted out. And soon. I am not going to let him come between us."

"There's no way that can happen."

Patrick threw his napkin down. "There are a hundred ways, a thousand."

"I can't turn my back on Daisy."

"I'm not asking you to. Daisy isn't the issue. Bren is. He's using Daisy to get to you. And doing a bangup job."

"Patrick," Ann grabbed his hand, "I love you. Whatever I felt for Bren died a long time ago."

"I know you love me. I'm not questioning that. But love isn't always enough."

"Stop it. You scare me when you talk that way."

"Why?"

"You never talked that way before."

"I never had to. I'm concerned, Ann. We have something very good, I want to protect it."

"Do you think I'd risk what we have?"

Patrick took her face in his hands. "Not deliberately."

"Not any way at all."

He kissed her. "That's what I wanted to hear." He smiled. "I suppose you're anxious to get upstairs to Daisy."

"Do you mind?"

"No, I don't mind. But you're pushing too hard with her."

"I have to. She doesn't like me."

"She doesn't like anybody. She's not used to affection, she doesn't trust it."

"I sensed that. That's why I'm doing everything I can."

"Everything is right. You took her to the doctor, to the dentist, to have her hair cut, to enroll at school. You took her shopping for clothes, for dolls and toys and books. You play games with her, read to her, teach her to sew. That's quite a lot in a week. It may be too much."

"Do you think so?"

"Don't press, darling. Children are like puppies, they need time to sniff you out."

"I'll remember that," Ann said as they went to the door. "And I'll work everything out with Bren this morning. That's a promise."

Patrick stopped. "This morning?"

"He's . . . coming over here. He wanted to spend time with Daisy, and he wanted to see her school. I said I'd take him to see it."

"Mornings are for work. Why isn't Bren at his job? I thought the whole point of our taking Daisy was so Bren could get settled in his job."

"Well, he's having some problems."

"Problems," Patrick said tersely. "Now why doesn't that surprise me?" He walked quickly into the hall, Ann hurrying behind him. "What else haven't you told me?"

"Nothing. I—"

"Next thing I know, he'll be moving in with us. Shall we ready the other guest room?"

"Patrick, you're upsetting yourself for no reason."

He stopped at the foot of the stairs. "I am under constant pressure at the hospital. I don't want pressure in my own home."

"There won't be any."

"There already is. We're arguing, Ann. Or hadn't you noticed?"

"*Yes*, I noticed. Can't we talk about it?"

Patrick started up the stairs. "I haven't time. I have to go to work. Interesting arrangement we have here. I go to work and my wife spends the day with her ex-husband."

Tears started in Ann's eyes. "Patrick, *please*," she called after him.

Patrick continued up the stairs. He didn't look back. His face was flushed, he felt a fierce pounding in his head. He was angry, angry at Bren, at Ann, at himself. He and Ann had quarreled before, but they'd been minor quarrels, easily solved, immediately forgotten. This, he knew, was different, for the words he'd spoken in anger would linger uneasily between them, perhaps for a long time.

"Hi, Patrick," Buddy said, coming out of his room.

"Morning. If you wait while I shower and dress, I'll drive you to the hospital."

"I wouldn't want any special treatment." Buddy smiled slightly.

Patrick didn't see Buddy's smile. His jaw tightened as he went into his bedroom. "I'm in no mood for your nonsense this morning." He slammed the door behind him.

Buddy stared at the closed door, then turned and went down the stairs. He saw Ann sitting on the bottom step, wiping her eyes.

"Ma, what's the matter?"

"Nothing."

Buddy sat beside her. "Ma, tell me."

"Patrick and I had an argument."

"Is that all? He and I argue all the time."

"It's not the same thing."

Buddy looked closely at his mother. He saw her anxiety, her trembling hands. "If Patrick did something to hurt you, I'll—"

"Be quiet, Buddy. *I* did something to hurt Patrick."

"You? I don't believe that."

"I didn't mean to hurt him. But I did."

"No."

"*Yes*. The worst part is . . . I'll probably do it again."

6

"Dr. Lansing to nine, stat . . . Dr. Lansing to nine, stat."

The ninth floor of Rhinelander Pavillion was in chaos. Shrill, ear-splitting music blasted from room 902, reverberating through the corridors. Nurses and aides crowded the entrance of the room, gesturing, shouting to be heard above the noise. Patients were out of their beds, jostling each other to get a better view. Undelivered dinner trays were stacked on carts abandoned haphazardly by an elevator.

Matt Lansing burst through a side door and raced down the corridor. He dodged the dinner carts and pushed his way into the crowd.

"We've got trouble, Matt."

"No kidding. You nurses get these patients back to their rooms. Ruth, Ellen, move it! Get them back to bed. The rest of you get back to work. Now!"

Matt ran into 902. *"My God,"* he said, staring in disbelief.

A patient was backed against the wall, his arm

locked tightly around a nurse's throat.

"Don't come any closer," he warned, holding a broken, jagged vase to the nurse's face.

"Take it easy," Matt said. "Nobody's going to hurt you. Just take it easy. Peg," he said to the terrified nurse, "try and stay still. You'll be fine, we'll get you out of this."

The resident, Dr. Roth, looked helplessly at Matt. "I don't know what happened. Peg came in to ask Mr. Boyd to turn his radio down. He exploded. He grabbed her and then smashed the vase."

"What's he here for?"

"Pneumonia. He was due to be released tomorrow."

The bathroom door opened and another patient edged into the room. "He's nuts, that's his problem. Nutty as a fruitcake."

"Please, Mr. Williams," Dr. Roth said, "go back inside."

"All day long he has his radio turned up high. All night long he drinks wine with his visitors. You don't know the trouble I had. Now this. He's a fruitcake."

"Get back inside, Williams. Now!" Matt said. "And stay there," he added as the door closed.

Matt looked closely at Mr. Boyd. He was sweating profusely. His eyes were wild and distended, his lips a purplish color.

"What medication is he on?"

"Penicillin. That wouldn't do it."

Matt saw a cigarette burning in the ashtray. He recognized the sickly sweet smell. "It's pot. He's smoking pot."

73

"I never saw that reaction to pot."

"Maybe there's something else in it. Roth," Matt turned to him, "walk slowly out of the room. Call security. Alert psychiatric. *Go* . . . slowly now, no sudden moves. And make sure the corridors are cleared."

"Where's he going?" Mr. Boyd asked, raising the sharp points of glass closer to Peg's face.

"Take it easy, Boyd. He has patients to see. Why don't you let the nurse go with him?"

"No."

"C'mon, you don't need her. I'll stay in her place."

"No." He was breathing heavily, having trouble focusing his eyes. "She has to . . . has to . . . stay."

"What do you want?" Matt asked quietly. "Is there something you want? Something we can get you?"

"No."

"You look tired. Why don't you lie down, just for a moment? Your eyes are tired, Boyd. How about taking a nap?"

"No."

Matt heard Dr. Roth's footsteps running along the corridor. He looked at Peg. She was crying, the tears slipping silently down her face. Her lips were bitten bloody.

"You're doing fine, Peg. Try and hold on a little longer."

"Where's . . . where's the other . . . guy?" Mr. Boyd asked, blinking his eyes rapidly.

"He has other things to do. So does the nurse. Why don't you let her go now?"

"We'll all go."

He shoved Peg forward, keeping her between himself and Matt. He stumbled and a spike of glass grazed Peg's cheek. She screamed.

"Boyd," Matt said, struggling to keep his voice calm, "you can hardly walk. Let the nurse go. Sit down and we'll talk. Let me help you."

"Move, lady." Mr. Boyd pushed Peg toward the door. "Get out of my way," he said to Matt.

"I can help you. Let me help you."

"Get away . . . away from me."

Matt backed out of the room. There was a uniformed security guard to the left of the door. Four other security guards were positioned along the corridor. The nurses and residents stood in two quiet groups at the nurses' station.

"Turn that radio off," Matt instructed the guard. "Keep the patients inside."

Mr. Boyd lurched into the corridor, half pushing, half dragging Peg with him.

Dr. Roth came up to Matt. "What the hell do we do now?" he asked worriedly.

"Have the pot sent up to the lab for analysis. Then come back." He lowered his voice as the music stopped and absolute stillness fell on the ninth floor. "I'm going to grab him."

"Are you—"

"Do it!"

Matt watched Mr. Boyd. His breathing had become labored and his eyes looked glazed. There was a tremor in his arms and legs, yet his grasp on Peg remained firm.

"Can you hear me, Boyd?"

75

"Hear you," he repeated tonelessly.

"Let the nurse go. You don't need her."

"Need her," he repeated again.

He wove back and forth, the shattered glass moving closer and closer to Peg's throat. She began to sob. Her tears flowed freely, streaming down her face.

"Okay, it's done," Dr. Roth said, coming back. "Are you sure you want to try this?"

"I have to. He's out of his mind, God only knows what he'll do next. Roth, I want you to talk to him. Talk loudly and keep talking. I'm going to try to get behind him."

"What'll I say?"

"Say anything, he won't know the difference."

Dr. Roth began talking and Matt moved away. He took tiny steps, advancing inch by inch for what seemed like an eternity. He heard Dr. Roth's loud, shaky voice. He heard Mr. Boyd's responses, slurred now and incoherent. He looked at Peg, at the weapon so close to her throat, and took a deep breath.

Matt lunged then, grabbing Mr. Boyd's arm, holding it high in the air. "Now, Peg!"

Peg broke loose and crumpled to the ground. The ninth floor sprang suddenly to life, as if awakened from a spell. There were cries and shouts, people running in every direction. Doctors and nurses hurried to Peg. They lifted her onto a gurney and wheeled her away, her sobs echoing through the corridor.

The security guards hurried to assist Matt. Mr. Boyd flailed away at them all. He kicked and punched and bit, slashing Matt's forehead before he was subdued. It took four men to get him on the gurney, four men to secure the restraints on his arms and legs.

"Take him to psychiatric," Matt said. "I'll call them as soon as I can."

Blood spurted from Matt's forehead and spilled down his face. He took a handkerchief from his pocket and held it to the wound.

"That's a bad gash," Dr. Roth said. "Let me take care of it."

"It can wait . . . Ladies and gentlemen, let me have your attention . . . Quiet, please . . . The emergency's over. Take a moment to collect yourselves, then go to all the rooms and reassure our patients. Be sure they know there's nothing more to worry about." He smiled. "You were great, by the way, thanks for the cooperation."

"Hey, Chief Resident," Buddy O'Hara called out, "you're doing a swell job. It's a whole new look in hospitals . . . music blaring, nurses getting attacked, patients smoking dope. What's next? Orgies?"

Matt stared impassively at Buddy. "I'll see you in the lounge in ten minutes. Be there."

"I'm going off duty now."

"You're going to the lounge."

Buddy hesitated. He knew everybody was watching them, waiting to see who would prevail. "I'll see you tomorrow," he said with a nonchalance he didn't feel.

"The lounge. Ten minutes. Or it's your ass in my sling."

Matt turned and walked away, Dr. Roth at his side. Dr. Roth said nothing, taking small sidelong glances at Matt as they walked. Matt's features were serene, but his eyes were twin pools of dark black fire.

"Why are you following me?" Matt asked.

"I want to look at your forehead. I think you'll need stitches."

"It's nothing."

"Look at your handkerchief."

Matt's handkerchief was bright red, soaked through with his blood. The blood dripped off the cloth and trickled down his fingers. "Okay, so I need stitches."

"Let's do it now. There may be glass in there."

"I don't feel any glass."

Dr. Roth stopped at the door of a utility room. "I had a surgical tray set up."

"All right, let's get it over with. Don't be too fancy, I have things to do."

They went inside. It was a narrow room with a sink, an examination table, and one chair. Syringes, vials of medication, and gleaming surgical instruments were arranged on a broad metal tray. Dr. Roth went to the sink and scrubbed his hands.

"The scar shouldn't be too bad," he said.

"With this face, who'll notice?"

"Every nurse at Rhinelander Pavillion."

"Don't believe everything you hear." Matt laughed.

Dr. Roth put on a pair of thin surgical gloves. He disinfected the wound, then probed it gently, tipping Matt's head up into the light.

"No glass, you're lucky."

"I'm also in a hurry."

"It won't take long."

Dr. Roth filled a syringe. He injected the clear liquid into Matt's forehead and then stepped back, preparing the sutures. He pressed the reddened skin around the wound.

"How does that feel?"

"Numb, get on with it."

Dr. Roth swabbed the wound again, then began stitching the raw flesh together. "I'll make it as even as I can."

"Roth, there's going to be an inquiry into this incident. Did you know about the pot? Did anyone?"

"*No.* Boyd was on oxygen the first five days, he wasn't smoking anything."

"When he got off the oxygen?"

"Boyd's been a goddamn pest. But the problem was noise, not pot. His radio going full blast, his visitors going full blast. He drove everybody crazy."

"What did you do about it?"

"Well . . . nothing. Hold on," he said as Matt moved his head, "just one more stitch. Are we supposed to be doctors or babysitters?"

"Both, sometimes. You'll have to learn that the hard way."

"It's always the hard way, in medicine." He tied the last suture and snipped off the end. "Finished. Eleven stitches, all even. Do you want to see them?"

"I'll pass."

Dr. Roth taped a sterile gauze bandage over the stitches. He filled another syringe while Matt rolled up his sleeve.

"Ouch," Matt said as the antibiotics were injected into his arm. "You have a heavy touch with a needle."

"I know. I'm working on it. I still practice on oranges, five minutes every day. Have you had a tetanus shot?"

"Yep." Matt stood up. "I'm covered. You've been very thorough, thanks."

"You're welcome, Dr. Lansing."

"I'll need a full report on Boyd, chapter and verse. On my desk first thing in the morning."

"You'll have it."

Matt went to the door. "Thanks again."

He walked out of the room, turning left and then right, on his way to the lounge. He thought about Buddy O'Hara, about his deliberate, ill-timed rudeness. It was an old story, and he was tired of it, he thought, opening the door to the lounge.

"You're late," Buddy said.

"What of it? I don't work for you, you work for me."

"Temporarily."

"What's that supposed to mean? No, never mind, I'm not here to play word games. I'm here to warn you."

"About what?"

"About your big mouth. You tried to humiliate me in front of the staff. I won't stand for that. I'm warning you . . . *don't* try it again."

Buddy's blue eyes were icy. "Or?"

"Or you'll be one miserable resident. Push me too far and you'll be one miserable *ex*-resident."

"Didn't you ever hear of free speech?"

"This hospital isn't a democracy."

"What is it? A monarchy? And you're the king?"

"I'm your boss, that's good enough."

"Another screwup like today and you won't be anybody's boss."

Matt jammed his big fists into his pockets. He sat on a couch at the far end of the room, putting a safe distance between himself and Buddy. "You're asking for it, O'Hara. You're more trouble than all the other residents combined."

"I'm a damn good doctor. The best. I'm worth it."

"Not to me."

"Who cares?"

The muscles around Matt's mouth tensed. "I thought I was beyond surprising. But you astonish me. What the hell's the matter with you, O'Hara?"

"There's nothing the matter with *me*."

"I know we've never been friends—"

"The word you're looking for is 'enemies'."

"If we're enemies, it's your fault. What have I done to you to make you behave this way? You've been on my back ever since I arrived at Rhinelander Pavillion."

"Then you should be used to it."

"We have to work together. We can't, if you keep throwing stones at me."

"Maybe I have my reasons."

"*What* reasons? Why do you dislike me? Why do you dislike everybody?"

81

Buddy took a step toward Matt and then stopped. "That's not true."

"It is. Why don't you have any friends here?"

"I have friends."

"No. You have admirers, people who appreciate your skill, your abilities. But you have no friends. You chase them away with your temper, your arrogance.

"Buddy," Matt said quietly, "I know you had some trouble during med school. You pulled out of it. You had some trouble during your internship. You pulled out of that. But now you're digging a hole too deep to pull out of."

"Like hell I am. I have a contract."

"Sure, but it has all the usual clauses. You can be suspended or canceled for cause."

"No. *No,*" Buddy paced the room, his hands chopping at the air. "*Nobody's* going to get rid of me. *Nobody.* Do you *hear* me?"

Buddy pounded the table, his temper building out of control. Matt sat up straight. He knew this wasn't just another of Buddy's tantrums. He saw fear in his eyes. He saw panic.

"*Do you hear me?*" Buddy demanded again.

Matt rushed across the room. "The entire hospital can hear you," he said, pushing Buddy into a chair. "Calm yourself, what's the matter with you? Buddy . . . Buddy!" he shook him.

Buddy looked up at Matt, confused. He glanced quickly around the room and then sat back, mopping his forehead.

"Are you all right?"

"Yes. I . . . would be, if people gave me half

a chance."

Buddy's voice was flat. Matt saw that he was spent, all played out.

"Get some rest, we'll talk another time."

"We can talk now, I don't care."

"Go home and get some rest." Matt started toward the door. "We'll talk tomorrow. We've both had bad days." He looked back at Buddy. "I want to help. Won't you believe that?"

"No."

"You believe no one. You trust no one. How can you live like that?"

"Trust is for kids."

"You'll be a lonely man if you think that way."

"I have my work. If you don't take it away from me."

Matt was surprised. "I don't want to take your work away from you. I don't want to take anything away from you. I'm here to help your career, not hurt it. How can I convince you of that?"

"You can't."

"There has to be a way to get through to you. I'm going to find it."

"Leave me alone." Buddy turned his chair around, turning his back on Matt. "Leave me alone."

Buddy leaned forward in his chair, huddled as if against a chill. Matt knew it was useless to say any more. He left the lounge, going to the nurses' station.

One of the nurses smiled at him. "Is the war over? Who won?"

"Not funny."

Matt reached for the phone. He spoke briefly with the lab, at greater length with psychiatric. He hung up the phone then, resting his elbows on the desk.

"This day is never going to end," he said.

"We have hot coffee."

"No, thanks, I have to get downstairs. How's Peg?"

"She's sleeping. They're keeping her overnight for observation."

"I'll stop in later."

Matt went to the elevator. He rode down to the second floor, using the time to put the day's events into perspective. He was upset about the Boyd incident, but he was far more upset about Buddy O'Hara. Something was wrong there, he thought, very wrong.

7

Matt passed through the empty outer office and knocked on Patrick's door.

"Come in."

"Can I talk to you?"

"Come in, sit down. How is your head?"

Matt drew a chair up to Patrick's desk. "A few stitches. Luckily I have a hard head."

"I congratulate you on your bravery." Patrick smiled. "That was a nasty situation."

"You heard."

"I saw. When security was paged I decided to see what it was all about. You took a big chance."

"There was no other way."

"Perhaps not." Patrick capped his pen and folded his hands on the desk. "What happened?"

"I'm not sure yet. Boyd was smoking marijuana, the lab is analyzing it now. There's no history of mental illness that we know of . . . I'm assuming there was something in the drug."

"The nurse?"

"She's all right."

Patrick sat back. "I'm not holding you responsible for what happened, if that's what you want to know."

"It isn't."

"Why are you here?"

"I came to report the incident, to answer any questions."

"My question would be . . . how did the patient's marijuana go undetected in the first place? Your answer would be . . . let me take a wild guess . . . nurses and doctors don't want to be cops."

"They don't."

"I've fought that battle before. And lost. Well," Patrick sighed, "the paperwork begins. I'll need reports from you, the lab, the ninth floor residents and nurses. One set for me, one for Dr. Murdock, one for Eve Lawrence. How long?"

"Within twenty-four hours."

The telephone rang and Patrick reached for it. "Dr. Dain here . . . yes, hold on. The lab," he said, handing the phone to Matt.

"Dr. Lansing . . . yes . . . yes . . . are you sure? . . . okay, call Dr. Graves in psychiatric, he's expecting your call."

Matt returned the phone to Patrick. "They found PCP in Boyd's marijuana."

"Very well. I want to be informed every step of the way on Boyd. In writing. Copies to Dr. Murdock and Eve Lawrence. Clear?"

"Perfectly."

"Good. Anything else?"

"Yes. I'd like to talk about Dr. O'Hara."

"We've had that talk before. I see no need to have it again."

86

"This is different."

"I heard the exchange between you and Buddy. You have the authority to handle it. I'm confident you did just that." Patrick looked thoughtfully at Matt. "Is Buddy the real reason you're here?"

"I told you I came to report the—"

"By rights you should have reported to Dr. Murdock, and you know it. What's really on your mind, Matt? The truth."

"Buddy's on my mind."

"In some ways Buddy's like a child, trying to see how far he can go, how far he can push people."

Patrick went to a cabinet at the side of the room. He opened the door to a compact, well-stocked bar. "A drink?"

"No, thanks."

Patrick poured a bourbon and carried it to his desk. "You see that, don't you?"

"I see that," Matt said slowly.

"But?"

"I don't know. Nothing I can pinpoint exactly."

Patrick sat down. "Something's bothering you about Buddy. What is it?"

"He . . . seems to be under a lot of pressure," Matt said carefully.

"Most residents are."

"Not all the time."

"Buddy does it to himself. If there's an easy way and a hard way, he will choose the hard way. I've given up thinking I could change that. I don't think you can."

"I'm responsible for him. I'd like to try. He doesn't think his work is appreciated."

"Did he tell you that?"

"Only indirectly. He's not about to pour out his heart to me."

Patrick sipped his drink. "Most residents need reassurance once in a while. If that's what you're talking about, fine. Anything beyond that . . . no."

"Buddy's more complicated than most."

"How well I know that. How well we all know that. Everyone at this hospital has spent an inordinate amount of time on Buddy O'Hara. We recognized his potential, we wanted to nurture it. In med school, in his internship, he had everyone's support. Well, now he's a resident. He's at the point where he must do it by himself."

"I'd like to relieve some of the pressure, if I can."

"Why? Why the sudden interest in Buddy? You and he were at each other's throats not long ago."

"I always believed his bluster. Today I realized it's an act, maybe a defense. He's scared."

"Everybody's scared."

"Not the way he is."

Patrick stared at Matt. "What happened between you two?"

"Nothing important. The usual argument."

"Don't spare my feelings. If there's anything I should know, I want to know it. Now."

"I saw a different side of Buddy today. It surprised me, that's all. If I can help, why not?"

Patrick took more of his drink. He was troubled by Matt's attitude. He knew Matt was a shrewd man, a man not given to easy emotions or quick sympathies. His new concern for Buddy was unlike him and his reticence on the subject made it the more disturbing.

"Buddy's made progress in the past few months," Patrick said quietly. "He still has a *long* way to go, of course. I think he'll make it . . . If not, if he can't, the time to find that out is now."

"I don't look at it that way."

"You wouldn't, at your age."

Matt smiled for the first time since he'd come into Patrick's office. "Age has nothing to do with it."

"I'm afraid it has. You're old enough to see the glory in our profession, young enough to discount the reality."

"I was *born* a realist."

"All right. Here is a realistic question: why are you so suddenly worried about Buddy?"

"You're putting me in a difficult position."

"Answer me, Matt."

"He's very . . . tense. Too tense."

"There's a normal tension in residency."

"This isn't normal tension. This is dangerous tension. Haven't you seen it?"

Patrick looked down at his desk. With all the problems at home he knew he'd paid scant attention to Buddy lately. He thought about dinner the night before. Buddy had been quiet, but then they'd all been quiet, deep in their own conflicts.

"I haven't noticed anything unusual."

"It's there. The normal tension of residency is bad enough. *This* worries me."

"Medicine isn't for the faint-hearted. Every good doctor I know, and that includes you and me, has some small core of steel in his character. *Has* to, because that's where the tough decisions are made."

"Buddy has enough steel for a fifty-story building. He just has to learn how to use it to his advantage."

"What do you propose?"

"I'd like to take him off rotation and put him on the wards."

"The wards? There's nothing but pressure in the wards."

"That's the kind of pressure Buddy may thrive on. He'll have more direct responsibility. He'll have more of a sense of accomplishment. He needs that."

"We prefer second or third-year residents in the wards. Ward patients don't have private doctors, so we prefer more experienced residents."

"I know. But Buddy can do the work. He can do anything, once he gets his emotions under control. And he won't be alone there, there are supervising residents."

"You're serious about this."

"I think it'll boost his self-confidence. I think as he gets more confidence, the tension will ease. I have another reason."

"I'm all ears."

"Well, he's dating a ward nurse. Wait." Matt held up his hand. "That's not as dumb a reason as it sounds. Buddy has no real friends here. I think it's important for him to work with someone who cares about him. He needs that kind of contact."

"Amazing," Patrick shook his head. "Is there *anything* you haven't thought of?"

"I was an intern when you came to Rhinelander

Pavillion. I studied the way you solved problems. You dealt with the whole of a problem, not bits and pieces. It was a useful lesson."

"Meaning?"

"In my place, you'd be making the same pitch."

"I'm not in your place. I'm in my place."

"Even better. You can approve my request."

Patrick smiled. "You have everything figured out."

"I try, Dr. Dain."

"I have no objection to your request. As for approving it, that's up to Dr. Murdock. The chain of command is Dr. Lansing to Dr. Murdock. I do not want that chain broken in matters of hospital policy. Do you understand?"

Matt stood up. "I'll tell Dr. Murdock it's okay with you."

"No, you won't. You will *ask* Dr. Murdock if it's okay with him."

"Just wanted to see if you were paying attention."

"Satisfied?"

Matt shrugged. "Sometimes it works, sometimes it doesn't."

"Hospital policy aside, if there's anything I can help you with, I'm here. Don't—" Patrick stopped as the door opened and Ann came into the room. "Hello, darling."

"I got here as soon as I could, traffic was awful," Ann said, brushing her hair back from her face. "Oh, you're busy . . . I'll wait outside."

"Nonsense." Patrick went to her. "I want you to meet Matt Lansing. Matt, my wife Ann."

"Hello, Mrs. Dain."

"I've heard a lot about you. I'm sorry for the interruption."

"A beautiful woman is never an interruption."

"Well," Ann said, startled, "thank you."

"Isn't he something?" Patrick laughed. "In another life he was Errol Flynn. Have a drink with us, Matt."

"I wish I could, but I have reports waiting. It was very nice meeting you, Mrs. Dain."

"Thank you. We want you to come to dinner one night. I'll call you."

"I'll look forward to it. Goodnight, Goodnight, Dr. Dain," Matt closed the door behind him.

"He's charming."

"You noticed. Sit down, darling, I'll get you a drink."

"Did I interrupt anything important?"

"We were all finished." Patrick mixed the drinks and carried them to the couch. "I was beginning to worry."

"Traffic was impossible. Patrick, Hollis told me you called and wanted me to come to the hospital. He didn't say why. Is something wrong?"

"I want to take you to dinner. If I'd called you, you would have found a dozen different excuses not to go."

"Daisy—"

"Will be fine. Hollis will see to everything."

"I was going to read *Winnie the Pooh* to her tonight."

"Hollis is capable of reading *Winnie the Pooh*. Ann, we've been like strangers this past week. Ever since our argument. We need a night to ourselves."

"I know we do."

"Then you don't mind?"

"Mind?" Ann kissed him. "I think it's wonderful."

"I reserved a corner booth at Giovanni's. We'll have wine and candlelight and we'll hold hands under the table."

"You're a nice man, Patrick Dain."

"I happen to love my wife. Did I ever tell you about my wife?"

"No, I don't think you did."

"Well, I love her, you see. I love her wide eyes . . . I love her kindness . . . I love the way she fits into the crook of my arm when we lay in bed."

"You'll have me crying in a minute."

Patrick smiled, looking at her. She was wearing a red wool Galanos suit with a matching three-quarter length cape lined in dark mink.

"And I love her eccentricities."

Ann looked up. "What eccentricities?"

"You took the bus over here."

"How did you know?"

"You always take the bus. You wear designer clothes and take the bus."

"I remember times I didn't even *have* bus fare. And the designer clothes are your idea."

"Because I want you to have everything. Everything beautiful and special and fine . . . Ann, are you crying?"

"I'm just so glad we're talking again, laughing again. This week was so terrible."

"It's over now."

93

"Oh, I hope so."

"What do you mean?"

"Daisy's still with us. As long as she is, there are going to be problems."

"It's been two weeks. It shouldn't be much longer."

"I don't know about that. Things aren't going too well for Bren."

Patrick sighed. "Daisy is a nice little girl, we'll manage. What's wrong with Bren?"

"Everything, to hear him tell it. Patrick, I'm afraid to talk about this, I don't want us to argue again."

"No more arguments."

"You may change your mind . . . I . . . I had to lend Bren some money. Not a lot," Ann added anxiously. "Enough to get him through the next couple of weeks. He thinks the job thing may be settled by then. I had to, Patrick, I—"

"I don't care about the money."

"You ought to, it's yours."

"Ann, you have your own money now. I arranged it that way because that's the way I wanted it."

"You didn't expect me to spend it on Bren."

"How you spend your money is up to you."

"He's broke. He was talking about applying for welfare. I hated to think of Daisy being brought up that way."

"Why doesn't he just get a job? Any job?"

"You don't know Bren. He won't take just *any* job. If he does, he won't keep it. He never did. He always found something wrong . . . the job was too menial, or he couldn't get along with the boss, or the hours were bad. He always found a reason. I know him, it has to be the job he wants or it won't work."

"How about president of IBM? Would that do?"

Ann looked away. "You wanted to talk about this, I didn't."

"I'd like to know what's going on. That's not unreasonable. Daisy will be with us another couple of weeks?"

"Patrick, you said yourself she's a nice little girl."

"Daisy is getting used to a life Bren will never be able to give her. And we're getting used to Daisy. That's not healthy."

"I don't know what else to do. What can we do?"

"I'll have a talk with Bren."

"You said no more arguments."

"No arguments. Talk."

"It won't do any good. He says I nagged him. I did. I nagged, I threatened, I begged. Look how far that got me."

"He's after something, Ann, it's about time I found out what."

Ann took a sip of her drink. "Are you going to offer him money?"

"Perhaps."

"He won't take it."

Patrick's eyes widened. "He won't? He sent you out to work and took your money. He sent his second wife out to work and took her money. He's back in New York and taking your money *again*. He's probably cadging nickels and dimes from

Daisy's allowance."

"Patrick, don't."

"Have I said anything about Bren that isn't true?"

"It's the way you say it."

"What way is that?"

Ann ran her hand through her hair. "Bren can't help what he is. He came to America with big dreams. All his dreams fell apart, one by one. That . . . changed him."

"A great many people came to America with big dreams. Many of their dreams fell apart too, but they supported their families, they built good lives for themselves."

"Bren's always been sensitive. I'm not defending him but—"

"Of course you're defending him." Patrick took a deep breath. He finished his drink and sat back. "I suppose that is your right," he said quietly. "But I intend to have a talk with Bren. That is my right. Ann . . . you really believe you owe him something, don't you?"

"I don't know. We have *so* much."

Ann had given him that explanation before. He hadn't been satisfied with it then and he wasn't now, though he decided not to press the point. He knew there were old emotions, old hurts, churning around in Ann; he knew she would have to deal with them in her own way, in her own time.

"A couple of more weeks won't do any harm," he said gently. "You and Daisy will have time to finish *Winnie the Pooh*."

Ann rested her head on Patrick's shoulder. "I

met Bren when he was fourteen. He'd been in America a year. He was so full of plans and dreams and hopes. He wanted to be a writer."

"Oh?"

"We married in our last year of high school. He worked during the day and wrote at night. He wrote a few things . . . I liked them, but everybody turned them down. So he decided to write full-time and take a part-time job. But Buddy came along, and Jill. It was okay for a while, then it wasn't okay. We were living on potato stew, always behind in the rent. Bren's writing never came to anything. He gave up on it. He gave up on working too."

"I'm sorry, darling."

"He was drinking all the time. He said his spirit had been killed. He said I killed it. One day he left and never came back."

"Ann, you can't believe that was your fault."

"I don't know . . . I only know I don't want to talk about this anymore tonight." Ann wiped her eyes. "I want to go to Giovanni's and hold hands with my husband. Deal?"

"Deal."

Patrick straightened his tie and put on his jacket. He took his coat from the closet and draped it over his arm. They walked to the door, then stopped, looking in the direction of David's office. They heard loud, angry voices, and the sound of something crashing to the floor.

"David and Lola," Ann said. "I rode upstairs with them. Lola was very mad, David was very upset. It's serious, isn't it?"

"All marriages go through rough spots."

"They were married about the time we were. They've been as happy as we've been. And now—"

Patrick put his finger to Ann's lips. "Whatever you're thinking, don't. They'll be fine. So will we. I guarantee it."

8

It had been raining for the past three days, but during the evening the rain had stopped, leaving the air clear and tranquil. The February sky was starless, deep gray-blue.

Patrick turned away from the window, back into the glare of the E.R. He glanced at his watch. "What's keeping Lola?"

"Here she is," Matt said.

Patrick looked up to see Lola leading a small child into the room. She was thin and small-boned, about four years old. Her dark hair was cut short in a ragged cap around her face. Her skin was so pale it was almost translucent.

Patrick drew in his breath, for the child had been badly beaten. The area around her eyes was bruised and swollen. Her mouth was puffy and discolored, and a line of stitches ran from her cheek to her chin.

"Her name is Susan," Lola said, lifting her onto the examination table. "That's all we were able to get out of her."

"Hello, Susan, my name is Patrick."

"Hello," she said stiffly, trying not to move her lips.

"She was found in the lobby," Matt said. "Nobody knows when or how she got there. We're guessing that whoever did this to her got scared, left her here, and took off. She was gushing blood."

"Poor little kid." Patrick stroked her head. "Have the authorities been notified?"

"I want to check her into pediatrics first. I want to do a complete workup, skull series, chest x-rays, blood, urine."

"I agree with that," Lola said.

"What have you done so far?"

"We disinfected her cuts and bruises, sewed up her face, checked for broken bones. This isn't the first time she's been beaten. Her back and upper thighs are all scarred."

"She has some chest congestion too," Matt said. "That's another reaon she should be in pediatrics."

Patrick looked into Susan's tiny face. His heart turned over, sickened by the violence done to the child. He patted her hand. She was so thin, her knuckles were sharp angular ridges.

"Malnutrition."

"Probably," Lola said.

"Susan," Patrick bent to her, "would you like to spend the night with us? We'll get you a big malted with a great big straw."

The child nodded her head up and down. She tried to smile but the effort was too painful. She nodded again.

"Good girl. We'll put you in a nice big room with

lots of other children and lots of toys. You'll like it."

He turned to Matt. "Any tags in her clothing? Anything at all?"

"Nothing. We checked our lost-child flyers too, just in case. Nothing there either."

"All right, check her into pediatrics. Put Dr. Warren in charge, he's had some experience with battered children . . . Susan, don't you worry about anything. We're going to take good care of you. You'll feel better very soon."

Matt lifted the child into his arms. "Okay, Susan, let's go for a ride on the elevator," he said, carrying her out of the room.

Patrick sat down. "I never get used to it."

"There are a lot of sick people out there."

"Yes." Patrick looked at Lola and then looked again. "Speaking of sick . . . you look awful."

"Thanks," she said, making notes in a manila folder, "but flattery will get you nowhere."

Lola had not been herself for several weeks, but now, in the brutal light of the E.R., Patrick saw how much she had changed. She'd lost weight, there were deep hollows in her cheeks. There was a pasty cast to her complexion, and her eyes were bloodshot, ringed with dark shadows.

"Lola, you look ill."

"I'm not ill. I'm a perfectly healthy woman whose marriage happens to be going to hell. As soon as I figure out how to cope with that I will. Until then, what you see is what you get."

"Your marriage?"

Lola closed the folder. "C'mon, Patrick, don't kid a kidder. You know we've been battling. It's all over the hospital."

"I knew something was wrong."

"You don't have to be delicate. We've had some real donnybrooks in David's office. You must have heard them."

"Once or twice."

"Well, didn't you wonder? More to the point, hasn't David confided in you?"

"Not a word. I've asked him, but you know David."

"I thought I did." Lola sat down. "Now I'm not so sure."

"It can't be that serious."

"Can't it?"

"Do you want to talk about it?"

"No. You and David are old friends and these things can be messy."

"You and I are old friends too."

"Not as old as you and David." Lola smiled slightly. "We didn't sail out boats together in Central Park. We didn't go off to Groton together. We weren't Whiffenpoofs together."

"You should talk to somebody. Why don't you talk to Ann?"

"Maybe I will."

"The night of our anniversary party . . . David said something about your working too much."

"I've been putting in more time here, that's true. But that's not the cause of our trouble. Things got bad at home and I turned to my work. But things got bad at home *first*. That's the sequence and David knows it."

"I wish I could help."

"You have your hands full. You don't look all that spiffy yourself."

"We have our little upsets at home too. I am up to my neck in O'Haras."

"How's it going?"

"I pray daily for guidance." Patrick smiled. "At the moment it's Sam Porter I'm worried about. He was released from CCU this afternoon."

"I never thought he'd leave here under his own power."

"Andrew DeWitt pulled him through. But for how long?"

"Have a drink, Patrick, relax."

"Good idea. Come up to the office and have a drink with me. Have two."

"No, I've even lost my taste for booze." Lola laughed suddenly. "Now you know how serious it is."

"Why don't you take some time off?"

"That's the last thing I want. What would I do with it? Think about all the things I don't want to think about?"

"I don't like the sound of this. You're not going to give up on David, on your marriage?"

"That question implies I have a choice."

"Don't you?"

"There are choices and there are choices."

"We're very cryptic tonight."

Lola stretched her arms above her head. "We're very tired tonight." She went to the door. "I have to get back to work. Will you see that Eve Lawrence gets the proper forms on Susan?"

"I'll take care of it." Patrick followed her out. "I have a few patients to see, but she's working late. Why don't you like Eve?"

"Who says I don't?"

"Well, do you?"

"I don't like her, I don't dislike her. I'm neutral. I'm Switzerland," Lola said, walking away.

David and Eve were seated on the velvet couch in Eve's office. The bright overhead lights had been dimmed, replaced by the gentler lights of the lamps on the end tables. Classical music drifted softly through the rose-scented air.

"Are we done with the paperwork?"

David closed the last file. "Done and done."

"Hallelujah." Eve gave David his drink. "On to better things."

"What did you have in mind?"

"Oh," Eve ran her finger along the back of his hand, "anything that suits your fancy."

"You're a very suggestive lady."

"Is that a complaint?"

"I'd sooner tear out my tongue."

Eve moved closer to him. She kissed his forehead, his cheek, his neck. She kissed his lips, lightly at first, then insistently.

"Make love to me," she said.

"Eve," he put his glass down and pulled her to him, "Eve."

"Make love to me."

"Here?"

"You won't be coming to my place tonight. And

this is such a lovely couch." She unbuttoned her blouse, tossing it on the floor. "It's a new adventure. Adventure is the spice of life."

She stepped out of her skirt and stood before him. He saw the rise of her breasts, the curve of her hips under the thin silk slip. He took off his jacket and tie.

"Hurry, David," she said, lying down.

David undressed and joined Eve on the couch. He stripped away the last of her clothing and gazed at her.

"You're so beautiful."

Eve drew him to her. Their bodies pressed together, their mouths moved hungrily on each other. They were consumed by the moment, by each other. They didn't hear the knock on the door.

Patrick stood frozen at the edge of the room. He blinked his eyes several times, unwilling to believe what he was seeing.

"I beg your pardon," he said curtly, slamming the door as he left.

Patrick walked along the corridor in a daze. He was stunned by David's behavior, saddened by it. He went into his office and poured a drink. He walked around the room, sipping his drink, stopping at the bookshelves, at the wall of paintings, at the windows.

He sat down for a while, leaning back in his chair. Lola kept coming into his thoughts. Did she know the truth about Eve and David, he wondered. She was a proud woman, he could imagine her pain.

Patrick set his drink down. Some of the liquid splashed on his desk, splattering a stack of papers.

He took his handkerchief and sopped up the liquid, brushing off the papers. He crumpled his handkerchief and threw it down.

"Patrick?"

"Not now."

David, neatly combed and dressed, crossed the office and mixed a drink. He took a large swallow of bourbon and then sat down.

"This is extremely embarrassing."

"To say the least."

"I'd like to explain."

"I'm not your conscience."

"But you are . . . You always play by the rules."

"I was brought up to play by the rules. So were you."

"I'm a big boy now."

"If cheating on your wife makes you a big boy. I take it this has been going on for some time."

"I don't know how it started," David said quietly.

"The hell you don't. Somebody makes a pass. That pass is completed or it isn't. I don't know if you were the passer or the passee, but either way you had a choice."

"It was only a flirtation, at first."

"And now?"

"I don't know."

"Surely you've thought about it."

"I haven't thought about anything else. This isn't easy for me, Patrick."

"If you're waiting for sympathy, don't."

"Not sympathy. Understanding."

"Are you in love with Eve?"

"No."

"Is she in love with you?"

"No. We're . . . attracted to each other, that's all."

"I'd expect that answer from a kid. You're no kid. You're risking everything . . . your marriage, Lola, and for what?"

"Don't you think I've asked myself that same question?"

"I think you're a horse's ass, but that's beside the point."

"You're my friend, *be* my friend."

"David, I don't want to see you throw away everything on a meaningless affair. I don't want to see you hurt. And you will be, if you go on this way."

"I love Lola, but I've always had the feeling that her work comes first. Eve . . . makes me feel important."

"Lola is a dedicated doctor. That doesn't mean she loves you any less."

"Her hospital obligations always seem to take precedence."

"Your hospital obligations take precedence, why shouldn't hers? It's actually worse for her. She's in emergency medicine, a completely unpredictable service."

"I know," David said impatiently, "but I don't know if that's the kind of marriage I want."

"Since when? Since Eve?"

"Leave her out of it."

"I wish I could. The events of this evening make that impossible."

"It's not Eve's fault."

"She's hardly an innocent bystander. Which brings me to another point. What you're doing is bad enough, but to do it *here*, practically under Lola's nose, is unforgivable."

"Don't worry, I'm not forgiving myself. There will be no repeat performances here."

"Here. Then you intend to continue seeing Eve?"

"Probably, yes. I need time to think, to put things in order."

"For a man who values order, you are certainly making a mess for yourself."

"Patrick, something was missing from my life. I don't know what, exactly, I only know it was missing . . . Then I came across a young, beautiful, desirable woman."

"Young, beautiful, desirable, *and* easy."

"Y   make it sound coarse."

"*Romeo and Juliet* it isn't."

"I didn't expect you to approve, but you don't have to be nasty."

"You need a kick in the pants, David. I'm happy to oblige."

"I have to do this my way."

"Where is *Lola's* way in all this? Have you *looked* at her lately? She looks terrible."

David got up. He walked back and forth, his mouth a tight line. "She's working herself to death."

"I'm not surprised. There's nothing for her at home."

"That's a cheap shot."

"You had one coming."

"We're obviously at an impasse."

"In more ways than one. You and I and Lola and Eve have to work together. How can we, with this hanging over our heads?"

"Eve won't make any trouble."

"She already has. Do you think I would have Eve and Lola at the same staff meetings now? Don't you realize the complications?"

"All I need is time. I'll work it out."

"Either that's wishful thinking, or your brain's gone soft."

David turned to Patrick. "Lola doesn't know about Eve."

"You really are a horse's ass. Lola probably knew about Eve fifteen minutes before you did."

"She doesn't know. She suspects."

"She knows now."

They swung around to see Lola framed in the doorway. She was very pale, save for two spots of bright color high on her cheeks. Her eyes were somber, shrouded with pain.

Patrick put his head in his hand. David didn't move. His face was gray, his lips parted soundlessly.

"Let me get you something," Patrick said. "A drink? Coffee?"

"No."

David took a step toward her. "Lola—"

"Don't say anything, David. I don't want you to say anything." She sat at the edge of the couch, hugging her arms around her. "I want to talk to Patrick. Alone."

"Lola," David said, "please listen to me. I—"

"Don't come home tonight. It will take me a while to clear my things out of the apartment. Don't come home until I've gone."

"I don't *want* you to go," David said desperately. "Please let me explain."

"I want to talk to Patrick. Alone."

"David," Patrick said in a low voice, "I think Lola needs a moment. Why don't you wait in your office."

David looked at Patrick. He looked at Lola, then went reluctantly to his office door. "We can work this out, Lola. I *know* we can," he said, going inside.

Patrick poured a cup of coffee. He added a jigger of brandy and took it to Lola.

"I don't know what you heard, but don't do anything hasty."

Lola took a sip of coffee. She put the cup down and pushed it away. "I heard the truth. I knew it all along, I tried to convince myself I was wrong."

"Talk to him, Lola."

"I don't have anything to say."

"He does."

"He's too late, Patrick, I want a week off."

"Of course. Dr. Rogers can take over for as long as you need."

"A week. I have to pack, find a place."

"I'm not trying to excuse David's behavior, but—"

"Thank you for that."

"But you two had a good marriage. It's worth fighting for. You fight for your patients, for your staff . . . it's time to fight for yourself."

"I'm all fought out." Lola left the couch. She

110

walked halfway across the room and stopped, looking at Patrick. "It's not the playing around that bothers me so much. It's the dishonesty of it. David was always absolutely honest, his integrity was absolute."

"Sometimes men get a little lost when they reach their forties."

"He betrayed me, Patrick. And himself. And our marriage." Lola went to the door. "I'll see you in a week."

"If there's anything I . . ." he began, but she was gone.

David came back into the office. He sat down, got up, sat down again.

"Well, did you hear?" Patrick asked.

"I was listening at the door. God, I didn't mean to hurt her. I *never* meant to hurt her."

"You have a certain naivete, David. You had it thirty years ago, you still have it."

"I'll talk to Lola tonight. We'll straighten it out."

"Don't even try. She's hurt and angry and tired."

"I don't want her to leave." David swallowed hard. "She *can't* leave."

Patrick looked sadly at David. He knew it would be a long night.

9

It was after ten when Patrick arrived home. He hung up his coat and put his medical bag on the top shelf of the closet. He took a bulky package from his pocket and walked toward the stairs.

"Ann? . . . Hollis? . . . anybody here?"

"Me."

Patrick turned to see Daisy, in a long quilted bathrobe and fuzzy pink slippers, standing outside the kitchen.

"You're up awfully late."

"I was getting a glass of milk. Ann said I could."

"Well come here, I have something for you." He sat on the bottom step, putting the package in his lap. "Do you remember we talked about getting you a pet?"

"I want a pony."

"You can't have a real pony. I explained that. But this may help."

"For me?"

"For you."

Daisy tore the paper off the package. She stared at her gift, a tan cloth horse with a mane and tail of

112

dark brown yarn.

"Do you like him?"

"His name is Alfie and he's handsome."

"And what do you say?"

"Thank you, Patrick."

Daisy smiled. It was only a brief half-smile, a little shy at that, but Patrick was satisfied. She'd seemed more relaxed recently, more like a child, and he was convinced she was finally coming out of herself.

"You have to take good care of Alfie."

"I will. He can sleep in my bed."

"Fine."

"I have a new bed."

"You do?"

"With ruffles."

"It sounds very pretty. Where's Ann?"

"Upstairs. With Poppa. They're in my room. My room has all new stuff."

Patrick frowned. "What kind of stuff?"

"All kinds."

"I see. Run along, have your milk now, Droopy. No dawdling."

She went off to the kitchen, Alfie clutched to her chest. Patrick started up the stairs. He stopped near the top of the landing and looked into Daisy's room. Ann was pointing to something, Bren at her side. They were laughing.

"Ann?" Patrick called.

"Patrick." Ann ran into the hall. "I'm so glad you're home. Wait until you see what we've done with Daisy's room."

"Hello, Patrick." Bren grinned.

"Still here?"

"You and I were supposed to have a talk. I came at eight on the dot. Seems you were delayed."

Patrick kissed Ann. "Let's see what you've done."

He walked into Daisy's room. He hardly recognized it, for it had been entirely redecorated. There was a ruffled white canopy bed, near it a child-sized rocking chair with a huge Raggedy Ann doll. There was a child-sized table and chairs, a desk, and a vanity with a ruffled white skirt. There were several bureaus and two wide bookcases. The walls had been covered with daisy-springed wallpaper.

"Do you like it?" Ann asked eagerly.

"I'm overwhelmed."

"But do you like it?"

"It's lovely . . . it must have taken a long time."

"The paperhangers came this morning. The furniture came this afternoon. Bren helped me get the last pieces in place."

"It's so nice to have a man around the house."

The smile left Ann's face. "You're upset."

"I'm not upset." Patrick walked out of the room.

"Where are you going?"

"I'll be in the library. Don't let me disturb you."

He hurried down the stairs, Ann and Bren close behind. He went directly to the library, sitting down at his desk.

Bren poured himself a drink. "Don't you want to have our talk, Patrick?"

"Not tonight. Call me tomorrow, we'll make another appointment."

Bren stood where he was, taking long swigs of his

114

drink. Patrick looked at him. He shook his head.

"You've had the company of my wife, the run of my apartment, the use of my bar. Is there anything else I can do for you?"

"Can't think of a thing." Bren smiled his crooked smile. "Anything I can do for you?"

"You can leave."

"Patrick," Ann said quickly, "you asked Bren to come tonight."

"Now I'm asking him to leave. Goodbye, Bren."

"I'll just finish my drink."

"Take the bottle with you. Take *all* the bottles with you if you want, but *go.*"

Ann looked nervously at the two men. "Patrick—"

"Dammit, Ann." Patrick slammed the desk with his fist. "I've been working since seven this morning and I'm tired. No more conversation. *Goodbye,* Bren."

Bren put his glass down. "Thanks for the dinner, Annie Laurie. I'll find my way out."

Bren's departure was followed by several minutes of deep silence. Ann sat on the couch, lacing and unlacing her fingers. Patrick lit a cigarette, watching the gray smoke curl lazily through the air.

"Bren was here at your invitation," Ann said finally.

"I called you at eight o'clock. I told you I would be late. There was no reason for Bren to stay."

"He was helping me with Daisy's room."

"Ah, yes. Daisy's room. How long have you been planning it?"

"A couple of weeks."

"And you never said a word."

"I didn't want to bother you. Patrick, I don't want to talk about this when you're so upset. You said there'd be no more arguments."

"I said a lot of things. So did you. Talk is cheap."

"I don't know what you mean."

"That room looks awfully permanent to me."

"Daisy can take the furniture with her when she goes."

"When she goes? When is she going? It's been five weeks."

"Bren—"

"Oh, I know . . . poor Bren is having problems . . . things aren't going well for poor Bren. What else is new?"

"Sarcasm isn't going to help."

"When does it end, Ann? Or doesn't it?"

"There's a *child* involved."

"*We're* involved. Our *marriage* is involved. Daisy could stay here forever and I wouldn't mind. But where Daisy is, Bren is. And *that* I will not tolerate much longer."

"He's sticking to the schedule. Except for tonight, he's stayed out of your way."

"But not out of yours."

Tears stung Ann's eyes. "If you don't know how I feel by now."

"I don't know because you don't know. You have to face the truth, Ann. Daisy isn't Jill. This isn't fifteen years ago. Bren isn't your husband."

Ann was very white. She turned away. "I can't listen to this. I won't."

"I'm not giving you a choice this time. You have

116

a lot of thinking to do. You have to come to terms with the past. And with the present. When you do, you'll know where you want to be. With me. Or with Bren."

There was profound silence. Then from Ann's throat came a sound that might have been a choked cry. "Patrick," she said with great difficulty, "all this because of a *room?*"

"I come home to find you and Bren acting like young-marrieds inspecting their daughter's nursery. A cozy, domestic picture. But there's something wrong with the picture, because he's not your husband and she's not your daughter."

"If it looked that way—"

"It looked that way."

Ann fell back against the couch. "I'm so sorry. I really am."

"I don't want you to be sorry. I want you to face the demons. Put the past to rest, one way or another. We'll have no peace until you do."

"It took me so long to forget the past."

"You didn't forget it, don't you see that? It's always been there, haunting you. *Deal* with it, once and for all."

Ann wiped the tears from her eyes. She stared unhappily at Patrick. "What if I can't?"

Patrick swiveled around in his chair. He looked toward the windows, to the twinkling lights of the city. His head ached, the lights bothered his eyes. He turned back to Ann.

"Where is Buddy?"

"He's out."

"Again?"

"He came home, changed his clothes, and went out again. I can't tell him what to do anymore, he's not a little boy."

"Have you tried?"

"Yes, I've tried. You always told me I tried too hard."

"Did you talk to him tonight?"

"He didn't give me a chance . . . Why?"

"How does he seem to you?"

"All right." Ann sat up straight. "Why?"

"I wonder if he isn't getting lost in the shuffle around here. Daisy gets all the attention, there isn't much left over for him."

"Is something wrong with Buddy?"

"I don't know. But he can't work all day and stay out all night."

"He doesn't have to stay out all night. Or are you blaming that on Daisy too?"

The telephone rang and Patrick reached for it. "Yes? . . . this is Dr. Dain . . . when?" He looked at his watch. "Yes, I see . . . is Dr. DeWitt there? . . . and call Dr. Murdock . . . well try the Yale Club, if he's not there, try the Atheltic Club. I'll be right over."

Patrick hung up. "Sam Porter's back in the hospital. He's dying."

"Oh." Ann's hand went to her mouth. "He was doing so well, what happened?"

Patrick walked to the door. "I'll stay at the hospital tonight. There's no point in my coming home."

Ann ran after him. "What do you *mean*, no point?"

Patrick started to speak, then changed his mind. He took her hand and held it for a moment. "It will be late. I'll stay at the hospital."

"You can't work all day and stay out all night either."

He brushed her forehead with his lips. "I'll call you in the morning."

Patrick hurried through the E.R. He stopped as David came out of one of the treatment rooms.

"Well?"

David shook his head. "You don't want to go in there."

"Is it over?"

"Andrew's doing his best, but . . ." He shook his head again.

"I want to see Sam."

David put his hand on Patrick's arm. "Not this way."

Patrick shook him off. "I want to see Sam."

He went inside. He saw Dr. DeWitt, Dr. Rogers and a nurse bent over Sam. Sam lay on the examination table, tubes running into his nose and arm. His face and body were the color of chalk, his lips a ghastly blue. He was gasping for air, his face twisted in a frozen mask of pain. Patrick looked at the heart monitor. The tracings were rapid and faint.

"Andrew?"

Andrew DeWitt didn't answer. He concentrated on Sam, massaging his chest, his eyes darting to the monitor. The nurse gave him a syringe.

Andrew injected the stimulant into Sam's heart

muscle, looking again at the monitor, silently counting off the seconds. He repeated the rhythmic heart massage while Sam's chest was covered with cream and a defibrillator was moved into place. The electricity shot through Sam's body.

"Again. Stand clear."

The electricity crackled and spat. They all looked to the monitor. The tracings slowed for a moment, then quickened.

"Again."

Once more Sam's body heaved up and down. His eyelids fluttered. There was a final gasp, then silence.

"Straight line!"

"Shock him again!" Patrick cried.

Andrew put his stethoscope to Sam's chest. He nodded at the nurse. She drew a sheet over Sam's face.

"Andrew, *no.*" Patrick grabbed him.

"I'm sorry." He took a towel from the nurse and dried his damp face and head. "I did everything I could. He had no heartbeat when he was brought in. We pulled him back. There just wasn't enough live tissue there." Andrew sighed. "He put up a hell of a fight."

"Why did you let him go home?"

"There was nothing more we could do. And he wanted to go home. He wanted to sign a will. He wanted to see his dog."

"Bess?"

"You know how he felt about that big mutt. Patrick, he told me he wanted to die at home, in his own bed. Sam taught anatomy for a long time, he knew what was going on."

"I can't believe he's gone."

"Excuse me, doctors," the nurse said. "We . . . uh, have things to do here."

Andrew steered Patrick into the corridor. "I know he seemed ageless, but he was seventy three. He had a good life."

"Are you okay?" David asked.

"Yes. Where's Gracie?"

"She's upstairs, under sedation. The first shot didn't work, we gave her a second. She'll sleep for a while. She needs that. I called her son, he's calling the rest of the family. She won't have to go through this alone. There are children, grandchildren, even a few great-grandchildren."

"Sam had a request," Andrew said as they walked toward the lobby. "If there's a memorial service, he wanted only happy recollections."

"There are plenty of those. Do you remember his last birthday party?"

"I remember he told dirty jokes in Latin."

Patrick smiled. "We can omit that particular recollection from the service."

"Everybody has at least one funny anecdote about Sam. We'll collect the best of them."

"Will you make the arrangements for the service?" Andrew asked.

"We'll see to it."

"Let me know as soon as it's set. I'll clear my schedule . . . *Damn*, I wish I could have done more for him."

"There's no one better than you, Andrew. If you couldn't do it, it couldn't be done."

"They're all tough to lose, but some are tougher than others."

"Who's for a drink?"

"Not me," Andrew said. "I'm operating at seven in the morning." He checked his watch. "Time to go. Goodnight, Patrick, David."

"Goodnight. Thanks for everything."

Andrew left and David turned to Patrick. "My car is parked around the corner. Can I drop you at home?"

"I'm not going home."

"You're not?"

"No."

"Where are you going?"

"To my office. I'm going to have ten or twenty drinks and collapse on the couch."

"We have a meeting in your office with orthopedics first thing in the morning."

"Perfect. I won't have far to go."

"Why aren't you going home?"

"Ann and I need a little distance. Bren has her tied in knots. I'm trying to be patient, but it's beginning to get to me."

David followed Patrick into the elevator. "Why don't you give him a check and tell him to get the hell out?"

"I've been waiting for Ann to tell him to get the hell out. Needless to say, it's been a long wait."

"Ann's not the type to do that."

"She certainly isn't when it comes to Bren. She's like a child around him, unsure, indecisive. She's supporting him now. Did I tell you that?"

David didn't reply. Patrick glanced at him as they

122

walked through the darkened, deserted corridor.

"Well, say something."

"I'm not exactly an expert on marriage. Lola will testify to that."

"Say something anyway."

"If Ann can't handle him, it's up to you."

Patrick turned on the lights in his office. David went to the bar. "What do you want?"

"Nothing. I was kidding about the ten or twenty drinks. But not about the couch." He flopped down, loosening his tie. "I intend to have a talk with Bren, but that won't solve the problem."

"Why not?"

"Because the problem is Ann. She's caught between the past and the present. Bren knows that."

"If you give him what he wants he'll clear out."

"I don't *know* what he wants. Oh, he wants money, but that's not all he wants."

"What more is there for someone like Bren?"

"Revenge. In some strange way he blames Ann for his failure. I think he wants to pay her back."

"All the more reason to get rid of him."

"I could buy him off, sure. But he could always come back. It would start all over again."

"Where does that leave you?"

"Between the legendary rock and the legendary hard place."

"We've been playing chess for twenty-five years." David smiled. "Don't tell me you can't outwit him."

Patrick clasped his hands behind his head. He stared up at the ceiling. "Don't underestimate him.

Bren's a crafty son of a bitch."

"I've heard the same thing said about you. In the same tone of voice."

"I keep telling myself the answer is to wait him out. Then I see Ann getting in deeper and deeper and I explode. He has me playing *his* game, and losing."

"Not for long."

"I wouldn't count on that. He's using his poverty, and Ann's guilt, *and* Daisy. That's potent stuff."

"Doesn't Ann see what he's doing?"

Patrick looked at David. "I'd give quite a lot to know the answer to that question. I'd give everything."

10

Patrick pressed the intercom button. "Yes, Jean?"

"Mr. O'Hara is here."

"Send him in."

Bren strode into the office. "Good morning to you, Patrick."

"Good morning." Patrick looked at him. He was wearing an old sweater and jacket, but he carried a new, expensive camel's hair coat. "There's coffee on the table. Help yourself."

"Never touch it."

Bren hung up his coat with elaborate care. He sat down and lit a cigarette, staring at Patrick through the smoke. He smiled.

"Well, how much are you going to offer me?"

"Who says I'm going to offer you anything?"

"I know your type. When you have a problem, you write a check. That's the way it's done."

"Don't hold your breath."

"It's you who's holding his breath. I've upset your applecart, Patrick. Isn't that so?"

Patrick sipped his coffee. "When you first

appeared on our doorstep, you said something about joining a trucking company. Is there really a trucking company?

"There is for a fact. P&L, over on Ninth Avenue."

"But you have no intention of joining it."

"No." Bren glanced around the office. "Look at you, Patrick Dain. Born into the lap of luxury and living there all your life. Why should I drive a truck?"

"What does one thing have to do with the other?"

"Oh, it's simple. I fell into a pot of gold. I like it there."

"You like having Ann support you?"

"Why not? She's my wife."

"*Was.*"

"That's right. I was her *first* husband, her *first* love. A woman doesn't forget her first love, especially a woman like Annie . . . Then there's Daisy, my ace in the hole."

"You've given this a lot of thought."

Bren stubbed out his cigarette. He smiled slowly. "I'll never forget that summer day in Southie. A hot day it was, not a breeze anywhere. There I was, reading my newspaper. What do I see? My Annie . . . wearing fine clothes, standing in front of a fine house, holding hands with a fine new husband. And the husband is rich. *Rich.* Well, right away I got to thinking."

"And scheming."

"I went straight to the library. I looked you up in a big book. There was more than a page on the Dain family. Bren, my boy, I said to myself, it took a while, but your ship finally came in."

"That newspaper article appeared seven months ago. What took you so long?"

"There were complications."

"Do tell."

"My wife was still alive then. I couldn't come to New York with Daisy *and* Irene, could I? No advantage there. You see what I mean, Patrick?"

"Indeed I do."

"I talked it over with Irene. We talked about it for weeks. Looked at it from every angle. We finally decided Daisy and I would come to New York and get what we could."

"I know that game. It's called Family Fraud." Patrick sat back. He was uneasy, for he didn't understand why Bren was talking so freely. "Do you know that you're incriminating yourself?"

"Me? How would I be doing that? This is a private conversation. You could repeat it, but I'd deny it. Annie never thought I was too smart. She wouldn't believe I planned this out."

"I could be recording this conversation."

"But you're not." Bren grinned. "New York is a great city, you can buy anything here." He took a pen from his pocket and held it up. "This is the first thing I bought. It's called a detector. If there's any recording going on, this pen gives a signal. It cost a pretty penny . . . but you have to spend money to make money. Isn't that so, Patrick?"

"*Why* are you telling me this?"

"Because I want you to squirm. I want you to know how well I've planned, and how long." Bren's eyes glinted. "I want you to suffer."

"You are telling me Irene is alive?"

"No. That was another complication. Irene got sick. Then she got sicker. Then, God rest her soul, she died."

"Poor Irene."

"A sad day it was."

"Of course that means you don't have to share the loot."

"You could look at it that way."

Patrick was quiet for a moment. His eyes narrowed slightly. "How did Poor Irene die? Terminal greed?"

"She died of the fever."

"What fever is that?"

"The lung fever."

"You must excuse me," Patrick said. "I don't understand sophisticated medical terms. *What* lung fever?"

"She had the influenza. Being the kind of woman she was, always worried about money, about paying bills . . . she went to work anyhow. It got worse and worse. It went to her lungs. She passed away a week later."

"Couldn't they help her at the hospital?"

"Irene wouldn't have any part of hospitals."

Something twisted in Patrick's stomach. A small doubt grew larger. "You took care of her at home?"

"Day and night." Bren smiled. "Except for the last night. The doctor was there that night. He was with Irene when she died. I never saw a man try so hard, but she was halfway to heaven by then."

"Where was Daisy?"

"She said a proper goodbye to her Ma. After that she sat in the parlor with the neighbors."

"The neighbors were there?"

"And the priest."

"Irene's death had a lot of witnesses."

"That's a funny kind of word to use."

"Is it?"

"You don't know the Irish. Nobody dies alone in an Irish neighborhood. When the time comes, friends and neighbors are there."

"What a pity Irene's time came so soon."

"Yes, a pity."

"But, as you said, that leaves more money for you . . . How do you intend to get all this money, by the way? Ann has a sizable bank account, but it's hardly the great fortune you have in mind."

"Annie might leave you."

"She might."

"There'd be a settlement."

"No, there would not."

"We'd take you to court."

Patrick smiled briefly. "The Dain attorneys would chew you up and spit you out."

"They wouldn't get the chance. I've seen you with Annie. You love her. No matter what, you'd want to make things easy for her. That means a big fat settlement."

"So you get the money, and you get Ann."

"As soon as I get control of the money, it's goodbye to Annie. I'll leave and take Daisy with me. Annie won't be expecting that." He grinned. "She'll break into a hundred pieces."

Patrick stiffened. "You hate her that much?"

"She ruined my life."

"That's a lie, O'Hara! That's the lie you've been telling yourself to excuse your own failures."

"There's no telling what I might have been . . . if it hadn't been for her, pushing at me, always *pushing* at me. Well, it's my turn to live, her turn to have nothing."

Patrick saw the naked loathing in Bren's eyes. The frustrations of his life had turned into a burning, sick malevolence.

"That's my plan. And you'll have to watch it happening . . . knowing there's nothing you can do about it. What do you say now, Patrick?"

"I say you should see a doctor. I think you need help."

"Help is it? A million or so in my kick is all the help I'll need."

"You'd better hope you win the Sweepstakes. That's the only way you'll see money like that."

"I'm willing to listen to your offer. I like a good laugh."

"There is no offer."

"That saves us time."

"Ann has to be the one to tell you to leave."

"She won't."

Patrick left his desk. He crossed the room, pouring a cup of coffee. His hand was shaking, shaking with rage and with fear, for he realized Bren was more dangerous than he'd guessed.

"Your plan depends on Ann leaving me."

"She'll leave you. Not right away, but she'll leave you."

"Ann loves me."

"That she does."

Bren got up. He walked around the room, glancing at the books, at the paintings. After a while he went over to Patrick.

"But I've got Annie confused, on the run. She'll make one mistake after another until she feels she *has* to leave you. Little mistakes at first. Like dressing up Daisy's room . . . that was a mistake, wasn't it, Patrick? The mistakes will get bigger. One day I'll get Annie into bed and then—"

Patrick slammed his cup down. He whirled around and smashed his fist into Bren's face. Bren staggered back. He fell against the couch, sliding down to the floor. Blood spurted from his lip.

"You hit me! And you, a doctor!"

"You want a chance to get even? Come on, I'm right here."

Jean rushed into the room. She saw Bren lying on the floor, Patrick standing over him. "Should I call security?"

"No. Leave us alone."

"But—"

"*Go,*" Patrick said and Jean backed out of the room.

"Come on," he demanded, "give me an excuse to take you apart bone by bone."

"You'll pay for this, Patrick."

Patrick pulled Bren to his feet. "We will see who pays. And how much. Now get the hell out of here."

Bren grabbed his coat and ran to the door. "You'll *pay.*"

David hurried in from his office just as Bren ran out. He saw the blood running down his face. "Jean

131

said . . . was that Bren?"

"Cowardly bastard!"

"Would you mind telling me what's going on?"

"I punched him. He almost died of fright. I wish he had."

"Well, I'll be damned. You still have it. You still have your killer right hook."

Patrick looked at his hand. He flexed his fingers. "He deserved it."

"Maybe we could get a hospital boxing team together . . . you, Matt Lansing, Buddy."

"I tell you he deserved it."

"I believe you."

"That bastard is out to destroy Ann."

"What are you going to do?"

"I'm going to stop him." Patrick poured a jigger of brandy and gulped it down. "I have a call to make, David. I'll see you later."

"We have a meeting at the medical school in one hour."

"Right."

Patrick opened his telephone directory. He turned to the phone and dialed a number.

"John Simpson, please, Patrick Dain calling . . . Hello, Mr. Simpson, Patrick Dain here . . . I have a job for you . . . can you come to my office at six tonight? . . . good, I'll see you then, goodbye."

Patrick hung up. His eyes were as cold and hard as blue marble.

John Simpson sat across from Patrick. He was a balding, conservatively-dressed man in his late forties. He made notes on a long yellow pad.

132

"His name is Bren O'Hara," Patrick said, "recently of Southie, in Boston. I am particularly interested in knowing all of his activities between July and January."

"His full name?"

"Brendan Paul O'Hara. His wife's name was Irene. I want to know *if* he was married, *if* his wife is deceased, and if so, *how* and *when* she died."

John Simpson looked up. "Yes, I understand."

"O'Hara says there was an illness. I want to know everything about that illness. I want to know everything about the day she died."

"Have you the names of friends or neighbors?"

"No. Discretion is absolutely essential in that regard, Mr. Simpson. I would not want his friends to tell him of this investigation."

"You may be assured of our discretion. Are you aware of any employment?"

"I don't think O'Hara was employed. The woman, Irene, may have worked at a place called Eddie's Diner. He has a six year old child, Daisy O'Hara. She didn't attend school. She had a friend named Alfie."

"Children are often helpful, without knowing it, of course."

"I'm told a priest and doctor were present at Irene's death. They would probably be neighborhood people."

"Have you a picture of O'Hara?"

"Sorry." Patrick slid a slip of paper across the desk. "This is the address of his rooming house. You'll have to take it from there. He's in his early forties, about six one, sandy hair, brown eyes."

"Has he any special hobbies or interests?"

"He's a heavy drinker."

"That's often *very* helpful."

"When can you start?"

"Immediately. Our operatives will start arriving in Boston tonight."

"You have your work cut out for you. Medical records are difficult to secure."

"We have our methods."

"And the people of Southie are leary of strangers."

"Leave that to us."

"Time is important. Put as many men on it as you need."

"You will have a complete account of O'Hara's actions during those seven months."

"I want every detail, I don't care how small."

"In our experience, answers usually come from small details. Of course every investigation has its own focus. In this instance, we will focus on anything that might be suspicious."

"That's correct."

John Simpson put his notepad in a black leather attache case. He closed the case and locked it, returning the key to his pocket.

"If it's there, we'll find it. The preliminary report will be ready in a week."

"Contact me here. I'd rather not be called at home."

"That's no problem, Dr. Dain. This is a business matter, it will be handled that way."

"O'Hara *must not* know."

"Please don't worry. We are the very best at

what we do." He permitted himself a quick smile. "That's why our fees are astronomical."

Patrick stood up. He walked John Simpson to the door and the two men shook hands.

"Thank you for coming," Patrick said.

"Feel free to call me at any time. Goodnight."

"Goodnight."

Patrick went back to his desk. He felt a moment of exhilaration. The Simpson-Croft agency was large and efficient. They would probe into every part of Bren's life, all the secret places, the dark, hidden corners. Soon, he thought, he would have a way of dealing with Bren O'Hara.

Patrick looked at the stack of papers on his desk. He began separating them, putting some into a folder, others into his briefcase. He looked up as Eve Lawrence came into the room. She looked sleek and beautiful in a tawny-colored wool dress and dark brown boots.

"Hello, Eve."

"I was on my way home. I took a chance you'd still be here."

"I'm here, but not for long. What can I do for you?"

"Why wasn't I at the med school meeting? Or the budget meeting last week?"

Patrick closed one folder and opened another. "You weren't needed there."

"That's not true. I always went to those meetings before."

"Things change."

"Level with me, Patrick. Ever since . . . ever since that night you walked in on David and me . . ." She sighed. "Am I being punished?"

"You know better than that."

"You're freezing me out. Why?"

"I'm trying to keep the peace. Your little romp with David is causing big problems."

"My personal life is my business."

"Not when it affects this hospital."

"How is it doing that?"

"Lola knows about you and David."

"He told me. He also told me he would handle things."

"David has done an extremely bad job of handling things. So have you. Besides, Lola isn't about to be *handled*."

"Lola isn't even here."

"She's coming back on Monday. What do I do then? I can't have a war on my staff. I won't."

"Why does there have to be a war? We're all adults."

"Use your head, Eve. There are bound to be frictions, tensions, God only knows what else."

"And your solution is to freeze me out?"

"I'm doing what I think is best, for now."

Eve leaned forward. "What's best for Lola and David . . . what about what's best for me? I'm not in this alone, why should I alone be penalized?"

Patrick threw a handful of papers into his briefcase and snapped it shut. "You're an excellent administrator, Eve, but Lola and David are doctors. I can replace an administrator. It would be very difficult to replace Lola or David."

"That's completely unfair."

"You know what doctors of their caliber earn on

the outside. How many of them want to work at hospitals, for hospital salaries? Damn few."

"Patrick, are you saying my *job* is on the line?"

"I hope it won't come to that. Should I have to choose, you know where the ax will fall."

"I've worked long and hard to get where I am. David means nothing to me, compared to my job."

"That's blunt."

"I mean it to be. I'm willing to trade. David for my job."

Patrick recoiled from her words. "For such a beautiful woman you can be very ugly."

"Lola and David are your friends; you'll protect them. I have to protect myself."

Patrick gathered up his briefcase and medical bag and went to the door. "I used to like you, Eve. I don't anymore. But if it's possible to protect your job, I will."

"*If?*"

"I'm fresh out of guarantees . . . for anything."

11

Buddy jammed his key into the lock and pushed the door open. He dropped his coat and bag on a chair and walked into the center hall. He saw Hollis, a gray apron drawn across his middle, polishing the brass fittings on the hall table.

"Hello, Hollis."

Hollis looked around. "Good afternoon, Dr. O'Hara. Lovely day, isn't it?"

"Where's Ma?"

"I believe she's in the kitchen."

"Thanks."

Buddy turned toward the kitchen. He started to open the door, then stopped. He stood there for several moments, biting down on his lip. Hollis watched him. He seemed troubled, edgy.

"Can I do anything for you, Dr. O'Hara?"

Buddy shook his head. He went into the kitchen. Sunshine spilled through the open windows. A light breeze fluttered through the room, lifting the leaves of the plants. Ann stood at the large oak table, humming as she prepared a small tray.

"Ma?"

"Buddy," she smiled, "how nice to have you home so early."

"It's my afternoon off."

"I suppose you'll be running right out."

"I want to talk to you."

Ann put a fresh rose into a bud vase and put the vase on the tray. "As soon as I take this to Daisy."

"Ma, I want to *talk* to you."

Ann looked up at him. There was a paleness about his mouth, an unnatural brightness in his eyes. She reached for his forehead.

"Do you have a fever? You look sick."

He pushed her away roughly. "Don't do that!"

"Buddy, what's wrong?"

"Everything's wrong. You know it, don't play dumb."

"Let me take this tray to Daisy and then we'll—"

Buddy knocked the tray from her hands. It clattered to the floor with a terrible noise, glasses and plates splintering into a hundred pieces. The rose lay in a pool of milk and juice. Buddy stomped on the rose until the petals were in shreds.

"*That's* how much I care about Daisy's tray."

Ann clutched the back of a chair. "Will you tell me what's *wrong?*"

"Where were you today?"

"I was here."

"Right, you were. Where were you *supposed* to be?"

Ann glanced away. "I had a reason."

"*What* reason? It was bad enough that you didn't go to Sam's funeral, but to miss the memorial service . . . The entire hospital was there. *With* wives and husbands. *Patrick* was the main speaker."

"I know, but—"

"You should have seen him. He kept looking at the door, waiting for you to come in. I'll never forget the look on his face when he realized you weren't coming at all."

Ann sat down. "Buddy, please *listen* to me. Daisy was sick. I couldn't leave her."

"Daisy has a cold. Patrick checked her last night. He said she had a cold. Didn't you believe him? He's the best diagnostician in the city."

"I called Bren this morning to let him know. Bren said—"

"*Bren* said? Who gives a damn in hell what *Bren* says? He's a liar. He always *was* a liar. He'll always *be* a liar."

"Bren said Daisy's had a little trouble with asthma."

"Don't you think Patrick would recognize asthma?"

"Bren said it can start as a cold and then get worse in a hurry."

"Naturally you take his word for it."

"Daisy's my responsibility."

"Your responsibility? She's become your whole *life*."

"That's not true!"

"You have some soft deal here. Patrick pours out his love on you, he pours out his money. You're like a princess in a fairy tale. And *this* is how you treat him. Any other man would have kicked you out on your ass by now."

140

"Don't talk to me that way, I'm still your mother."

"When you remember. When it doesn't interfere with Daisy."

"You're being mean," Ann said, tears moistening her eyes.

"Somebody has to bring you to your senses. You're throwing your life away. Why? For *Pop?* He left you flat. He left you and two kids flat."

"He's back now; I can't help that."

"When did he come back? When he found out you were in the chips, that's when."

"I don't want to talk about this anymore."

"That's too damn bad, because we're *going* to talk about it. Maybe you've forgotten how it was before Patrick, but I haven't."

"I haven't forgotten either."

Buddy's forehead glistened with perspiration. He stared into space, his eyes burning too brightly. "Jesus, scratching around for every penny, scratching around just to make it through each day . . . But that wasn't the worst part. The worst part was the loneliness. It seemed like we didn't belong anywhere, like nobody wanted us." He clenched his fists until his knuckles were white. "It's happening all over again."

"Nothing's happening."

"Patrick and I don't always get along, but I know what he is. He's a *good man*. He *cares* about us."

"Buddy, nothing's happening . . . Buddy?"

He looked at Ann. She was frightened by his expression. There was something wild and desper-

141

ate in it, something very close to hysteria.

"It's not that bad . . . *listen* to me, it's not that bad."

"You only see what you want to see."

"But Patrick understands."

"Do you think Patrick's going to take much more of this? You haven't been any kind of mother since Pop and Daisy got here. I doubt you've been any kind of wife."

"That's not your problem."

"It is." His big hand hammered the table. "It *is*. Once I had a father, then I didn't have a father anymore . . . Then I had a stepfather, soon I won't have a stepfather anymore. Maybe I shouldn't care, at my age. But I do. I need to feel I'm a part of something. I need to feel someone, besides me, gives a damn if I live or die."

Ann went to Buddy. She tried to put her arms around him but he shook her off.

"I care, I always will."

"If it doesn't interfere with Daisy."

"Buddy, I know it's hard to understand someone else's pain when you have your own. But I'm asking you to try . . . All those years after your father left I felt awful guilt. It was like a weight I carried around with me."

"What guilt?"

"I wondered if it was my fault he left. I wondered if I'd asked too much of him."

"That's ridiculous."

"There were years when you wondered too. When you were about thirteen, you accused me of driving your father away. You said you'd never forgive me."

"I was a kid, Ma, I was hurting. I needed to put that hurt on somebody else. It wasn't your fault."

"I was never sure of that. I'm still not. To this day, Bren says it's *all* my fault."

"And you believe him?"

"I have the chance, now, to make his life better."

"God," Buddy groaned. "Do you want Pop *back?*"

"I don't want him back. I want to make his life better. It's something I have to do."

"*Why?*"

"If I owe him a debt, that will settle it."

"You *don't*. You don't owe him one damn thing. He's using you, Ma. And you're using Patrick."

Ann went to the sink. She poured cold water over her hands and wrists, splashed it on her face. "Don't be so quick to judge."

"At least my eyes are wide open. I'm not blinded by a lot of stupid, dreamy notions."

"You think I am?"

"What would you call it? You're so busy with your imaginary guilt, you can't see what you're doing to anybody else."

"Maybe it's not imaginary."

"No?" Buddy jumped up. "How did Pop get to be the injured party? He takes a ten year walk . . . he comes back to dump his kid and sponge off you . . . and *you* owe *him* a debt?"

"He was my husband."

"Patrick *is* your husband."

"Buddy, if you'd only try to put yourself in my place."

"Your place is the last place I want to be." He knocked the chair aside and went to the door. "Your place stinks!"

Ann ran after him. "Where are you going?"

"Out. If I don't get out of here I'm going to go crazy."

Ann watched helplessly as he stomped through the hall. He grabbed his coat and marched out. The door crashed closed behind him.

Hollis bent over the hall table, arranging a bowl of fresh flowers. He'd heard almost all of the argument, one of many arguments he'd heard in this house recently. The family was coming apart, he thought worriedly, coming apart more each day.

"Hollis, I'm sorry for the . . . shouting."

"People have their little tiffs, eh, Mrs. Dain?" he said calmly.

"There was . . . an accident in the kitchen. Some dishes broke."

"I'll see to it straight away."

"Could you take a glass of juice to Daisy? I'm a little tired."

"Juice it is. And perhaps a biscuit or two?"

"Yes, a biscuit."

"Dr. Dain is upstairs."

"He is? So early?"

"A bit of headache, I believe, Mrs. Dain. He'd like to see you."

"Yes, all right."

Ann walked slowly up the stairs. She felt groggy, as if she'd been without sleep for a long time. She paused at the top of the stairs, trying to compose herself for Patrick. He wouldn't understand, she thought, anymore than anyone else understood. She sighed, for she wasn't sure she understood herself.

The master bedroom was actually a suite of rooms containing a bedroom, sitting room, two baths, and two dressing rooms. It had a spectacular view. Tall buildings glittered in the sun by day, twinkled with lights at night. The sky was endless, changing with the seasons, with the hours. The East River rolled and shifted in bright, silver-tipped currents.

The bedroom was done in blues and greens, here and there a splash of white, a splash of yellow. The desk and dressers were fine old mahogany, burnished over many years to a soft gloss. There was an antique brass bed, dressed in Porthault sheets and antique quilts. A woven wicker trunk sat at the foot of the bed, a hand-knitted Sonia Jaworsky afghan folded on top.

"Come in, Ann."

Patrick was stretched out on a long, white linen chaise. He was tieless, his shirt sleeves rolled up. He tossed his newspaper away.

"Well, come in. I'm not going to bite you."

"Hollis said you weren't feeling well."

"I have a headache. I had no meetings scheduled, so I decided to let them get along without me for a day."

"Would you like some tea? I'll get you some tea."

"I'd like you to sit down."

Ann pulled a chair closer to the chaise. She sat down then got up again. "I'll get you some aspirin."

145

"I took two aspirin at the hospital." He stared at her. The sun caught the golden highlights in her hair. The blue of her blouse matched the blue of her eyes. "You look very pretty today."

"Patrick, I'm sorry about the memorial service."

"I want you to stop apologizing to me."

"I can explain," Ann said quickly. "I called Bren to let him know about Daisy. He said she's had some trouble with asthma. I was afraid to leave her."

"Her lungs are absolutely clear."

"But he said—"

"He lied."

"Why would he do that?"

"His plan is to disrupt our lives as much as possible."

Ann sat down. "Plan? Bren couldn't plan from Monday to Tuesday without losing interest."

"He can when it suits his purpose."

Ann looked out of the window. She watched a ribbon of cars moving across the bridge. She longed to be in one of them. She longed to be anywhere but in this room. "I just can't believe Bren's cooking up a sinister plan for us."

"Why not? Because once upon a time he was handsome and charming and had pretty dreams?"

"He doesn't have much character, but he was never cruel."

"Buddy would disagree."

"Buddy doesn't know, he was only a child."

"A child left high and dry by his father."

"Bren is weak, I'm not denying that."

"Some people can get away with anything," Patrick said softly. "They're called sensitive, or they're called weak, and that excuses them any wrong."

Ann thought she heard something strange in Patrick's tone. She looked at him curiously. "You haven't said anything about my missing the memorial service. You don't seem angry, you don't even seem upset."

"Oh, I was upset."

"Then talk about it. Don't keep it inside."

"I'm not going to feed your guilt. I've probably done too much of that already. I leave the guilt to you and Bren to work out between yourselves."

Ann played nervously with her pearls. "You sound as if you don't care anymore."

"I care. I care enough to pull back. That's not easy for me. I am used to taking charge, to getting my own way."

"Pull back how?"

"I love you very much, Ann, but you have decisions to make. You must make them alone."

"Why won't anyone understand? I'm just helping Bren to start a new life. I know I've made mistakes, big ones . . . but as soon as he's settled, this will be over."

"I'm telling you, and I'm telling you for the last time, that Bren is playing dangerous games with our lives. He's deliberately leading you into mistakes, as you call them . . . Daisy's phony asthma, for example. Bren is using your guilt and your memories to accomplish his ends."

"It doesn't matter what he's doing. I know what *I'm* doing."

"Do you?"

"Give me credit for a little common sense."

"You're not a schemer. You're no match for Bren."

"I've heard enough of that from Buddy."

"I wish you'd pay more attention to him. He's as nervous as I've ever seen him."

"We're all nervous."

"Bren isn't."

Ann went to the desk. She moved a paperweight to the left and then to the right. "I don't like your attitude."

"Why not?"

"You don't seem to have much faith in me."

"I repeat, you're no match for Bren. He's not rational. His mind is twisted. I know. I spoke with him at length."

"You hit him. How rational is that?"

"He got what he deserved."

"In *your* opinion," Ann said sharply.

"Yes, in my opinion. I was there, you weren't. If the day ever comes when I can be intimidated by a Bren O'Hara, I'll take to my bed with a very large bottle of Seconal."

"Okay, you're the better man. You don't have to keep reminding me of it."

"For God's sake, Ann, that's not what I'm talking about at all. This isn't a question of vanity."

"Bren is broke and he's alone. I'm trying to help him. Is that so terrible? Do you want to call the firing squad?"

"*I'm* not victimizing you. Don't talk as if I am."

"*Nobody's* victimizing me. I can think for myself. I can make my own decisions."

"That's all I'm asking you to do."

"Are you asking me or *daring* me?"

"Wait a minute." Patrick sat up. "Am I the bad guy all of a sudden?"

"I didn't say that. Who's being sensitive now?"

"I'm trying to be reasonable."

"Try harder!"

Patrick was distracted by a knock at the door. "Yes?"

"It's Hollis, sir."

"Come in."

Hollis entered with a tray of sandwiches. "I've brought lunch." He put the tray on a table near the chaise. "Chicken sandwiches, shrimp salad, apple tarts, coffee and tea. Will there be anything else?"

"Thank you, Hollis, this is fine."

"Miss Daisy has eaten. She's in bed, watching television."

"Fine."

"She's watching a soap opera. In this soap opera," Hollis said slowly, "I gather that a young woman has been abducted by the mob and is being forced into prostitution. They have her tied up in a cellar at present. An effort, I believe, to break her spirit."

"Good grief, Hollis, see if you can find a more suitable program. If you can't, shut off the set and give her a book."

"Yes, Dr. Dain."

"Her Snoopy book," Ann suggested.

"Excellent idea, Mrs. Dain."

Hollis left and Patrick looked at Ann. "I don't think Daisy should have a television in her room."

"I'll speak to her about what she watches."

Patrick poured coffee. "Hungry?"

"I shouldn't have snapped at you, Patrick. I didn't mean what I said."

"We've both said things we didn't mean."

Patrick lit a cigarette. He inhaled deeply, watching the burning ash turn orange, then gray. "Ann, I asked Hollis to make up a bed for me in the sitting room. I'll stay there until we know where we are."

The color drained from Ann's face. She felt the room tilt and she put her hand to her head. "You're leaving me?"

"I'm not going far."

"But you're going."

"Yes."

"Why?"

"So you can think clearly. So I can."

"For how long?"

"Until you can tell me, honestly, how you feel about Bren. Until you can tell me if you are my wife . . . or Bren's."

Ann felt as if a thick rope were tightening around her throat. She rose unsteadily and made her way to the door. She groped blindly for the doorknob and left the room.

Patrick slumped back against the chaise. He stared at the closed door and it seemed to him that all the light in the room had gone.

12

March winds swept through the city. Windows rattled, trashcans were turned on their sides, and trees, still bare with winter, bowed. There was a brief, heavy snowstorm, and then a week of rain. Curtains of water, driven and lashed by the wind, washed over streets and buildings in rushing torrents. When the sun came out, the city shimmered in brightness.

The sun felt good on Patrick's face. He paused to enjoy it a moment longer, then turned and went into Rhinelander Pavillion. He was halfway to the elevator when he heard the page.

"Paging Code 1, to E.R. . . . Paging Code 1, to E.R."

Patrick reversed his course and hurried through a passageway to the E.R. He saw David run in from a side door.

"David," he caught up with him, "what have we got?"

"You know that construction site on Fifth Avenue? The wind just about blew it away. Pedestrians were hit with flying glass, flying steel, flying everything."

"How many?"

"We're expecting at least eighteen casualties. It may go higher . . . the streets were crowded, people were on their way to work."

Patrick draped his stethoscope around his neck. He dropped his coat and bag at the nurses' station and rushed to E.R.

"We're in for a rough one today," David said.

All the treatment rooms were in use, doctors and nurses running back and forth with equipment and medication. The remaining casualties lay on gurneys stretched from one end of the corridor to the other. Some cried and moaned in pain, others lay in rigid, eerie silence.

Blood was everywhere. It was on the casualties, on those who attended them, on spattered walls, on pieces of clothing hastily torn away and thrown to the floor. One doctor's starched white jacket was bloodied from neck to waist, while another doctor had a bloody handprint blazoned on his chest. There was a large metal pail filled with bloody swabs and gloves.

"At least there's no chaos this time," David said, for there was little panic and no confusion.

"Thank Matt Lansing for that. Look at him, crisp as lettuce."

Matt was in the center of the corridor, directing triage. He saw Patrick and David and waved them over.

"What do you want us to do?" David asked.

"Each of you take one end of the corridor. Move the serious cases into the first lane. We're clearing the treatment rooms as fast as we can."

"Have you called O.R.?" Patrick asked.

"They're standing by. Fielding is doing surgical triage. Most of the worst injuries are to the head and hands and legs, the exposed parts of the body."

Patrick and David went off in different directions. Patrick worked his way through the far end of the corridor, horrified by what he saw. Some of the casualties were unrecognizable for the blood streaming down their faces.

One woman had dozens of glass splinters imbedded in her cheek like a grotesque row of pickets. One man's chin had been smashed by the force of the blow he'd received, bits of bone jutting through ripped flesh. A man on the gurney behind him was spitting out broken, bloody teeth.

Patrick transferred the more serious cases, then did what he could for the others. He disinfected and bandaged cuts, applied tourniquets to bleeding veins, and temporary splints to broken bones. He ordered x-rays, and blood replacements, and sedatives. He talked with those patients who wanted to talk, murmured encouragement to those who could only stare.

By eleven o'clock each of the casualties had been treated and his team of grim-faced doctors, nurses, students, and orderlies dispersed to the treatment rooms and E. W. Patrick wearily peeled off his surgical gloves. He saw Buddy working intently over a patient and he went to him.

Buddy's patient was a woman in her late fifties. Blood oozed from her scalp and from both her eyes.

"I can't see, I can't see," she moaned over and

153

over again. "Help me, I can't see . . . I can't see."

"This is Mrs. McKell," Buddy said. "She's been sedated twice, I'm afraid to give her any more."

"Gloves!" Patrick called and a nurse slipped a fresh pair on his hands.

Patrick leaned over Mrs. McKell, flashing a light into her eyes. He saw tiny glass splinters in the retinas, and one large shard of glass stuck in the corner of the eye.

"The glass is in one piece, but—"

"I know," Buddy said. "Dr. Kramer's ready for her, but I have to get this one piece of glass out first."

Buddy checked the restraints on her arms and legs, then carefully, gently taped her eyelids open. In sterile gloves, with a large, sterile tweezer, he reached for the piece of protruding glass.

"Easy, Mrs. McKell . . . easy does it . . . we're almost there."

Buddy removed the glass and then packed the side of her eye. He put a light dressing over the packing.

"Don't worry, Mrs. McKell," he squeezed her hand, "you'll be fine." He looked around. "Orderly? . . . take her to Dr. Kramer in ophthalmology. Stat!"

Patrick smiled at Buddy. He was proud of him, pleased by the way he'd handled himself. He was about to congratulate him on a job well done when he heard Matt call his name.

"Let's see what that's about."

They walked over to Matt. Buddy was tired, but he felt good, for he knew he'd been at his best this morning. He'd taken case after case without hesitation or strain or error, and all under Patrick's watchful eye. He felt suddenly closer to Patrick, closer than he'd felt in months.

"Quite a morning, huh?"

"Quite . . . and you were—" Patrick stopped as he reached Matt. "Matt, you deserve a medal! I've never seen an emergency go so smoothly."

Buddy's face fell. He'd been expecting a word of appreciation, even praise, from Patrick, but his kind words had gone instead to Matt Lansing. He turned and quickly walked away.

The incident took only seconds, but Matt noticed and understood. He ached for Buddy, for in those seconds he'd looked so disappointed, so alone.

"Matt, did you hear me?"

"I'm not the only one who heard you."

"What?"

"I like medals, Dr. Dain, but not in front of Buddy."

Patrick looked around to see Buddy disappear through a door. "Is that contest still going on?"

"Buddy's been working his heart out. He deserves a pat on the back."

"You're right, of course. I'll be sure to see him later. How do we stand here?"

Matt consulted his clipboard. "We received twenty-four casualties. Ten were treated and released, thirteen were admitted, one died."

"I'd like you to handle the paperwork with Eve."

"Dr. Murdock usually—"

"I'd like *you* to do it. And make certain all the records are in perfect order, there will be lawsuits

155

all over the place."

"Yes, sir."

"Did you want me for anything else?"

"Senator Josephson was admitted a few minutes ago. He asked to see you."

"Why was he admitted?"

"He fell in the shower. He may have broken his ankle, they have him scheduled for x-rays. The senator is in," Matt looked again at his clipboard, "room 1509."

"On my way."

"Can I go with you, Dr. Dain? I've always admired Senator Josephson."

"Have you?" Patrick smiled. "Well, come along then."

They walked to the end of the corridor and rang for the express elevator. Patrick glanced at Matt.

"I see you're still worried about Buddy."

"He needs encouragement."

"You told me he was doing well on the wards."

"He is. I've ordered his supervising resident to give him a free hand and lots of praise. That's helped."

"But not enough?"

"Not as much as I'd hoped," Matt said as they stepped into the elevator. "Some days he's wound tight as a spring. He won't let himself believe we're on his side."

"That sounds familiar."

"I know you're trying to be neutral, Dr. Dain, but it would help if he knew you appreciated his work."

"I'll have a talk with him. *Another* talk."

"If you don't mind a suggestion . . . visit him in the wards. He sat up almost all last night with one of the patients there. He didn't have to, but he did. He did a damn good job."

"In other words . . . let him show off."

"In those words."

They got off at the fifteenth floor and headed for 1509. Matt was startled by the crowd of reporters and photographers gathered outside the room.

"I wonder what it's like to be followed around by the press everywhere you go."

"Is that sympathy I hear?" Patrick laughed. "Don't be deluded. He loves it."

"How could anybody love that?"

"It's all part of the ambition game. Without the press, he might as well fold his tent and go home."

Patrick and Matt pushed through the crowd. One of the senator's aides stepped away from the door.

"We've been waiting for you, Dr. Dain . . . Who's he?"

"This is Dr. Lansing."

"He'd better wait outside."

"*You'd* better not give me orders. Now get out of my way."

"The senator said *only* you."

Reporters and photographers began to surge forward. Microphones were thrust out, questions were shouted.

"They're going to get the idea you're hiding something." Patrick smiled.

"Oh, all right!"

The aide opened the door and Patrick and Matt went inside.

Room 1509 was one of four large private suites at Rhinelander Pavillion. It had a sitting room, bedroom, and bath, each painted a cool bottle-green.

The sitting room was carpeted in blue and green, furnished with a couch, a desk, several captain's chairs, and a portable refrigerator. There were bowls of fresh flowers and current issues of half a dozen magazines.

Patrick and Matt passed through the sitting room into the bedroom. It was a spacious room, with walk-in closets, and three built-in color television screens placed side by side. The curtains were a crispy ivory and green stripe, matching the stripe of the sheets and pillowcases.

Senator Josephson was sitting up in bed, scribbling notes on a ruled pad. He was a handsome man. His profile was smooth, his thick dark hair shot with silver streaks.

"Hello, Doug," Patrick said, reading his chart.

"Patrick, it's good to see you again. I wish the circumstances were happier."

"Senator Josephson, Dr. Lansing . . . Dr. Lansing, Senator Josephson."

"How do you do, sir. It's a pleasure to meet you. I'm a fan of yours."

"Thank you, Doctor. I hope you feel that kindly in November."

"They mean well."

"Don't we all. How do you feel?"

"I took a fall in the shower. I fell smack on my ankle."

Patrick went around to the side of the bed. "Does

that hurt?" he manipulated the ankle.

"Yes."

"And that?"

"Yes. I can't put any weight on it at all."

"You'll be going to x-ray soon. You may have a fracture."

"Will I have to stay here?"

"Not for long. Where is Lenore?"

"She's on her way here. I wanted to talk to you about that. Dr. Lansing, would you mind if I talked to Patrick alone?"

"*I'd* mind," Patrick said. "Dr. Lansing is here at my invitation . . . Don't worry, you can trust him."

"Well, I fell in the shower, but not the shower at home. I was . . . uh, at a friend's."

"Gee." Patrick laughed. "What a surprise."

"But if anybody asks, I fell at home. Lenore will back me up on that. If anybody asks you why Lenore didn't come with me to the hospital, tell them—"

"I have no intention of telling anybody anything, Doug. I have always felt that given enough rope, you would hang yourself."

"You sound pleased at the prospect." The senator grinned.

"I wouldn't break down and cry."

"Don't pay any attention to him, Dr. Lansing, we've been friends forever."

Patrick nodded. "Or does it just seem that long?"

"Maybe I should leave," Matt said.

"No, stay here. I consider this part of your education."

"Is that a compliment, Patrick?"

"When's the last time I gave you a compliment?"

"I see what you mean. I withdraw the question."

"Do you two always kid like this?" Matt asked.

"Only one of us is kidding."

"Patrick doesn't entirely approve of me. I'm imperfect."

"There is an example of the senator's keen analytical mind."

"Patrick, of course, is perfect. He's always been perfect. That's why they named a cathedral after him."

"And there," Patrick laughed, "is an example of the senator's keen wit."

"Well, I'm glad you boys are enjoying yourselves." Lenore Josephson walked into the room. "Laugh and the world laughs with you."

Lenore Josephson was blond, of medium height and weight, and exquisitely dressed. She had been a pretty woman once, but now there was a hardness about her eyes and mouth.

"I brought your things, Doug." She put a suitcase at the foot of the bed. "You'll want to change into a robe before the photographers come in . . . Hello, Patrick."

"Hello, Lenore . . . Mrs. Josephson, this is Dr. Lansing . . . Dr. Lansing, Mrs. Josephson."

"How do you do, Mrs. Josephson. Would you like to sit down?"

She looked Matt over. "You could dig out a robe and pajamas from that case."

"Lenore!"

She shrugged. "He seemed anxious to do something."

"I don't mind, Senator."

Matt opened the suitcase and carefully removed a dark blue robe and lighter blue pajamas. "Can you sit a little straighter, Senator? I'll help you into these."

"Lenore," Patrick said, "you haven't changed a bit."

"Don't waste your sarcasm on me. Twenty years of marriage to Doug have made me immune to sarcasm." She lit a cigarette. "How is Ann? I invited her to a lunch a few weeks ago. She didn't come."

"Ann's been busy."

"Oh? Anything important?"

"Not by your standards."

"Is that good or bad?"

Patrick smiled. "Do you care?"

"Not especially. How is Doug's ankle?"

"It may be a fracture. They'll be taking him to x-ray soon."

"He can't go anywhere until we get this press business over with. They're waiting outside, *drooling.*"

Patrick looked at Doug. He was in his pajamas and robe, his hair neatly parted and brushed. "Do you want to see the press now?"

"Just a minute on that."

Senator Josephson summoned his two aides from the sitting room. "Do we have our stories straight? Do we know what we're going to say?"

His easy manner had vanished. His eyes were cool, and there was a harshness in his voice.

"Let's review it. Phil," he said to the taller of the

aides, "if they ask why I didn't call an ambulance?"

"We thought," Phil said, "that an ambulance would take too long, so I drove you here myself."

"Check. If they ask why Lenore didn't come with us?"

"Mrs. Josephson was out shopping at the time of the accident. She didn't learn about it until she returned home."

"Check. Lenore, have you got that?"

She blew a puff of smoke in his direction. "Got it."

"Dave," he said to the other aide, "have the doormen been taken care of?"

"Yes, and the garage guy too. We're in the clear."

Matt had been watching the interplay between the senator and his aides with growing disbelief. He looked at Patrick. "I don't understand."

"They're rehearsing their lies."

"Lenore," the senator said brusquely, "fix your lipstick. And get rid of that damn cigarette."

Lenore put out her cigarette and applied a fresh coat of lipstick. "All right?"

"Stand at the side of the bed here," he instructed. "Smile and say as little as possible. And try to look like a concerned wife. *Force* yourself."

Matt looked at Patrick again. "This is terrible."

"Welcome to big-time politics."

"Are we ready?" the senator asked.

"Yes, sir," the aides replied in unison.

"Okay, open the floodgates."

Patrick drew Matt into a corner. "Should any questions come your way, you have *only* two answers . . . 'no comment', or, 'we're waiting for the x-rays'."

"I hate this. This is terrible. I'm sorry I came with you."

"Now, remember, Lenore—"

"Shut up, Doug," she snapped.

"Just do your job . . . Showtime, everybody," Doug Josephson said, convivial once more.

Phil ushered in the press. They formed a circle two deep around the bed, spilling over to jam the doorway. Cameras and microphones and notepads were readied to record every word, every gesture. Doug Josephson greeted many members of the press by name, laughing and joking with them. Lenore smiled graciously, nodded a few times, then looked away.

"We have no statement," Phil said, "but we know you have questions . . . anytime you're ready."

"A little equipment problem here," a cameraman shouted, "hold it a second."

Patrick looked at the press people. He looked at Doug's aides and at Doug, then he looked at Lenore. There was something disturbing in her expression and he took a step forward to get a better look. She was smiling, but it was a threatening smile. There was a chilling serenity in her eyes.

"Christ!" Patrick said.

"What's the matter?" Matt asked.

"There's going to be trouble."

"What trouble?"

"Lenore . . . look at Lenore!"

13

The first few questions went to the senator. Patrick moved around the edge of the crowd and grabbed Phil's arm.

"Later, Doctor."

"Listen to me, you have to get the press out of here," Patrick said urgently. "Make any excuse, but get them out."

"Are you crazy?"

"Phil, do it, *please.*"

Phil glanced at him scornfully and then turned his back. Patrick returned to Matt.

"Get to the phone in the sitting room. Call the switchboard. Except for the nurses' station, I want all outgoing service cut off on this floor until further notice. And have the express elevator grounded in the lobby. *Now*, Matt."

"Senator?" one of the reporters called out, "your meeting with the President next week is widely regarded as a showdown. Will you have to postpone your meeting?"

"I'd like to discourage the idea that it's a showdown . . . there is no truth to the rumor that the President and I are meeting at high noon in the White House corral." He waited for his laugh and then went on. "But to answer your question, this won't interfere with our meeting. I'll be there if I have to hop all the way."

"Senator, how will your accident affect your golf game?"

"I've announced my promise to break eighty this year," he answered with mock seriousness, "and our party keeps its promises."

Most of the reporters, satisfied with the interview, prepared to leave. A few remained where they were, ready to ask a question or two of the senator's wife.

"Mrs. Josephson, is it true the emergency number was busy, and you had to drive the senator here yourself?"

Lenore looked out at the smiling faces. She smiled back. "No, that's not true."

She paused. She looked at Doug. Patrick tensed, for he saw the expression on her face.

"You see, my husband's accident happened . . . at the apartment of his current mistress."

There was a shocked silence, then pandemonium. Cameras and microphones engulfed the Josephsons. Questions flew through the air, lost in the noise and confusion. Doug Josephson tried to stand, but couldn't. He sat down again. He sat so still he might have been dead.

Phil rushed to Lenore's side. "Mrs. Josephson," he shouted, "they don't know you're joking. Tell them you're joking!"

Lenore held up her hand. The crowd quieted,

waiting for her next words.

"Since I wasn't present at my husband's accident this morning, I can only simulate it for you."

Lenore snatched a pitcher of water from the bedstand and poured it over Doug's head. The water streamed through his hair and splashed down his face.

There were shouts and squeals. Cameras clicked frantically, the room suddenly ablaze with flashing light. Senator Josephson's face turned white, then red, then a kind of purple. He tried to smile, but managed only a dazed grimace.

Patrick fought his way through the crowd. He wasn't sure what he should do, for the situation, he knew, was beyond help.

"Have a nice day." Lenore laughed.

She pushed her way to the door. Several reporters followed her, many more dove for the phones.

Patrick bent over Doug. "Listen to me, *listen* to me." He shook him. "The phones have been shut off on this floor. The express elevator has been stopped. They'll have to walk down, or take the slow elevator. That gives you a couple of minutes to think of something and beat them to the lobby."

"Yes . . . yes," Doug said. "Phil, you stop them in the lobby. Tell them we've scheduled a press conference for this afternoon."

"*Not* here," Patrick said.

"Schedule it at my office," Doug said. "We'll think of something to say."

"Senator, what if we don't?"

"We will. We always do."

"Matt," Patrick said, "have them send up the express elevator and a security guard. Phil and *only* Phil is to use that elevator."

"Yes, sir." Matt ran out.

"Dave," Doug said, "we have to get moving on this. Call Craig, and Johnny, and my lawyers. Call Lenore's doctor. Maybe we can say she's having a breakdown."

Patrick looked at him in disgust. "Doug, I didn't buy you time so you could tell lies about Lenore."

"Maybe she *is* having a breakdown. How do we know? Why else would she . . . I mean, why . . ."

"Where can I get a secure phone?" Dave asked.

"My office is on the second floor. Tell Jean I said you could use my phone. It doesn't go through the switchboard."

Dave left and the third of the senator's aides, the man who'd been guarding the door, came in.

"It's really hit the fan this time."

"We'll come up with something," Doug said angrily. "We need a goddamn good solid story and we'll find one. This is my *career*, kiddo. No damn dizzy broad is going to ruin it."

A white-jacketed attendant came in with a wheelchair. "Senator Josephson for x-ray?" he asked.

"Patrick, I have no time for that now."

"Fifteen minutes, that's all it will take."

"Can't you move something in here?"

"We have to x-ray your leg and your back as well, just to be on the safe side."

"Maybe it's escaped your attention, but there is no safe side anymore. I'm in freefall, Patrick, and

167

Lenore just cut the cord on my parachute."

"You can use the time to organize your thoughts. It has to be done."

"*Now?*"

"Yes. Doug, I want you out of here as soon as possible. I can't have this hospital turned into a circus, and that's what it's going to be. We'll look at the x-rays, give you what treatment you need . . . but if a stay is indicated . . . there's Walter Reed and there's Bethesda and there are helicopters to take you there in no time."

"You're kicking me out?"

"We can't handle the security." Patrick and the attendant helped Doug into the wheelchair. "Once this gets out we'll have the rest of the press, and curiosity-seekers, and screwballs . . . We can't handle that." Patrick nodded at the attendant and he wheeled Doug out. "I'll see you back here in half an hour or so."

Patrick looked around the room. The floor was strewn with cigarette butts, and used film boxes, and bits and pieces of crumpled paper. The bed was soggy with small puddles of water.

"Dr. Dain." Matt tapped his shoulder. "Mrs. Josephson has gone and Phil is talking to the press in the lobby. I've had the phones turned back on, and called housekeeping to clean the room and change the bedding."

"Thanks, Matt, you have a second medal coming. Lloyd," he said to the aide, "I suppose you have a lot of calls to make."

"No . . . I don't think so."

"You have time, the senator will be gone for a while."

"No, I'm not making any calls. If the senator goes down in flames, I'm not going with him."

Patrick shook his head. "Your loyalty is genuinely touching."

"In politics there are only winners and losers. It's lousy, but that's the way it is."

"Matt, let's get out of here."

They walked into the corridor and went directly to the elevator. "You're very quiet," Patrick said.

"I'm sorry I saw any part of that. He made me sick, she made me sick, they all made me sick. I'm sorry I found out the senator is . . . what he is."

"Doug is a terrible womanizer and Lenore is a terrible snob. They deserve each other. But they don't deserve to be destroyed in public by each other."

"Is that why you tried to help him out?"

"That, and a sense of history."

"History?"

"Doug is his party's fair-haired boy."

"So?"

"So, the party expected he'd be moving into the White House in four years. If that plan is ruined, I prefer it not be ruined here."

They got off the elevator and walked to Patrick's office. "I must warn you again to be careful, should any questions come your way. I don't want the hospital drawn into this mess."

"I understand. Actually, I'd like to forget about the whole thing."

"That," Patrick smiled, "may not be so easy." He opened the door to his office. "See what I mean?"

David was at his desk, talking on the phone. Jean

169

was talking on another. Eve paced back and forth, looking grim.

"Well, the gang's all here . . . Hello, gang."

"Patrick," Eve spun around, "what in God's name *happened?*"

Patrick sat down. He stretched out his legs. "All hell broke loose."

"We know *that*. What happened?"

"Coffee, Dr. Dain?" Matt asked.

"Please."

David hung up the phone. He hesitated a moment, then took it off the hook. "The switchboard's been swamped with calls. Everybody who can't get through there is calling you or me. What the hell did he do?"

"Doug broke his ankle while in his girlfriend's shower. He and his aides carefully planned their lies. Then Lenore told the press about the girlfriend and poured a pitcher of water on Doug's head." Patrick took the coffee and gulped it down. "End of story."

"She didn't!"

"She sure as hell did."

David laughed. "I wish I'd seen it."

"Oh, you will. On any number of front pages."

"Where does that leave us?"

Patrick gulped the last of the coffee. "That's the problem. I've told Doug we'll treat the ankle, but if he needs hospitalization, it can't be here."

"We'll have to issue a statement," Eve said.

"You can issue a statement on his condition, as soon as we know what it is. Also, you are to say that the senator will be released today. I want us disassociated from this as soon as possible."

"Don't we have to say something about the . . . incident?" Eve asked.

"What incident?"

"I see." Eve nodded.

"We will issue *one brief* statement. The statement will be limited to the senator's *medical* condition. Period. The End. David, will you write it?"

"Yes, Jean's on the phone with x-ray now."

"What if they want the names of the doctors who were in the senator's room?"

"What doctors?"

"Okay, I get the message. David, you'll get the statement to me as soon as it's ready?"

"I will. Not a word to anyone until then."

"Eve," Matt said, "we have work to do on the Code 1 this morning."

"I'll call you when the Josephson business is done," she said, leaving.

"How did Doug take it?" David asked.

"I think he's going to try to wriggle out of it."

"Impossible."

"I don't know about that. Do you remember his nickname at Yale?"

"Slick. Everybody called him Slick."

"Umm. Has the news gotten around the hospital yet?"

"Can't you hear the buzz? They don't know exactly what happened, of course . . . all sorts of stories are flying around."

"I hope you've cautioned them—"

"I personally called each floor and laid it on the line. For all the good it will do."

"What are the latest figures on the Code 1?"

"One dead, five in critical. Two of those are still in surgery. Matt, I meant to congratulate you, you did a beautiful job."

"Thank you, Dr. Murdock. I'd like to check the admissions now, if it's all right."

"You'd better wait," Patrick said, "until we see how this story turns out."

Jean held the phone out to Patrick. "Dr. Clary in orthopedics. He wants to talk to you."

"Dr. Dain here . . . yes . . . yes . . . I agree . . . no, absolutely not . . . no . . . no . . . well, that is my final word . . . the senator's staff will make arrangements for transportation . . . good . . . good, thank you, Doctor."

Patrick hung up. "A hairline fracture. Clary wanted to keep him here for a few days, but there's no spinal damage, no reason he can't go to Washington."

The phone rang and he waved at Jean. "No calls."

"We ought to get out of here," David said.

"I have to get back to Doug anyway. Do you want to come?"

"I suppose I should."

"Matt?"

Matt's black eyes were unusually subdued. "I'd rather not, I'd really like to forget this. And I have patients waiting."

"I'm sorry it was so rough on you."

"Part of my education, that's what you said. Can I get back to work now?"

"Yes, go on."

Matt looked vastly relieved. He went to the door. "Dr. Dain, you won't forget about . . . the wards?"

"I won't forget. By the way, Matt, don't you think it's time you called me Patrick?"

"It's time." He smiled broadly. "Thank you, Patrick."

The door closed. David looked at Patrick. "So you've finally made up your mind about him."

"After what I saw today, why not?"

All the phones seemed to ring at once. David and Patrick went to the door. "Sorry, Jean. Tell them we've gone fishing."

David and Patrick walked into 1509. Senator Josephson was sitting in a wheelchair, his ankle in a cast. He was dressed in a dark business suit, a dark tie, and a light blue shirt. Phil and Dave were at his side, going over their notes.

"Doug," David smiled, "I came to say hello."

"And goodbye. Your pal is kicking me out."

"You understand our problem. After all, you're the best little problem solver in Washington."

"I don't need another smart ass," Doug said, then smiled. "I take it you've heard about Lenore, the wicked witch of the east, west, north, and south."

"What are you going to do?"

"Whatever I have to."

"Meaning?"

"I'll make a statement, let the dust settle, and go from there. I expect to be returned to office. I expect to be your beloved senator for another term."

"Remember, you promised me dinner at the White House."

"You'll get your dinner. And you'll sleep in the Lincoln bedroom. This is a detour along the road, not a dead end."

"I hate to interrupt, Mr. President," Patrick said, "but how is your ankle?"

"It feels better in this thing. Look, it would really simplify my life if I could stay here."

"Sorry."

"You'll *be* sorry." Doug smiled. "When I do get to the White House, I'll have your taxes audited for the past twenty-five years . . . I'll have you *drafted*."

"I wouldn't be a bit surprised. Have you made your plans?"

"We have a helicopter in two hours. We'll hold the press conference in Washington. The New York press will be ticked off, but that can't be helped."

"What are you going to say?"

"Lenore has been under a severe strain. Our marriage has been under a severe strain. It's true that I didn't spend the night at home, but Phil and his wife will swear I spent the night at their apartment."

Patrick looked at the ceiling. "What if your girlfriend decides to go public?"

"She won't."

"Your last girlfriend was all ready to write a book and go on talk shows."

"She changed her mind."

"I know. I received an invitation to the opening of her new boutique, on the ground floor of her

174

new townhouse."

"You see? There's always room for negotiation. I was also more careful this time. The lady in question isn't going public. *Her* career couldn't stand that."

"Dr. Dain," Phil said, "you knew something was going to happen. How?"

"I looked at Lenore. Do you ever look at her, do *you*, Doug?"

"For twenty years."

"You may look, but do you see? I saw her eyes today and I knew she'd finally had enough."

"Patrick, she wants me to be in love with her. I'm not. I haven't been in love with her for fifteen years, maybe longer."

"There is a thing called divorce."

"I had to look ahead. I was an aspiring politician. Fifteen years ago divorce was unthinkable for a politician."

"Now?"

"Now, maybe. I'll put out a few feelers. If the response is positive, then that may be the answer. If the response is negative, then Lenore and I resolve the severe strain in our marriage, have a joyous reunion, and wind up on the cover of *People* magazine."

"Just like that?"

"Just like that. Today's press conference is the key. I'm going to be very sincere. I'm going to wear my glasses."

"Doug," David smiled, "I say this to you as a friend . . . you are the bottom of the barrel."

"Being a nice guy is not the approved route to the

Presidency. It's happened a few times, yes, but not often."

"Do you really believe the voters are going to swallow this?"

"I won't be hurt too much with the mens' vote. And the women will squawk at first, but I have the old sex appeal going for me there. I'll beat this, wait and see."

"Well, Doug," Patrick said, "have a good trip. I don't have to wish you luck, you have the old sex appeal going for you."

"I'm asking one more time . . . let me stay here. We're friends, does the hospital come before friends?"

"The hospital comes before everything. It comes first."

Patrick and David left. They walked to the elevator in silence. "What do you think?" David asked finally.

"I think Doug will get to be President, and I'll get a tax audit and a draft notice."

"I was wondering about Lenore. She must hate him."

"She has every reason to."

David's eyes darkened. "I wonder if Lola hates *me* that much."

"You know damn well that Lola doesn't hate you at all . . . *yet*."

"Is that a warning?"

"Loud and clear."

14

The wards occupied the third floor at Rhinelander Pavillion. They were clean, functional
rooms, long and deep, with unadorned tan walls and
plain white blinds. There were four beds to each
ward, the sheets and pillowcases standard white
hospital issue.

Buddy O'Hara walked into ward 301. Dinner
trays had been removed and the patients were
reading, or napping, or watching small black and
white television sets attached to metal poles.

"How are you feeling, Mr. Lewis?" Buddy took
his pulse.

"Better, much better then yesterday. It's thanks
to you, Doctor, you done it."

Mr. Lewis was a thin, graying man in his middle
fifties, his teeth badly stained by nicotine. An i.v.
ran into his wrist.

"Time for another shot?" He held out his arm.

"It won't hurt," Buddy said. He swabbed the arm
with alcohol, then smoothly injected the clear
liquid. "There. You'll be on this medication
another day or two."

"All these needles, I'll look like a junkie."

Buddy checked his chart. "Any more nausea?"

"It's better than yesterday, but I still ain't got no appetite."

"Don't worry about that. In a few days you'll be hungry as a bear."

"Even thinking about food makes me sick."

"That's to be expected for now. In a few days, you'll be making up for all the meals you missed."

Patrick came up behind Buddy. "What do we have here?"

"Mr. Lewis was an emergency admission. Acute gastroenteritis with dehydration and elevated sugar."

"I been throwing up for three days." Mr. Lewis smiled. "Thought it was something I ate."

Patrick looked at his chart. "How do you feel today?"

"Like I'm gonna live. Yesterday I thought I was a goner. The doctor here, he done it. He stuck with me all night, talking to me, giving me medicine. It wasn't no fun, but he stuck. Look at him, looks like a kid, don't he? But he ain't no kid where it counts."

"Dr. O'Hara is one of our best," Patrick said.

"Hey, in my book he's *the* best."

Buddy turned to Patrick. "We're giving fluid replacement to correct the electrolyte balance, and companzine for the enteritis. The sugar's started to go down."

"Good. You're in good hands, Mr. Lewis. But the next time you feel ill, don't wait so long to come to us."

"Don't worry, the doctor already read me the riot act about that."

Patrick looked at the patient in the next bed. He was a black man in his late forties. He tossed restlessly from side to side.

"This is Mr. Smithe," Buddy said. "He was admitted through the Clinic. There's been continuous abdominal discomfort after meals, a weight loss of ten pounds in four weeks."

Patrick read his chart. "Did the G.I. show anything."

"It came back negative. I have him scheduled for a gallbladder series tomorrow morning."

"Hello, Mr. Smithe, I'm Dr. Dain. Can you tell me what's been bothering you?"

"It hurts something terrible after I eat."

Patrick went to his side. He gently probed the abdomen. "Here?"

Mr. Smithe winced. "Yeah, that's the spot."

"How about there?"

"There too."

"Any nausea or vomiting?"

"An hour after I eat I get to feeling nauseous."

"Does all food bother you, or just certain things?"

"I already give up anything spicy or fried. That's the worst."

"Have you been nervous or worried lately?"

"Tell you the truth, I was worried I had cancer. Doc O'Hara told me not to worry about that," he flashed a bright smile, "so I give up worrying too."

A nurse came into the ward then. She was young and slim and pretty, with reddish hair and gold-flecked, teasing brown eyes.

"Hello, Doctors," she said in a soft, sweet Southern voice. "Hi there, Mr. Smithe, are you feeling better?"

He sat up and pulled the bedtray toward him. "If that's more medicine for me, Sally, I'll be feeling worse."

Sally put a handful of foil packets on the tray and poured a glass of water. "I know what you mean," she said. "At home, if I was feeling poorly, Mama just picked some herbs and that was that. But in a hospital it's pills, pills, pills. Isn't that true, Dr. O'Hara?" She winked at Buddy.

Patrick saw Buddy color slightly and he smiled. Buddy had been dating Sally Tarlton for almost six months. If there was any serenity at all in Buddy's life, he thought, it came from Sally, for she was bright and happy and infinitely gentle.

"Mr. Smithe," Buddy said, "these are the radioactive iodine pills I told you about. You have to take them tonight so we can get a clear picture of your gallbladder tomorrow."

"So many? I'll be glowing in the dark."

"We want your gallbladder to glow in the dark." Buddy smiled. "Take them all by seven o'clock, then nothing but water until we get our x-rays."

Mr. Smithe shook his head. "I guess you know what you're doing."

"Don't worry about him," Mr. Lewis called from his bed. "He's the *best*."

"There you are," Patrick laughed, "you have the word of a satisfied customer . . . Dr. O'Hara, I'd like to see you for a moment."

"I want to check the other patients. I'll meet you in the lounge."

"Very well. Sally, walk along with me." Patrick led her to the door. "Goodnight, gentlemen." He waved as they turned into the corridor.

"You haven't been to dinner recently, Sally. We've missed you."

"Buddy hasn't been in what you'd call an entertaining mood. He comes over to my little place and we order Chinese food and watch the TV."

"How does Buddy seem to you?"

"Mighty unhappy. Sometimes his face is so long it's practically scraping the floor."

"Does he talk about his problems?"

"Some. I don't think I should tell you what Buddy talks about, Dr. Dain. No offense intended."

"None taken. But I'm worried about him. I'm looking for a way to get through to him."

"Well, now you mention it, I've been worried myself. Buddy's one big bundle of nerves. He jumps at the slightest sound, and sometimes he can't sit still. He walks back and forth, back and forth. I get worn out just watching him."

"What is he nervous about? Do you know?"

"That's not for me to say, Dr. Dain."

"I'm not asking you to betray a confidence. But is there anything you can tell me? Can you give me a clue?"

They reached the nurses's station and Sally slipped behind the desk. "You know Buddy better than I do."

"That's no longer true. We used to talk about things. We don't anymore. He's never home. He comes home to change his clothes, to sleep. I *sense* his tension, but I don't know what to do about it."

"Buddy's struggling to find a place for himself."

"He has a place."

"Can I be frank, Dr. Dain?"

"I wish you would."

"Buddy feels like an outsider. It's a feeling he's had for a long time. It went away for a while, but then it came back stronger than ever."

"An outsider?"

"Coming from the south, I understand. It's a feeling that you're different from everybody else . . . maybe not better, maybe not worse, but different. It makes for a loneliness way deep down."

"I know he felt that way once."

"He still does," Sally said quietly. "Buddy wants desperately to belong somewhere."

"But he *does* belong."

"Make him believe that."

Patrick looked away. "We're . . . having problems at home. I knew they were affecting Buddy, but until now, I didn't know how much. That's what you're talking about, isn't it?"

"I think I've talked enough. Ordinarily I'm a plain old chatterbox, but I shouldn't be chattering about Buddy." The phone rang and Sally laughed. "Saved by the bell."

Patrick walked on down the corridor to the lounge. He poured a cup of coffee and sipped it slowly. He thought about Buddy, about his years of rage and anxiety. Buddy's childhood had been marked by fear and the fear was with him still.

"Sorry to keep you," Buddy said, walking into

the lounge. "Mr. Smithe is running a temperature, I wanted to add antibiotics to his i.v."

"That's all right. Relax, have some coffee."

"No thanks. You wanted to talk to me?"

"I wanted to talk to you this morning, but you ran away before I had the chance."

"I seemed to be in the way."

"Nonsense. You did a great job and I wanted to tell you so."

"You mean it?"

"Your work was excellent, Buddy. Do you remember Mrs. McKell from the Code 1?"

"Sure, the woman with the glass in her eyes."

"She's lost the vision in her left eye, but her right eye will be unimpaired . . . and the credit for that goes to you."

Buddy's whole face lit up in a smile. "I should say something humble, but I'm not going to."

"Enjoy the moment. You earned it."

"I've waited a long time for . . . my work to be noticed."

"I've been following your work all along, you know that."

"You never say anything."

"I say as much as I can, without sounding partial. I have to wear two hats, Buddy. I'm not only your stepfather, I'm Chief of Staff. It wouldn't do to play favorites, even though I want to sometimes."

"Do you? I mean . . . am I really a favorite?"

"You've been a challenge, and a torment, and a few other things I shudder to remember." Patrick laughed. "But you've been a great pleasure as well. I've watched you develop and grow into a fine talent . . . a little better, a little surer each year."

Buddy basked in the warmth of Patrick's words. He felt a surge of strength and confidence. He felt renewed.

Patrick studied Buddy's expression. He realized how hungry the young man had been for recognition, for approval. "I'm proud of you," he said.

"When I saw you in the ward, I thought you were there to check up on me."

"Not at all. I've been getting excellent reports on you from the wards. I decided to visit the scene of your success."

"I love this service. I can make a difference here, the patients need me."

"It was kind of you to sit up with Mr. Lewis. Not many of our doctors would have bothered."

"He was scared. Poor guy, he's all alone in the world."

Patrick looked thoughtfully at Buddy. "Do you ever feel as if you're alone in the world?"

"Me? Yes, once in a while. Why do you ask?"

"We haven't talked much lately. I've hardly seen you. I do occasionally hear you pacing around in your room late at night. What keeps you up so late?"

"Nothing special."

"Communication is important, Buddy, especially in times of stress."

"You're trying to say something, I don't know what."

"I'm trying to ease into a small conversation about what's going on at home."

"No! I'm in a good mood now, the best mood I've

been in for a long time. I don't want to get depressed, Patrick. Not now!"

"I don't want to depress you. But you're upset and we ought to talk about it."

"What there to talk about? I know you moved into the sitting room."

"How do you know that?"

"I saw Hollis fixing the bed in there. I saw ties and shirts on the dresser. It wasn't hard to figure out."

"All right. Your mother and I need time alone to think. A lot has happened to our lives in a short time."

"You don't have to cover for her. I know it's her fault."

"You're being too hard on your mother, Buddy. She's in a tough spot too. She's only doing what she feels she must."

"No matter who it hurts!"

"Have you been hurt?"

"I . . . I'm not talking about myself."

"I think you are. You feel left out, and I don't blame you. Ann's been preoccupied, I've been preoccupied, and you've been left out. I see that now and I'm sorry. I'm apologizing, Buddy. It wasn't deliberate, it just happened."

"*You* have nothing to apologize for. It's Ma who's . . . ruining everything."

"Things are a long way from being ruined. Nothing irrevocable has been said *or* done."

"Yet."

"We're having some bad times, yes. Good marriages survive bad times."

185

Buddy walked to the window. He turned and walked to the coffee machine. He poured a cup of coffee, then put it on the table.

"Pop is leading her down the garden path and she's too dumb to see it."

"Dumb is the last thing your mother is."

"She's obsessed by him and Daisy."

"No. She's obsessed by the past. That's quite different."

"Well, I don't see the distinction. Anyway, it was a crummy past. It was hell. Who needs to remember it?"

"Ann needs to remember. She has to remember it now so she can forget it forever."

"Patrick, you don't know how Pop is. You don't know how he can be. He's spent all his life conning people. He's good at it, it's the only thing he *is* good at. He's conning her, *again,* and she can't see it."

"Right now, Ann is remembering the good times."

"What good times?"

"There must have been a few."

"What are a *few* good times compared to *years* of pure hell?"

"Ann will remember those years of pure hell soon enough."

"Pop won't let her. He just about has her convinced that the bad years were *her* fault. Next he'll have her convinced that there *were no* bad years."

"I love your mother and she loves me. I have faith in that."

"You're not fooling me, Patrick. You're cool on

186

the outside, but inside you're as worried as I am. More."

"Never assume."

"I don't have to assume. I know how much Ma's hurt you."

"Let's say I was . . . unprepared. Let's leave it at that."

"I can't. This has been on my mind since Pop came back."

"Buddy, I understand. The three years your mother and I have been married gave you the only security you've ever known. And now, you see it all slipping away."

"Because it is."

"No. I believe we'll work out our problems. But even at the worst, even if we *don't*, your life needn't change."

"How can you say that?"

"In the first place, your financial security is already insured. I've seen to that."

"I'm not talking about money. We've been a *family*."

Patrick's eyes were steady on Buddy. "No matter what happens, you and I will still be family. We will still be friends."

"That's the kind of thing people always say."

"*I* mean it."

"Why are you talking about this now?"

"I want you to know you're not alone. Stop brooding, stop imagining things. If you don't, your nerves will give out."

"My nerves are fine."

"They're not fine. You're too edgy, Buddy. You

haven't been sleeping well, and from the look of you, you haven't been eating well either. Add it up. What do you get?"

"Any first-year resident."

"Wrong."

"Do I get another guess?"

"Don't guess. Look in the mirror."

"C'mon, it's not that bad. The nurses still flirt with me, I must look okay."

Patrick smiled. "I don't want you to run yourself into the ground. Learn how to pace yourself. Learn how to relax."

"Work is my relaxation."

"Work is work. Relaxation is something else entirely. It's time you learn the difference."

"Maybe you're right."

"You're agreeing too easily. Are you humoring me?"

"I've always been open to advice."

"Open to advice? *You?*" Patrick laughed.

Buddy shrugged his shoulders. He smiled. "It's the new me."

"Can I offer the new you a suggestion? Have a talk with your mother. Patch up your differences."

"I'm not ready for that."

"The gulf between you is only going to widen. You don't want that to happen. Your mother certainly doesn't."

"I'll think about it."

"Don't think about it. *Do* it."

"I promise I'll think about it."

Patrick stood up. "I suppose that's better than nothing." He looked at his watch. "And I suppose

I should be getting back to work. Coming?"

They walked to the door together. Patrick draped his arm around Buddy's shoulder. "I'm glad we talked," he said.

"So am I. I appreciate your coming to the wards to see me."

Patrick glanced at him. "Well, Matt thought I—" he stopped, for he realized he'd made a grave mistake. "Buddy, I—"

"No!" Buddy twisted away from Patrick. His eyes were wild with anger, perspiration dampened his brow. "I should have known! I thought *Pop* was a con man. He has nothing on you! You had me *believing* your song and dance. But you were just saying what Matt wanted you to say."

"That's not true. Listen to—"

"Sure, Matt tells you to throw the poor kid a bone and you do it. You'd do anything for Matt Lansing! He's the greatest thing since penicillin! He's everybody's hero!"

"Buddy." Patrick grabbed Buddy's shoulders. "I insist you listen to me."

Buddy's face was red. The veins in his temples throbbed. "What for? So you can tell me more lies? Go to hell and take Matt with you."

"Are you *jealous* of Matt? I like him, but *you* are a part of my family."

Again, Buddy broke away from Patrick. "Not anymore!"

"It's true that Matt asked me to speak to you. He thought you deserved some recognition. I heartily agreed. I didn't lie to you. I meant everything I said. *Everything*."

"Bullshit!"

"How do I get through to you?" Patrick implored him. "Matt's not your enemy. I'm not your enemy. We're both on *your side*."

"I don't want you there," Buddy shouted. "I don't want anything from anybody ever again."

"Don't hurt yourself this way."

"As if you cared! As if anybody cared!"

Patrick was shaken by the look in Buddy's eyes. It was a look of anger, but beyond the anger was a deep, devouring panic.

"Buddy, you're drowning in self-pity. You're going down for the third time."

Buddy lurched to the door. "I won't be missed."

"Let us *help* you. Your mother and I—"

"My *mother* has Daisy. *You* have Matt. I hope you'll all be very happy."

Buddy ran out the door. Patrick heard his footsteps pounding down the corridor. A door slammed in the distance, and then there was quiet.

Patrick leaned against the wall. He was exhausted. He felt as if every bit of energy had been drained out of him. He stared into space, seeing nothing.

"Things aren't good, are they?"

Patrick turned. He saw Sally Tarlton standing there. "Things couldn't be worse."

15

Hollis was waiting in the hall when Patrick got home. He was unsmiling and he seemed anxious.

"I'm so glad you're here, sir."

"That makes one of us." Patrick handed over his coat and bag. "I'm afraid to ask, but what's happening?"

"You've had more than twenty calls about the Josephson matter. The messages are on your desk in the library."

"Throw them away. I'm not taking any calls about the senator."

Patrick looked toward the stairs, toward the sound of the argument raging above his head. He heard Buddy and Ann shouting at each other.

"How long has that been going on?"

"An hour, off and on. Dr. O'Hara is packing. Mrs. Dain is attempting to stop him. He seems quite determined, sir."

"The O'Haras are a determined lot. I used to find that charming."

Patrick went to the stairs. He listened to the angry voices rising and falling. "I remember when there was laughter. Now . . ."

Hollis looked genuinely distressed. "I do wish I could be of help, sir."

"We'll work it out. Don't worry."

Patrick walked up the stairs and went to Buddy's room. He stood in the doorway and looked inside. Closets and dresser drawers were open. Clothes were heaped carelessly on the bed, flung over the backs of chairs. A heavy canvas bag was stuffed with books.

Buddy snapped a suitcase shut and put it on the floor. He began tossing shirts and sweaters into a smaller suitcase.

"What's this?" Patrick asked.

"Patrick," Ann ran to him, "you have to do something." She was tired and drawn. Her hair fell unnoticed into her eyes. "Please, won't you try?"

"What are you doing, Buddy?"

"What does it look like I'm doing?"

"Where are you going?"

"That's none of your business."

"Buddy," Patrick said impatiently, "you have to leave a number for the hospital, if not for us."

"I'll be at Sally's until I can find an apartment."

Patrick looked closely at Buddy. His eyes were hard and cold, but his hands were shaking. "Do you know what apartments cost these days?"

"I earn a salary, I have money. *My* money, not yours. I don't need a duplex on Sutton Place. All I need is a bed somewhere."

Ann grasped Patrick's hand. "Can't you do anything?"

"Apparently not."

"Talk to him."

"*Talk?* I've talked, I've explained, I've apologized, I've pleaded. All to no avail."

Buddy glared at Patrick. "You also lied. You forgot to mention that."

"What is he talking about?" Ann asked.

Patrick led Ann to a chair and sat her down. "Buddy believes there is a plot against him. He believes me to be the chief conspirator."

"That's right, patronize me."

Patrick pushed a pile of clothes aside and sat on the bed. He sighed. "Look, you are certainly old enough to leave . . . But must you leave this way? Must you leave in anger?"

Buddy scooped up his ties and socks and threw them into the case. "That's the way I feel."

"Have you considered the way your mother feels?"

"Yes, and I don't care."

Patrick heard Ann's small cry. He looked at her, then looked back at Buddy. "Very well. I don't intend to argue with you anymore. If you want to leave so badly, leave."

"Patrick!"

"That's the way it is, Ann. Enough is enough."

"He doesn't want me here," Buddy shouted, "he never wanted me here."

"Believe what you want," Patrick said. "I'm through beating my breast."

"Are you through lying?"

"I didn't lie to you. I have never lied to you. You're too busy looking for villains to recognize the truth when you hear it."

Buddy emptied a drawer into his suitcase. "Nothing you can say will change my mind."

"I don't want to change your mind. I once told you I had a low tolerance for punks. You are behaving like a punk. You want to be a tough guy, well, *be* a tough guy. But *not here.*"

"Patrick," Ann said weakly, "Buddy doesn't mean it. Try to understand—"

"No! That's all I've heard for three months . . . understand the circumstances, understand this, understand that. And by God, I've tried. But I'm drawing the line here and now."

"Watch it," Buddy sneered, "you're tarnishing your halo."

Patrick threw up his hands. "I used to look forward to coming home. But no more."

"Don't blame me for that," Buddy said quickly.

"I'm tired of the shouting. I'm tired of the hostility. And since you mention it," Patrick said to Buddy, "I am especially tired of *your* big mouth."

There was a loud thud as Buddy closed his suitcase. "My heart bleeds for you."

"When you're ready to behave," Patrick said, "you'll be welcome here. Not before."

"Don't hold your breath."

Buddy slung his book bag over his shoulder. He picked up the suitcases and stalked to the door.

"Do you need any money?" Patrick asked.

"I don't need anything from you."

Patrick took Ann's hand. Together, they followed Buddy into the hall. "Aren't you going to say goodbye to your mother?"

"Bye, Ma."

"Buddy," Ann beseeched him, "we can't leave things like this. Will you call me? When will I see you?"

Buddy stopped near the stairs. He looked at Ann for a long moment. "We'll probably run into each other . . . sometime."

Ann slumped against Patrick. He put his arm around her. "Don't prolong this. If you're going, go now."

Daisy came out of her room then. She stared at Buddy's luggage, then looked up at him. "Where are you going, Buddy?"

Buddy's eyes blazed. His mouth trembled. "You! Get the hell out of my way!"

Patrick was appalled at the depth of Buddy's rage. He rushed to Daisy and pulled her back. "Go to your room," he said quietly. "And close the door."

"You!" Buddy screamed after her. *"It's all your fault."*

Patrick waited until Daisy was gone, then looked darkly at Buddy. "What's the matter with you? She's only a child."

Buddy's eyes blurred with tears. He turned, stomping and bumping his way down the stairs. Patrick watched him go. He saw Buddy kick his suitcases through the center hall. He heard him shout at Hollis. There was a brief silence, then the crash of the front door as Buddy left.

"Well, he's gone."

Ann ran tearfully to the bedroom. Patrick shook his head. "God bless our happy home," he muttered to himself.

Patrick went into Daisy's room. She was lying on the bed, hugging Alfie to her. Her face was very quiet and sad.

He sat at the edge of the bed. "You mustn't worry about anything. Buddy was upset, that's all."

"Why does Buddy hate me?"

"He doesn't hate you."

"Poppa says he does."

Patrick brushed her bangs away from her eyes. "Your poppa is mistaken. And Buddy hollered at you because he was upset. He didn't mean what he said. Sometimes people say silly things when they're upset."

Daisy hugged Alfie closer, tugging at the bow she'd tied in his brown yarn mane.

"Alfie looks quite handsome this evening."

Daisy turned her enormous eyes on Patrick. "Do you hate me?"

"*No*, I don't hate you. What a question!"

"Poppa says you do."

"He's wrong. As a matter of fact, Miss Daisy O'Hara, you have stolen my heart away."

"What does that mean?"

"That means you are my favorite little girl in the whole, wide world."

Patrick had meant only to pacify Daisy, but he realized he'd spoken the truth. His affection for her had grown steadily over the months. He'd enjoyed watching her progress, enjoyed making her smile. He remembered his pleasure the first time she'd laughed out loud. He knew that he'd begun to think of her as his own daughter.

"Shall I tell you a secret?"

196

"Okay."

Patrick stretched his arms far apart. "I love you *this* much."

A light came into Daisy's eyes. She smiled and it was the full, open smile of a happy child. "Thank you, Patrick."

"Do I get a hug?"

"No," she said, still shy about her feelings.

"Ah, *la belle dame sans merci.*"

"What does that mean?"

"That means the beautiful lady without mercy. How about a kiss? Could you manage that?"

"Okay." She leaned forward and kissed him quickly on the cheek. "You say funny things."

"I try. Always leave 'em laughing." Patrick winked. "Follow that advice and you will go far." He tucked the blankets in around her. "It's late, time to go to sleep."

"Is Ann coming to say goodnight?"

"Ann has a headache. You'll see her in the morning."

"Would you read me a story?"

"It's past your bedtime, Droopy. And tomorrow is a school day."

"A *little* story?"

"No sale. It's the sandman for you."

Patrick switched off the lamp and turned on the night-light. He went to the door. He paused, glancing back at Daisy.

"If anybody says anything . . . silly to you again, just remember," he stretched his arms far apart. "*This* much."

Daisy settled her head on the pillows. "I will."

"Goodnight. Sleep well."

Patrick walked along the hall to the sitting room. He went inside and closed the door, relieved to be alone. He hung up his jacket and took off his tie, then poured a large brandy. The brandy calmed him. He drank it gratefully and poured another.

Patrick carried his drink to the couch. He sat down, gazing around the room that had been his home for the last few weeks. It was a comfortable room of medium size, done mostly in tans and greens. The furniture, of dark oak, had been in the Dain family for generations. There was a daybed and, near the fireplace, an easy chair upholstered in a tan and black check. A six-foot rubber tree stood in the corner, dwarfing a dozen small cactus plants arranged around its base.

"May I come in?" Ann hesitated at the doorway.

"Of course." Patrick looked at her. She was wearing jeans and a red plaid blouse. Her hair was brushed away from her face and tied with a red ribbon. She looked very young and very tired. "Do you want a drink?"

"No . . . How is Daisy?"

"She's all right, everything considered."

"What did she say?"

"She asked if you were coming in. I made your excuses."

"What else did she say?"

Patrick sipped his brandy. "Daisy wanted to know why Buddy hated her. I assured her he didn't. She asked if I hated her. I assured her on that point too."

Ann sank into a chair. "Daisy looked so

198

vulnerable, so small."

"She is both those things. I wish Bren would remember that."

"Bren?"

"He's been filling her head with a lot of cruel ideas. Bren told Daisy that I hated her. He told her that Buddy hated her . . . You don't seem surprised."

"I'm not. I know how jealous Bren is."

"I'm afraid Buddy's explosion lent credence to what Bren said. The timing couldn't have been worse."

"Buddy doesn't hate her, you know. He *doesn't*."

"Yes, I know."

"I never saw him that way before."

"Neither did I."

"Is Buddy . . . is he . . ." Ann was unable to finish the sentence.

"Buddy is in bad shape."

"But he was doing so well. Just a few months ago, you told me he was doing beautifully."

"That was before . . . before our lives changed."

"Patrick, we took a little girl into our home. That's *all* we did. How can the addition of one little girl cause so much grief?"

"Daisy hasn't caused the grief, but in a way she's been the catalyst. She's made you remember things. While you are remembering your past, Buddy is remembering his. And it scares him to death. He also sees the changes in this household. That scares him to death. He's living in constant fear."

"I didn't mean to, but I pulled the rug out from under him."

"These last three years he's had security, the security that's eluded him all his life. Rightly or wrongly, he sees it disappearing. He feels threatened."

"Buddy's an adult. I never dreamed he'd react this way."

"Chronologically, he's an adult. Emotionally, he's still a young boy fighting for approval, for love."

"Well," Ann said dully, "you warned me this might happen."

"You're not the only one at fault. I let Buddy down too. I knew he felt threatened by Matt Lansing. Instead of dealing with the problem, I laughed it off. I made it out to be a simple competition between residents. It was far from that."

"How is he threatened by Matt?"

"He isn't."

"You mean it's all in . . . in Buddy's mind? He's *imagining* things? Patrick?"

Patrick drained his glass. He walked to the windows and stared down at the river. The water looked black and cold.

"Patrick, answer me!"

"Buddy takes small incidents and magnifies them *all* out of proportion . . . to the point where he now believes everybody is against him."

"Are you saying he's . . . ill?"

"I don't know."

"What do you mean you don't know? You're a doctor."

"I am not a psychiatrist."

200

Ann rose from her chair, then sat down again. She rubbed her hands nervously across her knees. "You think he needs a psychiatrist? . . . *Do* you?"

"I don't know. At the very least, he needs a rest."

"Give him a leave of absence. You can do that. You have the authority to do that."

Patrick turned around. He leaned against the windowsill. "He wouldn't take it. Furthermore, he would see it as another part of the plot to get rid of him."

"I'll *make* him take it."

"I'm sorry, Ann," Patrick said as gently as he could, "but at this moment, you have very little influence with Buddy."

Ann said nothing. She considered Patrick's words, considered the ferocity of Buddy's words earlier in the evening. She felt a heaviness in her arms and legs, a lethargy dragging her down. She forced herself to sit up straight and think.

"Someone must have some influence with Buddy."

"Sally Tarlton. *Maybe.*"

"Well?"

"Well, it would be unfortunate if Buddy thought that Sally, his last ally, had joined in the plot."

"Will you stop using that word!" Ann said angrily.

Patrick poured a fresh drink. "There is another side to this. It's possible that Buddy's work is the only thing holding him together right now."

"You can't be sure of that."

"I plan to talk to Adams in psychiatry tomorrow. Perhaps he can give me guidelines. Ann, it might be a good idea if Daisy . . . spent a few days with Bren. We'll put them up at the Plaza. It might help Buddy to know Daisy is . . . away."

"I thought of that five minutes after Buddy stormed in here tonight. But we can't send Daisy to Bren because Bren isn't here. He went to Southie yesterday."

Patrick's head snapped up. "Southie? How do you know?"

"I took him to the airport myself. I bought his tickets."

"Why did he go?"

"I don't know. I don't care. Buddy is the issue, not Bren."

"I'll do everything I can. Let's see what Adams has to say. He's a good man, I trust him."

"Do you think it's . . . very serious?"

"The O'Haras are strong." Patrick smiled slightly. "They're survivors. Buddy gets grit from you, nerve from Bren. He'll come through this."

He looked at his watch. He took a notebook from his pocket and went to the phone. "I have a call to make."

Ann remained where she was. Patrick looked pointedly at his watch. "It's a business call, and it's getting late."

Ann went to the door. "Tell me again he'll be all right."

"He'll be fine."

"When you say it, I believe it . . . Goodnight, Patrick."

"Goodnight."

Patrick heard the door close. He looked in the

202

notebook and then dialed the phone. "John Simpson, please, Patrick Dain calling . . . hello, Mr. Simpson, Patrick Dain here, sorry to disturb you at home . . . yes . . . could you come to my office tomorrow morning? . . . good . . . yes, thank you."

Patrick hung up. Bren's sudden trip to Southie concerned him, but he resolved not to think any more about the O'Haras tonight. He kicked off his shoes and walked to the bathroom. He stripped off his clothes and stepped into the shower.

Patrick stayed in the shower a long time. He soaped his head and body, and then turned the hot water up full. A misting steam rose in the glass enclosure, relaxing his muscles. He adjusted the shower nozzle until prickles of icy cold water stung his tired neck and shoulders to life. After several minutes, he turned off the taps and wrapped himself in a thick terrycloth robe.

He walked into the sitting room, rubbing at his head with a large towel. He stopped, for Ann was curled up on the daybed. She was wearing a negligé of ivory satin. The bodice was ivory lace, cut low over the swell of her breasts. Her hair spilled over her shoulders in gleaming honey waves. Her lips were rouged a soft pink.

"I couldn't sleep," she said.

"I'll . . . get you a pill."

"I don't want a pill."

"Ann . . ."

She went to him. She turned him to her. The satin gown clung to the curves of her body. Her perfume drifted in a cloud around her. She kissed him, then traced the outline of his mouth with her fingers.

Patrick took Ann in his arms. He crushed her to him, his lips on hers. He slid his hands over her body and he felt the fire rage within him.

Ann's gown fell to the floor. Patrick lifted her into his arms and carried her to the bed. He knelt beside her, caressing her body, and the fire became a madness of love. She slipped the robe from his shoulders and pulled him to her. They kissed and touched and murmured to each other in the shadow light of the moon. Their bodies met in wave after wave of sweet ecstasy and for them, then, that was the only truth.

16

It was seven thirty in the morning when Lola Shay arrived at the hospital cafeteria. It was nearly empty, most of the doctors and nurses having scattered for morning rounds. A lone busboy was clearing away the breakfast debris, loading trays and stacking them on a stainless steel cart.

Lola spotted Eve Lawrence sitting in a corner by the window. She was wearing something red and silky, and the sunlight dappled her golden hair. Even at a distance, Lola scowled, Eve was beautiful. She took a deep breath and walked across the room to Eve's table.

"Good morning."

"Good morning, Lola. Thank you for coming."

Lola sat down. "You've been very persistent. I decided to get it over with." There was a plate of danish and a carafe of fresh coffee on the table. She poured a cup of coffee and pushed the danish away. "Well, what do you want?"

"I'd like to talk."

"What would you like to talk about? The weather, politics, the new spring fashions?"

"Please, can we have a brief truce?"

"Okay, a truce. But I have a short attention span, so get to the point."

"David is the point."

"That figures."

"I did a stupid thing. I apologize."

Lola frowned. "Is that supposed to make everything all right? It doesn't."

"It's a place to start. I'm trying to find the right words."

"The rights words for what?"

"For an explanation."

"If you're planning to bare your soul, forget it. I'm not interested."

"Lola, I haven't seen David . . . socially, in two weeks. I want you to know that."

"Why?"

"You're his wife."

"How kind of you to remember. But *estranged* wife is more like it."

"You wouldn't be estranged if it weren't for . . . for what happened."

"Oh, I understand now. You're going to get us back together. Eve Lawrence, matchmaker. If that weren't so grotesque, it would be funny."

Eve glanced away. "I don't blame you for being bitter."

"Sure you do. You think I'm making much ado about nothing."

Eve looked up. "It was just an affair. David and I never loved each other."

"Is *that* supposed to make everything all right?"

"It didn't mean a thing to either of us."

"You have a lot to learn, Eve. I could accept an affair based on love. What I *won't* accept is cheap philandering. Cheap sex is all the rage and marriage is a joke, but *I'm* not laughing."

"I told you I was sorry."

"You're not sorry," Lola said sharply. "I know your type very well. A new affair every month and you couldn't care less. You're not sorry, but you *are* worried. What are you worried about?"

"My job."

"Your job? What does your job have to do with anything?"

"Ask Patrick."

"I'm asking you."

"Patrick has been excluding me from hospital business wherever he can. My authority is shrinking away to nothing. He's already told me that you and David are more important to the hospital than I am. If somebody has to go, it's me."

Lola sat back. "Is that when you stopped seeing David?"

"The hell with David! There are a hundred Davids out there, a thousand. My *job* is important."

Lola had sensed the coldness in Eve long ago; she wasn't surprised by it now. She stared at her impassively. "What do you want from me?"

"Talk to Patrick. He'll listen to you."

"Why should I?"

"We're both women, Lola. We both had to fight to get where we are. We should support one another, regardless of our other quarrels."

"Do you *really* expect me to help you?" Lola laughed.

"As hard as it is for a woman in medicine, it's just as hard for a woman in business."

"If you'd kept your mind on business, you wouldn't be in this spot."

"I picked the wrong man, I admit it. Married men are easiest for me, but I picked the wrong married man. That's a mistake I won't make again."

"God, you're a bitch!"

"I'm a woman who's worked very hard to get somewhere. I had no time for family, for marriage. I'm a working woman, I take my fun where I can."

"You're an insult to working women. Lots of women, myself included, have worked harder and longer than you ever have . . . and never found it necessary to stray into someone else's garden."

"That's beside the point."

"Is it?"

"Yes. I want to be judged by my work, not my personal life. Patrick has no complaint with my work, it's my personal life he objects to."

Lola turned her coffee cup around and around. "A hospital is a delicate mechanism. If it doesn't run smoothly, it doesn't run at all. Patrick dislikes tensions among the staff. He's said so often enough."

"Look, I fell into a stupid thing with David. I wasn't thinking. I'm thinking now and I'm all through with that."

"Does David know you're through?"

"Why, does it matter?"

"Oh," Lola glared at Eve, "it might matter to David."

Eve shook her head impatiently and the sunlight

rippled through her hair. "He doesn't care any more about me than I care about him. It was . . ." she shrugged. Her pretty hands fluttered in the air.

"Let me help," Lola snapped. "Just one of those things."

"*You're* the one he loves."

"And you're giving him back to me. For a price."

"Is it such a bad bargain?"

"It's despicable. But I'll make you another bargain."

"Anything."

"I'll talk to Patrick . . . on condition that you and David do what you wish to do. That is, if you and he wish to continue seeing each other, go ahead. If you don't, don't. The choice is yours and David's."

"That doesn't make sense. You *want* me to see David?"

"It's entirely up to the two of you. Either way, your employment here won't be jeopardized. You have my word on that."

"I don't understand."

"The damage has already been done. My marriage is over. If you and David wish to see each other, there's no reason you shouldn't."

"Your marriage doesn't have to be over."

"That's up to me. I've made my decision."

"If your marriage is really over, Patrick will have my head."

"No, he won't. He'll take his cue from me."

"What cue are you going to give him?" Eve asked suspiciously.

"I'm not going to carry a grudge. The shock has worn off, the pain will too, in time. I don't like you, but we're professionals, we can work together without rancor."

"You were angry when you came in here. Now, you're very accommodating. Why?"

"Why not? If David wants you, let him have you." Lola smiled cooly. "That's revenge enough for me."

"That hurt."

"It was supposed to. Not that I believe anything hurts you very deeply."

"Losing my job would hurt me. My job is all I have."

"That's your own doing. You're smart and young and beautiful, Eve. Your life can be anything you want it to be."

"I want success."

"You have success."

"Not the kind I'm talking about. I need two more years here, for my resume. After that, I can go anywhere. To a large medical center, to a large corporation. Anywhere! Top of the world."

Lola looked at her watch. She rose. "Top of the world? Jimmy Cagney said that in a movie once, just before he blew himself up."

"Patrick," Lola poked her head into his office. "Do you have a minute?"

He looked up. "I always have time for you. Come in."

"Can we talk, or is a meeting about to start?"

"My seven o'clock meeting just broke up. I'm

free as a bird until nine. What can I do for you?"

"Lay off Eve."

"I beg your pardon?"

Lola sat down across from Patrick. "I saw Eve this morning. She told me what you said to her."

"Refresh my memory."

"Don't be coy."

"Lola, I say a lot of things to a lot of people."

"Eve's worried about her job."

"Oh, that."

"That. Did you really threaten to fire her? How medieval!"

Patrick smiled. "I didn't threaten to fire her. I said that *if* there was a conflict, she knew where the ax would fall."

"Yes, I see the difference."

"I told her the truth. If there *is* a conflict, who goes? A doctor or an administrator? This is more than a personal problem, it's a hospital problem."

"Well, I've solved your problem. Nobody goes."

"I'm happy to hear that. Peace in our time, that's my motto."

"Aren't you bursting with curiosity? Don't you want to know what happened?"

"I don't believe you and Eve have become best friends. Therefore, it must have something to do with David."

"It does." Lola looked at David's office door. "Is he in there? I wouldn't want him listening at the keyhole."

"He's at a meeting with Matt. He'll be a while."

"Promise me you won't repeat this conversation to him."

"I promise."

"Eve and I had a talk this morning. I told her to feel free to see David, if that's what they wanted."

"What? . . . Lola, how could you do such a thing?"

"I told her my marriage was over, there was no reason they shouldn't see each other."

"You, of all people, giving up." Patrick shook his head back and forth. "*Why?*"

"I knew David hasn't seen Eve lately. I didn't know until this morning that it was *Eve* who pulled the plug. I didn't know *you* had forced her to."

"What are you getting at?"

"I want David to make his own decision. I don't want it made for him by Eve, or by you. Eve doesn't give a damn about him. It's fun and games for her. But I don't know how David feels. I have to know."

"He's tried to talk to you."

"A bunch of excuses and a bunch of platitudes, that's not want I want. I want to know how he *feels*. Listening to Eve talk about him . . . I realized I still cared. David's a jerk sometimes, and he's hurt me, but I still care."

"I never doubted it."

"I did. These past few weeks I wanted to kill him. I lay in bed at night thinking up exquisite tortures to inflict on him. When I saw the pictures of Lenore dumping water on Doug's head, I knew exactly how she felt."

"Don't compare David to Doug."

"Granted, Doug's a big-league rat and David's only an amateur. I still got a vicarious thrill looking at those pictures."

"I am sure Lenore spoke for a lot of women." Patrick smiled.

"I don't want to be one of those women. I know what kind of marriage I want. It's up to David to decide what kind of marriage he wants, or if he wants marriage at all."

"Of course he does."

"David was single for a long time after his first marriage. He became accustomed to lovely young women pampering him, pouring attention on him. He was king of the hill." Lola laughed. Her green eyes twinkled. "And what a hill it was!"

"He *married* you."

"And proceeded to have an affair with Eve."

"He regrets it now."

"Does he? Or does he merely want to have his cake and eat it too? There's a lot of kid in David."

"I assure you, he's growing up in a hurry."

"We'll see about that. That's why I gave Eve my blessing. That's why you're going to give Eve your blessing. To see what David decides."

"All right, if that's the way you want it."

"That's the way it has to be, for David's sake as well as mine. There'll always be an Eve somewhere. I won't go through this a second time. Lenore made that mistake years ago and look what happened. She and Doug are miserable."

"I understand what you're doing, but don't be impatient. Give David some time."

"I'm not going to draw this out," Lola said firmly. "If we don't have a life together, then I have to start building a life alone." She looked thoughtfully at Patrick. "We're all going through trials by fire, aren't we?"

"It hasn't been fun."

"I admire the way you're hanging on."

"I'm hanging on because I'm afraid to let go. What began as a small ripple is now a giant wave swamping all of us."

"Daisy too?"

"She's a perceptive child, she notices things. But I'm particularly worried about Buddy."

"His work has been excellent."

"His work is fine, his *life* is a mess. He moved out of our apartment."

"Personally, I think it's time he was on his own."

"That isn't why he moved out. He moved out in protest, in rage. It was a terrible scene."

"Buddy's always been volatile."

"Not this volatile. His anger is eating him alive." Patrick's blue eyes clouded. "I tried to calm him. I failed."

"Maybe therapy would help."

"He won't accept help. In his present mood, I wouldn't dare suggest it."

There was a knock at the door and David walked into the office. "Is this a private party? May I intrude?"

"You may," Patrick said.

"Hello, Lola."

"Hello, David."

"You certainly look pretty. I like your dress, is it new?"

"Out with the old, in with the new."

"I was wondering," David smiled hopefully, "are you free for lunch?"

"Sorry, I have an appointment."

"How about dinner?"

"Sorry."

"Could we have a drink after work? I'd like to see your new apartment . . . I'll bring champagne."

Lola went to the door. "Another time."

"When?" David called after her, but she was gone. "Well," he turned to Patrick, "I really swept her off her feet. Call me irresistible."

"Your approach is wrong."

"I've tried all kinds of approaches. Lola keeps brushing me off like a pesky fly."

"You do have your pesky moments."

"You're such a comfort, Patrick. Do you practice, or does it come naturally?"

Patrick searched around for his pen. He began initialing the memos that were stacked neatly on his desk. "Are you looking for sympathy again?"

"I wouldn't turn it down."

"Forget about yourself for a while. Think about Lola."

"I am thinking about Lola. Why was she here? Hospital business, or conversation?"

"A little of both."

"What did you talk about?"

"Nothing important."

"That explains everything," David said tersely. "Thank you for your clarity."

Patrick looked up. "It was an ordinary conversation. I didn't take notes."

"At least you *had* a conversation with Lola. That's more than I can say."

Patrick looked closely at David. His careful

grooming did nothing to disguise the strain of the last weeks. He was obviously tired, and his mouth was tightly drawn. "Lola still cares," Patrick said softly. "As for a hint, all I can tell you is what I've already told you. Grow up. And be quick about it."

"Did she mention Eve?"

"Eve's name came up, yes."

"Lola hasn't . . . forgiven me for Eve. She probably never will."

"You say that as if it's over between you and Eve."

"It is, more or less."

Patrick was startled. *"More or less?* That's not good enough. That's not nearly good enough."

"I want Lola back."

"What about Eve? Do you want her?"

David stared down at the floor. He frowned, tracing a pattern in the rug with the tip of his shoe. "I don't know," he said finally. "I don't know."

"When you do, talk to Lola. She'll talk to you, *when* you know what you want."

"I don't understand what's the matter with me." David spoke so quietly he might have been speaking to himself. "The choice should be so simple. Eve is only a fling. I *love* Lola. And yet I hesitate. I don't understand."

"Why don't we have dinner tonight?" Patrick offered. "We'll talk."

"You always go straight home."

"It's rather complicated at home." He paused. "I could do with an evening out. What do you say?"

"I'll bore you to death with my problems. Can you stand that?"

216

"We'll bore each other. What are friends for?"

David smiled. "You have a deal."

"Good. Now, tell me about Matt. Was he any help?"

"Matt is incredible. He finished the drug inventory. He was right, we have unexplained shortages in forty percent of the services. Codeine and barbiturates, but also antihistamines and antibiotics. Apparently, our people are helping themselves to whatever they want."

"Damn! I thought we had a good control system."

"So did I. It was Matt who instituted spot checks. Now he's devising a whole new system. He's going floor by floor, starting with the wards."

"Did you talk to him about Buddy?"

"I instructed him to keep an eagle eye on Buddy. He was way ahead of us on that too."

"What did he say?"

"He didn't say anything directly, but it's clear he thinks Buddy is in a precarious state."

Patrick absently played with a paperclip, twisting it out of shape. "I have an appointment with Adams this afternoon . . . I don't know if Buddy should be continued on staff."

"Don't take his work away from him. That may be the last straw."

"With Buddy, *anything* may be the last straw."

17

"Buddy." Sally Tarlton stopped him in the corridor. "Come take a look at Mr. Lewis and Mr. Smithe."

"What's the matter?"

"Mr. Smithe's temperature is up again. Mr. Lewis doesn't feel well at all."

"I saw them an hour ago on rounds."

Sally stood with her hands on her hips. She tilted her head up, her mouth in a pretty little pout. "Are you going to give me a hard time, Buddy O'Hara? Or are you going to come with me?"

"Do I have a choice?"

Sally strode into 301 and Buddy followed after her. They stopped first at the bedside of Mr. Lewis.

"How are you doing, Harry?" Buddy asked.

"Not so good. I have this headache. And my chest, it feels kind of heavy."

"What's his temperature?"

"100.8," Sally said.

Buddy put his stethoscope to Harry's chest. "Take a deep breath . . . that's it, once more . . . again . . . sit up please," Buddy moved the stethocope to Harry's back. "A deep breath . . . once more . . . Is anything else bothering you?"

"I feel kind of achy."

"Since when?"

"It come on me all of a sudden."

Buddy checked his pulse and blood pressure. He listened to his lungs a second time.

"So, Doctor, what's the story?"

"You have some congestion, Harry, that's why your chest feels heavy. It's nothing to worry about, a virus."

"You'll fix it." Harry Lewis smiled trustingly. "I ain't worried."

Buddy made a brief notation on his chart. "Sally, continue the antibiotics. I want a white count, a blood culture, and a smear." He patted Harry's hand. "Get some rest now."

They moved on to Mr. Smithe. He had the blankets pulled up around his neck. He was shivering.

"Temp is 101," Sally said.

"George, how do you feel?"

"About like him." He nodded toward Harry Lewis. "A headache, my chest feels full, plus I got chills. You think we caught it from each other?"

"You know what they say, Mr. Lewis." Sally smiled, smoothing his blankets. "A hospital's no place for sick people."

"Fine time to be telling me, Sally," he chuckled. "Doc, what'll this to do my gallbladder operation? They put me down for tomorrow morning."

"We won't operate while you're running a temperature. We'll get rid of this bug first, then

219

reschedule the operation."

Buddy bent to listen to his lungs. "Take a deep breath . . . again . . . once more . . . once more . . . It's nothing serious. This will add a few days to your stay here, but that's not so bad, is it?"

"I'll be climbing the walls. Sally, tell me the truth. Will I ever be getting out of here?"

"You surely will. And you'll feel good as new. That's a promise, neighbor to neighbor."

Buddy took a handkerchief from his pocket and wiped his damp face. "Neighbor to neighbor?" he asked.

"Mr. Smithe and I both come from Paroo County. I went to school with his fourth-cousin on his daddy's side, Cora Slocum Smithe. How about that!"

"Sally's my tie to home," George Smithe said.

Buddy scribbled a notation on his chart. "Continue the antibiotics. White count, culture and smear," he said to Sally. "George, get some rest."

"I will Doc. I'm too cold to get out of bed."

Buddy and Sally left the ward. Buddy was quiet, mopping his brow. Sally glanced at him.

"Don't tell me you're coming down with something."

"No, I'm fine."

"You don't look fine . . . Buddy, what's the matter with those men?"

"Nothing, a virus."

"If it's only a virus, why are you tampering with the charts? Why did you lie to Dr. Zabar this morning on rounds?"

"I didn't lie."

"You didn't let anybody examine Mr. Smithe or Mr. Lewis."

"Why should I?" Buddy snapped. "They're *my* patients."

"You didn't tell Dr. Zabar about their temperatures."

"That information is on the charts."

"Buddy, *wrong* information is on those charts. You have their temperatures at 99.6, just high enough to account for the antibiotics. You confirmed those temperatures to Dr. Zabar. I heard you."

"So I lied. So what? I'm twice the doctor Zabar is."

"He's your supervising resident."

"Who cares? Zabar's just putting in time here until he can go into private practice. He doesn't give one damn about anything else."

Sally put her hand on Buddy's arm. "I still don't understand why you didn't tell the truth."

"Look, those men have infections. I have to do something about it before somebody finds out."

"What kind of infections? Staph?"

Buddy hesitated. "Rush those tests through the lab *stat*."

"Staph? Is that it?" Sally asked softly.

"Could be." Buddy wiped the moisture from his forehead.

"One of the first things they told us in nursing school was that staph spreads through a hospital like wildfire. We have to—"

"The hell with nursing school! I went to *medical* school, I know what I'm doing."

Sally drew away from the harshness in Buddy's voice. Pink color rose in her face. "I didn't mean to overstep my place. You know that, don't you, Buddy? It's only that I'm worried. We have to report this. We'll need help."

They came to the nurses' station. Buddy took Sally's hand in his. "I'll do everything that has to be done. I'll take care of everything. You have to believe me," he said insistently, "I need you to believe me."

"But . . . it's contagious. There are other patients in that ward. We can't have things getting out of control. You wouldn't want that, I know you wouldn't."

"I'll start treatment as soon as I get the test results. Everything will be okay, you'll see."

"Buddy," Sally said gently, "why can't we tell Dr. Zabar or . . . somebody?"

"That's what they're waiting for! They've been waiting for me to make a mistake! This is it, they'll get me for it!"

"They? Who are they?"

"Patrick, Matt, all of them. They've been waiting, just waiting, for an excuse to throw me out."

"But you haven't made a mistake."

"They've been waiting all this time. This is it. They'll use it against me." Buddy's voice was ragged, his breath came in short gasps. His eyes were unfocused, swimming with tears. "They'll get me for it. They will."

Sally took a moment to collect her thoughts. For the first time in the months she'd known Buddy, she was frightened for him. He was immobilzed by his fear. He babbled on, crying, making little sense.

"Buddy," she turned his face to hers, "honey . . . it's all right. Buddy, you have to calm down . . . c'mon, you can do it. Calm yourself." She stared into his eyes. "Somebody's bound to come by, do you want them to see you this way? *Do you?*"

Buddy recovered himself slowly. He dried his eyes, blew his nose. Sally gave him a glass of water and he drank it down. She brought a cold cloth and pressed it to his head.

"Is that better?"

"Yes." He took a deep breath. "I . . . I don't know what happened. I'm afraid . . . Sally, I'm afraid they'll find out. Promise you won't tell Patrick or Matt. *Promise.*"

"Of course I promise, Buddy," she said soothingly.

"I mean . . . about anything. Promise you won't tell about Smithe or Lewis either."

"I promise . . . just get hold of yourself."

"I'm okay now."

Sally brought more water. Buddy drank it thirstily. "I guess I better change my shirt," he said, for his shirt was soaked through.

"Maybe you should lie down for a while."

"Hey," he smiled weakly, "I'm not an invalid. The tension built up . . . it was probably a good thing I got it out of my system."

"Well," Sally said slowly, "you're the doctor. But a little rest never hurt anybody. You didn't sleep too well last night, you know. I think you're plain wearing yourself out."

"Me? I'm strong as a horse."

"Even a horse knows when to take a rest."

"I could use some aspirin."

Sally opened a desk drawer and removed a bottle of aspirin. She shook two tablets into her hand and gave them to Buddy. "Would you like a cup of tea? We keep the hot water going all day around here."

"No, thanks." Buddy swallowed the aspirin. "I'm going to change my shirt and get back to work. Sally . . . I appreciate everything. I hope I didn't scare you" He flushed. "I must have seemed pretty silly . . . But everything's going to be okay. I swear."

Sally saw a group of residents walking toward the desk. "Company's coming."

Buddy glanced over his shoulder. "I better get out of here. Sally . . . don't worry," he said, then took off down the corridor.

Sally leaned against the counter. Her head throbbed, her hands were cold. She felt a deepening sense of dread, for she was certain now that a tragedy was in the making. She wanted to call Patrick, but she knew, in the light of her promise, that she could not. Her head pounded until she thought she would scream.

The residents stopped at the desk, laughing and talking all at once, ready with their jokes, their complaints.

"Before you ask," Sally said, "the other nurses are either making beds or giving out medication."

"Is that O'Hara running like a thief?" one of the residents asked.

Sally forced herself to smile. "There's work to

be done."

Buddy stopped at the end of the corridor, looking back at Sally. He was ashamed of his behavior, but above all, he was pleased that she was on his side. He stood there another moment, then went through a door into the residents' locker room.

It was a long, tan room, lined with metal lockers and worn canvas chairs. To Buddy's relief, it was empty. He splashed water on his face, closing his eyes as the coolness washed over him. He combed his hair and changed his shirt, slipping into a fresh white jacket. Carefully, he transferred the contents of his pockets, then closed the locker and left the room. He pushed through the swinging doors to the women's wards.

Buddy was about to check on a patient when he saw plumes of black smoke rising from the nurses' station. He ran the few steps to the desk.

The nurse on duty was almost asleep, her eyes half-closed, her chin resting on her hand. A cigarette had fallen out of the ashtray, landing on a stack of folders and setting them on fire. The flames leapt from the desk, curling dangerously toward the nurse's long dark hair.

Buddy grabbed a jacket from the coat rack and threw it on the flames. "Nurse Parker!" He shook her with one hand, trying to smother the fire with the other. "Nurse Parker!"

She blinked her eyes and looked around. A strangled cry came from her throat as red-hot sparks flew into her face. She jumped up, stumbling and tripping in her confusion.

"Get the extinguisher," Buddy yelled, beating

frantically at the spreading fire. "The extinguisher! There, on the wall."

Several nurses ran out of the wards to the desk. One nurse ripped the extinguisher from the wall and thrust it at Buddy. He struggled with the trigger, then sprayed a thick coat of foam on the blaze.

The corridor filled with shouts and screams. Buddy took a second to assess the scene. "Keep the patients in their rooms," he ordered. "Don't panic, it's under control."

A line of fire began creeping up one wall. Buddy blasted at it until the extinguisher was empty. Someone put a new extinguisher in his hands. He sprayed the walls and the shelves and the baseboards. He stood on a chair, directing the foam at the ceiling. By the time he was finished, the whole of the nurses' station lay under a cover of white. Buddy and the nurse at his side dripped foam from head to toe.

"Good job, Doctor," she said.

Buddy looked up at the ceiling. "That's one great sprinkler system we have," he said in disgust.

"How did the fire start?"

"Parker can answer that. Where the hell is she?" Buddy looked across the desk. He saw her then, an attractive young woman with a dazed expression, swaying slightly from side to side. "Get her into the nurses' room, Angie. Now."

"Shouldn't I call Dr. Lansing?"

"Get Parker. *Now.*"

Buddy sloshed through the foam to the room behind the nurses' station. He pulled a chair over to the lamp and then waited, tapping his foot impatiently.

Angie guided June Parker into the room. "She's not feeling well, Doctor."

"And I think I know why. Sit down, Parker." He flashed a light in her eyes. "What are you on?"

"On?" She yawned, rubbing her eyes. "On?"

"Get her purse," Buddy said.

Angie began to protest, but something in Buddy's look stopped her. "Yes, Doctor." She took the purse from a locker and brought it to him. "Here it is."

"Open it. Dump it out on this table."

Angie did as she was told. "Oh, boy," she said, for along with the cosmetics and keys and money and cigarettes, there was a bottle of pills. The bottle was labeled:

RHINELANDER PAVILLION
THIRD FLOOR WARDS
PHENOBARBITAL 30 MG

"Is that what you were looking for?" Angie asked.

"Something like it. Parker was nodding off at the desk. The fire was all around her, and there she was in la la land. Another few . . . Did you know anything about this?" he demanded.

"She's a good nurse. We never had any trouble with her."

"Until now?" Matt Lansing entered the room. He was outwardly calm, but his mouth was pale. "What does June have to do with this?"

227

Buddy tossed the bottle of pills at him. "Everything, hotshot. I love the way you run a hospital. The sprinkler systems don't work, the nurses are stealing dope."

Matt looked at the bottle. He bent and looked into June's eyes.

"How many fingers am I holding up?" he asked.

"Three?"

"Angie," Matt said, "get her a bed, have her checked over. Have a blood sample sent to the lab."

"Sure, Matt." Angie nodded, helping the young woman to her feet. "I'm sorry about this, we really didn't know."

"It wasn't your fault, don't worry about it."

"Is there anything else I can do?"

"Call Dr. Murdock's office. Tell him he'll have my report this afternoon."

"He should have your resignation," Buddy jeered.

Angie eased the young woman out the door. Matt looked at Buddy. "I've asked you not to speak to me that way in front of the staff."

"Who cares?"

"I'm running out of patience with you."

Buddy laughed. "Is that supposed to scare me? Tough luck, it doesn't."

"Damn it all, Buddy, you are living proof that a good deed never goes unpunished."

"What good deed?"

Matt turned away. Buddy came after him. "*What good deed?*"

He grabbed Matt by the lapels. He was a big man, but Matt was bigger. He reached out and slammed

Buddy against the wall. He held him there, his eyes narrowed into fierce black slits.

"Don't you ever put your hands on me again," he said, then let Buddy go. He walked to a far corner of the room. "This has got to stop. You're driving me crazy."

Buddy was suddenly very calm. He sat down. "What about the pills?" He smiled.

"What about them?"

"The great Matt Lansing finally made a mistake."

"What mistake? What are you *talking* about?"

"I know you suspected me. All along you thought I was stealing the drugs."

Matt frowned. "I never thought any such thing."

"That was your plan, wasn't it? You were going to say I stole the drugs. They'd have to kick me out then, and you'd have the hospital all to yourself."

"Buddy, you're not making any sense."

"But your plan's no good anymore. Parker was stealing the drugs and everybody will know about it now. Your plan didn't work." Buddy smiled serenely.

"There was no plan."

"I checked my locker every day, just to be sure you didn't plant anything in there to use against me."

Matt's mouth dropped open. "Buddy . . . can you hear yourself? Do you know what you're saying?"

"I've been one step ahead of you all along, Lansing. You're not going to get me. You can try, but I'll always be one step ahead of you."

Matt sat down heavily, dumbfounded by Buddy's

words. He clasped his hands tightly together. "Do you really believe I'm out to get you?"

"It's no secret."

"Why? Why would I want to get you?"

"You want to be top man here, Lansing. You won't be, not while I'm around. I know what you are. Maybe I'm the only one in the whole hospital who knows what you are."

"What am I?"

"A fraud. Everybody thinks you're so great. Everybody is wrong, and I'm going to prove it."

"Have you told Patrick what you believe?"

"Patrick is on your side. But he won't be on your side much longer. I'll see to that. I'll see to that if it's the last thing I do."

A nurse knocked at the door. "Excuse me, Dr. O'Hara. Mrs. Munoz is back from x-ray. Can we give her breakfast now?"

Buddy looked up. He stared at the nurse as if he didn't recognize her. He felt a fog moving in on him. He was bewildered, and for a moment he didn't know where he was.

"Mrs. Munoz, Doctor? Can she have her breakfast now?"

Buddy blinked. He stood up. The fog disappeared as suddenly as it had come. "No, not yet," he said. "I need a fasting sugar on Mrs. Munoz. Let's get a CBC while we're at it. How is she doing?"

"She's hungry."

Buddy went to the door. "That's a good sign."

"Buddy," Matt called, "wait a minute."

"Yes?"

"You've . . . had a difficult morning. Are you up

230

to working today?"

"Yes, I'm up to it."

"You must be tired. Can you do your best for the patients while you're tired?"

"Lansing, I'm worth more on my worst day than you are on your best."

"Here," the nurse threw a towel at Buddy, "you're all wet."

"I could take that two ways."

"Please do," she said as they left.

Matt closed his eyes, trying to figure out what to do next. If he had been worried about Buddy before, he was many times more worried now. Buddy was disturbed, he thought to himself, perhaps seriously so.

Matt sighed, for he knew there were no options. He would have to go to Patrick. He would have to recommend leave for Buddy, and if the leave was refused, suspension.

18

Buddy was waiting for Sally when she returned to the nurses' station. He sprang to his feet. "It's three o'clock, where have you been?"

"I had to wait for the lab reports. I didn't want to seem too anxious."

"Well?"

"It's staph. Both Mr. Lewis and Mr. Smithe." She took two folded sheets of paper from her pocket and gave them to Buddy. "See for yourself."

He read the reports. He turned away. "I'll start treatment right away."

"Buddy, those men should be isolated. There are other patients in their ward."

"Don't worry. I'll innoculate the others. They'll never know the difference."

Sally went around the side of the desk and sat down. She took a long appraising look at Buddy, trying to decide the best way to handle the situation. "You know how I feel about you," she said softly, "I have your best interests at heart. You believe that, don't you?"

"This is no time to—"

"It's the best time," she interrupted. "Because I have to tell you . . . you can't get away with this. Mr. Lewis has developed a bad cough. And both men are obviously feverish. A doctor, a nurse, *somebody* is bound to notice, regardless of what you put on the charts."

"I'll stay with them until lights out. In the morning, you and I will take over again. Nobody will get near them."

"There are *rounds* in the morning."

"You'll take Lewis and Smithe to x-ray before rounds. You'll keep them there until rounds are over."

Two nurses came back to the desk. Buddy led Sally into the nurses' room and closed the door. "Nobody will notice. I have everything planned."

"You know there isn't anything I wouldn't do for you. But there are lives involved. What we're doing is wrong."

Buddy encircled her wrist with his big hand. "I know what I'm doing. You have to help me. You promised you'd do it my way."

"You're hurting me . . . Buddy, you're *hurting* me."

He pulled his hand away. He saw the impression of his fingers on her pale skin. "I'm sorry. Are you okay?"

Sally rubbed her wrist. "I want you to listen to me. We have to move those men to isolation."

"No! I can't do that on my own. I'd have to report it."

"Then let's report it. It's not your fault those men are sick. Nobody will blame you."

233

Buddy stared at Sally. There was an ominous look in his eyes and she took a step backward. "Don't you understand," she tried again, "there's nothing to blame you *for.*"

"We're not going to report it. You gave me your word and I'm holding you to it."

Sally saw that it was useless to argue. Buddy wasn't thinking clearly; she realized that he had not been thinking clearly for months.

"All right." Her voice was so low it was almost a whisper. "All right."

Buddy relaxed. He smiled. "I'll pump them full of staphcillin. They'll be fine in no time flat."

"Yes, all right." She went to the door. "I'm off duty now. I'm going home."

"I'll see you later. Sally . . . you're not mad at me?"

"No, I'm not mad."

"I'll take you out to dinner tonight, how about it?"

"We're both tired. I'll defrost some chops and make a salad. There's half a pecan pie left too."

"Are you turning down a night on the town?"

"We wouldn't enjoy it, tired as we are."

"I guess not . . . I'm sorry about everything, Sally. But I'll make it up to you. Trust me a little longer. Say you trust me."

Sally recognized the desperate pleas in his voice. Her heart turned over. "Of course I trust you. I love you, Buddy O'Hara, just remember that," she added, going quickly from the room.

"Are you still here?" one of the nurses asked. "Sally? . . . Hey, what's the matter with you?"

Sally didn't reply. She hastened through the corridor, oblivious to everything but what she had to do now. She stopped to catch her breath, then went into the doctors' room.

"I've been cooling my heels here for ten minutes," Dr. Zabar said gruffly. "I've got things to do, what do you want?"

Sally regarded him silently. He was tall and skinny, with curly dark hair and horn-rimmed glasses. She knew he was not an easy man to talk to.

"C'mon, Sally," he prodded, "I haven't got all day."

"There's a problem," she said.

"What problem?"

"Ward 301. Two of the patients have staph infections. The lab confirmed it."

"301? Those are O'Hara's patients."

"That's right."

"Why tell me? Tell him."

"He knows."

"So what's your problem?"

"Buddy doesn't plan to report it. He wants to handle it on his own."

Ted Zabar stood up. "On his own? Without isolation?"

"That's right."

"No wonder you look like you've been through a wringer."

"I'm afraid the staph will spread to the other patients, maybe the whole floor."

"It's a possibility."

"That's why I'm reporting it to you."

"Oh, no you don't. We never had this conversation." He started toward the door. "I don't know anything about anything."

"Dr. Zabar! *You* are Buddy's supervising resident."

He turned around, staring at Sally over the top of his glasses. "I'm also under orders from Matt. I'm to give O'Hara a free hand and plenty of encouragement. Those are my orders, presumably from the top."

"Under the circumstances, those orders are void. And you know it."

"All I know is I'm not going to be the one to make waves. I have too much to lose."

"The patients have more to lose."

"Don't get sanctimonious with me. Save it for O'Hara."

"Buddy needs help."

"If you think I'm going to put my ass on the line for him, you're crazy. I've been waiting for him to get his. I'm glad I won't be disappointed."

"My God, this is a *hospital.* Can we forget all the other stuff and think about the *patients?*"

"Did you ask your boyfriend that question?"

"I told you, he needs help. He's . . . been working too hard."

Ted Zabar laughed. "Tell the story any way you want, but don't tell it to me. Tell Matt. Or go to the top, go to Murdock or Dain."

"I . . . can't do that."

"Why not?"

"I can't, that's all. I reported it to you. You have to act on my report."

"Not a chance. I'm through here July 1. On July

2, I join my uncle's practice on Seventy-second Street. It's a thriving practice, Sally, I want a piece of that action. But my uncle insists I finish my training here first. That means I don't make any waves between now and July 1."

"I'm not asking you to make waves," Sally's eyes flashed, "I'm asking you to do your *job*."

"You're asking me to turn O'Hara in to his *stepfather*. The messenger always gets blamed for the bad news. I refuse to get involved."

"I've already made my report," she said implacably. "You're already involved."

"There was no report. We never had this conversation. I don't know anything about anything."

"Don't you care about the consequences?"

"I care about Ted Zabar, M.D."

"I've come across some rotten people, but you're the worst yet. You make me ashamed that we're in the same profession."

"Don't flatter yourself. You're in bedpans and dirty bandages. I'm a doctor, I call the tune."

"You're a disgrace."

"I'm no worse than your boyfriend. We're both playing the angles."

"Buddy's . . . not well. What's your excuse?"

"What's O'Hara doing here if he's not well? Would he be here if his stepfather weren't Chief of Staff?"

"Dr. Dain has nothing to do with it."

"Everybody takes care of their own. Including you. I don't see you running to Dr. Dain."

"In point of fact," Sally said cooly, "you, Dr.

Zabar, are my boss. You are the supervising resident on the third floor. I am *supposed* to report to you. And I did."

"There was no report. Hang yourself, if you want to, my neck is staying well away from the noose."

"I'm talking about a contagious infection. You can't avoid the problem. What about morning rounds?"

"What about them?"

"Those men are obviously ill."

"As you pointed out, this is a hospital. Should they be obviously healthy?"

"You know what I mean."

"Yeah, I know. I'll be called away just before we reach 301. And nobody else is going to be anxious to get involved with O'Hara's patients either. We all got the word from Matt: Hands off."

"That was then, this is now."

"Tell that to Matt."

Sally wasn't getting anywhere and she knew it. She knew she would have to find another way. "Who's the duty doctor tonight?"

"I am. There's no easy way out, is there?" Ted Zabar took his glasses off. He blew on the lenses and wiped them clean. "If you want to make a grand gesture, you'll have to go to Matt yourself. But you won't do that." He put his glasses back on. He smiled, and it was a nasty smile. "You don't want to take the flak any more than I do. I'm considering my career, what are you considering?"

"I'm considering Buddy."

"I'll bet you are. I'll bet it was fun cozying up to Dain's stepson, cozying up to the Dain millions."

Sally slapped his face. "You're disgusting," she said, incensed. "I don't take kindly to talk like that." She looked at him warningly. "I'm not likely to forget it."

Out in the corridor, Sally removed her starched white cap and smoothed her fine, reddish hair. She was flustered, angry with Dr. Zabar, but angry with herself too, because she had failed. She wanted to go home, where she could think in peace and without distraction, where she could put things into perspective.

"Sally, is anything wrong?"

She looked up to see Matt Lansing standing there. She was relieved to see him, for there was something reassuring in his presence. His broad shoulders, his rock-like jaw radiated strength, but she knew there was more to it than that. There was his kindness, a calm, unwavering light shining in the blackness of his eyes. Sally knew that he was, by any definition, a good man. She longed to tell him the truth, but her promise to Buddy held her back.

"Sally? What is it? Can I help?"

"Oh, I'm just plain tired. We all had extra work today. The fire made the patients jumpy as fleas."

"Buddy handled the situation very well. He kept his head."

"I heard about that."

"I have the feeling there's something you want to tell me. Is there?"

"I always got a dopey look on my face this time of day. Pay no attention."

"It's a lovely face, not dopey in the least." Matt

tipped her chin upward. "Long have I admired you from afar, you and your come-hither smile."

"I know you're kidding, but I love it."

"Who's kidding? You are lovely, too lovely to have such sad eyes. Are you sure I can't help?"

"It's . . . personal. I have to work it out for myself."

"If you change your mind, I'm a good listener."

"I appreciate it, Matt, thanks." Sally walked a short distance away, then came back. "I don't mean this to sound forward, but could I have your home phone number?"

Matt wrote the number of a slip of paper and gave it to her.

"Don't worry, I know your heart belongs to Buddy."

"Thanks." She tucked the paper in her pocket. "I expected you'd understand. I won't use it unless . . . unless it's important."

"Anytime. If I'm not there, my service will know where to reach me."

Matt opened the door to the stairwell. He thought about Sally as he walked downstairs. He was certain she'd wanted to talk about Buddy and he wished she had, for that would have made his task easier. When Matt got to the second floor he saw Patrick walking just ahead of him.

"Patrick? Can you spare a few minutes for me?"

Patrick turned. "Certainly. I wanted to talk to you anyway. It's about Buddy."

"What about him?"

"Well, I talked with Dr. Adams in psychiatric today. I told him everything I could about Buddy. I was completely honest."

"Adams knows his business. What did he say?"

"He talked a great deal about ego damage. The withering away of the ego, so to speak, under real or imagined assault. Adams feels that Buddy's childhood problems were real, his later problems largely imagined. But you don't want to hear all this."

"Yes, I do. I'm very interested."

"You are? It's pretty dry stuff."

"Please, go on."

Patrick looked questioningly at Matt. "Very well. Adams talked about patterns of ego damage. He feels that since the damage occurred so early in Buddy's life, and since it was untreated, the natural consequence is for the pattern to grow stronger and stronger . . . until it overwhelms him."

"It's not irreversible, is it?"

"No. But he recommends intensive therapy. And as soon as possible. There's the rub. How do I get him into therapy? How does anybody get him to do anything?"

They walked into Patrick's outer office. "Hello, Jean. How's my schedule so far?"

"Nothing that can't wait."

"Good. Hold my calls for a while."

They went into his office. Patrick hung up his jacket and went to his desk. He glanced at his messages, then sat down.

"Adams also talked about Buddy's paranoia. It was hardly necessary, I knew that much myself." Patrick picked up his messages. He shifted them restlessly from hand to hand. "I suppose we all knew."

241

"But can it be treated?"

"As part of the whole picture, yes."

"What does he think is the best course for Buddy now, right this minute?"

Patrick noticed the intensity in Matt's voice. There was a peculiar alertness in his manner too, as if he were fearful of missing something. "What's bothering you?" he asked.

"You know Buddy's been on my mind. I'm interested in this."

Patrick wasn't satisfied with Matt's answer, though he knew it would be useless to press him. "Psychiatrists are not the most specific people in the world, as you know."

"He must have an opinion."

"We discussed a forced leave of absence for Buddy. The pros and cons of it. There are many of both."

Matt was growing more anxious; it was an effort for him to remain in his chair. "What's the bottom line?" he asked, his eyes riveted on Patrick.

"Adams is *against* a leave. He thinks that work is the single slender thread holding Buddy together. Cut that thread . . . and he will go to pieces."

Patrick got up. He went to the window and looked out at Central Park. The park had always reminded him of happier times. It was where he'd played with Tony when Tony had been small. It was where he'd proposed to Ann. It was where he and Buddy had gone for lunch on the first giddy day of Buddy's residency.

He turned back to Matt. "It's only an opinion, of course, but it's an *informed* opinion."

Matt was slumped in his chair, thinking about what Patrick had said. *He will go to pieces.* The words had not surprised him, for he had suspected as much, yet they'd given the situation a grim finality. To separate Buddy from his work was to risk his sanity.

"Matt?" he heard Patrick's voice coming from far away. "Matt, did you hear what I said?"

"Yes . . . yes, I heard."

"Well, there you have it. I've made a decision, subject to your approval."

Matt's eyes opened wide. "Decision? *Adams* made the decision. We can't disregard his advice."

"There is the hospital to consider. There are patients to consider. Buddy is responsible for *lives*, Matt."

"But Adams said he'd be all right as long as he had his work."

"That doesn't exactly fill me with confidence. Adams gave me an opinion, not a guarantee. There's a difference."

"What is your decision?"

"Buddy can continue here, provided he begins therapy immediately."

"If he refuses?"

Patrick's mouth tightened. He shrugged. "Then he will accept a leave or go on suspension. Matt, there really is no choice. Suppose Buddy makes a mistake . . . suppose he panics at the wrong time. We cannot take the chance."

"I know Buddy. Suggest therapy to him and they'll hear the explosion in New Jersey."

"I've thought about this very carefully. There is

no other choice."

"How are you going to approach him?"

"Through Sally Tarlton, if she agrees."

"She will. She'll do what's best for Buddy. He's lucky to have her in his corner."

"He has a lot of people in his corner. If he'd only . . ." Patrick sat down. He ran a hand through his dark hair. "I'll speak to Sally in the morning. We are agreed?"

"I'm only sorry it had to come to this."

"At least we know where we are. That's progress, of a sort. What did you want to talk to me about?"

Matt didn't reply. He'd planned to remove Buddy from the duty charts right away, but that was before Dr. Adams had intervened. *He will go to pieces.* The words echoed loudly in his head.

"Matt? Don't tell me you're having memory lapses at your tender age."

"I . . . it was about the fire. I wanted to tell you how well Buddy handled things."

"That's all beside the point now, isn't it?"

"It shows he's functioning."

Patrick picked up a pencil, then threw it down. "For how long?"

19

Sally awoke with a start. She sat up, dimly aware of the bad dream she'd had, of the bad dreams that had awakened her several times during the night. She looked over at Buddy. He, too, had had a fitful night, tossing and kicking, gnashing his teeth. She saw his face clearly in the light of the moon. Even in sleep, he was tense, his jaw clenched in response to some unimaginable pain.

Sally slipped out of bed. She found her robe and slippers and left the bedroom, tiptoeing through the darkened apartment to the kitchen. She switched on the lights and put water on for tea. She looked reluctantly at the clock. It was only one a.m. and she sighed wistfully.

Sally had always liked the dark, silent hours of morning, but not now. Now she yearned for day, for the comforting clatter of people and traffic in the streets outside her windows. To be awake and alone in the middle of this night meant that she would have to think. It meant that she would have to call Matt Lansing and tell him the truth, all of it.

Her kitchen shelves were lined with jars of herbs,

herbs from home to be brewed into tea. Instead, Sally put a teabag into her cup and poured hot water over it. It sat there until the water turned a deep brown. She threw the teabag away, and as she did so, she saw her wrist, blue-black where Buddy had grabbed it earlier that day. Gingerly, she felt the side of her mouth. That, too, was bruised, for Buddy had kissed her with such violence that even he had been frightened. He'd gone to sleep then, to his nightmares, and shortly after, she had gone to hers.

Sally opened the cookie jar, extracting the slip of paper with Matt's telephone number on it. She sipped her tea and stared at the number. She stared at it until the digits seemed to dance off the paper. The phone was at her elbow. She moved the paper closer to it, her long, slim fingers trembling. She looked at the phone. It appeared to grow larger and larger, spreading itself out to cover the kitchen table.

For one moment, Sally thought about calling her family. In the sad times of her life, in the worried times, they had always soothed her. They had always known what to do. She thought about her parents; her mother, a homemaker and member of every civic committee in the town, had always been scrupulously fair and truthful; her father, a history professor at the university, had never done a dishonest thing in his life. She knew what they would want her to do now.

Sally reached for the telephone. She was about to lift the receiver when the phone rang. She jumped. Her heart hammered in her chest.

"Hello?"

"Sally Tarlton?"

Sally recognized Ted Zabar's voice. "Dr. Zabar, what's wrong?"

"This is an anonymous call," the voice said gruffly. "Tell O'Hara that Mr. Lewis is in critical condition."

"Dr. Zabar, wait," she said, but he hung up.

Sally wanted to cry, but there was no time for tears. She dialed Matt's number. "Matt . . . I'm sorry, it's Sally Tarlton . . . you have to help me."

She explained as briefly and clearly as she could. There was the briefest pause when she finished, but then Matt calmly gave her instructions and said goodbye.

Sally ran back to the bedroom. She washed her face and rinsed her mouth. She tied her hair back and then pulled a skirt and blouse from the closet.

"Buddy? . . . Buddy?" she called as she dressed. "Buddy, get up."

"What is it?" His sleepy voice drifted across the room.

"We have to get to the hospital now. Get up, honey, get dressed."

"What's going on?"

"There's . . . an emergency. The hospital called."

He stumbled out of bed. "What kind of emergency?"

Sally pretended not to hear, for Matt had instructed her not to answer Buddy's questions.

"Hurry up, honey," she said.

He staggered into the bathroom. He turned on

the tap and put his head under the cold water. He dried his face and then hurriedly threw on his clothes.

"I'll get a cab and meet you downstairs," Sally said.

Buddy stared at her, forcing her to meet his gaze. "It's 301, isn't it?" His voice was flat; it was dead. "Isn't it?"

"They didn't say."

"Tell me. I have to know."

"Yes. It's 301."

They left the apartment in silence. Sally hailed a cab and gave the driver the address. She took Buddy's hand, patting it reassuringly, though he was beyond reassurance. He stared straight ahead, still and unblinking.

"It's going to be all right," she said to him, but if he heard, he gave no reply.

"This is it." The cab braked to a halt outside of Rhinelander Pavillion.

Sally paid the driver. She got out of the cab, pulling and tugging at Buddy until he followed her. She rushed him through the deserted lobby to the stairs.

Halfway up the stairs, he stopped. "No," he said.

"Buddy, honey, come with me. Everything is going to be all right," she added gently.

"No."

"Buddy, it's just a few more steps . . . you can do it . . . come on now . . . *Buddy*."

He looked into her eyes. "No. I can't."

"You can. Take my hand . . . go on, take my hand."

He held her hand tightly, as if it were a lifeline, following behind her until they reached the corridor. The corridor lights were dimmed and the wards were dark; only 301 was brightly lit.

Buddy stopped again. It took all of Sally's strength to move him, painful step by painful step, to the doorway.

Matt left Mr. Lewis' bedside and came to the door. He looked at Buddy and he knew that it was all over for him.

"I'm sorry, Sally," he said quietly, "but I didn't want Buddy left alone."

The sound of Matt's voice seemed to stir something in Buddy. He dropped Sally's hand and walked unsteadily into the ward.

"Buddy, don't." Matt tried to restrain him.

"Mr. Lewis is my patient." He shook Matt off.

He pushed a nurse aside and stared down at Harry Lewis. Harry was perspiring heavily, wheezing with every labored breath he took. He managed a wan smile when he saw Buddy. He tried to speak, but a fit of coughing overwhelmed him. It was a deep, wracking cough and he clutched his sides in pain.

Buddy froze. All the color went out of his face. His legs were weak and he felt light-headed. He frowned, for he couldn't remember where he was. He looked around, but all of the people in the room were strangers to him. The fog closed in then, warm and soft and almost blue. He floated in the sheltering mist, as if he were weightless in a place of perfect peace.

Matt went to the foot of the bed. "Nurse, all the

patients in this ward go to isolation, *stat.* Continue staphcillin, add penicillin G, 20 million units i.v. I want chest x-rays p.a., white counts, cultures, electrolytes, input-output." He wrote the orders in his large, flowing script. "Start Mr. Lewis on ice packs, and D5W i.v. Vitals every half hour until the fever breaks." He gave the charts to the nurse. "Get some orderlies and get it moving."

"Yes, Doctor."

"I'll help," Sally said.

"I need you here for now. Nurse, where's Zabar?"

"He didn't feel well. He said he was going somewhere to throw up. Unquote." She scurried out.

"Liar," Sally muttered.

"We'll deal with Zabar when the time comes. Right now," Matt glanced at Buddy, "do you think you can get him to Patrick's office?"

Sally looked at Buddy and her eyes filled with tears. "He's in another world. He's sick, he's really sick."

Matt put a steadying hand on Sally's shoulder. "We have to hold on a little longer. We can't afford to fall apart now. I know how hard this is for you, but please hold on."

Sally wiped her eyes. "I'll try."

"I don't want to risk setting Buddy off. Do you think you can ease him to the door?"

"I'll try."

She went to Buddy and took his hand. "Come along with me, honey. We're going downstairs now."

Buddy heard a voice. It was a sweet voice, low and kind. He looked around to see where it was coming from. He saw a pretty young woman with pale skin and reddish hair. He smiled at her.

"Who are you?"

"I'm . . . Sally. Come along with me now, Buddy."

"Where?"

"We're going downstairs."

Buddy blinked. The fog swirled around him, wisps of blue as light as gossamer. "Why?" he asked.

"Because I . . . don't want to go alone. Please come with me."

He followed her meekly, taking short, uncertain steps. He was confused, trying to remember something that was just outside the range of his memory.

Matt bent over Harry Lewis. "We're going to move you to another room. You have an infection, but we know what it is and how to treat it. There's nothing to worry about."

"What's . . . Dr. O . . . Dr. O'Hara . . ." he struggled to speak between coughs, "what's . . . matter?"

"Dr. O'Hara is tired. Don't worry about him, don't worry about anything. Save your strength."

Matt walked into the corridor. Buddy looked at him. The fog thinned, then lifted. He remembered where he was and why he was there. He began to shake. Within seconds, his whole body was shaking uncontrollably.

"Matt!" Sally called.

"Get the door."

She opened the door and Matt swept Buddy through it to the stairway.

"He's dead," Buddy cried. "Is he dead?"

"Nobody's dead," Matt said calmly, steering Buddy down the stairs. "Another step . . . that's it . . . another step . . . one more . . . one more."

They reached the second floor and together Sally and Matt propelled Buddy through the corridor to Patrick's office. Matt got the door open and turned on the lights. He pushed Buddy inside and sat him down on Patrick's couch.

"Isn't there something you can give him?" Sally asked.

"Patrick asked me to hold off on drugs until he got here." He checked his watch. "That should be any minute."

"Buddy's suffering *now*."

Buddy was hunched over, shaking, his chest heaving with choked sobs. His right hand beat furiously at the couch.

"Sally, you'd better leave."

"I won't leave him like this."

"I'm thinking of your safety."

"Buddy wouldn't hurt me."

"Not intentionally."

"Not any way."

"Buddy doesn't know what he's doing. Things could get very ugly very fast."

"I don't care," Sally said evenly. "I won't leave him. He needs help."

"There's nothing you can do for him now."

"I can be here."

Matt looked at his watch again. Buddy's condition was getting worse by the minute. His face was paper white, his eyes stark with terror. His sobs were successive cries of misery, each one more terrible than the one before.

"Talk to him, Sally," Matt said. He pulled her back. "But keep your distance."

"Buddy . . . Buddy, can you hear me?"

Patrick burst through the door then, David close behind. Patrick tossed his bag down and went to Buddy. He stood over him, too saddened, too shocked to speak.

"He needs sedation," Matt said, "he can't take much more of this."

Patrick nodded. "10 milligrams diazepam. There's some in my bag."

Patrick sat next to Buddy. He took a handkerchief and wiped Buddy's face and head. "Take it easy . . . we're with you," he said, piling pillows behind his back.

Matt brought the syringe. Patrick rolled up Buddy's sleeve and swabbed his arm. "We need help here, David."

David and Patrick held Buddy's arm down while Matt injected him. "Is that going to be enough?" Matt asked.

"I don't know."

Buddy saw shadowy forms moving around him. He thought he recognized Patrick, but he wasn't sure. The forms moved away and he thought he saw Sally. She was standing a few feet away from him, framed in a soft golden light.

"Sally? Is that you?"

"I'm here, Buddy."

She walked toward him, but David stopped her. "Don't get too close."

"I just want to sit with him."

"Give the sedative a chance to work."

"You're treating him as if . . . as if . . ." she turned away, for she couldn't bear to finish the sentence.

"Matt, what's the status of 301?" David asked.

"We've isolated them. It's too soon to tell how bad it is. One of the patients is critical. Staph pneumonia, temp 104. It's going to be touch and go for the next twelve hours."

"All the patients on that floor will have to be tested. It may have gone beyond 301."

"I've given the orders for tests. David, they're short-handed in isolation. I should be there to supervise."

"Go ahead, we'll handle this. Take Sally with you."

"I want to stay," she protested.

"There's nothing you can do here, but Matt needs your help in isolation."

"I can't leave Buddy . . . I can't. What's going to happen?"

"Patrick telephoned Twin Oaks. Dr. Turnbull is on his way here."

"Twin Oaks . . . The sanitarium?"

"Buddy needs help," David said gently. "There is no better place."

"You're taking him away?"

"Sally, Twin Oaks is the finest sanitarium in the East, possibly in the whole country. We should be thankful he's going there."

"But . . . why does he have to go away? We have a . . . psychiatric department right here."

David stroked her head. "Think how Buddy would feel, being a patient here. Think of his pride. It would be very difficult for him. You must see that."

Tears stood in her eyes. "But . . . he'll be gone."

"You can visit him there. It's a beautiful place, with trees and lawns and gardens."

"Sally?" Patrick called.

They all turned around. Buddy looked dazed, but he was calmer. His sobs were quieter and he'd stopped flailing at the couch. The raw edge of fear was stilled.

"Sally, I think it's best you go with Matt now. You'll see Buddy very soon. I'll arrange a car and driver any time you wish."

"Can I talk to him now?"

"He wouldn't know you were talking to him." Patrick went to Sally. He hugged her. "You're a nurse. I needn't explain this to you. Buddy's had a breakdown. We knew it was coming. We tried . . ." Patrick's voice faltered. He cleared his throat. "We tried to head it off. We failed."

"What's going to happen to Buddy?"

"He'll get help. You want him to get help, don't you?"

"I want anything that'll make Buddy well. I'm just upset because he's going so far away."

"It's not that far. Connecticut isn't the moon. Don't make this harder than it already is, Sally. Believe me, we're doing the right thing. We're

255

doing the *only* thing."

Sally kissed Buddy lightly, then ran to the door. "Coming, Matt?"

"Coming. Patrick, I'm sorry."

"Thanks, Matt. For everything."

Buddy didn't notice them leave. He stared into space, his sobs faint but steady in their anguish.

David sat down. "Don't you think you should tell Ann what's happened?"

"No. I told her there was an emergency at the hospital and I'd be staying the night. That's all she has to know for now."

"You're not being fair to her. She has a right to know."

Patrick looked at his watch. "It's past three. Bad news always seems ten times as bad when it comes in the middle of the night. I can't do that to Ann."

"She'd want to be with Buddy now."

"Of course she would. At the moment, however, I'm considering Buddy's interests, not Ann's."

"That sounds as if you're blaming her for this."

"Well," Patrick sighed, "she had a hand in it. So did I, for that matter. But the person I really blame is Bren. It's going to be my great pleasure to destroy him. He'll be the sorriest man in New York when I'm finished with him." Something cold and unyielding came into Patrick's eyes. "I made a mistake underestimating him, but he made a *bigger* mistake underestimating me. Simpson's final report is due in a few weeks, and that's the beginning of the end for Bren O'Hara."

Patrick bent over Buddy. He smoothed the hair

back from his face. He straightened up and looked at his watch again. "Where the devil is Turnbull?"

"Here I am."

Jonas Turnbull walked into the office. He was a portly man in his fifties, with gray hair and a placid smile. He was dignified and hearty at the same time, reminding many of an English squire.

"Hello, Patrick."

"Jonas," Patrick nodded. "You remember David."

"Indeed I do. Hello, David . . . And there's Dr. O'Hara." He pulled a chair over to Buddy and sat down. "Hello, Dr. O'Hara, I'm Jonas Turnbull," he said conversationally. "We met at a party last Christmas. Do you remember?"

Buddy continued to sob quietly. His mumblings had become indistinct and Jonas leaned forward to hear him. "I can't make out what he's saying."

"He thinks he's killed a patient," Patrick explained tiredly. "That is tied in somehow with the plot against him."

"Ah, yes, the plot." Jonas flashed a light in Buddy's eyes. He checked the reflexes in his arms and legs. "Well, what we have here is hysteria. His unconscious fears have taken control of his conscious mind. What sedation has he had?"

"Ten milligrams diazepam."

Jonas opened his medical bag and filled a syringe.

"What are you doing?" Patrick asked.

"Dr. O'Hara needs stronger sedation. We must relieve the pressure on his mind. In addition, the drive to Twin Oaks is not short. It's to his advantage that he sleep . . . There we are." He injected Buddy and threw the syringe away. "He will be under heavy sedation for the first few days, in order to give his mind the rest it needs. After that, our work will began in earnest."

Patrick looked at David. "I'm going to Twin Oaks with Buddy. I'll be back as soon as I can."

"Don't worry about a thing. I'll handle everything here. If Ann calls—"

"Tell her nothing! I'll tell her in my own way . . . in my own time."

"The car is downstairs," Jonas said. He went to the door. "Carl, please come in."

A Twin Oaks attendant entered the room. He was a massive man, dressed in dark slacks, dark blazer, and a gray turtleneck sweater.

"Carl, this is Dr. O'Hara. He will need assistance going to the car."

"Yes, sir."

Carl pushed a wheelchair to the side of the couch. He lifted Buddy into the chair, carefully tucking a blanket around him. He secured the straps and wheeled him out.

"Shall we go?" Jonas asked.

David put a hand on Patrick's shoulder. "Twin Oaks is the best. Buddy will recover."

"*Will* he recover, Jonas?"

"You told me that Dr. O'Hara has been battling all his life. This will be his biggest battle."

20

The sky was beginning to lighten when the cream-colored station wagon neared the grounds of Twin Oaks. They had been driving for an hour and a half, though, to Patrick, it seemed much longer. Buddy had slept through the trip, Carl keeping a watchful eye on him, checking his pulse every fifteen minutes. Patrick had spent the time talking to Jonas, filling in the small, potentially important details of Buddy's life. Once or twice he'd slipped into the netherland between wakefulness and sleep, but those respites had been brief, providing no real rest.

"We're almost there," Jonas said. "We're on Twin Oaks property now."

"Is all of this yours?"

"We have a hundred acres, most of it in trees." He smiled.

Patrick rolled his window down, inhaling the sharp, clear air. Here, at the edge of the property, there were trees as far as the eye could see. He imagined the trees a few weeks hence, in Spring, when their branches would be full and green and new again.

"Your place isn't far from here, is it?" Jonas asked.

"About thirty five miles. It's very like this, trees and wildlife . . . and the blessed quiet."

"We find the quiet valuable. It's a relief from the jingle-jangle of the city."

The station wagon turned into a long, wide driveway. They drove for several minutes, past meticulously clipped boxwood hedges, past a grove of graceful willows, before Patrick saw Twin Oaks.

The main house of Twin Oaks was a vast white mansion that dated back to Colonial times. It was set amid broad, rolling lawns and flanked by two towering oak trees which were at least as old as the house. Flower beds, waiting for warmer weather to bring them to riotous color, bordered the flagstone path. There was no sign, no special marking to identify Twin Oaks as a sanitarium. By design, it looked like a magnificent private estate, a relic of older and gentler days.

"I'd heard it was beautiful," Patrick said, "but I didn't realize *how* beautiful."

"Thank you," Jonas said, getting out of the car. "We have another building behind the main house. And there are cottages a quarter mile away. The tennis courts are to the left, the picnic grounds to the right."

"Picnic grounds?"

"The kitchen makes up picnic hampers for our patients to enjoy with their guests. It's friendly and peaceful. Everything we do here is geared to those principles."

Carl eased Buddy out of the car. He settled him in the wheelchair, bundling him up against the brisk country morning. "Room 4, Dr. Turnbull?"

"If you please. We'll be right along. And Carl, tell Dr. DuShan we've arrived."

"Yes, sir." Carl wheeled Buddy away.

"We have a few minutes, Patrick. Would you care to see the grounds?"

"Later, perhaps. Now, I'd like to see Buddy safely bedded down. He shouldn't be left alone."

"Our ratio of staff to patients is four to one. Dr. O'Hara will be carefully watched at all times, I assure you."

"Sorry, Jonas, I didn't mean to tell you your business."

"Your anxiety is understandable, but unnecessary. Don't let the luxury fool you. We're a serious facility with a dedicated staff. Mark DuShan will be one of Dr. O'Hara's therapists. He's a brilliant young doctor who's researched extensively in delusional paranoia. I'd trust my own son to him."

"I want you in charge of Buddy's case, Jonas."

"I will remain in charge. Beyond that, I must ask you to trust my judgement."

As they walked to the front door, a brown and white collie bounded up to Jonas. His tail wagged wildly, his ears flopped up and down in excitement.

"Well, good morning, Happy," Jonas bent to pat him. "I'll have my kiss now," he said and the dog licked his cheek. "There's a good fellow. Say hello to Dr. Dain."

The collie raised his big paw and Patrick shook it. "Hi, boy." He scratched his ear. "Is he your dog?"

"Happy is everybody's dog." Jonas gave him a final pat. "Go have your breakfast now, I'll see you later." The dog threw his silky head back, then romped across the grounds. "A good-natured animal can make all the difference to our patients. He's our fourth Happy. I consider him part of the staff."

They walked into Twin Oaks. An attendant stepped forward and took their coats. Like Carl, he was neatly groomed, dressed in dark slacks, dark blazer and a turtleneck sweater.

"Good morning, Dr. Turnbull." He gave him a chart. "They need your signature on both copies."

Jonas looked at the chart and Patrick glanced around the hall. It was long and deep, with dark wood floors and soft beige walls. A brass American Eagle sat atop a handsome mahogany console. Above the console was an oil portrait of General Gates.

"That's one of our treasures," Jonas said. "It was painted a year after the Revolutionary War."

"I don't know what I was expecting . . . but I certainly wasn't expecting this. It's . . . not much like a hospital."

"Does that disturb you?"

"A little, yes."

"But it shouldn't!" Jonas smiled brightly. "Nobody ever relaxes at a hospital. We *want* our patients to relax."

"It looks as if people can come and go as

they wish."

"We don't handle violent cases here. And," Jonas pointed to the molding around the ceiling, "of course, our security is excellent."

Patrick looked up. He saw closed-circuit television cameras set discreetly into the molding.

"Nobody comes or goes without our knowing it. Does that ease your mind?"

"Considerably."

A woman came up to them then. She was about thirty, with a sunny smile and light blue eyes. She was dressed in navy wool slacks and a yellow silk blouse.

"Nurse Mayo," Jonas said, "this is Dr. Dain. Mayo will be Dr. O'Hara's day nurse."

"How do you do." Patrick took her hand. "I hope Buddy won't be too much for you."

"Don't worry about that." She smiled, and the corners of her eyes crinkled. "If there's anything I can't handle, there are two attendants stationed on each floor at all times."

"He's a nervous one, Mayo." Jonas nodded toward Patrick. "Won't take my word for anything."

"We're stricter than we look," she said. She had a nice voice, light and easy. "The patients adapt to our routine just like that."

"Is Dr. O'Hara ready for us, Mayo?" Jonas asked.

"Five minutes."

"Fine, we'll see you then."

"Good meeting you, Dr. Dain," she said and walked off to the stairs.

"I see you don't believe in uniforms either."

"Uniforms scare people. Patrick, what have you got against pleasant people in pleasant surroundings? Would you prefer something out of Charles Dickens?"

Patrick laughed. He realized that for the first time in many hours, in many days, he was beginning to relax. "You're right, Jonas. I'm being stupid. It's a beautiful place, and I'm glad Buddy's here."

"That's more like it. Come along, I'll give you the five minute tour."

Patrick saw the music room, with its gleaming baby grand piano and long, comfortable couches. He visited the sitting room, the billiards room, and at the back of the house, the airy, spacious dining room.

The dining room was done in old oakwoods and yellow and white checks. There were fresh flowers at every table. The tables, set for breakfast, sparkled with crystal, silver, and blue-banded white china. The blue linen napkins at each place were folded into the shape of butterflies. An antique patchwork quilt hung over the fireplace, opposite which was a wall of old pewter platters and mugs. The french doors at the end of the room opened onto a flagstone patio.

"Our patients spend a lot of time here," Jonas said. "We've tried to make the room as appealing as possible."

"You've succeeded."

"I think we can see Dr. O'Hara now. Follow me, Patrick."

They took the stairs to the second floor. Jonas greeted the two attendants sitting at desks at either end of the floor, then proceeded to Room 4. He knocked and they went inside.

Buddy's room was carpeted in dark brown, papered in a muted beige and green print. The polished brown wood shutters were open, letting in the amber morning light. There was a desk, a dresser, several easy chairs, a night table, and a large double bed.

Buddy was sitting up in bed, freshly shaved and washed. His blond hair, still damp, was brushed off his face. He wore wine-colored flannel pajamas. A matching wine-colored robe was draped at the foot of the bed.

"He's only half with us," Mayo said. "But his pulse is regular and his b.p. is 130/80 on the button."

"What happens now?" Patrick asked.

"Blood tests and x-rays. After that, a light breakfast. After that, sleep. We want Dr. O'Hara to sleep for the next few days because he *needs* sleep. Once he's rested, our work begins."

"Therapy?"

"First we have to get to know each other. When that is accomplished, therapy begins. His therapy will be intensive. It will be arduous." Jonas looked at Buddy. "He'll fight us, in the beginning."

"How do you know?"

"That's classic in cases of his kind."

"I'd like to talk to him before I go."

"Of course."

"Could we talk alone?"

"I can't allow that, Patrick. From now on, a member of our staff will be with Dr. O'Hara all the time. That's a hard and fast rule, no exceptions."

"You *are* stricter than you look."

Patrick sat at the side of the bed. "Buddy . . . can you hear me?"

Buddy looked up. He was befuddled. The pupils of his eyes were dilated and teary.

"Buddy . . . it's Patrick. I have to leave for a while. I'll be back very soon."

"Patrick? Where . . . are we?"

"We're in the country, in Connecticut. How do you feel?"

Buddy's eyes blinked rapidly. "Is he dead?"

"No. Your patient is alive, he's fine."

"He's dead." Buddy began to moan. "He's dead."

Jonas tapped Patrick's shoulder. "This is bad. I'm afraid you're upsetting him. You're reminding him of things best forgotten right now."

"I can't leave like this. I have to explain—"

"Explanations would be lost on him. As Mayo said, he's only half with us. Patrick, it's time to go."

Patrick stared at Buddy. A few months before he'd been brimming with youthful fire and strength; now he was pale and exhausted, literally broken.

"Patrick," Jonas said softly, "you knew you would have to leave him."

"I hadn't thought that far ahead."

"Well, you *do* have to leave him. And now is the time. Let's go downstairs . . . Come, Patrick, Dr. O'Hara is in good hands."

Patrick stood up. "I feel as if I'm deserting him."

"You're doing what must be done."

"I wonder if Buddy will see it that way."

"He will *not*, not in the beginning."

"Will he forgive me?"

"You're trying to help him, you don't need forgiveness for that."

"Buddy will hate me for leaving him here."

"Yes. Do you want love or do you want him to get well?"

"I want both."

"Then you must be patient. And you must let us do our job. Dr. O'Hara's inability to forgive is part of his illness. Until he is well, he will continue to hate . . . not only you, Patrick, but everybody. He believes everybody is his enemy. That is part of his illness. You can give him the opportunity to get well. Or you can let him sink deeper and deeper into his illness until his mind is destroyed forever."

"I brought him here. That speaks for itself."

Jonas smiled. "I will not tolerate meddling."

"No meddling, you have my word."

"We often have more trouble with our patients' relatives than with our patients."

"Jonas, you have my word."

"I think you can trust him." Mayo laughed.

Jonas nodded. "It's a good idea to have everything clear from the start. You do understand?"

"I do."

"Excellent! We can go downstairs now. There are a few forms for you to sign."

"There always are." Patrick looked at Buddy, then at Mayo. "Take good care of him."

"We all will, Dr. Dain."

Patrick and Jonas left the room and went to the

stairs. "If you'd like to rest for a while, we can make you quite comfortable," Jonas offered.

"Thanks, but I have to get back to the city. I have to tell Buddy's mother what's happened. It's going to be a blow."

"She must have suspected something was wrong."

"We both *knew* something was wrong. We didn't know the degree. Perhaps, in my case, I didn't want to know."

"That's not unusual. Facing a situation like this is never pleasant. Come," Jonas said, leading Patrick into his office, "sit down and relax."

Jonas Turnbull's office was an eclectic mixture of Early American and contemporary pieces. It was large without being forbidding, filled with plants and books and family photographs.

Patrick sat down. He looked around approvingly. "I wouldn't mind being a patient here."

"You would probably mind very much. Doctors are terrible patients."

"Do you get many doctors?"

"We get people from all professions."

"That doesn't answer my question."

"Within the limits of discretion, I will tell you what you already know—medicine is a high stress profession. Does it disturb you that doctors occasionally break down?"

"I suppose so."

"Why? Doctors are mortal men and women. They have no special protection, no special immunity."

"They have special responsibilities."

"That merely compounds the stress. Think about it, Patrick. Nobody blinks an eye if a doctor becomes physically ill . . . but if the illness is of the mind, well, that's a different story, isn't it? If the illness is of the mind, the doctor is disgraced."

"What are you getting at?"

"Dr. O'Hara's condition has been deteriorating for some time. Yet it went untreated."

Patrick lit a cigarette. He looked away.

"No, don't blame yourself. Blame the thinking of our profession. Doctors are supposed to be stable, ergo they *are* stable." Jonas smiled slightly. "Except that it doesn't work that way."

"I swear I didn't know Buddy's condition was this serious."

"It's possible you were too close to it. But is it possible that *none* of the doctors at Rhinelander Pavillion knew?"

"Obviously it's possible."

"Don't be disingenuous, Patrick. They saw, they knew, but they refused to *believe.*" Jonas sat back, puffing on his pipe. "I'm telling you this for a reason."

"What reason?"

"I want you to be aware of the complications. Dr. O'Hara's profession is a complication. He's a doctor, and so he'll refuse to believe he's lost control. We'll have more than the usual defenses to break through. That's why I'm prohibiting all visitors for two weeks."

Patrick looked up. "Two weeks? But surely his mother can see him?"

"No."

"Jonas, she'll be beside herself."

"You'll have to make her understand. I'll speak to her, if you'd like. But the decision is firm. We can't have outside distractions."

"She's his *mother*."

"Our patients come first. We do what's best for them. And we know exactly what we're doing."

"Can she telephone him?"

"No. I'd hoped I wouldn't have to say this . . . but I would have prohibited Mrs. Dain in any case."

"Jonas, *why?*"

"You gave me the background yourself. Dr. O'Hara has great hostility toward his mother now. He shouldn't see her until he's ready to deal with his anger. Also, by then, your family situation might be . . . calmer."

"This isn't going to help my family situation."

"Don't be too sure. Shock is often a spur." Jonas smiled. "Cheer up, Patrick. I met Mrs. Dain only briefly, but she seemed an extremely sensible woman. She may be trapped in the past, but we all are to one degree or another. Trust her."

"I've *been* trusting her. That hasn't gotten us very far."

"As I said, shock is often a spur. You must look on the bright side."

"You have a twisted sense of humor, Jonas."

"Not at all. There's a bright side. There's *always* a bright side. Buddy is getting help, that's one bright side. There are others. Look for them! Let's see some effort here!"

Patrick laughed. "Nobody's depressed around you for long."

"I'm not from the gloom and doom school. Don't believe in it." He placed a set of forms in front of Patrick. "Fill in the top section, sign the bottom. Take your time," he said, going to the windows. He opened the drapes and the sun poured in. "If it were a shade warmer we could breakfast outside."

"No breakfast for me. I have to get back."

"Well, we'll make up something for you to take in the car."

Patrick completed the forms. He read them over and gave them to Jonas. "Where is Dr. DuShan? I'd like to meet him."

"He left a note on my desk. He apologizes, but he's been detained in the other building. You'll meet him next time around."

"How will I know what's happening?"

"We'll phone you daily with a report. Of course, you can call us at any time." Jonas put the forms in a folder and marked it. "Some coffee before you go?"

"No, thanks. But I would like to use your phone. I want to catch Ann before she leaves."

"Certainly."

Patrick dialed his number. "Good morning, Hollis, is Mrs. Dain there? . . . where? . . . when? . . . no . . . no, I understand . . . no . . . I'll be home in a couple of hours . . . yes . . . yes, good-bye."

"Patrick, what is it?" Jonas asked. "You look a little grim around the mouth."

"Remember my wife? The extremely sensible woman?"

"Yes."

"Well, the extremely sensible woman has gone to meet her ex-husband. They're going apartment hunting."

"Now, Patrick—"

"No, no lectures! All I want is a car and driver. I'm going home to plan the destruction of Bren O'Hara. And I'm in a hurry!"

21

Ann and Bren got out of a taxi on East Sixty-eighth Street. It was a quiet, prosperous street lined with brownstones and shaded by London plane trees. Colorful flower boxes bordered many of the tall windows.

"That's the building. Isn't it lovely?" Ann asked, smiling. "I was so lucky to hear about it."

"I don't know about this, Annie. It looks too fancy for the likes of me. The boarding house is good enough."

"We've been all through this. If you have an apartment you can take Daisy on weekends. You'll have a home, a real home."

"I heard apartments in New York were very expensive."

"You heard right. Bren, this is something I want to do for you and Daisy."

"I don't know."

"At least look at the apartment. You said you would."

"I'll look, but I'm making no promises."

"We have to hurry," Ann rushed him to the

door, her sable-trimmed green wool cape fluttering behind her. "We have to see the owner before she goes to work."

They passed through the door into a small, immaculate vestibule. Ann found the name she wanted and rang the bell. The answering ring unlocked the door to the hall. The hall and stairway were carpeted in a deep velvety gray. There was a square chrome-framed mirror above an ebony console table.

"Here it is," Ann said, "the garden apartment."

Ann smoothed her hair and straightened Bren's tie, then knocked at 1G.

"Who is it?"

"Mrs. Dain. I called about subletting your apartment."

The door opened a crack. A thin, dark-haired woman peered at them over a chain lock. "Mrs. Dain?"

"Yes."

"Come in." She unlocked the door. "I'm Mrs. Royce. I don't have much time so I'll get to the point. It's a one year sublet, fully furnished. You have to take it as it is, and you'll be responsible for any damages. You also have to use our cleaning woman twice a week."

"I understand," Ann said.

"You said there was a child?"

"A girl, six years old. She'll be here on weekends."

"We have a seven-year-old daughter. Her bedroom should suit your girl. The rest of the apartment is child-proof, nothing to worry about there.

We learned about washable paint when our daughter learned about finger-painting."

"I know what you mean," Ann smiled.

"Well, look around. But don't take too long."

The living room was painted white, except for one wall of ruddy exposed brick. The facing couches were slipcovered in white cotton, strewn with plump pillows in vivid reds and blues and greens. A fringed red and gold Mexican shawl was folded over the arm of one couch. There were twin glass and chrome coffee tables and, nearby, a tub of bright paper flowers.

Beyond the living room was a dining area, and beyond that, an open kitchen of stainless steel and butcher board. There were two bedrooms at the back of the apartment, the larger of the bedrooms opening onto the garden.

"Can we go outside?" Ann asked.

"Okay, but don't take too long."

"Annie," Bren whispered, "I don't like the bum's rush she's giving us here."

"Never mind that. This apartment is a steal, go along with me." Ann opened the door to the garden. "Look, Daisy can play out here."

There were two tables and two chaises, each covered in heavy plastic wrapping to protect against winter. There was a built-in barbeque and a fluted bird bath. At the rear was a fenced plot of land large enough for a vegetable garden.

"Bren, it's perfect."

"I have to admit it's a pretty place. You know what I'm thinking, Annie Laurie? I'm thinking this is the kind of place we dreamed about when we were first married."

Ann turned. She looked through the glass doors of the garden into the apartment. It was, she thought, exactly the kind of place they'd dreamed about. It didn't seem so long ago. She remembered how they'd looked, how they'd talked, and a torrent of memories rushed over her.

She'd graduated from high school on a Friday and on Saturday they'd been married. Their honeymoon had been two days at Coney Island, in a white frame rooming house a block away from the ocean. They'd spent their afternoons at the beach, lying close together on the sand, planning their future. Bren had sketched their dream apartment in the sand and it had been very much like this one, down to the garden with its sun-whitened bird bath.

"I bought you a shawl just like the one on the couch there. Remember?"

"Yes," Ann said, and suddenly she felt sixteen years old again, her life stretching before her.

She thought about the shawl. Bren had bought it at a stand near the beach. It was cheap silk and crudely painted, but she'd thought it was wonderful. For a long time it hung over their bed at home.

"Mrs. Dain? . . . Mrs. Dain?"

Ann looked up. Mrs. Royce stood impatiently in the doorway, swinging a ring of keys. "I really have to get to my office," she said.

"I'm . . . sorry. I was daydreaming."

"Have you decided? There's another couple coming at six tonight, so you'd better make up your mind. I have to settle this today, my husband and I are leaving for California at the end of the week."

"Yes, we've decided. It's perfect."

They followed Mrs. Royce into the living room. "I hate to hurry people this way, but I warned you I didn't have much time. I asked my husband to stay and show the apartment, but *he* couldn't be late for work. It's all right if *I'm* late, but *he* can't be late. Men!"

She took a sheaf of papers from a manila envelope and gave them to Ann. "You can take the lease for your lawyer to look at, but you'll have to leave one month's deposit now."

"How much is it?" Bren asked.

"Why, it's a thousand a month, plus utilities, plus the cleaning woman. I explained all this to your wife on the phone."

"A thous—"

"Bren," Ann said quickly, "that part is all settled."

"But a thous—"

"*Please*, Bren. Leave this to me."

Mrs. Royce looked curiously at them. They were a strange couple, she thought, for the woman was well and expensively dressed, while the man's clothing was cheap and slightly ill-fitting. She wondered why the woman hadn't consulted her husband about the rental arrangements.

"You are Mr. Dain?" she asked.

"He's Mr. O'Hara," Ann said, "a friend of the family."

"Oh, I see."

Ann reddened. "No, you don't see. Mr. O'Hara is a *family* friend. My husband and I are helping him get settled in the city."

"I didn't mean to imply—"

"I'll sign the lease now, if you don't mind."

"I don't mind. But be sure, because once it's signed, it's signed. I won't have time to make other arrangements."

"I'm sure."

"Okay. There's an inventory sheet attached to the lease. Everything in the apartment is listed, along with the replacement value. If you break it, you own it."

"I understand."

Ann opened her handbag. She removed her checkbook and hastily wrote out a check. "This is the first month's rent, plus the security arrangement we discussed. I'll send future rent checks to you in California. And here," she took some papers from her handbag, "are the references you requested."

"Thank you." Mrs. Royce looked at the check. "If the bank says everything is okay, you can move in over the weekend. The cupboards are full, help yourself."

Bren smiled crookedly. "At these prices, we will. What are the neighbors like?"

"It's a quiet building. Everybody minds their own business. It's a nice neighborhood, also quiet. Your . . . Mrs. Dain has a list of shops in the area. Most of them deliver. Most of them offer charge accounts." She looked at her watch. "I really have to fly . . . Call if you have any questions. We'll be here until Saturday noon." She put her coat on and took her briefcase and purse from the table. "Here are the keys. They're all marked."

"I'd like to stay a while and check the kitchen supplies," Ann said. "Is that all right?"

"Just be out by five-thirty." Mrs. Royce went to the door. "I hope you'll be happy here."

"I will be," Bren said. "And good luck to you in California."

"Goodbye. Goodbye, Mrs. Dain."

The door slammed and Bren grinned at Ann. "She thought we were renting the place for hanky-panky."

"I know what she thought."

Ann averted her eyes, for she'd been shocked and angered by Mrs. Royce's rude conclusion. She wondered if other people were drawing similar conclusions. She thought about Patrick and her face colored again.

"People always said we looked good together, Annie Laurie. Like we belonged."

"That was a long time ago."

"Not so long. Anyway, what's time? A measure, that's all. Is it so important?"

Ann didn't answer him. She searched around in her handbag until she found a notepad and pen.

"Annie, did you hear me?"

"Let's see what you'll need for the kitchen. Can you cook?"

"I get by. When Irene was sick, toward the end, I did all of the cooking for me and Daisy. Hamburgers, stews. We didn't starve."

Ann walked into the kitchen. She opened the butcher board cabinets and began making notes.

"Of course," Bren said, "it wasn't the fancy stuff you have at your house. No caviar omelets for breakfast."

"We don't have caviar omelets for breakfast or any other time. We eat normal food."

"When's the last time you had a hamburger?"

Bren was standing very close to her and she stepped away. "Yesterday at lunch. With ketchup, not caviar."

Bren took a can from the cabinet and looked at the label. "Hearts of palm. Everybody's living the good life. Including me, now. This apartment comes dear, Annie."

"I have a generous allowance. I hardly spend any of it. It sits in the bank."

"Must be a lot of money by now."

"I guess."

"It must be wonderful to have money. Look what it buys. This apartment, for example."

Ann took the can from his hand and returned it to the cabinet.

"It's a nice apartment," she said.

"Are you going to tell Patrick about it?"

"Certainly. Why wouldn't I?"

"I don't know. It costs so much. And it's a romantic kind of place. With the garden by the bedroom . . . and the bedroom painted that soft kind of blue. Did you notice the bedroom, Annie Laurie?"

Bren was only inches away from her. His hair had always smelled of nutmeg and now the musky scent wafted around her. Bren was so close she felt his breath on her skin.

She remembered a day at the beach those many years ago. Their young flesh had pressed together and there'd been the scent of nutmeg. They'd wanted each other, wanted each other fiercely. They'd found a place underneath the boardwalk and there they'd made love again and again.

A thrill ran the length of Ann's body as she remembered. Bren moved closer and closer still. At the last second, Ann pulled away. She was sickened by her thoughts, by her feelings. Were these the feelings Patrick wanted her to remember, she wondered wretchedly.

"I . . . think the kitchen has everything you need," she said in a low voice.

Bren turned, hiding his smile. It was so easy, he thought. He'd almost had her; it would not be long before he did have her, and then her world would break apart, never to be whole again. It was hard for him to keep from laughing, for the revenge he sought was so near.

Ann drew her cape about her. "We can go now. Would you mind if I didn't drop you off at the boarding house? I want to get home. Patrick will be waiting."

"Not at all. I know you'll be having a lot to say to Patrick."

Patrick was sitting on the chaise when Ann walked into the bedroom. He was wearing blue jeans and a blue work shirt, the sleeves rolled up to the elbow. His hair was tousled, as if he'd just awakened from a nap.

"I'm sorry I wasn't here when you got home," Ann said.

"Hollis explained."

281

Ann took off her cape. She sat down and unzipped her high brown boots. "I rented an apartment for Bren. He can take Daisy on weekends, and maybe we can get Buddy straightened out. It's a nice apartment, Daisy will like it there."

"Good."

"It's expensive. A thousand a month."

"It's your money."

"The apartment is furnished. It has everything, we won't have to buy anything. And it's only a one year sublet, not a lifetime contract."

Patrick stared at Ann. Her color was too high, her speech too rapid. "Why are you so nervous?"

"I'm not nervous."

"You're talking very fast."

"I want to get it over with. I know Bren isn't your favorite subject."

"Bren hasn't interested me in some time. Except as part of a theory of justice." Patrick leaned back. "There isn't much justice in the world. But there's some. I intend to see that Bren gets what he deserves."

Ann didn't know what Patrick was talking about and she didn't want to know. There was something severe in his manner, something she had never seen before.

"You don't sound like yourself, Patrick."

"Come sit next to me."

She did as he asked. He put his arm around her. "I have to talk to you."

Ann's eyes narrowed. "Is it bad?"

"Let me start from the beginning."

"It's about Buddy."

"Yes."

Patrick began with the incidents at Rhinelander Pavillion the night before. He went on to talk about Twin Oaks and most, but not all, of Jonas Turnbull's conversation. He spoke in level, measured tones, now and again squeezing her shoulder.

Ann listened to the recitation in unbroken silence. Once or twice her hands went to her throat, but otherwise she was still. Her arms hung at her sides like dead weights. She felt removed, separated from her body.

Patrick brought her a pill and she took it without question. He settled her on the chaise and covered her with the afghan. "That's all I can tell you for now, Ann. Ann?"

She looked at him. Her face was blank, as if she couldn't see or hear or speak. Patrick leaned over her. He pinched her hard. She began to cry.

Ann covered her face with her hands. She felt the tears come and she didn't try to stop them. They were tears of grief and guilt and pain, a pain so deep she thought her heart would split in two. Her body shook with great choking sobs. She cried for a long time.

Patrick let her cry it out, for he knew there was nothing he could do, nothing he could say. Each of her cries cut through him like a knife, but he remained where he was, stroking her head.

Ann's sobs slowed. The hot, harsh tears became soft, almost caressing. She took the handkerchief Patrick offered and dried her eyes and face.

"Do you feel better?" he asked.

"I guess I had to get it out of my system," she

sniffled. "I think I always knew . . . this would happen. When he was a child . . ." A solitary tear slipped down her cheek and she brushed it away. "When can I see him? Can I go today?"

"You can't see him yet. Nobody can see him for a couple of weeks. That's the way Jonas wants it. We have to trust him."

"I'm not going to leave Buddy there alone. I don't care *what* Jonas says."

Ann's eyes sparkled with her old fiery spirit and Patrick was relieved to see it. She'd been, he thought, too passive for too long.

"Ann, Jonas is in charge and we're fortunate to have him. We must do what he wants. We must do what's best for Buddy, no matter how hard it may be on us."

"He'll expect to see me."

"He *will* see you, when Jonas approves."

"He'll be scared."

"I'm not saying this is going to be easy for Buddy. He's in for a fight, the fight of his life. But when it's over he'll be well."

Ann looked into Patrick's eyes. "Can you promise that?"

"All of the resources of Twin Oaks are behind him. They are considerable."

"That's an evasion."

"No, that's the truth. I had to get treatment for Buddy. I got the best treatment I could."

"But to leave him there. Why didn't you call me?"

"I did call you. You were out."

Patrick's words hit her with the force of a

physical blow. Ann was horrified, for she realized that while her son was being confined to Twin Oaks, she had been with Bren, remembering the stirrings of years ago.

Patrick saw the expression on her face. "I'm sorry," he said quickly. "I didn't mean to—"

"No, you're right. I should have been here."

"Ann, I made the decision to take Buddy to Twin Oaks. I made the decision without consulting you. By the time I called you this morning, the deed was done. Your being here would have made *no* difference. Stop punishing yourself!"

"And *why* didn't you consult me? Because I've been no help to anyone lately. Count on me for the wrong move at the wrong time."

"You're being silly."

"I'm taking a look at myself. I've been a terrible wife these past months. I've been a worse mother."

"Why do you insist on upsetting yourself like this? What good does it do?"

"It prepares me. Because when I *do* see Buddy, that's what he's going to tell me. That's what Jonas will tell me, if you don't get to him first. I might as well be prepared."

"Buddy resents us *all* just now."

"But especially good old Ma. Because good old Ma can't seem to get her priorities straight. Admit it, Patrick. Buddy needed my attention and I wasn't there."

"That's history now. The only thing that matters now is the future."

"The future! The future is all knotted up with the past."

"Unknot it."

"I knew you'd say that. Or something like it."

"What do you *want* me to say, Ann? Do you want me to rake you over the coals? Do you want me to scream and holler and carry on?"

"You have that right. While I've been playing Lady Bountiful I've let you down, I've let Buddy down. Maybe I need some sense screamed into me."

Patrick stood up. He went to the desk and lit a cigarette. "I'm getting tired of this. Every talk we have turns into an argument. No matter what side I take, you take the other side. I'm trying to make this easy for you, can't you see that?"

"I don't want you to make this easy for me."

"I'll see what I can do about sackcloth and ashes. Will that make you happy?"

"Happier than your protecting me all the time."

"I love you, Ann. Is it so wrong to want to protect the person you love?"

"It is if the person is me."

"For God's sake, *why?*"

Ann closed her eyes against the tears. "Do you know what I was doing while you were taking care of Buddy? *Do you?*"

Something cold and sharp gripped Patrick's heart. "What were you doing?"

"I was standing in a garden on Sixty-eighth Street. I was remembering my honeymoon with *Bren*. All of it. *All of it.*"

Patrick turned and left the room. The silence was deafening.

22

The decontamination crew marched through the third floor of Rhinelander Pavillion, a small army clad in green coveralls, caps, masks, gloves, and boots. They carried tanks of disinfectant and specially designed hoses and vacuums. The patients had been moved out of the south wing and the crew, working in teams of threes, swept into the wards, sealing them off until their work was completed.

Matt Lansing charted the time of their arrival, then walked in the opposite direction to the doctors' room. Most of the staff were assembled there, awaiting the start of the meeting that had been called.

Matt strode into the room. "Quite please, ladies and gentlemen. I want your undivided attention." He paused until everybody stopped talking. "I've heard some snickering about Dr. O'Hara. I don't want to hear it again. As many of you know, Dr. O'Hara has been working very hard. That hard work has resulted in nervous exhaustion. He's in a hospital, receiving treatment. Some of you find that amusing." Matt's stern black eyes scanned their faces. "I don't."

A coffee cup fell to the floor with a noisy crash. A doctor and two nurses bent to pick up the pieces.

"Leave it!" Matt ordered. "I'm not finished . . . However you might feel about Dr. O'Hara personally, he is a member of our staff and a gifted physician. He's ill, and that is *not* a joke. We're medical professionals. I expect professional behavior from every one of you. Are there any questions?"

Matt looked from face to face. The young doctors and nurses were subdued and clearly embarrassed. Many of them avoided his glance.

"My final comment on the subject is this—what happened to Dr. O'Hara could happen to any one of us. Think about that. Now, as to our emergency. We have five confirmed cases of staph pneumonia. One of those patients, Mr. Lewis, remains critical. All the other ward patients have been tested. Their tests are negative. I believe we've stemmed the contagion, but I want you all to keep a sharp lookout nevertheless. Those of you who have not yet had your shots are to have them *immediately*. Are there any questions?"

There were no questions and Matt nodded. "Nurse Tarlton and Dr. Zabar will stay. The rest of you are dismissed."

The staff filed out quietly, not looking at Matt, not even looking at each other. Sally Tarlton and Ted Zabar joined Matt near the door.

"What's this about, Matt?" Dr. Zabar asked.

"The three of us are wanted in Dr. Dain's office. It's about the way the Lewis and Smithe cases were handled."

"Why me? I'm not involved in that."

"Oh, you're involved, Zabar. You're involved up to your ears." Matt held the door open. "Let's get going."

"Matt," Sally tugged at his arm as they walked to the stairs, "have you heard any more about Buddy?"

"It's only been two days. You can't expect to hear anything substantial for a while."

They took the stairs to the second floor. Ted Zabar drew away when they reached Patrick's office. "I really don't see what this has to do with me."

"It's no use pretending. Dr. Dain knows everything."

"There's nothing to know."

"Get going. *Now*," Matt nudged him into Patrick's office.

Patrick was seated at his desk. David sat in a chair close by. Both men were absorbed in a stack of charts and lab reports.

"Good morning," Matt said.

Patrick looked up. "Well, if it isn't Tweedledee, Tweedledum, and Tweedledumest."

Ted Zabar stepped forward. "Dr. Dain, Dr. Murdock, I'd like to say at the outset—"

"Be quiet," David said. "We're not interested in what you'd like to say."

"But—" he began, then stopped, for David glared at him in warning.

"Sally, we'll begin with you," Patrick said. "We understand that you reported the staph outbreak to

Dr. Zabar. Is that correct?"

"Yes, sir."

"That's a lie!" Ted said.

"And then what, Sally?" Patrick asked.

"Dr. Zabar refused to do anything about it. He said that his residency was over on July 1 and he didn't want to make waves."

"Another lie!" Ted put in loudly.

"You were convinced he would not act on your report?"

"Yes, sir."

"Why didn't you report the matter to Dr. Lansing?"

"I had . . . personal reasons. I was wrong, I expect to be penalized."

Patrick glanced briefly at David. He sighed. "You're suspended without pay. I'll notify the nurses' committee and we'll decide on the length of the suspension."

Patrick sat back, pressing his fingertips together. "Now, Dr. Zabar, your turn."

"She's lying," Ted said angrily. "She never told me anything."

"You never met with her in the doctors' room?"

"No!"

"You never told her about your uncle's practice on Seventy-second Street?"

"I . . . no, I did not."

David swiveled around in his chair. "Do you supervise morning rounds?"

"Of course I do."

"Every morning?"

"Yes."

"Mr. Lewis and Mr. Smithe were running temperatures on the morning of the incident. They had chills and chest congestion. How did you miss their symptoms?"

"They were Dr. O'Hara's patients. I was under orders to give him a free hand with his patients."

"Did you notice their symptoms? Yes or no?"

Ted hesitated, for he could not now admit to seeing their symptoms or to ignoring them.

"Answer my question," David demanded.

"They looked a little feverish. But Dr. O'Hara assured me they were all right."

David consulted his notes. "Didn't Dr. Fong and Dr. Brooks come to you after rounds? Didn't they ask you to double check those two patients?"

"I . . . I don't remember that."

"*I* have their statements here. Would you care to see them?"

"Look, don't try to hang this on me. It's Dr. O'Hara's mess, not mine."

"It was reported to you. Why didn't you act on the report?"

"I didn't . . ." Ted shook his head. "It was *not* reported to me."

David looked at his notes again. "You were on the wards for twenty-four hours and you didn't notice anything wrong in 301. Is that your statement?"

"Late that night I realized Mr. Lewis was very ill. I called Sally and told her to get O'Hara."

David looked at Sally. "Did he call you?"

"It was an anonymous call. It could have been anybody."

"She's *lying* again." Ted took his glasses off and wiped furiously at the lenses. "Look, this whole thing is O'Hara's fault."

"Dr. O'Hara wasn't in his right mind. Were you in your right mind?"

"Yes."

"Then we must conclude that in twenty-four hours of duty you failed to recognize the symptoms of two seriously ill patients in your charge."

"You're twisting things around, but you're not going to get away with it. You can't take any action against me."

"We could," Patrick spoke quietly, "but we won't. However, what your uncle chooses to do about it is a different matter."

"My uncle?"

"Neil Zabar is an old friend of mine. He is a conscientious doctor and an honorable man. He is entitled to know the circumstances of this incident. And so he shall."

Ted sat down. He put his glasses on and stared vacantly at the floor. "You know how my uncle will react. Why are you doing this to me?"

"You are a doctor who has betrayed his oath. I have no doubt you'll do it again, the next time you find yourself in a tight spot. You're a dangerous man, Ted."

"Not dangerous, smart."

"How smart are you now?"

"All right! I've had enough of this. I'll tell you the truth."

"We know the truth. We gave you a chance to admit the truth. You lied. You'll have to accept the consequences."

"My uncle won't let me into his practice."

"I trust Neil Zabar to make the correct decision. You may go now."

Ted went to the door. "Tell O'Hara I hope he's in a rubber room for a *long, long* time. Tell him that for me," he said through a cruel, narrow smile.

David and Matt and Sally looked at Ted in shock. Tears sprang to Sally's eyes.

"I will relay your message," Patrick replied evenly, though his hands clenched into fists.

Matt moved closer to Sally. "Pay no attention to him. He's an idiot. And he's come to the end of the road."

"I wish that were true," Patrick said. "But I know his type. He'll wind up running a Medicaid mill and getting very rich."

"Can . . . can I go now?" Sally asked.

"Get some rest. I'll call you in a day or two."

"Does Buddy need anything? Is there anything I can send him?"

"We've sent some clothing and things along. Twin Oaks provides everything else he needs. Wait a week or so and send flowers."

Matt opened the door for her. "Are you okay?"

"Sure. Thanks, Matt. Thank you, Dr. Dain, Dr. Murdock."

Matt closed the door. "That wraps it up. The rest of the third floor staff is in the clear. Zabar told Fong that he'd take care of 301. Fong had no reason to disbelieve him. He relayed the information to the others and went about his business. It's all in my report. So, if there's nothing else . . ."

293

"There is," David said. "Now we come to Tweedledumest. You." He waved a piece of paper in the air. "What is this supposed to be?"

"That *is* my resignation."

"I won't accept it. Don't look at Patrick, he won't accept it either."

"I don't understand."

"Your resignation is rejected. The subject is closed."

"David, let's look at the record since I've been in this job. A patient went berserk and attacked a nurse, there was a fire, and there was a problem in 301."

"You're not responsible for a patient going berserk. And a nurse started the fire."

"Which leaves the problem in 301."

"Patrick and I have discussed that. You're not responsible for what happened. We can hardly expect you to check every patient every day. That's why we have supervising residents on each floor."

"It's more than that. I'm dissatisfied with my judgment. My judgment on Buddy was bad. It may prove to be fatal. In that respect, I'm responsible."

"Matt," Patrick said, "let me remind you that Dr. Adams in psychiatric approved your course of action. If *he* didn't know better, we weren't likely to. I agree that the line is thin, but this is a shared responsibility. All of us are responsible and none of us are responsible. I believe we did the best we could. Unlike Dr. Zabar, we acted in good faith."

"That doesn't make it all right."

"Nothing will ever make it all right. Nothing like

294

this has ever happened in my career before, or David's, or yours. We made a mistake that jeopardized our patients. And we will have to live with that knowledge always. I can think of no worse punishment."

"Neither can I."

"Then what are we talking about?"

"There's a *principle* involved here."

"Matt, we've considered your resignation. The answer is no. We all have a lot of work to do, I suggest we get to it. Let's start putting the pieces back together."

Matt was surprised by their decision but he was relieved too, for while his resignation had been honestly offered, he hadn't looked forward to leaving Rhinelander Pavillion. He knew that what had been ambition a few months before had become something far more important. In his new responsibilities he'd found a new dedication to his work. He'd found the commitment he'd been looking for.

"Are you going to stand there all morning?" Patrick asked.

"No, I'm going. I . . . want to thank you both."

"Keep us informed about the third floor."

Matt left the office. David looked across the desk at Patrick.

"I'm glad that's over. He was serious about resigning."

"I'd have been disappointed if he wasn't. He has strong principles. All he needs now is a little flexibility."

David laughed. "Like you?"

"I get more flexible by the minute. Events

295

change people. Things I wouldn't have done six months ago I'll do now, and gladly."

"You're talking about Bren."

"No, I'm talking about the *destruction* of Bren."

John Simpson opened his attache case and removed a thick black binder. He put the binder on Patrick's desk and placed a manila folder next to it.

"As you can see, the full report is quite lengthy. I have summarized the important points in a shorter report."

Patrick paced back and forth between the window and the desk. He was tense, more tense than he'd expected to be. "Is that all of it?"

"Had you allowed us additional time, we could have gone deeper. However, I think you will be pleased."

"Pleased?"

"Your suspicions were not unreasonable."

Patrick felt his heart thump. He stared at the reports. He had anticipated this moment for a long time, but now that the moment had come he wanted to be certain of his choice. He could order the reports destroyed or he could continue on the course he'd begun.

"What are the important points?" he asked finally.

John Simpson, expressionless, opened the folder. "Mrs. Irene O'Hara died at home, of pneumonia, in August of last year. The death certificate was signed by the family physician. There was no autopsy."

"Why not?"

"Irene's death had been expected. She had been

ill for two weeks. She had refused hospital treatment, but was attended by the family doctor. Her illness progressed along normal lines. Then her condition deteriorated suddenly. She went into coma. An ambulance was called, but she was dead by the time they got there. The doctor's records indicate respiratory failure due to pneumonia."

"I see nothing suspicious in that."

"Neither did we, at first. But something caught our eye. In tracing O'Hara's movements during his wife's illness, we discovered two visits to Boston doctors. The doctors were previously unknown to him and he to them."

"Go on."

"He complained of insomnia. He received prescriptions for sleeping pills."

"Are you sure?"

"Absolutely sure." John Simpson opened the binder and flipped through several pages. "Here we have copies of two prescriptions for a total of twenty sleeping pills."

Patrick looked over John Simpson's shoulder. "That says *Dennis* O'Hara."

"He gave an incorrect name and address, but it's *your* O'Hara. He's been identified. There is no question, no question at all."

"I see."

"One: why did he give an incorrect name and address? Two: if he needed sleeping pills for himself, why didn't he ask the family doctor he saw almost daily? Three: why did he have the prescriptions filled at two different pharmacies miles away from Southie?"

Patrick went to his desk. He sat down. "That's damning, but it's not conclusive."

"There is more. The O'Haras had a bad marriage. Their fights were well known. But when Irene became ill, O'Hara became very solicitous. He handled everything, including Irene's medication."

"So?"

"I refer again to the doctor's records. He was puzzled because Irene didn't respond to the medication he'd prescribed. He was forced to change it."

"That's not necessarily unusual."

"The point is, she didn't respond to the first medication because O'Hara *never* gave it to her. There was a capsule for the infection and a liquid for her lungs. We can only speculate that he emptied the capsules and filled them with something else, perhaps sugar. We *know* he never gave her the liquid."

"You couldn't possibly know that."

"But I could. I do. I told you that children are often very helpful. In this case, we struck gold with a neighborhood child named Alfie. Alfie was playing in the street by the trash cans when he found a bottle. He kept it because it was the right size for collecting fireflies. But first he had to empty it out. It was *full* when he found it. Full to the brim."

John Simpson reached into his attache case and brought out a large envelope. He opened the envelope and removed a clear glass medicine bottle, part of the prescription label still intact.

"This is it," he said. "Our lab took traces and

confirmed the original contents."

Patrick looked at the bottle. "Children make mistakes."

"Children are honest. As long as they don't feel intimidated, they are always honest."

Patrick picked up the binder and thumbed through it. He was amazed to see copies of doctors' confidential records, copies of half a dozen prescriptions, and statements from dozens of people, including a parish priest."

"How did you get all this?"

"Our ways are our ways. The how isn't important. Every single word is accurate. We stand behind every single word."

"This report runs three hundred pages."

"We are paid to be thorough."

"Obviously, with all this, you've formed an opinion."

"We don't give opinions. We give facts. The facts of O'Hara's investigation paint a very unsavory picture. One: he denies his sick wife the medication she desperately needs. Two: when that becomes risky, he feeds her an overdose of sleeping pills . . . sending her into coma, into death."

Patrick said nothing for a moment. His stomach churned and he felt shaky. The information, though not totally unexpected, sickened him. He had sensed the corruption in Bren from the beginning, but now he knew how pernicious that corruption was.

"Someone . . . must have known what was going on."

"I assure you that neither the neighbors nor the

doctor had any idea whatsoever. And the priest is an innocent man who sees only the good in people. They were all relieved that O'Hara was being kind to Irene. She hadn't had much kindness in her life."

"He couldn't have planned a thing like this."

"Irene's illness was sheer luck for O'Hara. He then improved on it, so to speak." John Simpson stared at Patrick. "You have been playing devil's advocate and playing it very well," he said in even, round tones. "We use a similar process in our business. But facts are facts."

"This report is interpretive."

"Not at all. It is factual. As a point of law, there is enough information for an exumation order. An autopsy would prove our facts beyond doubt."

"Are there other copies of this report?"

"We have one copy, in code. All other notes and materials have been shredded in accordance with company policy."

"I want your copy destroyed."

"I'll see it to immediately." John Simpson rose. "The information is yours to use as you see fit. There are many kinds of justice, Dr. Dain. We are merely a conduit."

"You're in a nasty business."

"Life is often nasty," John Simpson replied, unperturbed. "Unfortunately, there is no cure for that."

"*Lacrimae rerum.* That means tears in the nature of things."

"An apt phrase." John Simpson closed his attache case and walked to the door. "Please call if we can be of any further service to you."

"I sincerely hope that won't be necessary."

"I quite understand. Good day, Dr. Dain."

"Good day."

The door closed softly. Patrick's eyes were weary beyond imagination as he stared at the binder. Between its covers, neatly typed and spaced, was all the information he needed to prevent Bren from hurting anyone again. For Irene it was too late; but for Ann and Buddy and Daisy there was still time.

Patrick locked the report in his briefcase. He shuddered at the thought of reading it, but read it he would. He would read every word on every page, and when he had finished, he would read it again. *There are many kinds of justice.* Indeed, he smiled faintly. Indeed.

23

The first week of April brought low clouds and steady, gentle rains. The gray days lasted until the weekend, when the clouds lifted and the sky turned a brilliant cerulean blue.

Buddy O'Hara, in flannel slacks and a crew neck sweater, stood at the wide windows in Dr. DuShan's office. He sniffed at the air, for it had the good country smell of earth freshly washed by rain. He watched as the last glistening drops of water evaporated in the warmth of the sun.

Buddy leaned out of the window and whistled. Happy looked up, then bounced across the lawn to the house. He stood on his hind legs and put his damp paws on the sill, cocking his head while Buddy petted him. After a few minutes he dashed away, chasing a squirrel into the hedges.

"It's a beautiful day," Mark DuShan said, walking into the office. "Shall we talk outside?"

"No."

"As you wish."

Mark DuShan was not overly tall, neither good-looking, nor bad-looking. He was a calm, infinitely pleasant man in his late thirties, with large, friendly brown eyes and a quiet voice.

"Are you going to talk to me today?"

"I don't know."

Mark DuShan hung his jacket over the back of a chair and sat down. He opened a notebook and sharpened a pencil. "Let me know when you decide," he said equably.

Buddy had not made an easy adjustment to Twin Oaks. He'd awakened from a haze of sedatives to find himself in a strange room, in a strange place, surrounded by strange faces. For the first few days he'd been terrified, trembling piteously, unable even to speak his name.

Slowly, his fear waned, replaced by blind fury. For the next few days he'd been irate, hurling chairs and lamps and anything else he could lift, until he was put under restraint.

When his anger was exhausted, Dr. Turnbull pronounced him ready to begin. The schedule was strict. There were carefully supervised meals and vitamin supplements three times a day. There were therapy sessions with Dr. DuShan three times a day. There were whirlpool baths and vigorous massages in the morning and at the end of the day. He was offered, and allowed to refuse, the recreational therapy available at the hobby cottage.

Buddy's therapy sessions had gone poorly. He had refused to speak, refused to respond to questions, and so found himself staring silently at Mark DuShan for a solid hour each morning and again in the afternoon and evening.

Mark DuShan had shown no sign of giving in.

Buddy, out of frustration, out of boredom, began to cooperate. His cooperation was grudging, and sometimes erratic, for he talked freely at some sessions and remained mute at others.

"Dr. O'Hara, have you made up your mind?"

"Why do you keep calling me *Doctor?* That's all I hear around here. *Doctor* this, *Doctor* that."

"It's your professional title, you've earned it. Why shouldn't we use it?"

"It's not my title anymore."

"Why do you say that?"

"Look where I am!"

"Where are you?"

"In a goddamn loony bin, that's where. You can kiss my career goodbye, and my title with it."

"Why is that?"

Buddy came away from the window and sprawled in a chair. "Do you always talk in question marks?"

"Not always. I want to know how you feel about things. So I ask questions."

"I'm in here three goddamn times a day. You must know how I feel by now."

"We're a long way from knowing. You're still finding your way, Dr. O'Hara. I'm here to help you."

"The last guy who said that to me, got me put in the loony bin. Some help!"

"What guy was that?"

"There were two. Matt Lansing, the big deal Chief Resident. And Patrick."

Mark DuShan sat back. He flipped the tip of his tie up and down. "Do you remember anything about the night you were brought here?"

"No."

"Nothing at all?"

Buddy took a deep breath. "Maybe a little."

"Tell me about it."

"I don't want to."

"Why not?"

"Because you're on *their* side."

"Whose side is that?"

"Matt's side. Patrick's side. He's paying the bills. You have to do what he says."

Mark smiled. "You don't believe that. Why did you say it?"

"How do you know what I believe?" Buddy seethed. "I was practically kidnapped. I was taken to another state. I was drugged . . . And now everyday I have to sit here with you. That's what Patrick did to me. And you're on his side."

"Tell me what you remember about the night you were brought here."

"*No.*" Buddy pounded the arm of the chair. "I *won't*. We've been through this a thousand times. I won't tell you. I can't. I can't remember."

Mark made a notation in his book. He was certain that Buddy remembered quite a lot about that night, for whenever he had raised the subject, Buddy had reacted angrily. He knew that they would not get very far until Buddy was willing to confront his memory.

"You have visitors coming today, Dr. O'Hara."

Buddy looked up quickly. "Visitors? Who?"

"Your mother and stepfather."

Buddy bolted from his chair. "No! Stop them!

Call them up and stop them." He rushed to the desk and picked up the telephone. "Call them *now*."

"They're already on their way. They'll be here shortly."

"I won't see them. I won't. You can't force me to."

"I don't want to force you. The decision is yours."

Buddy looked warily at Mark. "What do you mean?"

"I mean that whether or not you see them is up to you. You're a grown man, capable of deciding whom you want to see."

"This is a trick."

Mark laughed. He took the phone from Buddy's hand and replaced the receiver. "It's no such thing. Why are you so suspicious?"

"I have to be. Everybody's out to get me. If I don't watch out . . ."

"Yes? Go on."

"I didn't mean that the way it sounded." Buddy seemed confused. He frowned. He shook his head, trying to clear it. "They were always waiting for me to make a mistake."

"They?"

"All of them. Matt especially."

"And did you make a mistake?"

"No." Buddy looked away. "I didn't."

"Everybody makes mistakes."

"Tell that to Matt. He's goddamned perfect."

"Dr. O'Hara, I'd like you to try and remember the night you were brought here. Did you see Matt that night?"

"I don't know. I don't want to talk about it."

"You'll feel better if you do."

"I can't. I can't remember." Buddy sat down. His hands shook and his upper lip beaded with perspiration. He looked pained. "I *can't*."

Mark studied Buddy. He knew that the memory was there, but that Buddy was fighting it. He conceded that little more would be accomplished in this session.

"You have visitors coming, so we'll cut this short. I'll see you this afternoon, Dr. O'Hara."

Buddy was relieved. He almost ran to the door, anxious to get away from Dr. DuShan and his constant questions.

"You will be informed when your visitors arrive," Mark said.

"My visitors can go to hell. They're the reason I'm here."

"The decision is yours. There are choices, you know. You may see them together, or you may see them separately, or you may see one and not the other."

"Don't complicate things."

But Mark had intended to complicate things, for he wanted to determine how Buddy would deal with his choices; if, after all, he would choose to see his mother or his stepfather, or if he would refuse them both.

"Well," Mayo said as Buddy entered the hall, "I hear this is a big day. You have visitors coming."

"They can go to hell."

Jonas Turnbull greeted Ann and Patrick at the

door. He noticed that they both looked tired, though Ann looked particularly hollow-eyed. He showed them to his offices, waiting until they were seated before he spoke.

"I trust you've been satisfied with our reports."

"Yes, but we'd like to know more," Patrick said.

"There's not too much more I can tell you yet. Progress at this stage is slow. I expect that to improve, but I cannot say when."

"His state of mind?" Ann asked.

"I'll be candid with you. Dr. O'Hara's thinking is often muddled. He has occasional, and brief, irrational episodes. Generally, these are brought on by fear."

"Fear of what?"

"Anything. Everything. He's lost his identity, you see. That is especially frightening to a person of Dr. O'Hara's temperament."

"I want to see him now," Ann said.

"Well—"

"No excuses! I want to see him now."

"Ann," Patrick said with unusual asperity, "let Jonas finish."

"I understand your impatience." Jonas smiled. "The problem is that we are not yet sure if Dr. O'Hara will agree to see anyone today."

"Does he know we're here?"

"I've sent word."

"You don't sound optimistic."

"Some patients are reluctant to see their families at first. It's nothing personal really. It's part of the clinial picture."

Jonas looked from Ann to Patrick. He'd last seen

308

them together in December, and he remembered being impressed by their closeness. Now, there seemed to be a distance between them; it was as if they were deliberately keeping each other at arm's length.

"I know this is a strain on you two," he said.

Ann laughed. It was a short, rueful sound. "We're used to strain. I don't know what we'd do without it."

An uncomfortable silence gripped the room. They were all glad when the intercom rang. Jonas took the call. He said a few words and then hung up.

"Please excuse me," he said, going to the door. "I won't be a moment."

"Well," Ann said, "we certainly put on a nice show for him."

"We're not here to put on a show for him or anyone else. You always worry about the wrong things."

"Thanks."

They said nothing more. Ann glanced at Patrick. She realized that they had, in fact, spoken very little to each other in the last two weeks. Patrick worked long, irregular hours at the hospital and when he returned home he closed himself in the library, reading from a thick, black binder. He had refused to discuss the contents of the binder with her, locking it in his private safe overnight, taking it to the hospital with him in the morning.

He had not inquired about Bren either, although he knew that she saw him at least twice a week— dropping Daisy off at his apartment on Friday, picking her up on Sunday night. It was odd, Ann thought, but Patrick had begun to act as if Bren no longer existed.

"Patrick," she said suddenly, "I still think we should tell Bren about Buddy."

"No."

"He's Buddy's father. He has a right."

"He has no rights."

"If he should hear about this—"

"The only way he will hear about this is if you tell him." Patrick stared into her eyes. "I forbid you to do that."

"Forbid?"

"Yes. You've done as you pleased and I haven't tried to stop you . . . But I *forbid* you to include Buddy in your Bren O'Hara fantasies."

Ann felt as if she had been slapped. She bit down on her lip and turned away. Her posture was rigid, her knuckles white.

Patrick hated himself for being so harsh, but he knew there was no other way. The situation with Bren would soon come to a head and Ann would then have a harsh decision to make. If they were not prepared for the days ahead, Patrick thought, they would surely fail.

Jonas returned to the office. "Will you come with me to the patio? Dr. O'Hara is on his way downstairs. I don't know his intentions, but I expect we'll find out."

They walked through the quiet hall to a side door. When they stepped outside the sun was rich and warm and a soft breeze rustled through the trees.

"We have a nice day for it," Jonas said. "Whatever *it* turns out to be."

They waited. Ann and Patrick stood still, staring anxiously at the door.

"What did he say?" Ann asked.

"Dr. O'Hara's language is colorful, but not always clear."

"Oh," Ann squealed, "there he is. He looks rested."

"He is."

Buddy stopped at the edge of the patio. "Not *her*," he said loudly. "I won't talk to *her*."

"Buddy—" Patrick began.

"No! If she stays, I go."

"That's all right," Ann said. "I just wanted to see you, Buddy. You look much better. You look fine."

"Get her *out* of here."

"Ann," Jonas took her arm, "please come with me. We'll be in my office," he said, leading her away.

"How are you, Buddy?" Patrick asked.

"I'm crazy, haven't you heard?"

"How do you feel?"

"How does anybody feel when they're dumped in a goddamn loony bin?"

Patrick sat down. "I see you haven't lost your fighting spirit."

"That's about all I haven't lost. Thanks a lot for ruining my career."

"Your career isn't ruined. It's there, when you're ready."

"My career is finished, and me along with it. Matt got what he wanted. You all got what you wanted."

"Nobody wanted this. Nobody wanted anything except to help."

"Is this what you call help? Having me locked up?"

"You're not locked up. Buddy, you weren't well. Something had to be done. You could be in some cold, impersonal ward with a lot of disturbed people, or you could be here. I thought you'd prefer to be here."

"I don't *belong* here. I'm only here because that's what Matt wanted."

"Matt had nothing to do with it."

"You're still taking his side. You take his side and lock *me* up. Why do you all hate me?"

"Nobody hates you, I least of all."

Patrick tried to read Buddy's expression. The hostility and fear were familiar, but there was something else. It was hopelessness, the hopelessness of a man who stood alone and unprotected in the world.

"I want you to be well," he said. "We all want that."

"Go to hell! You're not going to trick me twice."

"I'm not supposed to upset you," Patrick said quietly, "but I'll risk it. Buddy, you've had problems for many years. They simmered and simmered until they boiled over. *That's* why you're here. The healing won't begin until you admit your problems."

"I'm *not* sick."

"Don't you remember what happened at the hospital?"

Patrick realized that his question was a mistake. Buddy paled. His eyes clouded with pain and for a moment he looked like a desperate animal struggling to free himself from a trap.

Patrick went to him. "Buddy?"

"No! I don't want to talk about it."

"All right, we'll talk about something else. Let's sit down and relax."

"No."

"I have a message from Sally."

"You're lying."

Patrick took a sealed envelope from his pocket. He held it out to Buddy. "Sally asked me to give this letter to you. Please take it."

"She doesn't care about me. She hasn't come to see me."

"She's coming tomorrow. It's all arranged. Take the letter, Buddy."

He stared at the envelope. "How do I know it's really from Sally?"

"You won't know unless you read it."

Buddy grabbed the envelope and ripped it open. He recognized Sally's firm, angular writing. He scanned the two pages, then folded them into his pocket. "I'll read it later."

"Buddy, how about seeing your mother? Just for a minute?"

"I have nothing to say to her. Don't bother bringing her back here. I'm not going to change my mind."

Patrick sighed. He looked out at the grounds, then looked toward the west end of the patio. A dozen or so people were gathered in the dining room for lunch, white-jacketed waiters passing among them with menus. In the distance were the picnic grounds, with checkered cloths and picnic hampers spread out under the trees.

"May I join you for lunch?" Patrick asked.

"The dining room is for psychos only."

"Don't talk that way."

"That's the way it is. If you don't like it, it's too damn bad."

"Buddy, I know you're hurt. I know you think I did a terrible thing. But all I want is what's *best* for you."

"Yeah. With friends like you, who needs enemies?"

Patrick saw Buddy's dark, tormented eyes. "Is there anything you want? Anything I can get you?" he asked helplessly.

Buddy turned on him. "I want a new life," he cried bitterly. "Can you get me a new life?"

"I'm trying. Twin Oaks *is* a new life. It's a second chance. I'm begging you to take it."

"There are no second chances. I'm finished and you know it."

"You're not finished. Far from it. You're young and talented, there's nothing you can't do if you try. Don't look at this as the end of something. Look at it as the beginning. For your own sake, Buddy, *try*."

"The day you brought me here you finished me for good. Who wants a psycho doctor? Nobody. And my work was all I ever had. So thanks, Patrick. Thanks a lot."

Mayo came to the patio door. "Hello, Dr. Dain. Dr. O'Hara, it's time to freshen up for lunch."

"What if I'm not hungry?"

"It's a long time 'til dinner."

"I'll survive."

"You know Dr. Turnbull's rules. Besides," she smiled, "I hear the lobster is wonderful today."

"She's one of my keepers," Buddy said. "I have several."

"Buddy, wait a minute—"

"I have to go now. It's feeding time at the zoo."

24

"Well," Patrick said, walking into Jonas Turn-bull's office, "that was short and anything but sweet."

"I thought it wise to conclude your visit at that point."

"Were you watching?"

Jonas pointed to a long row of television monitors. "We're keeping Dr. O'Hara under observation for now. His temper is . . . shall we say explosive?"

"I had hoped for more progress." Patrick looked at Ann. She sat on the couch, sipping sherry and trying to smile. "I'm sorry about Buddy's attitude. He'll get over it, Ann, give him time."

"Quite right." Jonas nodded. "Time is one of our better tools."

Ann put her glass down. "Please don't humor me. I wanted to see my son and I did. I can be satisfied with that."

"We'll try again tomorrow."

"No, Patrick, I'm going back to the city."

"But we planned to stay in Connecticut over

the weekend."

"*You* planned."

"What about Buddy?"

"Another day isn't going to make any difference in his attitude. I'll be here next Saturday to try again."

"He might like to know you're here now."

"I'm going back to the city."

"There it is," Patrick shook his finger at Ann, "classic O'Hara stubbornness. I could write a book about it."

"What's stopping you?"

"Discretion! The better part of valor."

"And you're *so* valiant."

"*One* of us has to be."

Jonas stepped nimbly between Patrick and Ann. "Now, now," he said soothingly, "that's enough of that. You both want to yell at Dr. O'Hara, but since you cannot, you yell at each other. Foolish, isn't it?"

"I just want to go home," Ann said.

"How do you plan to get there?" Patrick asked. "With or without you, I'm staying at the house this weekend. I'll need the car."

"If necessary, I'll walk."

"Ann," Jonas said, "I have a car and driver waiting to take you home. If that's what you really want."

"That's what I really want. And the sooner the better."

"The car's in the driveway. I'll walk you out."

"Don't trouble, Jonas," Ann went to the door. "I'll find it. Patrick, will you call me?"

"Will you be home?"

"No," Ann snapped. "Robert Redford's taking me to Bermuda. I'll send you a postcard," she added, slamming the door as she left.

"I do like a woman with spirit." Jonas smiled.

"That's what I *used* to say."

Jonas poured two drinks and gave one to Patrick. "Try a little of this. It's guaranteed good for what ails you."

"Ann ails me. It's one argument after another."

"But that's healthy."

"Healthy? Jonas, you're bizarre. I think your work is getting to you."

"It's better to argue than to hide your feelings."

"We argue *all* the time."

"You're both wrestling with conflicts. Considering those conflicts, arguing is a healthy sign. You wouldn't argue if it were all over between you."

Jonas turned as Mark DuShan entered the office. "Ah, Mark, we've been waiting for you. Patrick, this is our Dr. DuShan. Mark, this is Dr. Dain."

"How do you do, Dr. Dain."

"Hello, Mark. Call me Patrick."

"Thank you."

"And now that we're on a first name basis, I can tell you I'm not overly impressed with your work."

"I'm sorry to hear that."

"What are you going to do about it?"

"I'm going to do my job. I'm good at it."

"How good?"

"Very good. But I'm not God and I don't do miracles."

Mark spoke easily and without any trace of

rebuke, yet Patrick felt as if he had been put in his place. "You're a little young, aren't you?"

"I'm not that much younger than you. And you run an entire hospital."

Patrick smiled. He liked Mark DuShan's direct gaze, his unruffled confidence.

"Well, Patrick?" Jonas chuckled. "What do you say now?"

"I don't think Buddy's going to get away with anything. I had to be sure. He has a way of pushing people."

"I don't mind pushing back." Mark smiled. "When it's appropriate. Tell me about your visit with Dr. O'Hara."

"Let's go outside. I could use some fresh air. Jonas, I'll be back tomorrow. Sally Tarlton will be here too."

"Excellent!"

Patrick followed Mark outside. They strolled leisurely across the lawn, stopping at a grove of willows.

"How does Jonas manage to be so damn cheerful all the time?"

"Do you disapprove?"

"I'm jealous. I wish I could find a silver lining or two myself."

"I can't offer silver linings, but I do see a glimmer of light in Dr. O'Hara's case."

"Oh? What's that?"

"He's done a lot of complaining, a lot of shouting and protesting . . . but he hasn't once demanded to leave."

"Is that significant?"

"I think so. I think he's accepted the fact of his illness. Not *admitted* it, but accepted it."

"He didn't seem very accepting to me," Patrick said as they walked on. "He kept insisting his career was over."

"Dr. O'Hara believes he's responsible for the death of a patient."

"Mr. Lewis didn't die."

"Dr. O'Hara *believes* he did. The thought terrifies him. He doesn't want that responsibility again. So he tells everyone who'll listen that his career is over. He's really trying to convince himself."

"Do you mean he's *through* with medicine?"

"No. But he's afraid. We have a *long* way to go."

A lovely, young blond woman came by on the arm of an attendant. Mark stopped. "Hello, Mrs. Marshall. How are you today?" he asked.

Mrs. Marshall nodded her head up and down but did not speak.

"Did you enjoy your lunch?"

Again, she nodded.

"That's good. I'll see you later, Mrs. Marshall," Mark said and the attendant walked her away.

"Can't she talk?" Patrick asked.

Mark glanced at him. "Everything you see and hear at Twin Oaks is confidential. Agreed?"

"Of course."

"Mrs. Marshall simply stopped talking one day. She refused to speak, to smile, to nod, to respond in any way at all. She literally shut the world out."

"Trauma?"

"None. We have absolutely no explanation for her behavior. After two months, we've succeeded in getting her to nod in response to questions. That's all."

"Are you telling me I'm going to have to be patient?"

"Our work is harder than yours, Patrick. We don't have blood tests or x-rays to guide us. It takes time. In some cases, a *lot* of time."

"In Buddy's case?"

"I'm not going to make any flashy promises. I've found the key to Dr. O'Hara's case, but it may be a long while before I unlock the door."

"Can I help?"

"Stay calm." Mark smiled.

"I'll try." Patrick stopped at a white Volkswagen. "This is my car. I'll be on my way now. Thanks for your time, Mark, I appreciate it."

Patrick turned to unlock the car door, but as he turned he thought he glimpsed a familiar figure sitting under a tree.

"Is that Lenore Josephson?"

"We're agreed that everything you see or hear at Twin Oaks is confidential?"

"Yes, of course."

"That's Mrs. Josephson."

"Is she . . . visiting someone?"

"She's a patient here."

"That's too bad." Patrick frowned. "Is it all right if I speak to her?"

"If it's all right with her, it's all right with me."

Patrick walked over to Lenore, Mark a few paces behind.

"Lenore?"

Lenore Josephson looked up from her book.

Patrick saw the gray shadows under her eyes, the deep hollows in her cheeks. Her hair, usually so precisely combed and groomed, hung limply on her shoulders. She wore a floppy blue shirt and wrinkled brown slacks.

"Hello, Patrick."

"I was visiting Buddy. I was about to leave when I saw you."

"Are you in a hurry, or can you stay and talk?"

"I have plenty of time."

"Does Dr. DuShan object?" Lenore looked at him.

"He does not. I'll leave you to your visit." Mark waved, walking away.

"Do you have a cigarette, Patrick?"

"Right here."

"Thanks," she said, leaning toward the flame of his lighter. "You wouldn't happen to have a scotch and soda on you?"

"I'm afraid not."

"It's a great place, but only the cottage patients have bar privileges." Lenore puffed on her cigarette. "Well, aren't you going to ask me?"

Patrick sat down next to her on the grass. "Ask you what?"

"What a nice girl like me is doing in a place like this. Sorry, I forgot . . . you don't think I'm such a nice girl."

"I never said that."

"You didn't have to."

"You weren't very kind to Ann. You're a snob, Lenore."

"Yes, I know. I was born in the wrong century,

maybe in the wrong country. Patrick, we're not friends, but we go back a lot of years. I can talk to you. I'm so sick of talking to shrinks."

"How do you feel?"

"How do I look?"

"Tired."

Lenore smiled. "You always were gallant. I feel as lousy as I look, if that's possible."

"I read something in the paper about you and Doug getting back together. What happened?"

"Doug's people put that story out. A lie, as usual. As a matter of fact, I asked Doug for a divorce."

"And?"

"Doug checked around and divorce wasn't in the cards. He said a resounding *no*."

"You don't need his permission. You can get your own divorce."

"Yes, and Doug could make my life awfully unpleasant."

"More unpleasant than it's been?"

Lenore stubbed out her cigarette. She stared straight ahead. "I'm here because I swallowed half a bottle of sleeping pills. It's happened before. The first time was a year ago. Doug could and would use that against me. I don't want the children to think I'm crazy, even if I am."

"Do you really want a divorce?"

"I love Doug. But Doug doesn't love, he uses. I've had twenty years of it. Twenty years of his women, his lies, his sarcasm. *Yes*, I want a divorce."

"Then do something about it."

"Doug has too much ammunition. And all the guns are pointed at me."

"You have ammunition of your own."

"What do I do with it? Doug seduces the press. He's charming and funny and talks a good game. They buy it. He's Mr. Charisma and they eat it up."

"Lenore, you have to try to help yourself."

"How? Doug plans to be President. Do you think he's going to let me get in his way?"

"After what happened at Rhinelander Pavillion—"

"Some people have short memories. And some people, important people, don't care about Doug's floozies." Lenore stood up. "Let's walk."

They started across the picnic grounds. Lenore's nurse seemed to spring from nowhere to trail them at a discreet distance.

"Is Mary Poppins watching me?"

"There's a nurse a few yards back, if that's what you mean."

"She doesn't let me out of her sight. What does she think I'm going to do? Hang myself from a tree?"

There was a hard edge in Lenore's voice and Patrick looked at her. "Come," he took her arm, "let's enjoy the day."

Most of the picnickers had gone; only a few porters remained to tidy the grounds. The air was clear and the sun was softer now, a pale gold. Patrick heard birds chattering in the treetops.

"Isn't it lovely here?" He smiled. He looked at Lenore and saw that she was crying. "Lenore, what is it?"

"They *are* floozies, you know. Cheap tramps looking for kicks. Every one of them."

324

Patrick offered his handkerchief, but Lenore paid no attention. "The one before this one was twenty-two. Twenty-two!"

"Take it easy, Lenore. Doug's the little boy who never grew up. He needs constant attention. It doesn't mean a thing."

"He has a *wife* for that. But his *wife's* not *twenty-two* anymore. So he's not interested."

Tears spilled from Lenore's eyes. Her hair fell into her face. Patrick was alarmed by the desperate tone in her voice. He got a firm grip on her arm, trying to slow her down.

"Lenore, take it easy," he said worriedly. "It'll be—"

"Twenty-two years old! How do I compete with that? Doug hasn't touched me in a *year*. Not *once*. Because I'm not *twenty-two* anymore."

Lenore broke away from Patrick. She started unbuttoning her shirt.

"Lenore, wait." Patrick ran after her, motioning to her nurse as he ran.

Lenore tore off her shirt. She danced around in a circle, naked from the waist up, waving the shirt around.

"Am I so bad?" she shouted. "I'm not twenty-two, but am I so bad?"

Patrick turned to see the nurse speaking into a small transmitter. He removed his jacket and ran after her. "Lenore! . . . Lenore!" he called.

Patrick came within a foot of her. He grabbed her, but she slipped out of his grasp. She ran a broken pattern through the grounds, cutting left, then right, then going straight ahead.

Patrick saw the porters staring at the strange scene. "Go back to work!" he yelled at them. "Mind your own business! . . . Lenore? Lenore?" he resumed the chase.

Lenore disappeared behind a cluster of trees. Patrick went around to the other side. He saw her standing there, her lips drawn back in a silent scream, her eyes bulging. He lunged at her, locking her in his arms, wrapping his jacket around her.

A small tan car drove up then. Two attendants leaped out. They took Lenore and gently bundled her into the car.

Patrick watched them drive away. He took a deep breath, too astonished to move.

"Excuse me, sir," Lenore's nurse said. "Doctor may want to speak to you. Would you mind coming along with me?"

"What? Oh, yes, of course."

They got into a second car. Patrick looked at the nurse. "I'm terribly sorry. I . . . I don't know what happened."

"Mrs. Josephson will be fine." She smiled. "Don't worry."

There was no sign of the first car, or of Lenore, when they reached the main house. Everything was quiet and serene; for a moment Patrick wondered if he had been dreaming.

Jonas Turnbull opened the car door. "Patrick, you've had quite a full day."

"I don't know what the hell happened." He got out of the car. "What happened?"

"You'll have to tell me," Jonas said as they went inside.

Jonas led the way to his office. Patrick took the waiting drink and finished it in one gulp.

"Another?"

"No." Patrick sat down. "Jonas, what's going on?"

"Mrs. Josephson is here because she tried to commit suicide. Obviously, you know that."

"I didn't until today."

"She was brought directly here from her home. The publicity would have been . . . unfortunate."

"That sounds like Doug."

"Do you know the Josephsons well?"

"I went to school with Doug. We've kept in touch."

"Mrs. Josephson is a very disturbed woman. It's important that you tell me what precipitated this incident."

Patrick reconstructed the afternoon as fully as he could. He spoke slowly, including every detail he remembered. Jonas sat at his desk, taking notes.

"That's all there is," Patrick said. "The next thing I knew, I was chasing her."

"Yes, I see."

"Do you make any sense out of that?"

"Unfortunately, I do."

"If Lenore is disturbed, Doug deserves full credit."

"Is that so?" Doug Josephson walked into the office. "I take enough abuse from my enemies, Patrick. I don't need it from my friends." He grinned. "How are you, pal?"

"You might ask how Lenore is."

"I got here a few minutes ago. I already know

how she is. Running naked as a jaybird through the woods. I didn't know the old girl had it in her."

"You see what I mean, Jonas. Doug is all heart." Patrick shook his head. "I think I'll take that drink."

"Help yourself. Senator, this really isn't a laughing matter. Mrs. Josephson is indeed ill."

"That's old news."

"Doug, have you really become such a bastard?"

"I know Lenore is sick. Am I supposed to be surprised?"

"Don't you *care?*"

"She's here. I didn't lock her in the attic. I've had problems with her before, Patrick. This is old stuff."

"That doesn't make it less important. *Do* you care? You didn't answer my question."

The smile went out of Doug's eyes. "I'm not sure you have the right to ask that question. I understand your boy is here. Is he?"

"Yes."

"And I understand *your* marriage hasn't been all sweetness and light recently."

"Senator," Jonas interjected quickly, "that's enough."

"No," Patrick said, "let him finish. Where did you hear about my marriage, Doug?"

"Is it true?"

"Yes." Patrick sighed. "It's true."

"When your life is running smoothly, talk to me about mine. Until then, get off my back."

A brief smile flickered at the edges of Patrick's mouth. He lit a cigarette. "Well, when you're right, you're right."

"It took twenty years," Doug laughed, "but you finally let me win an argument. And don't look so sad, Patrick. *Nobody's* life runs smoothly. I know, because that's what politics is all about . . . the dissatisfaction of the soul."

"I'm not up to philosophy just now, Doug."

"That's not philosophy, that's a line from one of my speeches."

"I didn't recognize it. I try not to listen to your speeches."

"For that, you owe me a drink. Come on, let's lift a jar or two. It'll be a while before I can see Lenore."

"Another time."

"There's no time like the present."

"Is that another line from one of your speeches? You need new material."

"Seriously, let's go somewhere and have a drink. I hate hanging around this place."

"Sorry."

Patrick stood up. He was exhausted; his head reeled. A dozen different images collided and crashed in his mind. He saw Buddy, sullen and defiant, then crying and trembling with fear. He saw Ann, jittery with confusion, trying to walk two paths at once. He saw Lenore rushing crazily through the woods. He saw Doug's devouring grin. He saw all of them together, running toward him, shouting words he couldn't hear, desperate words, angry words, words of grief.

"Patrick." Jonas was at his side. "Are you well?"

"Barely. But if I don't leave right now, you'll have to get me a room here."

"Perhaps I should have someone drive you to your house."

Patrick smiled. "I think I can manage. Doug, take care of yourself. And I'll take your advice."

"Advice?"

"To get my life running smoothly."

"There's no such thing. Believe me, it can't be done."

"We'll have to see about that. Won't we?"

25

"I'm so glad you came to visit," Ann said to Lola Shay. "And here's your reward, one martini extra dry."

Lola tasted the drink. "Perfect."

"We aim to please."

Lola settled back on the couch, looking at Ann over the rim of her glasses. Ann was wearing a slim black dress with white ruffled collar and cuffs. Her hair was pulled away from her face, showing off a pair of delicate pearl and gold earrings.

"You're very elegant for a Sunday afternoon."

"I have to go out later to pick up Daisy."

"At Bren's?"

Ann nodded. "She spends weekends with him. She doesn't like it, but she does it."

"Do you always dress so carefully to pick up Daisy?"

"The clothes are in my closet, I might as well wear them."

"Where's Patrick?"

"He stayed in Connecticut."

"Why didn't you stay with him?"

"Lola," Ann smiled, "I feel as if I'm being cross-examined."

"You are. We're friends, so I'll talk to you as a friend. I think you're being stupid. This business with Bren is nonsense, plain and simple."

"I don't know what you're talking about."

"Then I'll be blunt. I'm talking about your captain's paradise. A husband on Sutton Place, and a husband on Sixty-eighth Street."

"*Ex*-husband."

"Are you sure?"

"Lola!"

"Well," she smiled, "nobody ever accused me of being a diplomat."

"Obviously not."

"Do you want me to be diplomatic, Ann? Or can we relax and talk honestly?"

"Can I choose the subject?"

"There's only one subject . . . what you're doing to your life. I didn't say anything before because I thought you'd find a way to handle things. But now I'm worried."

Ann walked around the living room, absently straightening pictures and repositioning plants. "I have reasons."

"What reasons?"

"Bren's had a rotten life. *I* kept him from having the kind of life he wanted. I'm making it up to him now."

"What a lot of hooey!"

"I don't expect you to understand. You and Patrick and David were born into money. That's a different world. Everything was given to you.

Everything was done for you."

"Patrick and David, yes. But my father was a bus driver and my mother worked at the local bakery. There were five kids in the family and we all lived in a crummy little apartment over a pizzeria. We shared the place with the roaches."

Ann looked at her in surprise. "I didn't know that. You never told me."

"You never asked."

"I just assumed."

"Why? Because I buy my clothes at Saks? I didn't twenty years ago, I assure you."

"You should be able to understand what Bren went through, you went through it yourself."

"I have no extra sympathy for Bren. He's a parasite."

"He wasn't, not in the beginning."

"Jack the Ripper wasn't Jack the Ripper, in the beginning."

Ann sat down. She sipped her drink. "I see I'm not going to get very far."

"You're not going to convert me. I know what Bren is. So do you. But you won't admit it, that's the sad part."

"He *needed* a chance. I've given it to him and it's made a difference. He's changing, Lola. I can see it."

"Is he working?"

"Not yet."

"Not *yet*? He's been here four months."

"He's going to start looking. He promised and I believe him."

"You'll be a white-haired old lady by the time he

333

starts looking."

"You're wrong. Lola, he *is* changing. He's getting a whole new sense of himself."

"And what are you getting? A vision of your youth? Absolution for a failed marriage?"

Ann felt the warm blush on her cheeks. She looked away. "Is that so terrible?"

"You're paying a terrible price."

"I can't help it."

"Can't or won't?"

"I owe him. I owe myself."

Lola leaned forward, staring at Ann. *"Now* we're getting to it. This isn't just for Bren, it's for you. Because you're in love with a memory."

Ann wiped her eyes. "I can't help it. I . . . I keep remembering things. Patrick said I would. He was right."

"Patrick was *dead wrong.* He should have thrown Bren out by the seat of his pants. He should have stopped this thing before it ever began."

"He said he'd never be sure that way."

Lola finished her drink. She reached for the pitcher and poured another. "No man ever loved a woman more deeply than Patrick loves you."

"Don't you think I know that?"

"I thought you loved Patrick the same way."

"Lola, I *do.* It *kills* me to hurt him. I don't want to hurt him. I don't mean to . . . but I hurt him anyway. There's something inside me I don't understand."

"Have you tried?"

"The harder I try the worse it gets. Something is *driving* me. I don't know what."

"It sounds like you never got over Bren."

Ann slumped in her chair. "Buddy wasn't the only one affected when Bren walked out. Those first few days I thought I'd go out of my mind. I couldn't, because of the children. I still remember how they looked. They were stunned. They were so hurt. After a while I began to hate Bren. When I heard that he'd died, I was *glad*."

"They say there's no hate without love."

"I don't believe that."

"What do you believe?"

"I don't know. My son is sick, my marriage is coming apart, and I . . ." Ann dried her tears, fighting for control. "I'm letting it all happen and I don't know why."

"Are you prepared to lose Patrick?"

Ann picked up her drink. The glass slipped from her hand and shattered on the table.

"I'll take care of it," Lola said, mopping up the spill. "I'm sorry if the question upset you, but that's the question you have to ask yourself."

"I *can't* lose Patrick."

"You can't have Patrick *and* Bren."

"I don't want Bren, not the way you mean it."

"What way do you want him?"

Ann put her hand to her head. "Lola, please stop. No more."

"You were always a sensible woman. *Be* sensible."

"Please, leave me alone."

"You're going to listen to me, Ann. My marriage is in shreds because David and I were careless with each other. I never really considered his needs, and he never really considered my feelings. We took each other for granted and we're paying for it. The same thing is going to happen to you."

"No!" Ann said through her tears. "No! Patrick understands."

"God knows Patrick is understanding. *Too* understanding, if you ask me. But even Patrick has limits."

"As soon as Bren is settled—"

"You've been saying that for four months."

"Do you expect Bren to put his life back together overnight?"

"I don't *care* about Bren. I care about you. I care about Patrick. Ann, you have the kind of marriage everyone dreams about. It's straight out of a storybook."

"That was before."

"Before what?"

"Before Bren came back."

"The man you hate? The man whose death you cheered? So what if he came back?"

"He's unfinished business. I have to finish it."

"At your own peril."

"Yes. At my own peril."

Ann arrived at Bren's a little after six. She checked her hair in the hall mirror, then knocked on the door.

"Come in," Bren opened the door. "Come right in," he grinned. "And what's that you have there?"

"I brought the Sunday *Times*. There are a lot . . . of want ads."

"You think of everything, Annie Laurie. What

would we do without you?" He put the newspaper on a table. "Daisy," he called, "look who's here. It's our Annie."

Daisy ran to Ann, her small canvas suitcase bumping against her leg. "Hi, Ann. I'm all ready to go."

"Hi, sweetheart." Ann kissed her. "But we're not going yet. We're going to have dinner here."

"I'm not hungry."

"Something smells very good. I bet it's stew."

"I'm not hungry."

"Daisy, we have to eat."

"Let's eat at home."

Ann bent down to her. "Sweetheart, this is your home too."

"I like my other home better."

"See how it is?" Bren shrugged. "She's spoiled. The child can't enjoy her food anymore unless a butler serves it on platinum plates."

"Daisy," Ann brushed the bangs out of her eyes, "your Poppa's cooked a whole meal for us. We can't be rude."

"He can eat it. I want to go home."

Ann stood up. She gave her jacket and purse to Daisy. "Be a good girl and put these away for me."

"Do we *have* to stay here?"

"Yes, little girl," Bren said impatiently. "Now do as you're told."

Daisy slouched unhappily away. Ann was perplexed by her behavior, by her coolness toward Bren. "Aren't you two getting along?"

"Sure we are."

"Why doesn't Daisy like it here?"

337

"She's spoiled."

"She's the *least* spoiled child I've ever known."

"Patrick's probably talking against me, filling her head with lies."

"Patrick doesn't lie."

"You're a loyal woman, Annie. I always said that. Sit down, I'll bring the wine."

"No wine for me."

Ann glanced around the apartment. The couch was covered with old magazines and the ashtrays were overflowing. The glass tables were layered with fingerprints and crumbs and coffee stains. There was a fine coating of dust on the floor.

"It's a mess, Bren."

"The maid's coming tomorrow."

"Now who's spoiled?"

"When in Rome . . . Anyhow, I couldn't cook and clean too, could I?"

"People do."

He grinned. "I was never good at organizing things. You used to tell me that, if you'll remember."

Ann quickly stacked the magazines and put them in a corner. She took the dirty ashtrays to the kitchen.

"A house needs a woman's touch," Bren said, following her.

Ann tied an apron around her waist. "Never mind the soft soap. What can I do in here?"

"The supper's ready. You can dish it out, if you don't mind. I'll light the candles."

"Candles?" Ann smiled.

"Nothing but the best for the O'Haras. Isn't

338

that right?"

"Ann's not an O'Hara," Daisy said, standing at the entrance of the kitchen.

Bren turned around. "You're forgetting what I told you, little girl. Children should be seen and not heard."

"Yes, Poppa."

"Here, make yourself useful. Take the salad to the table . . . Annie, I don't like the way she's sassing me lately."

Ann went to the stove and began ladling the stew out. "Daisy was only stating a fact. I'm *not* an O'Hara."

"Sure you are. And you always will be. No piece of paper is going to change that."

"I'm Mrs. Patrick Dain."

Bren leaned over her. He ran his finger along the nape of her neck. "Then what are you doing here with me, Mrs. Dain?"

"I'm . . . I'm trying to get dinner on the table," she said, flustered. "I will, if you'll get out of my way."

He laughed softly. "Anything you say, Annie Laurie."

"Daisy, did you wash your hands?"

"Yes, Ann."

"Good." She put a bowl of stew in front of the child. "I tasted it and it's delicious. I want you to eat every bite."

Daisy made a face but said nothing. She picked up her fork and began separating the meat from the vegetables.

Ann brought the rest of the food to the table and

then sat down. She was aware of Bren's gaze on her. There was something bold in his look, as if he were laughing at a private joke only the two of them shared.

"Have you been drinking?" she asked.

"I take a social drink now and then, like any man."

"You know what I mean."

"Those days are over, Annie. Didn't I give you my word and all? I only drank heavy when I was unhappy. I've nothing to be unhappy about now. I've a fine apartment, a fine child . . . a fine woman sitting at my table."

Ann shifted around in her chair. She didn't like the intimacy in Bren's voice, the husky warmth. She tried to concentrate on her food, but she had little appetite.

Bren sensed her tension. He realized he was moving to fast.

"I like to have a joke once in a while," he said easily. "You'll forgive me, Annie, won't you?"

"Did you tell a joke, Poppa?" Daisy asked.

Bren reached across the table and tickled Daisy under the chin. "Eat your supper, little girl. Annie, no compliments for the chef?"

"The stew's great. Couldn't be better."

"Do you remember the day . . . we'd only been married a few months . . . and I decided to surprise you and cook supper?"

"No, I . . . *yes*, I do," Ann laughed suddenly. "What an unholy mess that was."

"But the fun we had that day! How about the fun?"

The memory came back slowly at first, then in a rush. She'd come home to find their tiny kitchenette full of dirty dishes and blackened pots. Vegetable peelings were all over the floor, and flour rose in a white mist from the counter top. The sink was stopped up, clogged with grease and meat scraps. Bren had smiled sheepishly as she'd inspected the stew simmering on the stove. It was a sickly concoction of undercooked meat and overcooked vegetables, awash in a watery gravy. They'd laughed about it, but later that night, they'd eaten it all.

Ann remembered that dinner. Their rickety table had been covered with oilcloth and set with dime store plates, but they hadn't cared. They ate the terrible stew and drank the cheap wine and held hands until it was very late. Bren talked about their future together and Ann listened, rapt, for everything seemed to lay before them bright and shiny as a child's dream.

Now, Ann looked around the table. This was the way Bren had meant it to be, she thought; good food and good wine and candlelight at day's end.

Bren's eyes were riveted on Ann. He watched the play of emotions on her face and he knew that his plans were falling into place. One more push, he thought exultantly, and he would have things exactly as he wanted them.

Daisy shook Ann's arm. "You look funny," she said.

"Do I, sweetheart? I was thinking about something . . . something long, long ago."

"In the olden days?"

341

"Well, after the dinosaurs but before the astronauts."

"What?"

Ann pushed her chair away from the table. "Help me clear the dishes away, Daisy."

"*Then* can we go home?"

"As soon as the dishes are done."

A dazzling smile broke through Daisy's gloom. Her big gray eyes twinkled, and there was a bounce to her step as she carried the dishes to the kitchen.

"Take your time," Ann cautioned her. "We don't want to break anything."

"I'll be careful."

"Look at her," Bren said. "She can't wait to leave."

"Daisy has to adjust to this new schedule. She's been moved around a lot, Bren, it's confusing."

"If I'd acted that way around *my* poppa I would have gotten what for. He'd crack the leather strap across my backside, no questions asked. That's how a child learns respect."

"That's not respect, that's fear."

"What's wrong with a little fear?"

"Ann," Daisy stared up at her, "I'm all finished."

"So quickly?" Ann saw that the table had been cleared. She heard the dishwasher humming in the kitchen. "That's very good, Daisy."

"Can we go now?"

"All right, we'll go."

"Stay long enough for coffee," Bren said.

"It's getting late, and Daisy has school in the morning. Thanks for dinner, Bren. I enjoyed it."

"We'll do it again next Sunday. I'll make something special."

"Here, Ann." Daisy gave her her jacket and purse. She pulled her toward the front door. "I'm all ready. Are you all ready?"

"Say goodnight to your father."

"Bye, Poppa."

"Where's my kiss, little girl?"

Bren bent down and Daisy kissed his cheek. "Thank you for dinner, Poppa," she said formally.

"That's better." Bren straightened up. He looked at Ann. "Next Sunday. Is it a date?"

"I . . . I don't know. We'll see."

"Say it's a date." He grinned. "At least say maybe."

"Maybe."

He opened the door. Daisy grabbed her suitcase and ran out. Ann turned to leave but Bren stopped her. He kissed her. It was a soft kiss, but there was no gentleness in it; there was power and challenge.

Ann pushed him away. "Bren!"

"For old time's sake."

"Don't ever do that again."

Bren wasn't bothered by the indignation in Ann's voice, for he'd felt her hesitate before she'd pulled back. There would be another time, a time when she would not pull back, and that time, he thought with satisfaction, would be soon.

"You're mine, Annie Laurie. I can't help how I feel."

"Goodnight, Bren."

Ann took Daisy's hand and hurried into the street. The evening was warm, but she felt a chill.

Her mouth was dry and her throat ached.

"Why did you kiss Poppa?" Daisy asked.

"That wasn't really . . . a kiss. Your poppa was playing a joke."

"Was it funny?"

"No. It was very silly."

They reached the bus stop and Daisy put her suitcase down. She fished in her pocket and drew out several quarters. "I can pay," she said.

"That's your allowance, save it for something you want." She gave her some coins. "You can hold the carfare."

"Can I put it in the box? It goes *chug* when you put it in the box."

"Yes. Daisy, I want to talk to you. You weren't very nice to your poppa tonight."

"I don't like Poppa."

"That's an awful thing to say."

"He doesn't like me either."

"Of course he does."

"He doesn't talk to me, or play with me. And he made me keep Alfie in my suitcase the whole weekend. Even for sleeping."

"Your poppa has a lot on his mind."

"He doesn't like me. He doesn't like any children." Daisy shrugged.

"That's not true."

"It is too. Mamma said."

"You must have misunderstood her."

"I didn't. Mamma said it wasn't my fault, but Poppa didn't like children. I knew that anyhow. Because he said children just made trouble trouble trouble."

344

Ann's lips parted but she didn't speak. Another old memory tugged at her. She reached for it, but it was too far away.

"The bus is coming," Daisy said. "I'll put the money in the box."

Ann stepped off the curb. Traffic was light, but she saw an empty taxi and she flagged it down.

Daisy smiled expectantly. "Are we going to take a *taxi?*"

"Yes."

Ann opened the door and helped Daisy inside. She gave the driver the address and then sat back, tiredly rubbing her eyes.

"Patrick always takes me in a taxi. You never took me in a taxi before," Daisy said.

"This is a special treat."

"Why?"

"I don't know, it just is." Ann patted Daisy's hand. "Be quiet for a while, sweetheart, I have a headache."

Ann looked out the window. Stores and apartment buildings flashed by, but she didn't see them. She was concentrating, trying to remember. The memory came tantalizingly close, then drifted away.

"Are you thinking about the olden days again?" Daisy whispered.

"Yes, the olden days."

26

Ann screamed. She sat upright in bed and turned on the lights. Her heart was beating very fast and her hands were cold and damp. She looked desperately around the room for the source of her terror. It was several minutes before she realized that the terror had been in her dream.

Ann put on her robe and rushed across the hall to Daisy's room. She opened the door and peered inside. Daisy slept contentedly, Alfie clutched in her arms. Ann quietly closed the door and went back to her bedroom.

She sat at the edge of the bed, taking deep breaths to calm herself. She felt dizzy and her head throbbed. With trembling fingers, she poured a glass of water. She drank it slowly, holding on to the glass with both hands.

Ann closed her eyes, forcing herself to think about her dream. She saw Bren and herself, recently married, in their old Greenwich Village apartment. The rain beat against the windows, but there was another, louder sound. It was the sound of a brutal argument.

Ann gasped suddenly, for she knew now what she had been trying to remember.

"It was that night," she murmured. "That terrible night in the rain."

Ann's memory of that night, buried for more than twenty-five years, came into sharp focus. She remembered everything as it had been then—the dingy beige walls of their tiny apartment, the rip in the arm of the old blue sofa, the aroma of spaghetti sauce cooking, and the drenching, incessant rain.

Ann stood at the window, watching the heavy rain pour down. She saw the water collecting in the gutters, making one big splash as cars passed by.

"I'm home, Annie Laurie," Bren said, closing the door behind him.

Ann ran into his arms. She kissed him and then drew back, giggling. "You're soaked."

"I am for a fact. They say all this rain is good for the farmers, but it doesn't do much for me."

Ann hung Bren's dripping jacket on the shower rack in the bathroom. She took a large towel from the radiator and brought it to him. "Spaghetti and meatballs for dinner. That'll warm you up."

Bren finished drying his hair and tossed the towel away. He pulled Ann to him and hugged her. "I like this better. Annie, is that a bottle of wine I see? What's the occasion?"

"It's very special. The most special there is."

"Have I forgotten an anniversary? Let's see, we've been married five months and ten, no, eleven days."

"It's not an anniversary. Sit down, I'll get

the wine."

She brought the bottle and two glasses to the sofa. "It's for a toast. I have wonderful news."

"Did I win the Sweepstakes?"

"More wonderful than that."

"Then tell me, woman. Or are you expecting me to guess?"

"I went to the doctor today."

"Annie—"

"No, it's *good* news. *Great* news. Bren, we're going to have a baby."

"A baby? Is he sure?"

Ann's young face shone. Her cheeks dimpled in a broad smile.

"Absolutely sure. Isn't that the most wonderful news in the whole world?"

"You're seventeen years old, a baby yourself."

"I'm a married lady and a mother-to-be."

"How far along are you?"

"Two months."

Bren took her hand. "Don't worry about it, Annie. I'll talk to Jack. He knows about things like that."

"I know about things like that too," she laughed. "In seven months we'll have our baby. Our own baby! Bren, I can't believe it."

"You can't keep it."

"What?"

"The baby. You can't keep it."

"What are you talking about?"

Bren looked at her sternly. "You know what I'm talking about."

"I *don't.*"

"Annie, there are doctors who take care of things like that."

"Take care of . . ." Ann jumped up. Her eyes were round with shock and pain. "Are you suggesting an . . . an . . ."

"An abortion. Yes, I am. And I'm not suggesting, I'm *saying*. That's the way it has to be. Anyhow, I hear it's a simple thing. A few minutes and it's all over."

"I don't want it to be all over. I *want* our baby."

"There's no use talking. My mind's made up. You can't keep it."

"Stop saying *it*. Call the baby he or she, but stop saying *it*."

"What's the difference? Don't make such a fuss."

Ann stared at him in disbelief, for she didn't know this side of Bren; this side was ugly and unfeeling. "I'm carrying your child. Don't you care?"

"There's nothing to care about. I didn't want a child. I didn't ask for a child. We're young, Annie. What do we want with a child? How would we take care of it?"

"I'll take care of the baby. You won't be bothered, I *promise*."

"How do we support it? We're barely getting by as it is."

"If that's all you're worried about," Ann said with relief, "you have your part-time job. And I can continue to work until the baby comes."

"And after that?"

"Well . . . I guess you'd have to get a full-time

job. But just for a while," she added quickly, "maybe for a year, just until the baby is old enough to leave with somebody. My mother would look after the baby while I was at work. I know she would."

"Babies get sick. They need a lot of attention. You'd never be able to hold a job."

"You would."

"And what would happen to my writing?"

"Bren, you could write at night. And on weekends. You'd have plenty of time."

"Dog tired from a job and trying to write too? With a baby yapping in the background at all hours? It's no good, Annie. I'll hear no more about it."

"You haven't been writing that much anyway," Ann said stubbornly.

"I'm in a dry spell. But it'll pass. And my luck will change. All I have to do is sell one piece and I'm on my way."

"Your writing isn't more important than a baby."

"It is to me. I want money, Annie, and success. A man doesn't get that with a baby hanging around his neck."

Ann covered her face with her hands. "My God," she cried.

"Don't go looking to God for help. What's He done for you lately except give you a kid we don't need or want."

"*I* want this child."

"I want a million dollars. Does that mean someone's going to knock on the door and give it to me? It's a hard world out there, Annie. A man can't be sentimental.''

"I don't care what you say. It's my body, it's up to me to decide. And I've decided."

"And *I'll* be stuck with the kid."

"You'll change your mind. Once the baby's here, you'll change your mind."

"I'm telling you straight out, Annie. I don't want any children. Not now, not later."

"But . . . we always talked about being a family."

"You and me together are family. We're all the family we need, and all I want."

"That's not all I want."

"Did you ever hear me talk about children? Did I ever once say I wanted a kid?"

"Not in so many words."

"In *no* words."

"Bren, children—"

"Children are trouble, trouble, trouble. That's *all* they are. Who would know better than me? Didn't I grow up in a houseful of 'em?"

"One little baby isn't a houseful."

"And you, tricking me like that." Bren's eyes flashed dangerously. "Every night before we went to bed I asked you was it all right. Sure it was, you said. But it wasn't, because there you are with one in the oven."

Ann blushed dark red. "I . . . I didn't know that's what you meant."

"What did you think I meant? Did you think I was asking permission? I was asking was it all right, was it safe?"

"I don't know about those things."

"Miss Prim and Proper doesn't know about those things," he sneered. "You spent too much time with the nuns at school, that's your problem. But no more. I'll be speaking to Jack in the morning. He'll tell us where we can go and that'll be the end of it."

"No."

"What did you say?"

"You heard me."

"I'm your husband. You'll do what I say."

"Not about this. This is our baby, and we're going to have him and love him and take care of him."

"Are you talking back to me?"

"Yes," Ann said firmly, though she took a defensive step backward.

A storm gathered on Bren's face. He went red, then white with anger, and the dark veins rose in his neck. His fury was huge. When he stood up he seemed twice his normal size.

Ann continued to back away from him. She was more scared than she had ever been in her life, and more confused, for she had never seen Bren this way. She dug her nails into the palms of her hands until they bled.

Bren loomed over her, enraged. His face was a ghastly white, ugly with wrath. His eyes were narrow, glazed slits.

"Please," she said, backed now into a corner.

"We're getting rid of it! Do you hear me?" he thundered.

Ann tried to move, but Bren's broad shoulders blocked her way. She ducked under his arm and ran. He grabbed a plant and threw it at her. It smashed against the wall and fell, dirt and clay and leaves, on the sofa. Ann screamed. She dashed out the door to the stairs. Gasping and sobbing, she ran down the four flights into the street.

The pelting rain soaked through her thin cotton housedress. The wind blew her wet hair across her face. She ran wildly to the corner, then stopped, for she didn't know where to go. She had no money with her, no friends nearby. She wanted her mother, but her mother was eighty blocks away.

Ann huddled in a doorway, weeping. Her heart beat so violently that she thought it would explode. She peeked out of the doorway. There were no people in the street. There were only a few cars, and those drove by quickly. She remembered her baby, and the thought of him, warm and protected, steadied her. She stepped out of the doorway, determined to walk to her mother's.

"What's the matter, miss?"

Ann saw a policeman come to a stop in front of her. He was a burly man, swathed in a heavy raincoat. "I . . . I have to get to my mother's."

He looked at her suspiciously. "What are you doing out on a night like this? And dressed like that?"

"Please . . . could you help me get to my mother's?"

"Hello, Officer."

Ann jumped at the sound of Bren's voice. He smiled, holding out his umbrella.

"You know this girl?" the policeman asked.

"She's my wife. You know how they get. We had

a bit of a fight and right away she's out the door." -

"Where do you live?"

"Right there, down the street," Bren pointed.

"You better take her home. Can't have her roaming the streets on a night like this."

"No!" Ann cried. "*Please*, I don't want to go."

"Officer," Bren said calmly, "she's pregnant. You know how they get when they're pregnant."

"I ought to. I been through it enough. Go along, missus, before you catch your death."

Bren pulled Ann underneath the umbrella. "That's right," he said. "It's not just you now, you have to think of the baby." He smiled. "Thank you, Officer. And goodnight to you."

"Bren, don't do this," Ann begged as he dragged her down the street.

"I'm taking you home where you belong."

"I want to go to Mamma's."

"You're not going to be one of those wives always running home to Mamma. Best you learn that now."

"You're going to hurt me."

Bren stopped walking and stared at her. "I'd never hurt you, Annie. I have a temper, like any man. But I'd never hurt you."

Bren pulled her along the street to their building. He pushed her inside. "Up you go."

Ann looked at Bren, then looked at the stairs, then looked at Bren again. "I'm afraid."

He laughed. "Of me? I'm your husband, not the bogeyman."

They walked upstairs in silence. Bren pushed her through the door, then closed and locked it. He threw the umbrella down and turned to her.

"We won't talk anymore about this tonight."

"All right," Ann whispered.

"Get into some dry clothes. Then clean up the sofa and get supper on. I'm hungry."

Ann moved swiftly through the apartment, doing as she was told. Bren sat down at the table. He pretended to read the newspaper, all the while watching her out of the corner of his eye.

"You look like a wet kitten," he said.

"I'm sorry."

"I wasn't complaining, mind you. I was making a comment."

Ann put the food on the table. "Some of the meatballs are . . . a little burned. I'm sorry."

"Annie, I don't want you to be afraid of me."

"I can't help it."

Bren stood up. "It's all on account of this goddamn baby. There was never a cross word between us until this goddamn—"

"Don't curse our baby," Ann said before she could stop herself.

Bren slapped her face. She staggered sideways, grabbing the back of a chair for support. She began to cry again, soundless, dry sobs.

Bren walked away. He walked from one end of the apartment to the other, then turned and retraced his steps.

"Okay, Annie. Okay. If you're so bound and determined to have it . . . I won't stop you."

Ann looked at him. "Oh, Bren, you won't be sorry."

"Sure I'll be sorry. So will you. But it's the kid

who'll be sorriest of all. You're doing him no favor bringing him into this world."

That had happened almost twenty-six years ago, Ann thought now, and in all the years since she'd kept the memory of that night locked away. She'd denied the memory, for she hadn't been able to face the pain.

Ann walked across the bedroom to the desk. She picked up a silver-framed picture of Buddy. The picture had been taken a few days into his residency and he'd been smiling. He had Bren's smile, she thought to herself, Bren's smile as she remembered it in the first months of their marriage. Ann returned the picture to the desk and went back to the bed. She sat down, hugging a pillow to her.

That rainy night had put a mark on their marriage, Ann knew. It had ended their innocence, and though they'd never referred to the incident again, it had changed them. She had seen something in Bren that had frightened her, and at the end, appalled her. She didn't know what Bren had seen, but she knew that he'd never forgiven her for Buddy's birth.

Ann remembered Buddy as a baby and she smiled. Buddy had been a fat, happy baby, into everything, walking early, talking early, sunny as a summer day. When his sister had come along he'd treated her with a reverence so grave it was funny. Later, when they'd gone off to school together for the first time, Buddy had practically burst with pride.

The joy of those young years had eluded Bren,

Ann thought sadly. He'd turned inward, turned to drink, turned to schemes increasingly desperate and vain. His disappointment had become bitterness, and his bitterness cruelty.

She'd continued to love him, if in a different way, and the children had loved him in the uncomplicated way of children. But their love hadn't been enough. Ann saw it all clearly now—a series of small cruelties leading to the final, large cruelty. She would never forget the faces of her children on the day they knew that their father had left them. That was the day she'd stopped loving Bren O'Hara.

Ann laughed out loud. She was lightheaded with relief, with her new, clear vision. She felt as if the most enormous weight had been lifted from her chest. It was possible, she thought, that she owed Bren something; if she did, that debt was being repaid. More importantly, she knew now that she had not loved Bren for many years. She knew that surely and without doubt; she would never have to question again.

Ann took Patrick's picture from her night table. She stared at it, wishing he, and not his picture, were here with her now. He'd been so wise. Somehow he'd guessed, or sensed, or known that she had to linger over the happy times with Bren before she could deal with the harsher truths.

"You're so smart," she said to his picture. "Patrick Grayson Dain, I love you."

Ann felt wonderful. She felt like laughing and crying, like dancing; if there had been a hat nearby, she would have thrown it in the air.

Ann left the bedroom and went downstairs. She was surprised to see Hollis sitting at the kitchen table.

"Good morning, Mrs. Dain," Hollis rose. "I hope I didn't awaken you."

"No, I never exactly got to sleep. But what are you doing up?"

"I don't sleep as much as I used to, Mrs. Dain. Age, I imagine."

"Hollis," Ann kissed his cheek as she went to the stove, "you are younger than Springtime."

He smiled. "If I may say so, Mrs. Dain, it's a great pleasure to see you in such a happy mood."

"It's a great pleasure to *be* in such a happy mood." Ann poured a cup of coffee and brought it to the table. "Sit down, Hollis. We have plans to make."

"Plans, Mrs. Dain?"

"I want to plan a special dinner."

"Certainly. For how many people?"

"Two. Dr. Dain and myself. Let's have all his favorite dishes. Rack of lamb . . . can we get a good rack of lamb for tomorrow night?"

"I'll telephone the butcher first thing."

"Rack of lamb then, and baked carrots, and potato soufflé, and a green salad with little croutons."

"Splendid," he nodded. "And for desert, Crème Brulé?"

"Hollis, we're so lucky to have you."

"Why, thank you, Mrs. Dain."

"If it's cool enough for a fire, we'll eat in the library by the fireplace. If not, we'll eat in the sitting room by the windows. How does that sound?"

Hollis smiled at the excitement in her eyes. She looked younger, calmer than she had in months, and he let himself hope that it was an omen of things to come.

"Does that sound okay?"

"It sounds lovely indeed."

"Don't say anything to Dr. Dain. I want to surprise him."

"Of course, Mrs. Dain. But the doctor's schedule presents certain problems. The timing of the meal . . . it wouldn't do to overcook the lamb."

"I'll have him home at eight. I don't know how, but I'll think of something."

"Everything will be ready."

"I'll pick out some flowers. And let's have candles, *lots* of candles. I want it to be pretty, Hollis. I want it to be happy. There hasn't been much happiness in this house lately, has there?"

"Looking at you now, Mrs. Dain, I'd wager that's about to change."

27

The pediatrics wing at Rhinelander Pavillion consisted of a small intensive care unit, an infants' area, and four large, airy wards. The wards were cheerfully wallpapered with pictures of clowns and balloons and carousels. There were bins of toys and shelves of books and games.

Patrick walked into the observation ward. Each of the eight beds was occupied, and the room rang with the high-pitched voices of children.

"Hi, kids." Patrick waved.

"Over here," Matt called.

Patrick went to the bedside of a plump, blond boy. His lip had been split and one side of his face was swollen and bruised. He stared impassively at the floor, but Patrick saw that his hands were clenched into fists.

"This is Jeff," Matt said. "He's five."

"Hello, Jeff. How do you feel?"

"Okay," the boy answered without looking up.

Matt drew Patrick aside. "His mother brought him into the E.R. She said he fell. They took precautionary x-rays and found several old frac-

360

tures. They also found an old scar on his back and one on his thigh."

Patrick took the chart from Matt. "What does the mother have to say?"

"We haven't asked her anything yet."

"Why not? Look at this chart. It's a good bet somebody's been knocking the child around."

"Eve Lawrence jumped all over Dr. Stern for admitting Jeff to pediatrics. She says we're on shaky legal ground."

"Good old Eve."

Patrick sat down next to the boy. "How did you hurt yourself, Jeff?"

"I fell."

"Where did you fall?"

"At home. In my room."

"Were you alone?"

Jeff looked up at Patrick. He started to say something, then changed his mind. He nodded.

"Where was your mother?"

"I don't know."

"And your father?"

"He's not home. He's away. He's working."

"Turn around, let me see your face." Patrick reached out to check Jeff's bruises. The boy flinched at the sudden movement. "I'm not going to hurt you. Just relax for a while." Patrick smiled at him. "There are plenty of toys. Do you like to play with toys?"

Jeff nodded.

"Good. Make yourself at home. Lunch will be coming soon." Patrick stood. "Matt, let's have a talk with his mother."

They walked to the doctors' room at the end of the corridor. Patrick looked at the chart once more, then went inside with Matt.

"Mrs. Desmond?"

"Yes. How's Jeff?"

"He's fine. He's resting."

Mrs. Desmond lit a cigarette. She was a fair, blue-eyed woman in her thirties. She wore an expensive gray wool suit and a sapphire clip. Her light hair was rolled prettily around the back of her head. Patrick noticed that her fingernails were bitten down to the quick.

"I'm Dr. Dain, this is Dr. Lansing. We'd like to ask you a few questions."

"Why? All I want to do is take Jeff home. You said he was fine."

"These injuries aren't serious. But we'd like to know how he got them."

"He fell. He was coming in for breakfast and he fell against the stove."

Patrick and Matt exchanged glances. "Mrs. Desmond, Jeff said he fell in his room."

"He did." She fidgeted in her chair. "He fell in his room and fell again in the kitchen . . . He's clumsy. He can't put one foot in front of the other without falling down."

"Has he had a neurological examination?" Matt asked.

"There's nothing wrong with Jeff." She shook her head impatiently. "He's just clumsy. Some children are like that. Now," she stood up, "I'd like to take my son home."

"Not yet," Patrick said.

"Why not?"

"We've found other injuries, old injuries, Mrs. Desmond. Quite a few of them."

"Look, I told you, he falls a lot."

"Who is Jeff's pediatrician?"

Mrs. Desmond threw her cigarette on the floor and stamped it out. She picked up her handbag and went to the door.

"Mrs. Desmond, we're *asking* for your cooperation. Don't force us to insist."

She leaned her head against the door. She didn't move, didn't speak. After a few moments she turned back to them, her glance fluttering between Patrick and Matt.

"Our pediatrician retired. We don't have anybody right now."

"What was his name? The man who retired?"

"I don't recall," she said weakly.

"Mrs. Desmond, you're making this extremely difficult."

"I don't know what *this* is. If you're accusing me of something, *accuse* me. Otherwise, I want to take my son and go."

"So many injuries are unusual in a boy Jeff's age," Patrick said carefully. "We're trying to get at the truth."

"I've *told* you the truth."

"I don't think so."

"I don't have to stand here and listen to this. You have no right. I could sue you. I *will* sue you."

"We're trying to help your son."

"He doesn't need any help. He's clumsy. He'll grow out of it."

"Where is your husband, Mrs. Desmond?"

Her eyes opened wider. She moved her handbag nervously from arm to arm. "Leave him out of this."

"If you don't give us the information we need, we'll have to ask your husband."

"Oh, that's funny. My husband? Let me tell you about *my husband*. He's away three weeks out of every four. When he is home, he's so busy with meetings and reports and conferences that he might as well be away."

"Nevertheless, he might be able to fill in some of the gaps."

"I'd be surprised if he remembered our son's name. He doesn't care about Jeff. According to my husband, Jeff is *my* department. He wants a perfect child, but none of the bother, none of the worry."

"It's hard raising a child alone," Matt said quietly.

Mrs. Desmond looked at him. "I know people do it, but I don't know *how* they do it. I have to run the house, and I have my own job . . . and my mother moved in with us after her stroke, and Jeff needs so much attention." She pressed her hand to her forehead. "Sometimes I . . . sometimes . . ."

Matt helped her to a chair. "Sometimes you have to strike out at somebody."

She grasped Matt's hand. "I have *all* the responsibility. He expects me to be a perfect wife, a perfect mother, a perfect hostess . . . and I *have* to work because we're living way above our heads. The pressure . . ."

"I understand," Matt said softly. "The pressure

364

builds and builds until you have to take it out on somebody."

Her shoulders sagged. Tears gathered in her eyes and splashed down her cheeks. "*God*, you must think I'm an *animal*, treating my own child that way . . . I can't help myself. Before I know what's happening . . . it's happened."

Matt gave her his handkerchief. "When did this start?"

"Two years ago. Claude, my husband, was made a vice president of his company. I don't know," she wiped her eyes, "everything changed. Instead of giving Jeff a little slap on the hand I . . . I really *hit* him. Instead of a spanking . . . it was a beating."

"Did you try to get help?"

Her eyes pleaded with Matt. "I was too ashamed. What kind of woman beats her own child? I kept changing pediatricians. I made up all sorts of stories. I had to change Jeff's school a few months ago. His teacher was beginning to get suspicious."

"Mrs. Desmond, hiding the problem isn't going to make it go away."

"I know there are therapy groups for people like . . . me. I went to one once. I got as far as the door. Then I ran like hell."

"Why?"

"The thought of being with those people . . . I couldn't take it."

"Those people are precisely the people you should be with. They share your problem. They understand it."

"Doctor, do you know what it's like to tell a group of strangers that you . . . beat your child? Do you know what that's like?"

"Do you?"

"I didn't have the courage to find out. I'm not a brave person. I'm not strong. When I think about it, I realize I'm not much of anything. I take out my frustrations on a helpless child. I know what that makes me."

"Mrs. Desmond," Patrick said, "you are going to have to get help. We won't turn Jeff over to you until you do."

"Half of me has been praying for someone to stop me. But the other half . . ."

"What about the other half?"

"I'm *frightened*. If Claude finds out about this he'll divorce me. He'll take everything. My marriage is no bargain, but without it, I'll have nothing."

"We sympathize, Mrs. Desmond, but Jeff is the issue here. He's being hurt physically and mentally. And the situation can only get worse. It's not just a question of his health, it's a question of his life."

"Please." She shut her eyes tight. "Please, I can't think anymore."

"Matt, I'd like a word with you."

They walked a few steps away. Patrick looked back at Mrs. Desmond. She was hunched over, crying, ripping her handkerchief to bits.

"We have to move on this, Matt. Any suggestions?"

"Dr. MacMuray in psychiatric. He's researched in the area of battered children. He knows his stuff. Let him talk to Mrs. Desmond. He can put her in touch with the right doctors, the right groups."

"Well, that's a place to start."

"Patrick, do you think we could keep this unofficial for now?"

"I don't know. There's a minor involved, that makes things complicated. I *do* know that we'll have to notify her husband."

"It's going to be hard on her."

"Jeff's welfare comes first. We have no choice."

They returned to Mrs. Desmond. "We'd like you to see one of our doctors," Patrick said. "His name is MacMuray. He's a psychiatrist who's familiar with this kind of problem. He can recommend the proper treatment for you."

"I'll . . . I'll make an appointment."

"We'd like you to see him now. Putting it off isn't going to help you or Jeff. Come with me, Mrs. Desmond, I'll introduce you to Dr. MacMuray."

"I don't want to go with you. Dr. Lansing, will you take me there?"

"Go on, Matt." Patrick nodded. "And stay with them until something is decided. I'll be in my office. Let me know."

"Are you going to call my husband? Do you have to?"

"We have to."

"That's the end of me."

"Your husband would have found out sooner or later. Mrs. Desmond, you're not in this alone. Your husband shares the responsibility for what's happened. It's time he started dealing with it."

"I'm *frightened.*"

"We'll help you," Matt said, leading her out. "We'll help you all we can."

*   *   *

"I'm talking about the hospital's *legal* position," Eve said.

"I'm talking about the hospital's *moral* position," David replied brusquely. "As long as I'm here, that comes first."

"It's my job to protect the hospital."

"It's our job to protect the patients. Quaint as that may sound to you."

David and Eve had been arguing for fifteen minutes. Now, Patrick decided that he'd heard enough. He swiveled around in his chair, banging a paperweight against the side of his desk.

"This is a waste of time," he said. "There's nothing to be gained in rehashing this."

"I want Dr. Stern reprimanded for his actions concerning the Desmond boy."

"*No*," David said. "Stern's actions were entirely *correct*."

"He didn't *know* that at the time. He was *guessing*. He could have landed us in the middle of a lawsuit."

"He had a bruised, bleeding child, and a stack of x-rays. He *wasn't* guessing."

"He accused the boy's mother."

"*Correctly*."

"He didn't *know* that at the time."

"Eve," Patrick said wearily, "it's done. If you need a scapegoat, paint the target on my back. But let's put an end to this."

"Mr. Desmond may have something to say about that."

"He *should* say thank you. Eve, we have legitimate doubts about the boy's injuries. Because of these doubts, we took steps to insure his safety. And, ultimately, Mrs. Desmond admitted that we were right. I don't see the problem."

"Million dollar lawsuits have been lost before because people didn't *see* the problem."

"For Christ's sake," David shouted, "there's a five-year-old child involved here. Is a lawsuit more important to you than his life?"

"Don't make me the heavy. I have a job to do. I'm trying to do it. If we're slapped with a summons a few months from now, someone is going to be held accountable."

"Eve, it won't be you. Does that ease your mind?"

"No, it doesn't. We must be the only hospital in the city without guidelines on cases like this. We were caught with our pants down."

"It's not the first time you were caught with *your* pants down," David said.

"Eve," Patrick put in hastily, "we haven't had to deal with this situation until now. The battered children we've seen have been brought to us by the police."

"Well, if Stern had given me a minute to check on procedure, this could have been avoided. But he had to rush right in."

"Dr. Stern did the correct thing. Period. We will stand behind him. Period. As for guidelines, okay. Talk to our lawyers and see what they say. But understand this . . . in no instance will a lawyer's decision take precedence over a doctor's decision."

"Hospitals aren't run that way."

"This one is."

"Maybe Eve would be happier at another hospital," David said. "Someplace where official policy is closer to her own thinking."

"Maybe I would."

"Don't let us stand in your way."

"Enough." Patrick slammed his fist on the desk. "I'm putting an end to this discussion. Eve, Matt will keep you informed about the Desmond matter. Is there anything else you want to talk about?"

Eve didn't reply. She stood with her arms crossed, glaring at David.

"Eve, is there anything else?"

"No." She went to the door. "Unless you're expecting thanks for all the support I *don't* get around here."

"I appreciate your efforts," Patrick said. "You're a good administrator, Eve. But medical judgments will always have priority. That's the way it is."

"Don't worry. I see *exactly* how it is."

"Well," Patrick said when she was gone, "would you care to explain?"

"Explain what?"

"You were a little rough on Eve."

"She'll get over it. She has a heart of pure granite."

"Go easy, David. Eve handles her job well. I'd rather not lose her."

"She won't leave here until she has something better lined up. Eve takes *very* good care of Eve."

Patrick looked at him. "Why all the animosity?"

"I didn't like the way she treated Dr. Stern. I didn't like her whole attitude."

"Is that all there is to it? What's really bothering you?"

"Eve didn't have one word of concern for the Desmond boy. Not one. Lola wouldn't have reacted so callously."

"Oh." Patrick smiled. "The truth at last."

"What truth?"

"David, you've been short-tempered for weeks. You've been moody and preoccupied and sour."

"While you, on the other hand, have been a barrel of laughs."

"I *know* what's bothering me. I *didn't* know what was bothering you . . . until now. Your fling with Eve is over. You want Lola back."

"I'm not going to get her back."

"Has she said that?"

"She hasn't said *anything*. She's civil. She smiles politely. She nods graciously . . . All in all, I get more warmth from my doorman."

"You're a big tipper."

"Not funny."

"David, the wounds need time to heal."

"These particular wounds may never heal."

"Lola loves you."

"She did."

"Still does. But she takes marriage seriously. You play at it."

"Playing isn't what it's cracked up to be. And that's the voice of experience speaking."

Patrick smiled. "I do believe there's hope for you yet."

The door opened and Matt walked in. His eyes were subdued; there was a weary slump to his shoulders. "Jean said you were waiting for me," he said.

"How did the Desmond thing turn out?"

"Mrs. Desmond has appointments with a psychiatrist and a counseling group. Whether she keeps the appointments remains to be seen." Matt sat down. He took a notebook from his jacket pocket. "I have the names and dates for Eve's records."

"What about *Mr.* Desmond?" David asked.

"MacMuray reached him in Los Angeles. Jeff will stay at the hospital until Desmond gets back from his trip. Thursday or Friday."

"Does he know the nature of the problem?"

"He does now. Frankly, I don't think he's going to be any help. He's mad as hell. He called his wife a monster . . . and a few other things I won't repeat. He doesn't see the sickness . . . only the shame."

"You look beat, Matt. Is the job getting to you?"

"It's not the job," Matt said slowly, "it's the things I *see* in the job."

"People are under terrible pressures these days. They react in terrible ways. We see the results here."

"No." Matt shook his dark head. "It's more than that. It's seeing what people *do* to each other. The thousand different ways they hurt each other. It isn't even intentional most of the time. It's *careless* hurt. That's the worst part. That's what I can't understand."

David glanced at Patrick. Patrick shrugged. "Out of the mouths of babes."

"What?" Matt asked.

"You hit us where we live," David said shortly. "You hit us in our guilt."

28

"Good evening, Dr. Dain." Hollis greeted Patrick at the door. "You look tired, sir."

"My usual condition. I had a strange message from Mrs. Dain. Is anything wrong?"

"Mrs. Dain is waiting for you in the sitting room."

"Hollis, is anything wrong?"

"Everything's *right*, sir," he smiled, "right as rain."

Patrick hurried past Hollis and up the stairs to the sitting room. "Ann?" he called. "Ann, what's going on?"

Ann opened the door. She was wearing a copper-colored gown of soft jersey. Her hair was piled atop her head in shining waves. There was a faint blush on her cheeks, and her eyes sparkled.

Patrick took a long look at her. "Well," he said, "I wasn't expecting . . . what is this about?"

She took his hand. "Come inside."

Patrick gazed around the sitting room in surprise. Candlelight suffused the room in pale gold. A small table by the windows had been set with silver and crystal and the first spring flowers of the season. Champagne cooled in a glistening silver bucket.

Patrick looked at Ann. "What are we celebrating?"

"Us."

"As I recall, we didn't part on especially friendly terms. What's happened since Saturday? What's changed?"

"I've changed."

"You look different. You look—"

"Happy? I am. And I want you to be happy. I want *us* to be happy together."

"We have . . . problems."

"Not anymore."

Patrick's heart leaped as he wondered if their nightmare was finally over. He looked into Ann's eyes and he saw the clear, untroubled love he'd known so well before the bad times had come. He saw Ann's smile, steady as a beacon, and his pulse quickened.

"Patrick, I've spent these months reliving my life with Bren. I got stuck in the past for a while. I got stuck in twisted dreams. But it's over now. It's over."

"Are . . . you sure?"

"I love you so much."

Relief cascaded over Patrick, washing away the pain and the dread. A feeling of joy swelled in his chest and rose into his throat. When he took Ann in his arms, he knew the promise of their future together.

"Patrick, I've been such an idiot."

"Don't talk that way about the woman I love. I do love you, Ann. Never more than at this moment."

"Do you think our lives can be the way they were?"

"Better. Because we're wiser than we were."

"You've been wise all along. You knew what I had to do."

"Don't give me too much credit, Ann. My patience was wearing thin. Another few weeks, another month, and I don't know—"

"Ssh." Ann pressed her fingers to his lips. "It's over."

"I've never heard prettier words."

Patrick sat down. Ann poured two drinks and brought them to the table. "Shall we have a toast?"

Patrick raised his glass to hers. "To all our tomorrows."

They sipped their drinks in blissful peace, savoring the sight of each other, smiling at each other, touching hands.

"You look wonderful," Patrick said.

"I feel wonderful, thanks to you. I thought . . . I was afraid it might be too late for us."

"Too late? Darling, we're just beginning."

"I'd like to tell Buddy that everything's all right. It may help him to know."

"We'll talk to Dr. DuShan this weekend . . . Can we have a whole weekend in the country, Ann? We'll walk in the woods, wade in the pond . . . stare at the moon like lovestruck kids."

"You don't have to convince me. From now on, where you go, I go. I've learned my lesson."

"Do you want to talk about it? About Bren?"

"Not yet. Not now. This evening is for us. The rest of the world can wait."

"My thoughts exactly." Patrick looked toward the door. "What's that?"

"That's your four-star dinner. Come in, Hollis."

Hollis wheeled a teakwood serving cart into the room. Daisy, in pink robe and slippers, tagged along behind him.

"Miss Daisy has come to say goodnight," Hollis explained.

"Goodnight, Ann." She kissed her.

"Goodnight, sweetheart."

Daisy threw her arms around Patrick. "Goodnight."

"Sleep well, Droopy."

"I will." Daisy took a couple of steps, then stopped and looked about the room. "Is this a party?"

"It most certainly is."

"Can I stay?"

"It's your bedtime."

"It's always my bedtime. I like parties better."

Patrick laughed. "You can have a party on your birthday. Any kind of party you want."

"*Any* kind?"

"Absolutely. Now scoot."

"Okay. Goodnight, Hollis."

"Goodnight, Miss Daisy. Straight to bed, no dawdling."

"I wonder if I should have said that. She'll want a pony at her birthday party."

"She'll settle for a magician," Ann said. "Look, there's some magic for you."

Hollis lifted the covers of the serving dishes. The roast lamb was scented with thyme, garnished with tiny mushroom caps. The plump baby carrots bubbled in a mint sauce, and the potato souffle rose in a puffy cloud.

"A veritable feast." Patrick smiled. "I could get used to this high living."

Hollis poured the champagne and then quietly left the room. Patrick looked at Ann. "Thank you," he said.

"For what?"

"For everything. For making everything perfect. For the love that went into tonight."

"You deserved a special treat."

"*You're* my special treat." Patrick took a sip of champagne. "Well, let the feast begin."

They talked and laughed all through dinner. There was no strain, no reservation, between them. They were two people in love, their struggles safely in the past, their future beckoning.

It was a leisurely evening. A half circle of moon dallied in the center of the windows for a while, then moved on. The sky was a tapestry of flickering stars, their lights falling on the shimmering blackness of the East River.

Ann blew out the candles and joined Patrick at the windows.

"What are you thinking about?" she asked.

"The day started out so badly . . . but it's ending with starlight and old brandy and a beautiful woman. I was thinking about how lucky I am."

Ann kissed him and all his senses seemed to come

alive at once. The smoothness of her skin, the fragrance of her perfume, the love in her eyes, all these rushed at him until his head swam.

"I want to make love to you," he said.

Patrick swept Ann up in his arms and carried her to the bedroom. He undressed her slowly, kissing the softness of her body as her clothing slipped away. Her nakedness pressed against him. He carried her to the bed and they embraced in a tenderness fired by passion. When their bodies met, they knew the storm and sweet reconciliation of love lost and found again.

It was five in the morning when Ann awoke. She drew the bedcovers about her and sat up. Patrick was at the desk, a large black binder open in front of him.

"Patrick, what's wrong?"

He turned. "I'm sorry, darling. I tried to be quiet. Go back to sleep."

"What's the matter?"

"This is no time to talk."

"It is if there's something to talk about. What is it? What's that black book you're always staring at?"

"Ann, we had such a wonderful evening. I don't want to break the spell."

She put her robe on and went to the desk. "What's in that book, Patrick?"

"A man's life."

"I don't understand."

"Ann, it's about Bren. Are we strong enough to

talk about him? Are we ready?"

"He can't hurt us anymore," she smiled. "We're immune."

"I . . . did something. You may not approve of what I did."

Her smile faded. "Tell me. Patrick, please tell me, you're making me nervous."

"I hired private investigators to look into Bren's past."

"What?" Ann sat down. "That's not like you at all."

"I had a few qualms. Not many. Ann, the day Bren came to my office . . . he said some awful things. He made some threats. I realized how dangerous he was. And I realized that I needed ammunition."

"What did you expect to find? What *did* you find?"

Patrick stroked Ann's cheek. "Are you sure you want to talk about this?"

"You can't tell me anything about Bren I don't already know, or suspect."

"I wish that were true."

"Patrick, I've spent these months examining my life with Bren. I know what he was. I know what he is. I know the ugliness in him."

"This is uglier than you imagine."

"Tell me what you found out."

"It concerns Bren and his wife Irene."

"Yes?"

"If you'll remember, Bren came to New York shortly after Irene's death."

"I remember."

"Irene had pneumonia. That was the . . . *official* cause of her death."

Ann heard the shading in Patrick's voice. It took her another moment to understand his meaning. "Did you find a *different* cause?"

"I'm afraid so."

"Bren?"

There was the smallest pause before Patrick replied. "I'm afraid so."

Ann tensed, but her gaze was steady. "How?"

"Irene may or may not have recovered from her pneumonia. But Bren intervened. He made certain that she did *not*. At first, he withheld her medicine. That must have seemed too risky, so he changed his plan."

Patrick paced the length of the bedroom. He was concentrating hard, choosing each word with great care.

"Bren," he continued, "got his hands on a quantity of sleeping pills. He waited. On the day of Irene's death, she had begun to show some improvement, but was still quite feverish. I believe that Bren gave her the sleeping pills in a glass of lemonade. I believe that he waited a while, then called the doctor. Shortly after the doctor arrived, Irene went into respiratory failure. Naturally, the doctor assumed the pneumonia caused her lungs to fail. An ambulance was called, but it was too late."

Patrick sat down. He wiped his forehead. "That's it."

"But . . . didn't anyone suspect?" Ann asked, dazed.

"No one. There was no reason for suspicion.

381

When you think about it, it's *fantastic*. It is *impossible* to make something like that look like natural causes unless *everything* falls *exactly* right. For Bren's purposes, everything fell exactly right. It couldn't happen again in a thousand years, in two thousand."

"Patrick, could there be a mistake?"

"I've read this report so often I know it by heart. The conclusion is inescapable. I also showed the report to David. Some years ago, he had a case along these lines—a man who gave his wife an insulin overdose. It all came back to him when he read this report. There's only *one* conclusion."

"But it's incredible. I can't believe Bren could plan something so complicated. I can't remember him ever planning *anything*. He didn't know *how* to think ahead."

"He learned."

"Why would he want Irene dead?"

"Money. Our money. Look at the sequence of events, Ann. Bren reads about us in the newspapers and a few months later his wife is dead and he's knocking on our door."

"I thought the timing was suspicious, but I never dreamed . . . is there proof?"

"Enough for an exhumation." Patrick gave the binder to Ann. "I've marked several pages for you to read. Are you up to it?"

"Yes."

"I'll get us some coffee."

Patrick left and Ann opened the binder. A dozen pages were marked with paper clips, many sentences underlined in red. She read the pages slowly, pausing to digest the multitude of small details. When she finished, she read the pages a second time.

Patrick returned with steaming mugs of coffee. "Well, what do you think?"

"I don't know what to say."

"It's all in the report."

"That's what I mean. I knew Bren was capable of terrible things . . . but I never dreamed he was capable of . . . of this."

Patrick sat down next to Ann. "Are you all right? You're very pale."

"It's the shock. Patrick," she looked at him wide-eyed. "I just had an awful thought. What about Daisy? He might hurt her."

"He has no reason to hurt her now. As a matter of fact, he needs her."

"We can't depend on that."

"Not indefinitely, no. That's why I've decided . . . we'll have to move for custody of Daisy."

"He wouldn't let you have her. If you push him . . . Patrick, I'm afraid."

"Don't be. Either way, Bren will have no choice in the matter."

"Either way?"

"This report leaves me with three options. I can do nothing. Or I can notify the Massachusetts authorities. Or I can handle it in my own way."

"You can't do nothing."

"No, I can't. Whichever of the two other options I choose, Bren will be in no position to retain custody of Daisy."

"*Whichever?* You *have* to notify the authorities."

Patrick got up. He walked around the room, his head bent in thought.

"You're scaring me," Ann said.

"Why?"

"Because I think you're going to try to handle this yourself. Because I think you're going to get hurt."

"I can take care of myself."

Ann ran to him. "You don't know what you're dealing with. Bren must be *insane* to have done that to Irene. There's no telling what he'll do next."

"Ann, there's nothing he *can* do. It's over for him. But there are people for whom it's *not* over. Daisy. Buddy. Their lives are just beginning. What would it do to them to know their father is . . . what he is?"

"Daisy is young. She's strong. But Buddy . . ."

"I don't know if he can stand another shock. I'd rather not find out."

"Maybe he wouldn't have to know."

"Things like this don't remain secret, especially when the Dain name is involved."

"You've given this a lot of thought. You've already made up your mind."

"No. I don't know what I'm going to do. I need more time, it's not an easy decision."

"Patrick, if Bren knows he has nothing to lose, he's liable to do anything. And he'll do it to you. He *hates* you."

"I'm aware of that."

"You're very calm about all this."

"I've had plenty of time to think about it. Bren can't hurt me, much as he'd like to. But he can hurt

384

Daisy and Buddy."

Ann picked up the binder. "I suppose I should read the whole report."

"It's extremely unpleasant reading. Irene worked and worked and worked some more. Bren did nothing but abuse her. She was only thirty when she died. There's a picture of her in there. She looks closer to fifty."

Ann put the binder on the desk. "Maybe I won't read it. It's beginning to sound too familiar."

"I'm sorry you had to know, Ann."

"Don't be sorry for me. Be sorry for Irene."

"I am."

"If only she'd left him!"

"She had a child, no money, lots of debts. She couldn't go anywhere. Unfortunately, she wasn't the kind of woman to kick Bren out." Patrick took Ann's hand. "You know the story, darling, you lived it yourself."

"But my story turned out differently."

"Thank God it did."

"Patrick, you said Bren made threats. What threats?"

"They're not important anymore."

"I have to know."

"He didn't threaten physical violence . . . he threatened emotional violence. Bren planned to destroy our marriage. He hoped that would break you, and me. It wasn't *just* money he was after. He wanted to punish us."

"Bren wanted to punish *me*. You were an afterthought. I remember the night he began to hate me." Ann sighed. "That was twenty-five years ago. He's carried that hate around ever since."

"His mind is twisted. It no longer matters why or how."

Ann opened the binder. She turned the pages until she came to Irene's picture. She saw the face of a once-pretty woman aged too soon by work and worry. Deep frown lines were etched into her forehead. Her hair was dull and sprinkled with gray. She looked mournful, as if she had not smiled in many years.

Tears welled in Ann's eyes. "I wonder if Bren thinks about her."

Patrick closed the binder. He turned Ann to him. "I don't want you to dwell on this. You'll make yourself sick."

"Bren has to pay for what he did."

"He will. One way or another."

29

The radiant May sunshine lit up the countryside as Sally Tarlton drove toward Twin Oaks. She drove slowly, stopping along the way to admire the untamed land. It reminded her of home. There were sunny ribbons of wildflowers, bright jagged patches of yellow and violet and white, growing in every direction. The trees were tall and proud and a hundred different shades of green. The birds flew back and forth between their nests, calling merrily to each other, playfully dipping their wings.

Sally passed a clump of tangled berry bushes and she smiled, for she remembered the wild berries she'd picked as a child. She would, she thought, take Buddy home one day. She would show him the bluebells and poke-daisys that grew near General Lee Creek. She would show him the Spanish moss and the honeysuckle and the ancient willows.

The landscape changed abruptly as Sally neared Twin Oaks. Here the grounds were neatly trimmed, the trees carefully pruned. She saw beds of daffodils and tulips, and as she turned into the driveway, she saw anemonies bordering the path.

Sally leaned over the steering wheel, staring out of the window toward the main house. She'd made the trip to Twin Oaks every week and sometimes Buddy had been at the door to welcome her. Now, she saw Mark DuShan standing there and her heart jumped. She parked the car and hurried to him.

"Is something wrong with Buddy?" she asked anxiously.

"Nothing at all. I didn't mean to alarm you. I wanted to talk to you."

Mark smiled at her. He liked Sally, and he'd decided that she would have to be the key that unlocked the door in Buddy's mind.

"What do you want to talk about?"

"I'd like to confide in you, Sally. May I?"

"Yes." She nodded.

"Buddy has made some progress. But that progress will stop unless he takes the next step."

"What can I do?"

"It's crucial for him to remember the night of his breakdown. I've tried and tried to lead him through it, but we stall at the same point each time. He's fighting me. I'm hoping he won't fight you."

"Do you want me to talk to him about that night?"

"You must do it subtly or he'll cut you off. Try little reminders. Small details are often the most important."

She reached into her pocket and removed a square white envelope. "I have a card for Buddy. It's from the last patient he saw that night, Mr. Lewis."

"That's perfect. Give it to him, but don't make a

fuss about it. I think he'll have a strong reaction to that card. Don't let him hide it. Try to draw him out."

"I understand."

"Sally, he may be angry with you for mentioning that night. The anger will pass, I promise."

"Anything that gets Buddy well is fine with me."

"One more thing. I usually monitor Buddy's visits on the screen in my office. This time I'd like to be closer. Do you have any objection?"

"I don't. Buddy might."

"He won't see me. I'll be just outside the door. It sounds sneaky," Mark smiled, "but I have my reasons."

"Are you expecting trouble?"

"Only temporarily. Are you game?"

"I'm game."

They went into the house. Mark led Sally down the hall to the music room. "Easy does it," he said as she went inside.

Buddy was sitting on the couch. He looked calm and rested, though his eyes were dark and far away.

"Hi, Buddy."

Buddy stood up. He kissed her. "I thought maybe you weren't coming."

"Why would you think a thing like that?"

"It's such a long trip. I wish you'd let Patrick get you a driver. I don't like the idea of your being all alone on these roads."

"I've been driving on country roads since I was fourteen. It's *city* driving that gives me the shakes."

"What if you have a flat tire?"

"You must think I'm an absolute ninny." Sally laughed. "If I have a flat, I'll change it."

"Do you know how?"

"My daddy wouldn't let us drive until we could all but take a car apart and put it back together again. I'm a pretty fair mechanic, if I say so myself."

"Really? I can't picture you sweating over some grubby engine."

"Southern ladies don't sweat, suh, they glow."

"I'll remember that." He smiled.

"One of these days you'll meet my daddy. I'm going to take you down home and show you off all over Paroo County."

Buddy glanced away. "Don't count on it," he said. "I'm going to be here a long time."

"You'll be leaving here before you know it."

"No. I'm . . . sick."

"You're going to get better. Everybody's pulling for you. Everybody's rooting hard as they can. With all that good feeling vibrating around, you can't help but get better."

"I'm not kidding, Sally. I can finally admit that I'm . . . sick."

"That's a positive sign right there. Every week, every day, you're getting better. Buddy, you'll be out of here in no time at all. I know it."

"You *don't* know. Nobody does."

"I know *you*. Someplace way deep down, you believe in yourself. You just have to find that place again."

"I don't think I can."

Sally stared into his eyes. "All you have to do is

try. Don't be afraid."

Buddy walked over to the piano. He ran his fingers lightly over the keys. "I always wanted to learn how to play."

"It's not too late. My sister's a whiz on the piano. You'll meet her when we go home. My family has an old red spinet—"

"Stop it! Why do you keep talking about going home? I'm not going anywhere."

"I want you to know my family," Sally said gently. "I want them to know you. They'll like you."

"Why should they? My *own* family doesn't like me."

"That's a big fat lie. And that's enough gloomy talk for one morning. Come sit by me and see what I brought you."

"Did you get the toy for Happy?"

"Come see for yourself."

Buddy returned to the couch and sat down. "Okay." He smiled. "Let's have the goodies."

Sally opened her large canvas tote bag. "Here we are," she said. "Milky Ways for you. A rubber bone for Happy. Peanuts for the squirrels. Notes from people at the hospital. And this." She gave him the square white envelope. "Open that one first. It's special."

Buddy took the card out of the envelope. He frowned, unable to make out the signature. "Who's it from?"

"Mr. Lewis."

Buddy dropped the card. "Mr. Lewis is dead."

"If he is, he's the healthiest looking dead man I

ever saw. He came by the hospital to ask about you. He wanted me to give you that card."

"He's *dead.*"

"Buddy." Sally turned his face to hers. "Mr. Lewis is fine. He's been fine for weeks."

Buddy swept the gifts off the couch. "You're *lying.* Why are you lying to me?"

"He *was* sick. But he got better. You're confused, honey. Think back. The last time you saw him, he was very sick. Do you remember that?"

Buddy jumped up. "No." He walked away. "*No.*"

Sally went after him. "Try and remember."

Buddy turned his back on her. He felt dizzy and weak. He had trouble catching his breath.

"Try and remember. We were in ward 301. It was late at night. I was with you. Matt was there too."

"*No.*"

"All the wards were dark," Sally continued, "except for 301. Do you remember?"

Fear began to crawl over Buddy. It started in his chest and spread outward to every part of his body. He felt cold, then hot; perspiration dripped from his forehead. He doubled over, straining for breath.

"Mr. Lewis was very sick," Sally said, fighting back her tears. "He had a terrible cough. Do you remember how hard he was coughing?"

Buddy began to tremble. The room dimmed. It went in and out of focus, narrowing, then lengthening, like the mirror in a funhouse. He staggered away, clutching at the furniture to steady himself.

"*God,*" he cried. "What's happening to me? I feel so . . . what's *happening?*"

Mark DuShan walked into the room. "Wait in my office, Sally," he said calmly. "Don't worry, we're almost there."

"Doctor, I—"

"Do as I ask. Please," he said and Sally ran out.

Mark closed the door. He locked it. "Dr. O'Hara?"

"I'm . . . going to faint."

"You won't faint."

"Help . . . me," Buddy gasped. "My head is pounding."

"Listen to me, Dr. O'Hara. It's late at night. You're at Rhinelander Pavillion. All the wards are dark except for 301. You're in 301. What do you see?"

"See? I . . . don't see . . . anyone."

"Who's in 301 with you? Who do you see?"

Buddy swayed slightly. "Fog. There's fog . . . the fog is coming closer . . . it's all around me."

"The fog is gone now. It's all gone. You're in 301. Who do you see?"

"Sally is there."

"Who else?"

"Matt. He's watching me . . . watching . . . waiting."

"Who else is there?"

"Nurses."

"Who else, Dr. O'Hara?"

"Nobody." Buddy shook his head. "Nobody else."

"There are patients in 301. You're there to see your patient. Your patient is very sick. Who is he?"

"No." Buddy began to cry. "No patients. No patients."

"Your patient is lying in bed. He's very sick. He has a terrible cough. Can you hear him coughing?"

Buddy shut his eyes. "Oh, God. Oh, God," he moaned.

"You're standing at your patient's bedside. What do you see?"

"No patients. There . . . are . . . no . . . patients."

"You're leaning over the bed. Your patient is looking at you. He's coughing. He's very sick. He needs your help."

Buddy screamed. It was a horrible sound, full of anguish and suffering. There were more screams, as sharp and desperate as the screams of Hell.

"Who do you see, Dr. O'Hara?"

"Mr. Lewis. It's Mr. Lewis. He's dying . . . Oh, God, he's dying. It's my fault."

"Why is it your fault?"

Buddy turned. He took a step, then fell down. He pulled himself up only to fall again. "I *can't*. I can't."

Mark helped him into a chair. "Dr. O'Hara, why is it your fault?"

"The infection. Staph. I didn't report it."

"Why didn't you report it?"

"Couldn't."

"Why not?"

"Couldn't. Couldn't make a mistake."

"Everybody makes mistakes, Dr. O'Hara."

"No, I couldn't."

"Why not?"

"Can't make mistakes. Can't. I have to be . . . the

best." Buddy's breath came in short, quick bursts. "Always have to be the best."

"Why?"

"I have to . . . show him."

Mark sat back. He relaxed a little, for he knew that the key had turned and the door was opening. "Why do you have to show him?"

Buddy's chest shook with sobs. His eyes were glazed, fixed in another time and place. "So he'll like me again. If he likes me . . . he'll come back. We won't be alone anymore."

"Who? Who'll come back?"

"He's gone. We're all alone now," Buddy said. His voice was strange, the voice of a child. "Jill and me and Ma. Ma says he isn't ever coming back . . . but he'll come back . . . if I'm very good, he'll come back."

"Who'll come back?"

"I don't want to talk about it."

"*Who'll* come back?" Mark persisted.

Buddy started out of his chair. "No, don't!" he shouted.

Mark held him down. "What do you see?"

"He's *hitting* me . . . it *hurts* . . . he's cursing me . . . and hitting me . . . Ma's trying to stop him . . . he's hitting *Ma*. There's blood . . . there's blood all over."

Buddy blinked a few times, as if he were coming out of a dream. His sobs slowed, then stopped. He looked around the room in confusion. Finally, Buddy looked up at Mark. "He left the next day and never came back. Until this past January."

"Who is 'he,' Dr. O'Hara?"

Buddy rubbed his eyes. He looked around the room again, still unsure of his surroundings. "What did you say?"

"I asked you who 'he' is."

"My father. I'm talking about my . . ." Buddy stared at Mark, his eyes round with surprise. "I don't believe it! For fifteen years, I thought it was my fault that my father left us. For fifteen years, I drove myself, pushed myself . . . because of *him*."

Mark smiled. "Exactly."

"But . . . why?"

"Consider what happened. Your father beat you that night. He spoke cruelly to you. And the very next day he was gone forever. Your child's mind put all those facts together, and put all the blame on your head. You grew up, but you continued to blame yourself. The guilt got stronger. Your father's reappearance was the last straw."

"Is it . . . over?"

"You tell me. How do you feel?"

"I don't know. I feel . . . different."

"We have a lot of work ahead of us. But the worst is over," Mark said. "Right now, you'd better have a shower and a nap. We'll talk more about this later."

Buddy stood up. His legs were weak, but this time he did not fall.

"Ready?"

"Wait a minute . . . was Sally here before?"

"Sally's still here. You can see her at lunch. After you've rested."

"She brought me a card. I want to see it."

Buddy went to the couch. He sorted through the

notes until he found the card he wanted. "I thought so. It's from Mr. Lewis," he explained, "a patient of mine. Wasn't that nice of him?"

"Very nice," Mark agreed, silently bidding goodbye to the last of Buddy's delusions.

Mark unlocked the door. Mayo was waiting in the hall.

"There were a few bets that you wouldn't come out of here alive," she said.

"Alive and well." Mark laughed. "Dr. O'Hara is all yours now. A shower, a nap, 2 milligrams diazepam."

"Yes, sir." Mayo looked at Buddy. His wet hair was pasted to his head. His shirt was drenched. "Dr. O'Hara, will you come with me?"

Buddy walked to the door. He turned to Mark. Twice he started to speak, twice he changed his mind. "Thanks," he said finally.

Mark watched as Buddy went off with Mayo. He was elated, for he knew that Buddy's healing had begun. He smiled broadly as Sally ran toward him.

"Does your smile mean what I hope it means?" she asked.

"The news is very good."

"You were in there so long."

"Buddy had a hard time of it." Mark nodded. "He had to remember painful things. But the remembering freed his mind."

"You mean . . . he's better? He's really better?"

"He really is," Mark said happily.

Sally eyes lit up. She beamed. "Dr. DuShan, I can't tell you how grateful I am."

"There's still work to be done, but the problems

are out in the open now. I must thank you for that. You kept at him."

"Will he forgive me?"

"He already has. Sally, you're going to begin to see a different Buddy. He'll certainly be less intense. There'll be other differences."

"Do you want to know if I'm prepared? I am."

"I didn't doubt it," Mark smiled at her. "Not for a moment."

Sally stood outside on the patio, waiting for Buddy. The scent of flowers drifted toward her, and somewhere a radio was playing Chopin, but she paid little attention. Her thoughts were on Buddy. It had been more than three hours since she'd left him in the music room and it seemed even longer than that. She ached to see him, to assure herself that he was all right, that his pain was gone.

"Buddy . . . Buddy, here I am." She waved.

Buddy saw her. He was at her side in four quick strides. "Sally." He hugged her. "Hey, I'm sorry."

"There's nothing to be sorry about."

"You must have been here for hours. I'm a little disoriented." Buddy shrugged. "I don't remember much of what happened. I remember being with you, but the next thing I knew I was talking to Dr. DuShan. And I was a mess."

They sat down. The sunlight caught and held in Buddy's blond hair. His eyes were a clear, serene blue.

"You're beautiful now." Sally ruffled his hair. "I hear it was a rough session. But a good one."

"I guess so. It was weird . . . For a while there, I

was eleven years old again. My father was beating hell out of me. And screaming, you never heard such screaming."

"You don't have to talk about it."

"I don't mind. See, my father's been at the root of my problems all along. Can you believe that? I mean, if I'd just let it all out when I was a kid, I would have been okay. If I'd yelled and cried and thrown my toys at the wall . . . but I didn't. I kept it all inside. Until finally, BOOM."

"Buddy O'Hara, I'm so proud of you."

"Proud? I've been a bastard. I've been impossible. I'm *still* half a basket case."

"You faced the truth. Mean and ugly as it was, you faced it. That makes me proud."

"It was DuShan. He kept pushing, pushing, pushing. He wouldn't give up."

"Aren't you glad?"

"Now I am. I feel different. My mind feels . . . vacuumed."

"*What?*"

"No kidding. It's as if someone put a vacuum in there and cleaned out all the cobwebs."

Sally leaned her head on Buddy's shoulder. "As long as I've known you, there's been an edge in your voice. You know what? It's not there anymore."

"Am I beginning to sound like a normal person? In time," Buddy smiled, "I may actually *be* a normal person. Who knows?"

"It's terrific to see you smile. Keep it up."

"Keep reminding me."

Buddy looked out at the grounds of Twin Oaks.

"Hi, Walter," he called. "How about billiards later on?"

The man, thirtyish, athletic-looking, nodded affirmatively and walked on.

"A friend of yours?" Sally asked.

"Sometimes we eat together. Sometimes we shoot pool. Do you know what he did?"

"Tell me."

"He bought a gun. Out of the blue, he got an urge to buy a gun and he did. Then, a week later, he went out and shot all the cars parked on Eighty-first Street. He shot sixteen cars and one moped."

"Why?"

"He doesn't know. That's why he's here. Twin Oaks is one fascinating place."

"You'll be leaving soon."

"Not until I'm completely well. I was thinking about this before I came downstairs. Sally, I want to go back to medicine."

"That's where you belong. It would be plain sinful to let your talent go to waste."

"But I won't go back until I'm healthy."

"Buddy, Dr. DuShan told me the worst is over. And he's right. I see the change in you already."

"I'm not going to rush it. I have too much to figure out. I've been terrible to Ma and Patrick . . . and Matt. Hell, I've been terrible to everybody. I have to know why. I have to get to know myself. Does that sound crazy?"

"It sounds like a man making peace with himself."

"What I'm trying to say is . . . it may take time. It could be weeks or it could be *months.*"

"I understand."

"It'll be a while before I can pick up my career. It'll be a while before I start leading a normal life."

"Buddy O'Hara, are you *warning* me?"

"I guess I am. Weeks, months, I don't know how long it's going to take. That's . . . a lot to ask of anyone."

Sally knew what he was trying to say. She smiled. "However long it takes, I'll be with you."

30

A dozen people were gathered in Patrick's office. The atmosphere here was festive, replete with champagne and hors d'oeuvres and a three-tiered cake marked CONGRATULATIONS.

"Well," Patrick came up to David, "do you think Matt will sign the contract?"

"I always say there's nothing like a little peer pressure to urge a man on. How can he refuse us *all?*"

"I love your subtlety." Patrick laughed. "I hope Matt feels the same way."

The intercom buzzed three times and the group quieted.

"Surprise!" they shouted as Matt entered the room.

Matt stopped. He looked around, then looked behind him to see if their greeting was meant for someone else.

"Come in, Matt," David called. "You're the guest of honor."

"I am? . . . Why?"

David waved a thick sheaf of documents in the

air. "This is your contract signing party."

Applause rippled through the room. Matt looked at all the smiling, expectant faces and he was genuinely touched. Two spots of color brightened his cheeks. His black eyes were luminous.

"Speech!" someone cried. "Speech!"

"Oh, no." David took Matt's arm, steering him to the desk. "Signing first, speeches later."

"Matt," Patrick smiled, "this whole party was David's doing. Don't let his intimidation go for naught."

Matt stared at the contracts. Suddenly he remembered his first day in medical school. He remembered himself as he'd been then, alone, vulnerable, yet unafraid. He'd been brash, and sometimes too sure. In those days, he hadn't known there were limits.

Now, he was glad that those days were behind him. His brashness had been mellowed by time and by responsibility. He'd learned well the limits of people, of medicine, of life, even as he recognized the infinite possibilities. Rhinelander Pavillion, he knew, had stilled the worst in him, and found the best.

Matt looked up. "David, are you certain?"

"Do you know the price of champagne?" David smiled. "Sign!"

"Patrick?"

"With my blessings."

Matt picked up a pen and signed all three copies with swift, broad strokes. "It's official." He grinned.

There was more applause, and the sound of

champagne corks popping. People crowded around, offering handshakes and congratulations. Several nurses planted loud kisses on his cheeks.

"How do you feel?" David asked.

"I'm overwhelmed . . . and I'm *very* grateful."

"We need you here, Matt."

"You and Patrick make a pretty effective team, with or without me."

"Yes. I handle the small and medium problems that come up almost daily. Patrick handles the big problems whenever they come up. But *you* make both our jobs easier."

"Mine too." Lola joined them. "Congratulations, Matt. Let me add some lipstick to your collection," she said, kissing him. "I'm delighted that you're staying. We all are."

"Please, this praise is going to my head."

"You'll hear a lot more before the day is over." David nodded toward the other guests. "Why don't you greet your admiring public?"

"I think I will. See you later."

Lola looked at David. "Why did you chase him away?"

"I wanted to talk to you. This seemed like a good opportunity. This seemed like the *only* opportunity."

"Oh, David, we have nothing to say."

"I have plenty to say."

"Such as?"

"I'm sorry, Lola. I've never been so sorry in my life."

"That doesn't change anything, even if it's true."

404

"Of course it's true!"

"What does it change?"

"*I've* changed. I want to talk to you about that. I love you, Lola, I want to talk to you about that too."

"You love me and I love you. But it wasn't enough to keep our marriage together, was it?"

"It's enough to put our marriage *back* together . . . if we want to . . . if we try."

"Probably. But how long would it *stay* together?"

David stared into Lola's cool green eyes. "It's not like you to be so hard."

"How should I be? You're acting like a bad child who expects to be punished and then forgiven. I don't want your apologies and I don't want to punish you. You misunderstand."

"No, I don't. I *am* sorry and you *do* deserve an apology. But that isn't all there is to it. More than Eve, more than my indiscretion is involved here. I know that."

"Do you?"

"I betrayed a trust. What's worse, I betrayed it casually."

A tiny smile played at the corners of Lola's mouth. "You *have* been thinking."

"In some respects, I'm not a very worthy character. I see that now. For too many years I did exactly as I pleased. I didn't take anything seriously. It was fun and games. That's a difficult habit to break. I admit I didn't try."

"What makes you think it's going to be any different now?"

"Eve's still available. I don't want her. This city

is teeming with available women. I don't want them either. You're the one and only woman I want, Lola. I've tried living without you. It's no good. It's miserable."

"That's flattering."

"It wasn't meant to be flattering. It's the truth."

"David, I don't know. This experience has been painful. It hurt like *hell*. I don't want to go through that again."

"I've learned something about pain myself."

"Maybe you have. I still don't know."

"Look, I didn't put any effort into our marriage. I'm ready to, now. I want to. I *want* our marriage."

"You say that today . . . but a month from today, or a year . . . *eventually*, some pretty little thing will come by, wiggling her hips at you. What then?"

"No pretty little thing is worth it. Lola, I didn't know what I was losing. I didn't understand the risk . . . Life is a matter of choices. I've made my choice and there's no going back."

She gazed out at the party. The guests stood in small groups, laughing, drinking, enjoying themselves. It had been a long time, Lola thought, since she'd enjoyed herself. There'd been a hollow space in her chest, a space only David could fill. She glanced at him and she felt a familiar warmth wash over the emptiness.

"Lola, can't we at least talk about it? Can't we try?"

"I'm . . . free tonight. We can talk. But I'm not promising anything. And you're not going to con me into anything. I have to be sure . . . *absolutely* sure."

"I'm only asking you to hear me out. I won't pressure you. I *couldn't* con you if I tried. Just say you'll listen."

"I'll listen."

Patrick came up behind David. "I've been watching you two," he smiled. "Do I detect good news in the offing?"

"I'll probably regret it," Lola said, "but I agreed to hear him out."

"Ah, the silver-tongued devil strikes again."

"Thanks a lot, Patrick."

"You're welcome. And what are you waiting for? The night's young, the neighborhood's full of romantic little cafes . . . Get going."

"We'll say goodbye to Matt."

"Don't interrupt him. He's trying to get to Holly. I think there's going to be good news there too."

"Matt and Holly?" David asked.

"Why not? They've been seeing each other for almost a year. His future's secure now. Look at him, he's obviously anxious to get to her."

Matt threaded his way through the crowd. He stopped often to exchange words and smiles with the assembled staff members, though he kept one eye on Holly.

"Coming," he called to her, pushing past the last group of well-wishers. "Here I am. I didn't think I'd make it."

Holly smiled up at him. Her blond hair was in soft ringlets about her face. She'd changed out of her uniform into a dazzling dress of bright cherry-red.

"Holly, you put every other woman in the room to shame. You look great."

"I bought this dress especially for the party." She spun around. "You like?"

"I like. But why didn't you tell me about the party?"

"It was supposed to be a surprise. Don't you like surprises?"

"Sometimes."

"You liked this one. I saw how you looked when you walked in. Your face lit up like a Christmas tree."

"I couldn't believe it. I never had a surprise party before. I never had *any* kind of party before."

"Never? What about birthdays?"

"Birthdays were like all other days. School and work and chores."

"Poor thing. You never had any fun."

"It wasn't quite that bad." Matt smiled. "All the kids I knew were in the same boat."

"I'll make it up to you. Marry me and you'll have as many birthday parties as you want. We'll have parties all the time."

Matt didn't speak. His eyes were thoughtful and very dark.

"Don't look so pained," Holly said. "I was only kidding. I like to kid you. I like to see you turn green whenever I mention marriage."

"You've mentioned marriage a lot lately."

"Maybe I've been overdoing it. I'll have to find something else to kid you about."

"But you're not kidding. You're serious."

"Serious? Me?"

"You want to get married."

"Yes, I want to. But," she added hastily, "I'm willing to wait."

"That would be a mistake."

"Okay, let's find a justice of the peace."

Matt took her hand and led her to the couch. "Sit down, Holly."

"Whoops. I don't like the sound of that."

"It's time we talked."

"Now? This is a party."

"Holly, I keep making excuses not to talk about us. I've put it off long enough."

"Forget what I said. I won't mention the subject again."

"You have every right to mention it."

"I'm happy with things the way they are, Matt. Let's leave it at that."

"I can't. Because you're not happy, not really. You're *waiting*. You're waiting for something that . . . isn't going to happen."

"That's what I call coming straight to the point."

"I'm trying to be honest. From the beginning, I told you I wasn't ready for marriage."

"And I accepted it."

"For a while, yes."

"Matt, you didn't say you'd *never* be ready. If I want to wait, what's wrong with that?"

"I care about you . . . I don't want you to be disappointed."

"I'm not the girl of your dreams. Is that it?"

"I love you, Holly. I love being with you. But that doesn't include marriage. I've seen what happens when people get married too soon. I'm not going to do that to myself or anyone else."

"How do you know it's too soon?"

"I know I won't marry anyone until I'm settled *inside*. I don't want to be another Senator Josephson. I don't want to be a rat."

"So that's it. You haven't been the same since you met him. Now I understand why."

"It's not just him. David and Lola had their problems too . . . it's no secret why. Do you think I'd put you through that?"

"You're making too much of this. Let's let things go on as they were. Then we'll see."

"Holly, I know myself. I *can't* give you what you want. I'm not ready."

"That's not it." She shook her head sadly. "If you really loved me, all this other stuff wouldn't make any difference. If you really loved me, you'd follow your heart, and to hell with caution."

"Holly—"

"No, that's all right. I've known how you felt all along. I guess I was hoping that lightning would strike . . . that you'd wake up one morning and decide you couldn't live without me."

"I do love you, Holly," he said gently.

"You're fond of me. And we have fun together. But that's not love. You're not the only one who made up excuses not to talk about us. *I* didn't want to talk about us . . . because I knew what we'd say."

"I'm sorry. The last thing I wanted to do was hurt you."

"I know that." Holly wiped her eyes. She smiled. "Lansing, you're *not* a rat. You're a bee who has to pollinate all the flowers . . . but when you finally meet the right woman . . . you'll marry her, and you'll go home to her every night, and you'll be happy. I'm just not the right woman."

Holly stood up. She took a glass of champagne from the table and drank it quickly. "I'm going to miss you."

"We'll see each other."

"But it won't be the same, will it?" She stood on tiptoe and kissed his cheek. "So long, Lansing."

Matt watched her cut through the crowd to the door. He sighed.

"Trouble?" Patrick asked.

"One door opens, another closes."

"No doors are closed to you anymore. Matt?" Patrick followed his gaze. He saw Holly leave the party. "Where is she going?"

"Away from me."

"Aren't you going to go after her?"

"*I* sent her away."

"That's not the smartest thing you've ever done."

"It may be the kindest. Holly was getting serious. She would have been hurt."

"You surprise me, Matt. Isn't marriage in your plans?"

"Someday. Right now, I'm a bad risk."

"I suppose you have a few more wild oats to sow?"

Matt smiled. "That's one way of putting it. I'm not ready to settle down yet. Holly said my attitude would change when I met the right woman. Maybe that's true."

"I guarantee it is. It's rather like being hit over the head with a blunt instrument. One's perceptions change."

"I can hardly wait."

"Matt, I'm curious. Why did you choose today, this party, to come to terms with Holly?"

"Job insecurity was the last excuse I had for not making a move. When I signed the contract, that excuse was gone. Holly expected me to say something. I knew I *had* to say something. And I knew it had to be honest . . . The Josephsons showed me what happens when people keep lying to each other."

"The Josephsons?"

"I was beginning to enjoy my rakish reputation. Then I met the Josephsons . . . I knew I didn't want to be like him. Nor did I want to be married to a woman like his wife."

"Their circumstances are . . . unusual, Matt."

"I'm not judging them. If anything, I'm grateful to them. They made me think."

"Showed you the error of your ways, did they?"

"They showed me sorrow. A marriage like theirs must be a special kind of agony."

Lenore Josephson floated around her bedroom in a cloud of barbiturates. She yawned a few times, but more often she laughed, for she felt light-hearted and a little giddy. She tottered from one end of the room to the other, poking at old photographs and mementos, at the souvenirs of her life.

Eight pieces of unopened luggage stood in the corner. The luggage had been left there the week before, when she'd returned from Twin Oaks. She'd refused to unpack or to have anyone unpack for her; only today had she understood why. She looked at the cases, giving each one a kick, then weaving away.

Lenore was dressed in a long pink lace nightgown with white lace straps. Her lips and cheeks were glossed with pink color and there were pink and white combs in her hair. She looked at herself in the mirror. All the hard edges were gone from her face. She laughed, for she looked soft and dewy and young again.

Lenore made her way to the bed. She fell back against it with a whoosh, gleefully bouncing up and down. The bouncing began to make her dizzy and she stopped. She sat up, reaching for the bottle of pills on her night table.

The bottle had been almost full two hours ago; now, only a handful remained. She shook the last pills out and swallowed them one by one, forcing them down with large gulps of water. She pulled the telephone onto the bed, cradling the receiver in her lap, dialing slowly. She got three wrong numbers before she heard Patrick's voice.

"Hello, Patrick . . . it's me . . . *me,* your old friend Lenore," she giggled. "No, I'm fine . . . fine and dandy . . . listen, I never felt better in my . . . in my . . ."

Lenore yawned. Sleep was beginning to close in on her now. She saw the blessed darkness coming nearer and she smiled, for with the darkness was peace.

"What's that, Patrick?" she asked, swaying from

side to side. "No, I'm not alone . . . my house-keeper is here . . . Patrick? . . . who's this? . . . Matt who? . . . do I know you? . . . Where's Patrick? . . . who's this? . . . Matt who? . . . I want Patrick . . . no . . . don't want to . . . talk . . . to you."

Lenore threw the phone on the floor. It was an effort to think, to remain upright, but she was not yet ready to let go.

"Just . . . another minute," she whispered. "Just give . . . me . . . one more . . . minute."

Lenore took a photograph and a small box from her night table. She ripped the photograph into long strips, tossing them into the air, watching them fall. She lay back on the bed then, carefully arranging the folds of her gown. She opened the box and removed a single shining razor blade. There was a smile on her face as she drove the blade into her wrist. She sighed. She closed her eyes and the darkness came.

Patrick pounded on the door on the Josephsons' apartment. A heavyset woman in a gray uniform opened the door.

"I'm not deaf. What is . . . Dr. Dain, is that you, sir?"

Patrick pushed past her into the apartment. "Where's Mrs. Josephson?"

"In the bedroom, I think."

"Show me. Hurry!"

"What is it, Doctor?"

"*Hurry*, Mrs. Pomeroy."

She led Patrick through a deep, paneled hallway.

"There." She pointed. "That's Mrs. Josephson's bedroom."

Patrick went inside. Lenore lay on the bed, framed in the lights of the bedside lamps.

"Lenore? Lenore, are you . . ." Patrick stopped. "My *God*," he said.

The white silk sheets and spreads were soaked with Lenore's blood. Thin, uneven lines of dried blood ran from the side of the bed to the floor. The razor blade was still clutched in Lenore's fingers.

Patrick raised Lenore's eyelids. Her eyes stared at him, unseeing, dead. Her skin was already cool to the touch. He took his stethoscope from his bag and placed it on her chest. After a moment, he put the stethoscope away and went to the door.

"Mrs. Pomeroy, where is the Senator?"

"In Washington, sir. What is it? Is Mrs. Josephson sick?"

"I'm sorry . . . Mrs. Josephson is dead. I want you to call the police." He looked at his watch. "It's seven thirty-four. Call the police. Tell—"

Mrs. Pomeroy ran into the bedroom. She saw Lenore; she saw the blood. She screamed.

"Mrs. Pomeroy." Patrick turned her away from the bed. "Don't. Let's go outside now. Mrs. Pomeroy . . . *Mrs. Pomeroy.*" He shook her. "Please listen to me. I have to call the Senator. I want you to call the police. Can you do that?"

"Oh, the poor woman. The poor woman."

Patrick walked Mrs. Pomeroy outside. *"I'll* call the police," he said. "I'll use this hall phone. But I want you to call Washington. I want you to . . . are you listening to me?"

"Yes, sir."

"I'll use this phone to call the police. You use another phone and get Senator Josephson on the line. Don't tell him anything, just get him on the line for me. Do you understand?"

"Yes, sir," she said, running into the study.

Patrick dialed 911. "My name is Dr. Dain. I'm calling from Two Hundred Gracie Square, apartment 22. There's been a suicide . . . yes, yes, that's right. I'll be waiting for you."

Patrick looked inside the study. "Do you have the Senator yet?"

"They're paging him now."

"Let me know when you get him."

Patrick went back to the bedroom. He stared down at Lenore. Her face, in death, was smooth and utterly tranquil. He noticed pieces of a photograph strewn on the bed and he bent over for a closer look. There were glimpses of a long white veil, of a bouquet trimmed with long white ribbons. It had been a wedding picture, he realized, Lenore's wedding picture.

Slowly, it dawned on him that Lenore had planned even the smallest details of her suicide. She'd dressed herself in a pretty gown, made up her face and curled her hair. And she'd taken no chances, for there on the blood-spattered table he saw the empty pill bottle. He saw no note, but the shredded wedding picture spoke more eloquently than any note could have.

He took a quilt from a chair. It was pink, the same pink as her gown, and he was certain she'd planned that too. He covered her with the quilt, drawing it

416

gently over her face. The special kind of agony Matt had spoken of was over for her now, he thought, though the thought was little comfort.

"Dr. Dain," Mrs. Pomeroy called in a quavering voice. "Senator Josephson is on."

Patrick went into the hall. "Thank you. Go lie down, Mrs. Pomeroy. I'll give you something for your nerves as soon as I'm finished."

"Yes, sir. I could use it."

Patrick crossed the study and picked up the phone. "Doug? . . . yes, it's Patrick. I'm afraid I . . . I have terrible news . . ."

31

"Hello, Jean," Patrick said, walking into his office. "Sorry to be so late." He glanced at the messages on his desk. "Anything I should know about?"

"Everything's under control here. I have a couple of important messages for David though. Did he come back with you?"

"He stopped off at ICU to check on a patient. He won't be long."

"You look beat."

"I am."

"How was the funeral?"

"Very private. It was family and close friends . . . and a large security force to keep the press at a distance."

"How's the Senator holding up?"

"It's hard to say. Whatever his feelings are, he's keeping them under tight rein."

"That's bad."

"Perhaps. Perhaps not. The older I get, the fewer answers I seem to have." Patrick hung his jacket on the back of a chair and sat down. "Jean, I'm expecting Mr. O'Hara shortly. Send him right in. And hold my calls if you can."

"Sure. Try the coffee, it's hot." Jean hesitated at the door. "Would you like a brandy or something?"

"Do I look that ragged?"

"Around the edges. I bet you'll be glad when this week is over."

"We'll all be glad."

Patrick leaned back. He stretched. Every muscle in his body ached with fatigue, for he'd had almost no sleep in the last few days. There's been endless meetings with the police, endless inquiries from the press. Doorbells and telephones rang constantly and at all hours. Doug Josephson had secluded himself at the Dains' apartment, night after night arguing noisely with his aides.

"Good afternoon to you, Patrick."

Patrick turned. He saw Bren standing in the doorway. He looked jaunty in a navy blue blazer and well-pressed gray slacks.

"Come in. Sit down."

"I'm getting tired of your orders. I didn't like being ordered over here today."

"What you like or don't like is of absolutely no concern to me."

"That's where you're wrong. *Everything* about me is of concern to you."

"Look, Bren, I'm in a bad mood. I'm certainly in no mood to spar with you. So sit down and shut up."

Bren's eyes narrowed. Something in Patrick's manner, something he couldn't identify, made him uncomfortable. "You're making a mistake trying to push me around. I'm holding all the cards."

"You're holding nothing."

Bren sat down. "That's news to me," he said.

"There's more news on the way. Get ready for it."

"What's this all about? Have you been working on Annie? Is that why I haven't seen her for two weeks?"

"Ann hasn't been feeling well. Didn't she tell you?"

"She told me. I didn't believe her. I think you've been giving her a hard time. You've been keeping her away from me."

"She's a grown woman. She makes her own decisions."

"With a lot of help from you."

"Sometimes."

"Enjoy it while you can. It's true I'm off schedule, but I'll get my Annie back. You'll see."

Patrick laughed. "*Your* Annie?"

"You heard me."

"Now you hear me. Ann's through with you. She wanted to tell you so herself. I asked her to wait."

"I know a lie when I hear one."

"You're an idiot, Bren. You took Ann for a nice, cozy walk down memory lane. But you walked her too far. She remembered what a miserable bastard you really are."

Bren flushed. He jumped up. "I'll not listen to anymore of this."

"Take one step and I'll stuff that chair down your throat."

Bren stopped. He didn't know what to make of

Patrick's attitude, of the steely assurance in his voice. His pulse fluttered. His stomach turned over as he wondered if his gamble had failed.

"Sit down," Patrick ordered and Bren complied.

"I think you're bluffing," Bren said after a moment.

"No, you don't. You think I'm telling the truth and you're beginning to sweat. I've played a lot of poker in my time. I know when a man is about to fold."

"What's on your mind, Patrick? Spit it out."

"Very well. I didn't call you here to talk about Ann. I want to talk about Irene."

"Irene?"

"That's right."

"Irene's dead and buried, God rest her soul."

"What I want to talk about is how Irene *got* dead."

Bren sat up straight. He stared at Patrick. "She died of the fever. The lung fever."

"Did she?"

"Don't take my word for it. Look at the death certificate."

"I looked at the death certificate."

"Well . . . then you know how she died."

"Yes, *I* know how she died."

Bren lit a cigarette. "You're talking in circles."

"And *you* know how she died."

"The lung fever."

"Try again."

"Why should I?"

"Confession is good for the soul."

Bren took short, quick puffs on his cigarette. He

began to feel sick and he stubbed it out.

"You talk a lot, Patrick, but you don't say anything."

"I'm on to you. I know what you did and how you did it."

"I did nothing!"

"Try again."

"Are you . . . accusing me of something?"

"I most certainly am."

"About Irene?"

"Obviously."

"You're crazy! I have the death certificate . . . right there in black and white it says—"

"It *says* wrong."

"That's what you'd like to think."

"That's what I *know*."

Bren took a deep breath. He cleared his throat. "There's nothing to know."

"The Moncrief Pharmacy. The Supreme 6 Drug Store. Do those names ring a bell?"

"No!"

"Try again."

Bren felt the room getting smaller and smaller. The walls seemed to swell. They expanded out toward him, cutting off his air. He wanted to run but he couldn't make his legs move. They were stiff and heavy as tree trunks.

"Well?" Patrick asked. "Where's all your big talk now? I'm waiting for you to say something."

"I've nothing to say."

"You got sleeping pills at those pharmacies, Bren. Of course you got them as *Dennis* O'Hara, but that's beside the point."

"I *never* got any sleeping pills."

"But you did."

"Prove it!"

"When I'm ready to, I will. Your picture has been identified. And I have copies of the prescriptions."

Bren's lips parted. "Copies?"

"That's right."

"You're lying."

"Look at me, Bren. Am I lying?"

"How could you have copies? How could you have *anything?* It's imposs . . ." Bren turned slowly to Patrick. "Have you had someone checking up on me? Is that it? I'll sue you for that . . . goddamn you, I'll take you to court."

"Don't talk to me about the law. Talk to me about sleeping pills."

Bren remembered the day he'd had the prescriptions filled. It had all been so easy, he thought; he hadn't even been nervous.

"Well?" Patrick asked again.

"Okay, I got the damn pills. What of it? A lot of people use 'em. It's no sin."

"The sin came later."

"What sin?" Bren asked dully.

"What did you do with the pills?"

"I . . . had trouble sleeping. I took the pills to sleep."

"No. You waited for the right moment. Then you dumped the pills in a glass of lemonade. Then you gave the lemonade to Irene."

Bren's tongue flicked at his lips. He eyed the door, but still he couldn't move.

"Isn't that what happened?"

"No!"

"Of course it is."

"I . . . took the pills myself."

"You gave them to Irene. You gave *all* of them to her at one time, in a glass of lemonade."

"No." Bren's voice was barely a whisper.

"Tell the truth, you'll feel better."

The day of Irene's death was clear in Bren's mind. She hadn't wanted the lemonade, but he'd insisted. He'd propped her up in bed and stayed at her side until she finished it all. She'd complained about the bitter taste and he'd blamed it on her fever.

Bren remembered taking the glass to the kitchen. He'd washed it in scalding hot water and put it away; then he'd gone back to sit with Irene, to wait. It happened quickly. Irene's eyelids closed in sleep and her breathing became labored. When the doctor arrived she was already in coma, her lips tinged with blue. Minutes later, she was dead.

It might have been a movie unreeling before him, so sharp were the details in his mind's eye. He could see Irene's body being wheeled out, the doctor and the priest following behind. He could see himself standing at the screen door. There'd been no particular expression on his face because there'd been no particular feeling in his heart. He remembered that he hadn't felt anything, anything at all.

"We have things to talk about," Patrick said.

Bren looked at him. "You've said your piece."

"You haven't said yours."

"I'm not going to."

"This isn't a game anymore, Bren. If you have anything to say, I advise you to say it now."

"I don't need your advice. I have Irene's death certificate. You're a rich man and all, but even your money can't change a death certificate."

"An exhumation can change it. And I *can* get an exhumation."

"I'll kill you first."

"No, I don't think so. It's over, Bren. You've lost."

"You're forgetting about Annie. She'll help me."

"Not a chance." Patrick pushed the phone toward Bren. "Call her. We both know what she'll say. Or do you still think I'm bluffing?"

"Maybe."

"Ann knows what you did to Irene. She read the investigators' report."

Bren's eyes twinkled. "Report? I . . . don't understand. I thought you might go nosing around. So I went back to Southie myself, to check. There was nothing."

"You shouldn't have gone back. You wound up getting drunk with one of my investigators. You wound up bragging about the score you were going to make on your ex-wife."

Bren sat back. He was suddenly very tired. He couldn't think, couldn't concentrate.

"You were out of your league from the beginning," Patrick said. "I warned you. But you wouldn't listen. Did you really think I would let you destroy everything I care about?"

"It was . . . a perfect plan," Bren murmured.

"You never had a perfect plan in your life. You could have written to Ann and asked for money. She would have sent it, as much as you needed. But that wasn't good enough for you. You had to have a grand scheme. You got rid of Irene and then you came to New York and threatened us. The day you threatened Ann was the day I had investigators on your tail."

"Nobody saw me." Bren shook his head. "Nobody knew."

"We know now, don't we?"

"It's . . . impossible."

"All I needed was time. *You* gave me the time I needed. You were so busy buying out the stores that you forgot about me. That was a mistake."

"Where's the report?"

"In a safe place."

"What . . . are you going to do with it?"

Patrick was silent. Until this moment he hadn't known what he was going to do with the report; now he realized that there'd never been any choice. He went to the liquor cabinet and poured two whiskeys. He carried the drinks to the desk and handed one to Bren.

"Well, Patrick?"

"I'm giving you the opportunity to go to the authorities yourself. If you do, I'll help you. I'll hire attorneys for you. I'll help in any way I can."

Rage cut abruptly through Bren's lethargy. His face turned crimson and his eyes glinted with hate. "*You* help *me?*" he shouted. "For hundreds of years it's been people like you *stepping* on people like me."

"Your failures are your own fault."

Bren shot out of his chair. His mouth was twisted and ugly. "Why do you think I fail? Why do you think I am the way I am? It's because people like you are *always* stepping on me, keeping me down."

"You're not making any sense."

"I *had* to do what I did. It was my chance. I saw my chance and I took it. You'd of done the same in my place."

"Bren, you're in no position to argue. If you don't go to the authorities, I will."

"All my life I waited for my one big chance to get somewhere. And all my life people like you kept me from it. But not this time. *Not this time.*"

"You're through. Face it."

A cry came from Bren's throat. He swung wildly at Patrick. Patrick grabbed his arm and pushed him away. He pushed him onto the couch and held him there.

"Don't move!" he said. "Don't move, just listen. *You* kept yourself from getting anywhere. Nobody else. You ran from every responsibility you ever had. You're a coward. And a damn fool."

Bren tried to break Patrick's grip but Patrick held firm. "It will be easier on you if you turn yourself in. And it will be easier on your children. For once in your sorry life, think about your children."

"What do you know about my life? You have your money and your lackeys and your fancy ways . . . I have nothing. It's not fair! Why should you have everything while I have nothing?"

Patrick walked away. "You're hopeless," he said disgustedly.

"I tried to change the odds. Just one time I wanted to come out on top. And I would have, if it hadn't been for you. Your kind isn't happy unless it's persecuting my kind."

"Persecuting? A woman is *dead* because of you. Do you expect me to forget that?"

"Irene was nothing to you. Why should you care about her life? *She* didn't even care. Her life was work and worry, there was no joy in it. I did her a favor getting her out of this stinking world."

"Bren, you're a sick man."

"Persecuting me won't bring Irene back."

"I'm sorry."

"Give me money and I'll go away. I won't be bothering you again, if that's your fear."

"I'm asking you, for the last time, to go to the authorities."

"I won't!"

"Then I will."

Bren's face was white. He stood up and walked unsteadily toward the door. Patrick saw the swollen veins in his pale temples, the blue lines at the edges of his mouth.

"Bren, you're in deep trouble. Don't make it worse."

"*You're* the one making it worse." Bren's fist struck savagely at the wall. "*You'll* be the sorry one for it. Call your precious authorities. Give 'em your precious report. Have your revenge. And I'll have mine."

Patrick looked up sharply. "Another threat?"

"You have something that belongs to me," Bren said through a vicious grin.

"If you're talking about Daisy—"

"She's my daughter. And I'll have her back. I'll have her back or kill us both in the attempt. Then," Bren threw the door open, "you'll see who's the sorry one. Then you'll see how *much* I hate you."

Patrick picked up the phone and dialed his apartment. "Ann, where's Daisy? . . . go to school and get her *now* . . . take Hollis with you . . . no, bring her straight here, don't stop for anything . . . Bren's going to try to grab her . . . *hurry*, Ann."

Bren plunged through the door to the stairs. He leaned against the railing for a moment, his eyes tightly shut. His chest heaved. He took a deep breath and then another and another. He saw his plans, his dreams, in ruins around him and he cried out in fury.

He felt like screaming, like tearing the hospital apart. His anger was like a fire raging in his soul. Patrick and Ann would not get away with it, he thought, dizzy with rage. Daisy was his last card and he would play it. This was one plan, he swore to himself, that would succeed.

Bren started down the stairs. He had to grope his way, for his anger made everything a blur. He couldn't remember being so angry before. There was a fiery gnawing in every fiber of his body, pushing him, urging him on. He was glad of it. It made him feel powerful and strong again.

Bren reached the ground floor and stamped through the lobby to the street. He thought about Daisy. He wouldn't go after her today, he decided, for they would be expecting that. He would wait until Monday, until she went to her dancing class. He would go to that class, he smiled thinly, and he would go well-armed. They wouldn't try to stop him; they wouldn't dare.

Bren hurried blindly along the sidewalk. He bumped into passers-by, into a beribboned baby carriage, oblivious to the curses hurled after him. He reached the corner and stepped into the street. Automobile horns exploded around him. He looked up as a green sedan flung him into the air.

There was a moment of chaos. Horns blared and brakes squealed. A woman screamed. Bren lay on the ground, his eyes open and staring, blood pouring from his mouth. The driver ran out of the sedan and gaped at the inert body.

"Don't touch him!" someone in the crowd shouted and the driver shrank back.

"It wasn't my fault!" he cried. "I had the light. You saw. You all saw. I had the light. He came out of nowhere. You're all witnesses."

A young woman pushed through the crowd. "There's a hospital right up the street. I'm a nurse there. I called them, they're on their way."

"Thank God! Is . . . there anything we should do for him?"

The nurse stared down at the bloodied body. She saw pieces of bone jutting out of the crushed skull. "An ambulance will be here any . . . there it is."

A red and white ambulance drew up alongside the curb. Two attendants jumped out. They checked for pulse and heartbeat, then strapped Bren onto a gurney and wheeled him inside.

The distraught driver watched the ambulance

pull away. "It wasn't my fault! Is he . . . dead? You're a nurse, tell me!" He saw a police car come to a stop. He ran to it. "It wasn't my fault, Officers. I had the light. I have witnesses . . ."

Bren was wheeled into the E.R. at Rhinelander Pavillion. A doctor hurried over.

"Traffic accident," the attendant said. "Don't bother. He's dead."

Patrick opened the door to Daisy's room. Ann rose to greet him.

"Did you tell her?"

"Yes," Ann said. "She's all right."

Patrick walked across the room. He bent down and kissed Daisy's head. "How are you, Droopy?"

"Poppa died today."

"I know. I'm very sorry."

"Poppa will be happy now."

"Oh?"

"He didn't like it on Earth. But he'll be happy in Heaven. There are angels there. Mamma said."

Patrick sat down. He took her small hand in his. "Do you want to talk about anything, Daisy. Do you have any questions?"

"Do I have to go to the grave?"

"You can if you want to. You don't have to go."

"I don't want to. It's spooky at the grave."

"Are you afraid? You shouldn't be," he said gently. "There's nothing there to hurt you."

"When I'm older I won't be afraid. I'm only six, you know."

Patrick smiled. "Is that all? I thought you were at least thirty."

"You're silly." Daisy giggled. "Patrick . . . where am I going to live now?"

"Ann and I want you to live with us. We want you to be our little girl."

"Will you be my poppa?"

"Would you like that?"

"Oh yes. But I don't want to call you Poppa. I'll call you Daddy. And Ann will be Mommy. Okay?"

"Mommy." Patrick smiled up at Ann. "How about it?"

"Sounds good to me."

"Well, that settles it, Droopy. We're a family."

"Forever?"

"Forever."

Daisy clapped her hands together. "Neato."

"It's bedtime, sweetheart," Ann said, tucking the sheets in around her. "It's late. Are you sleepy?"

"Alfie is sleepy."

"Sweet dreams to both of you." Ann kissed her. "Goodnight."

Ann and Patrick went to the door and turned out the lights.

"Am I really your little girl now?" Daisy called to them.

"Really and truly."

"Then can I have a pony?"

"No." Patrick laughed. "But I'll consider a puppy."

"Neato. I'm going to name him Cornelius."

"Go to sleep before I change my mind."

They went into the hall.

"She seems fine," Patrick said.

"I think she was always a bit scared of Bren. She doesn't have to be scared anymore."

Patrick put his arm around Ann. "We've got ourselves a little girl. Happy?"

"I love you. I'm married to the best man in the whole world."

"What a coincidence." He smiled.

"Yes?"

"I happen to be married to the best woman in the whole world. Have I ever told you about my wife?"

"Tell me. And don't stint on the adjectives."

32

Bren's funeral was on the first Saturday in June. They stood on a grassy knoll in a Westchester cemetary, Ann and Patrick, Lola and David, listening to the priest intone the prayers for the dead. When he finished, the bronze casket was lowered into the moist, freshly-turned earth. Ann stepped forward and dropped a single yellow rose into the void. She stared into the darkness for a while, then turned away.

"Thank you, Father," she said to the priest. "It was a lovely service."

"Mr. O'Hara is with God now."

"Yes, Father. Thank you."

They walked across the lawn to their cars. Ann hugged Lola and kissed David's cheek. "I appreciate your coming. It was very kind."

"Yes it was." Patrick nodded. "Why don't you come to Connecticut with us? We'll have a nice country weekend."

"You need time together," David said. "And so do we." He smiled at Lola.

"I'm happy for you two," Ann said.

"He *almost* has me convinced." Lola winked. "Meanwhile, I'm enjoying the wooing."

"In that case," David opened the car door, "let's not waste time."

Lola got into the car. She poked her dark head out of the window. "You know when David last opened a door for me? Never."

"It's the new me," David said, sliding behind the wheel. "How do you like it?"

"Very impressive." Patrick smiled.

They waved as the sleek red Triumph drove off. "Do you think they'll make it?" Ann asked.

"David's growing up. And Lola's an extraordinary woman. I think they'll make it with room to spare."

"I hope so."

"Shall we go? Are you ready?"

"Ready."

Ann was quiet during the ride to Connecticut, gazing out at the landscape. Pretty suburban towns gave way to prettier rural villages. There were farmlands then, with black and white cows grazing in the sun. Past the farmlands were great stretches of dense woods.

Patrick glanced at Ann from time to time but he didn't speak. Finally, about a mile from Twin Oaks, he pulled the car to the side of the road and turned off the engine.

"What is it, darling? Do you want to cry? Go ahead."

"I *don't* want to cry. That's what I've been thinking about. I haven't shed one tear for Bren. It doesn't seem right."

"You shed your tears while he was alive."

"For *me*, not for him."

"For both of you."

"He lived almost forty-four years. But no one will miss him. No one will mourn. How sad that is."

"It would have been sadder had he lived. For everybody. At least Buddy is free now. So is Daisy."

"I know."

"What else is bothering you?"

"I was thinking about Jill," Ann said and her eyes misted. "She was so young when she died. Yet she did more living in twenty-one years than Bren did in forty-four. Everybody loved her."

"She was a sweet girl." Patrick leaned over and kissed Ann lightly on the top of her head. "She was like her mother."

"Daisy reminds me *so* much of Jill. It's like . . . a second chance."

Patrick started the car. "Perhaps that's what God had in mind."

They drove past fields of wildflowers, past overgrown woodlands, until Twin Oaks came into view. The sun was high in the sky and the air was sweet with the scent of newly mown grass.

Ann looked up. She leaned forward. "Patrick, those roses!" she said as they turned into the driveway.

Even at a distance, the roses around the main house were spectacular. They'd bloomed only a few days before, and in their first bloom they were huge and lushly shaded. The pinks were the color of a blush. The reds were bold and sassy. They grew in masses around the house, in beds and on trellises, hundreds of them. Ann was overwhelmed.

"Buddy's going to be sorry to leave this behind," she said.

"Under the circumstances," Patrick smiled, "I hardly think so."

Jonas Turnbull opened the car door. "Hello, Ann," he said, helping her out. "I was sorry to hear about Mr. O'Hara."

"Thank you, Jonas. I don't like saying it, but it's probably for the best."

"I quite understand. You'll be glad to know that Dr. O'Hara took the news very well. He was moody for a day or so, but he and Mark DuShan worked it out."

"Are you sure?"

"Absolutely."

"Hello, Jonas," Patrick said. "What's the big surprise you promised us?"

"Dr. O'Hara is moving to one of the cottages. That is the final step before discharge. I expect he'll be out of here in a week or two."

"Oh," Ann squealed. "Really? Is it definite?"

"Actually, he could leave any time now. But he wants to put the last little pieces in place. We agree with his decision."

"Then he's . . . well?"

"He's a changed man. He knows himself. More importantly, he likes himself."

"But is he *well?*"

"Completely well. He'll always be on the sensitive side . . . that's a matter of his personality. That's part of him. We wouldn't want to tamper with that."

"You know Buddy wants to go back to medicine," Patrick said.

"There's no reason why he shouldn't. He's able to function, able to cope. This experience gives him an extra dimension to offer his patients."

"But the stress," Ann said.

"Dr. O'Hara is sensitive. That doesn't mean he can't handle stress. He's learned how to handle it. He's learned not to push himself. That was a large part of his problem, Ann. He set unrealistic standards. He set the standards of a *god*. I don't believe he'll do that again."

"I don't want him to rush right back in."

Jonas smiled. "That's exactly what he must do. You want to protect him, to coddle him. Don't. He was ill. Now he's better. Now it's time to go back to work."

Ann shook her head. "This is a controlled environment. What happens when Buddy has to face the outside world? The *real* world?"

"All our efforts are aimed at coping with the stresses of the real world. Ann, it wasn't the outside world that broke your son. The inner world, the world in his mind, *that* broke him." Jonas stared into Ann's eyes. "You're too polite to tell me, but I know what's upsetting you. Mrs. Josephson committed suicide a week after leaving Twin Oaks. She couldn't cope with the outside world. You're afraid that Dr. O'Hara may have similar difficulties."

"I'm sorry, Jonas. But it's on my mind."

"Of course it is. However, you must understand the vast differences between the two cases. I can't go into detail, but I can say this much . . . Dr.

O'Hara has a life to return to. Mrs. Josephson felt she did *not*. We were aware of that. We didn't want to discharge her. We urged the Senator to keep her here for treatment. But she wanted to go home and he agreed. The outcome was not a surprise to us. Everything considered, it was inevitable."

"I . . . didn't realize."

"That's confidential information, Ann. I told you only to help you see that there is no danger."

"I'm glad you did. Thank you."

"Can we see Buddy now?" Patrick asked.

"He'll be right along. It's a pretty day, and there are chairs under those trees. Why don't you wait out here? I'll send him to you."

Jonas left. Patrick and Ann strolled a few yards to a group of green and white striped canvas chairs.

"Feeling better?" Patrick asked.

"I could wring Doug's neck."

"Aside from that."

"Aside from that, I'm so relieved I could jump up and down and shout Hallelujah."

"I'd like to see that."

"You may yet. I may break out in song any minute. Oh, there's Buddy!"

Buddy walked down the path toward them. The sun glistened in his blond hair and his face was smooth and unshadowed. He looked young and fit. In an open-necked sport shirt and faded jeans, he could have been a college student on his way to class.

"Hello, Ma." Buddy hesitated, then he encircled Ann in a hug. He stared at her. "If you want to sock me," he smiled, "I'll understand."

"I don't want to sock you. I just want to look at you."

"Hello, Patrick." Buddy hugged him too. "Here's my chin. Make it a good one."

"I'll pass."

They all sat down. Buddy turned to Ann. "I'm sorry about Pop's funeral. I didn't want to go."

"I didn't expect you to."

"Are you okay?"

"I'm fine. And you're . . . *splendid*. Buddy, you look wonderful."

"Thanks. There's so much to say I don't know where to start . . . I guess I'll start with the most important thing. I apologize to both of you. I know I hurt you and I'm sorry," he swallowed hard, "because I love you both very much."

Tears came to Ann's eyes. "All the hurt is in the past."

"It is. It really is. I used to hurt inside. There was a dull ache all the time."

"No more?" Patrick asked.

"It's gone. I remember it, but even the memory is getting dim."

"You sound surprised."

"I am. I've never felt so good before. I feel . . . new. And I feel *ready*. I can't wait to get back to work."

"When will that be?"

"I'm going to stay here another week. Maybe two. Then it's *Dr.* O'Hara again." He looked at Patrick. "Matt came to see me yesterday. We had a long talk. It was a good talk. He's a good guy. Of course you knew that all along."

"Yes." Patrick smiled.

"Well, I was jealous. I envied him his talent and his popularity . . . and his sanity. I suppose you knew that, too."

"No, that was a guess."

"Matt asked me to come back to Rhinelander Pavillion. I know I could go to another hospital. But Rhinelander Pavillion is what I want."

"I couldn't be more pleased," Patrick said. "But you'll be in for some teasing, some ribbing. And it won't be subtle. Are you prepared for that?"

"I've learned how to laugh. I've even learned how to laugh at myself. I, Buddy O'Hara, have learned how to take a joke."

"You'll be sorely tested."

"I'm ready, Patrick."

"Yes, I believe you are. Pick your date and call Matt. He'll put you back on the schedule."

"We already settled that. I'm back on schedule as of July first."

"That's changeover day. That's the worst day of the year."

"What's changeover day?" Ann asked.

"The new interns and residents come in then. It's sort of a cross between bedlam and comic opera."

"I didn't pick that date to prove anything," Buddy said. "It just makes sense to start with the new staff."

"That's exceedingly brave."

"There's one more thing . . . When I leave here, I'd like to move back into my room until I find an apartment."

"Buddy," Ann put her hand on his arm, "you don't have to get an apartment. Not yet."

"Sure I do." He smiled. "I love you guys, but I'll be twenty-six years old next month. I should have my own place."

"Take as long as you want," Patrick said. "Find the right place. And if you need help with key money, don't by shy."

"It'll be fun being home again. I can get to know Daisy . . . Ma, don't look uncomfortable. I was jealous of Daisy. I'm not anymore."

"We're . . . going to adopt her."

"That's great! Listen, I know I was rough on her. I probably scared her to death. But I want to make it up to her now. I've been thinking about it. Do you . . . do you think she'd like a puppy?"

"She certainly would," Patrick laughed. "You must have ESP."

"There's a dog here. His name is Happy. He's well named, he makes *everybody* happy. Anyway," Buddy grinned, "I'd like to buy a puppy for Daisy."

"Make it small and friendly. In that order."

"Then it's okay?"

"Daisy will be your friend for life."

"Good." Buddy stood up. "Carol," he called, "over here."

A thin, freckle-faced young woman walked over to Buddy.

"Carol, these are my parents."

She smiled at Ann and Patrick. They exchanged pleasantries and then she continued on her way. "Don't forget backgammon tonight," Buddy called after her. "Carol had a breakdown too," he explained. "She refused to eat because she thought people were trying to poison her. She's better now."

"Do you know many of the patients?"

"Some. We're like survivors of a plane crash— eager to exchange horror stories. I've learned a lot about people. That's bound to make me a better doctor . . . I understand things now that I never would have understood before." Buddy laughed. "Am I babbling?"

"Not at all. But why do you keep looking at the path?"

"I'm expecting Sally. I'm dying to tell her all the news."

Patrick tapped Ann's shoulder. "I do believe that's our cue to leave."

Buddy colored. "I didn't mean to be rude. I wasn't trying to hurry you."

"We understand." Ann smiled up at him. "You want to be alone with your girl. That's nothing to be embarrassed about."

"Definitely not." Patrick slipped his arm around Ann. "I like to be alone with my girl too."

They walked toward the path. Buddy stopped at a small, circular flower bed and picked a daffodil. He gave it to Ann.

"We can have a picnic tomorrow," he said. "Just the three of us. Will you come back tomorrow?"

"We'll be here. Can we bring you anything?"

"I have everything I need." Buddy kissed Ann and gave Patrick a quick hug. "I really do." He grinned, waving as he walked away.

"Well, Ann, I needn't ask if you're happy. It's all

in your eyes."

"I have my two men back. Three, now that Tony's down from school."

Patrick glanced at his watch. "We should be going. Tony will be waiting for us at the house."

"I hope he'll stay the night."

"I guarantee he will. He plans to butter me up."

"Butter you up for what?"

"Tony is going to say 'Dad, I'd like to spend the summer in Europe. And I'd really like to do it right.' Freely translated, that means fork over the cash."

"How do you know what he'll say?"

"When I finished my junior year at Yale, I went to *my* father's house. I said, 'Dad, I'd like to spend the summer in Europe. And I'd really like to do it right.'"

"You're so smart."

"No, I have a good memory."

They paused at the car and looked over at Buddy. They saw him carefully pluck a bright red rose and cup it in his hands.

"One guess who that's for."

"There's Sally now."

Clusters of visitors were beginning to arrive but Patrick spotted Sally immediately. She wore a light, summery dress of pink voile. Her reddish hair spilled over her shoulders and her face glowed.

Buddy saw her at the same time. He called to her. They ran toward each other, into each other's arms. They kissed, and it was a kiss of infinite tenderness.

"Love is wonderful." Ann beamed.

Patrick held her to him. "Darling, let's go home."

FICTION FOR TODAY'S WOMAN

THE BUTTERFLY SECRET (394, $2.50)
by Toni Tucci
Every woman's fantasy comes to life in Toni Tucci's guide to new life for the mature woman. Learn the secret of love, happiness and excitement, and how to fulfill your own needs while satisfying your mate's.

FACADES (500, $2.50)
by Stanley Levine & Bud Knight
The glamourous, glittering world of Seventh Avenue unfolds around famous fashion designer Stephen Rich, who dresses and undresses the most beautiful people in the world.

LONG NIGHT (515, $2.25)
by P. B. Gallagher
An innocent relationship turns into a horrifying nightmare when a beautiful young woman falls victim to a confused man seeking revenge for his father's death.

BELLA'S BLESSINGS (562, $2.50)
by William Black
From the Roaring Twenties to the dark Depression years. Three generations of an unforgettable family—their passions, triumphs and tragedies.

MIRABEAU PLANTATION (596, $2.50)
by Marcia Meredith
Crystal must rescue her plantation from its handsome holder even at the expense of losing his love. A sweeping plantation novel about love, war, and a passion that would never die.

SOMETHING FOR EVERYONE—
BEST SELLERS FROM ZEBRA!

EPIDEMIC! (644, $2.50)
by Larry R. Leichter, M.D.
From coast to coast, beach to beach, the killer virus spread. Diagnosed as a strain of meningitis, it did not respond to treatment—and no one could stop it from becoming the world's most terrifying epidemic!

FIRE MOUNTAIN (646, $2.50)
by Janet Cullen-Tanaka
Everyone refused to listen but hour by hour, yard by yard, the cracks and fissures in Mt. Rainer grew. Within hours the half-million-year-old volcano rose from its sleep, causing one of the most cataclysmic eruptions of all time.

GHOST SUB (655, $2.50)
by Roger E. Herst
The U.S.S. *Amundsen* is on the most dangerous patrol since World War II—it is equipped with deadly weapons . . . and nothing less than a nuclear holocaust hangs in the balance.

AVALANCHE (672, $2.50)
by Max Steele
Disaster strikes at the biggest and newest ski resort in the Rocky Mountains. It is New Year's eve and the glamorous and glittering ski people find themselves trapped between a wall of fire and a mountain of impenetrable snow.

Available wherever paperbacks are sold, or order direct from the Publisher. Send cover price plus 50¢ per copy for mailing and handling to Zebra Books, 21 East 40th Street, New York, N.Y. 10016. DO NOT SEND CASH!

READ THESE ZEBRA BEST SELLERS

BESTSELLERS FOR TODAY'S WOMAN

ALL THE WAY   (571, $2.25)
by Felice Buckvar
After over twenty years of devotion to another man, Phyllis finds herself helplessly in love, once again, with that same tall, handsome high school sweetheart who had loved her . . . ALL THE WAY.

HAPPILY EVERY AFTER   (595, $2.25)
by Felice Buckvar
Disillusioned with her husband, her children and her life, Dorothy Fine begins to search for her own identity . . . and discovers that it's not too late to love and live again.

SO LITTLE TIME   (585, $2.50)
by Sharon M. Combes
Darcey must put her love and courage to the test when she learns that her fiancé has only months to live. Destined to become this year's *Love Story*.

RHINELANDER PAVILLION   (572, $2.50)
by Barbara Harrison
A powerful novel that captures the real-life drama of a big city hospital and its dedicated staff who become caught up in their own passions and desires.

THE BUTTERFLY SECRET   (394, $2.50)
by Toni Tucci
Every woman's fantasy comes to life in Toni Tucci's guide to new life for the mature woman. Learn the secret of love, happiness and excitement, and how to fulfill your own needs while satisfying your mate's.

Available wherever paperbacks are sold, or order direct from the Publisher. Send cover price plus 50¢ per copy for mailing and handling to Zebra Books, 21 East 40th Street, New York, N.Y. 10016. DO NOT SEND CASH!